PENGUIN BOOKS

PARNELL AND THE ENGLISHWOMAN

Hugh Leonard was born in Dublin in 1926, was educated at Presentation College, Dun Laoghaire, and then spent fourteen years as a clerk in the Land Commission. He was able to give up this job when he began to have some success as a playwright. He was Literary Editor of the Abbey Theatre from 1976 until 1977 and is a member of the council of the Dublin Theatre Festival. His plays include *A Leap in the Dark* (1957), *A Walk on the Water* (1960), *The Saints Go Cycling In* (1965), *The Au Pair Man* (1968), *The Patrick Pearse Motel* (1971), *Thieves* (1973), *Summer* (1974), *Irishmen* (1975), *Time Was* (1976), *Moving Days* (1981), *Kill* (1982), *Scorpions* (1983) and *The Mask of Moriarty* (1985). His real breakthrough came with *Da*, which in the United States won a Tony Award for the Best Play of 1978, the Drama Desk Award and the New York Critics' Circle Award. He also won the Harvey Award for the best play of 1979/80 with *A Life*.

Hugh Leonard has also written a number of plays for television, including *Silent Song*, which won the Italia Award for 1967, and his adaptations for television include works by Emily Brontë, Dickens, Flaubert, Maugham and Saki. He has also written a four-part drama series, *Parnell*, for BBC Television. *Home Before Night*, his autobiography, was published in 1979 and its companion volume, *Out After Dark*, in 1990. Hugh Leonard lives in Dalkey, outside Dublin, and writes a weekly satirical column for the *Sunday Independent* in between what he calls 'real work'.

PARNELL AND THE ENGLISHWOMAN

HUGH LEONARD

PENGUIN BOOKS

PENGUIN BOOKS

Published by the Penguin Group
Penguin Books Ltd, 27 Wrights Lane, London w8 5TZ, England
Viking Penguin, a division of Penguin Books USA Inc.
375 Hudson Street, New York, New York 10014, USA
Penguin Books Australia Ltd, Ringwood, Victoria, Australia
Penguin Books Canada Ltd, 2801 John Street, Markham, Ontario, Canada L3R 1B4
Penguin Books (NZ) Ltd, 182–190 Wairau Road, Auckland 10, New Zealand

Penguin Books Ltd, Registered Offices: Harmondsworth, Middlesex, England

First published by André Deutsch 1991
Published in Penguin Books 1991
10 9 8 7 6 5 4 3 2

Printed in England by Clays Ltd, St Ives plc

For Paule, wife and Parnellite, with love.

ONE

Eight guests had been invited; seven had come.

She looked at Willie at the far end of the table. His face was acquiring a familiar flush; they had waited dinner too long, and he had made the most of it. He allowed a waiter to recharge his glass. The manoeuvre completed, he gave her his best attention.

'Kate, my dear, shall we begin?'

She said: 'Another five minutes.'

If humiliation had shape and substance, hers would be an empty chair. The thought, fully formed, stepped gracefully into her mind. She admired it as not badly done, then again regarded the chair to her right. In absurd fancy, she instructed a waiter to take it away. Ah, then there would be a space, in itself as accusing as the chair. She saw her dinner guests move sideways at her command to obliterate the evidence. They did so, not rising but at a sit, the chairs clumping sideways like wooden beasts. The image caused an unwanted smile to tug at her cheek.

She had ordered dinner with especial care: consommé, sole with lobster sauce, jugged hare, calf's heart (she had decided upon it for no other reason than to inform her guest of honour with a batting of the eyelids and a blush, if she could manage it, that it was known as 'love in disguise'), guinea fowl, duck *à la suédoise* and leg of lamb. For dessert, a ratafia ice pudding,

1

a Bakewell and a fool. James, the head waiter, had suggested an Irish cheese to accompany the Stilton, the Leicester and the Sage Derby, again in deference to her guest. An Irish cheese! How had Thomas's Hotel come by such a curiosity? Again and to her dismay, she felt her eyes drawn to the chair. On her left, Justin McCarthy, M.P., sleek with London dinners, was telling his other neighbour of a book he had read. She heard him say, *'Dear Lady Disdain.'* No, it was not a book he had read; he was an author, and so of course it was a book he had written.

Her husband said: 'Kate, admit defeat.'

She had arranged the dinner for Willie's sake, and yet there was a hint of pleasure on his face, as if he were glad to see her discomfited. He stroked his fair moustache with a forefinger. She took an answering pleasure in the thought that he would one day be bald.

'Your lion,' he said, 'refuses to take the bait.'

Faces turned towards her. She saw Anna try and fail to seem sympathetic. The injustice stung.

'This time I have his note,' Katharine protested.

'And that is all you have!' Willie replied, his smile maddening. 'My poor innocent Kate' (he might have been performing sleight of hand for their guests' amusement), 'you have yet to learn that when you invite the Irish to dine you invite their bad manners as well.'

Mrs Justin McCarthy, on Willie's left, blinked. She looked towards her husband, who, with the malice of his trade and race, seemed doubly glad that he had come.

Katharine touched McCarthy's hand. She would be his accomplice. 'Do I, Willie?'

'With, of course, the' – Willie cleared his throat – 'the very rare exception.'

He spoke with a candour that forbade modesty. His accent, formed by school at Oscott, a year at Trinity College – more cloistered than any convent – and not much longer than that in the 18th Hussars, was proof of how far he had risen above the misfortune of being the son of a Dublin solicitor.

'I agree,' Katharine said. 'But *of course* there are exceptions.'

'Thank you, my dear.' (The fool was smirking.)

'Not at all,' Katharine said, springing the trap shut, 'I was referring to Mr and Mrs McCarthy.'

'Ma'am.' Justin McCarthy bowed to her.

There was laughter. Anna shrieked and said, 'Most handsomely deserved!' Mrs McCarthy, a creature of modesty, who would have felt unclothed without her fan, now brought it into play and sent a small gale down the table. A Mr Woffington guffawed and said, 'She's too clever for you, O'Shea.'

Willie smiled at Katharine with all of his face except the eyes. She waited for him to apologise to the McCarthys, but saw that he was too much occupied in nursing the wound to his vanity. She made an imploring face at Anna, who sprang into the void.

'To accept and then not to come!' she said. 'He must be every bit as dreadful as they say. How many times is this, Katharine? Three?'

Katharine shook her head: a woman angelically ill done by. Her mouth formed a silent and mournful 'Four'.

'*How* many? Then he has no breeding, none. Why on earth do you bother to invite him?'

'Ask my husband,' Katharine said.

'Ask me?' Willie's head came up.

'After all,' she said, 'Willie and Mr Parnell have qualities in common. They are both Irish —'

'She taunts me with my misfortune!' He giggled.

'. . . and every day they are privileged to sit and breathe the same air as Mr Gladstone. Well then, if Mr Parnell's star is in the ascendant, as it seems to be, why should not my husband's rise along with it?'

'Well said, Kate!' Willie glared at his guests as if challenging any one of them to doubt that he was the ablest man in Westminster. 'Why the deuce not? I daresay I can do the fellow a service or two. Quid pro quo and all that. Eh, McCarthy?'

3

McCarthy made no reply. Katharine bestowed on Willie the kind of smile that was to be expected from the supportive and affectionate wife of Captain William O'Shea, M.P. for County Clare. She allowed the smile to linger upon him like a dying sun, then made a signal to James.

She said: 'Let us begin. The man will not come.'

She wondered if any of her guests suspected – apart from Anna, who of course knew – that she and Willie no longer lived together. He had moved to Albert Mansions near Victoria, whereas she had remained at Eltham, across the park from Aunt Ben. Willie, a devout weekend Catholic, came on Sundays to take the children to Mass. At thirty-nine, he was still a breaker of hearts; his hair continued to curl, never mind that a new pinkness shone at the crown; his bearing was fierce and soldierly. And God, who tempered the wind to the shorn lamb, had endowed him with the cunning to suggest at first glance that he possessed what he conspicuously lacked: brains, taste and breeding. Katharine, a clergyman's daughter, believed in the fairness of the Almighty, who distributed His gifts so that intelligence, charm and handsomeness went to separate homes. God would not be so prodigal as to spoil Willie with a brain as well as good looks.

The Hussars wore a great quantity of gold braid; it was a commodity that had led to many marriages. Anna had fallen in love with a Lieutenant-Colonel Steele and, having married him, had as quickly fallen out of it, and Katharine, who was younger, did not learn by her example. Willie was dashing; and while he disliked being Irish he did not hesitate to play his soldier's role as if, instead of being born of woman, he had been written by Mr Boucicault. He was in turn a zephyr and a whirlwind; within the same hour he could plummet from impassioned lover, brooking no timidity, to forlorn wretch, determined upon a hero's death if, somewhere, a war could be found. She dreaded the occasions of their parting, for he marked these with heart-broken verses of his own; she was twenty and thought him a wonder, but her reverend father, whose pet she was, had imbued her with a thirst for poetry, and even the

4

headiness of first love did not blind her to Willie's dissimilarity to Lord Byron. She winced now as she recalled her private name for him: 'Boysie.'

He gave her a gold and turquoise locket on a chain of gold and blue enamel and besought her to marry him. She unhesitatingly refused. She thought him not quite *real*. He belonged, she believed, eternally on one knee: a waxwork suitor. She could see Willie vividly in his many selves: as soldier, reckless steeplechaser, good fellow, Prince Valiant, swearer of gallant oaths, even – God help her – versifier, but only mistily as a husband. She loved him to this side of distraction, but, as a properly brought up young lady, she knew not to burn her boats out of sight of a windward shore. Besides, her suitor had a rival. Katharine, as the youngest of eight, returned her father's adoration. One day, when she was ten, he had perched her upon the lap of Anthony Trollope. The Reverend John Page Wood did not tell his daughter that she was sitting astride the knee of a great man, but the great man was obliging enough to rectify the omission. Katharine saw her father wink at her, and thereafter in her mind and heart he was a compendium of perfections. Willie knew nothing of fathers, except that his own had had a Dublin accent of a nasality that was an affront to a fastidious ear; what he found baffling was that Katharine loved him (she said), but would not have him. Thrice spurned, he behaved impeccably, apart from writing her a farewell poem that was worse than all the others, and went with his regiment to Valencia, there to await word that she had recovered her senses. Instead, there came the unexpected news that the Reverend Wood had fallen ill and died, and that his best-loved daughter, crazed with grief, seemed herself determined to follow him to the grave. Willie, hearkening to the summons of Death the Matchmaker, returned hotfoot from Spain, proposed again and took tears for his answer.

As a prospective husband, he had seemed to her indistinct; in the actual event, the mists failed to rise. He sold his army commission and went into business with the proceeds. The venture collapsed, and before long he discovered in himself a flair for

5

bankruptcy. Like Katharine, however, Willie had an unwavering faith in the fairness of the Almighty. After no more than five years of marriage, for example, it occurred to him that all things under heaven had their purpose, and that the divine intention in filling the world with handsome women could be none other than to provide comfort for those worthy of it, among whom he counted himself. And God's benefice was not so easily exhausted, for two of His angels came to the rescue of the straitened O'Sheas. One of these was Mrs Benjamin Wood – Aunt Ben, whose wealth was such that she paid the novelist, Mr George Meredith, three hundred pounds a year to come and read to her. 'Mr Meredith,' she was heard to exclaim when he attempted to read from his own works instead of Molière's, 'your conceit is as wonderful as your genius!' She was a kindly soul and, in Willie's view, a paragon among aunts, inasmuch as she was not only wealthy but eighty-three, a widow, and childless. Katharine was her favourite niece, and Aunt Ben proved it by settling three thousand pounds a year upon her. With the money came a proposal that the O'Sheas and their children – for by now there were Gerard, Norah and Carmen – come and live in Wonersh Lodge across the park from her own mansion. No more repayment was asked for than that Katharine should be Aunt Ben's daily companion.

The second angel was a banker named Christopher Weguelin. He dined with the O'Sheas, pronounced Willie a genius *manqué* whose hour had yet to come, and arranged for him to return to Spain, this time to manage a sulphur mine. It would give him an occupation, it was agreed, until such time as Aunt Ben went to her reward and her relatives came into theirs. Willie was hardly on the boat-train to Dover than the altruistic Mr Weguelin presented himself at Eltham and, now that he had disposed of an inconvenience, proposed that he and Katharine retire to a bedroom. She sent him away. Later that evening, she stripped in front of her cheval glass and took stock of herself. She found much to dislike. Although she was not yet thirty, her figure, after the children and eight years of Willie, had become dumpy. Her nose was broad and there was an unbecoming slackness about her mouth. She was not a beauty, but at least her hair was an attractive auburn, her complexion was without flaw, and her eyes were blue and alert. She was intelligent, and she had presence. She would do. Next morning, she sent a note to Mr Weguelin inviting him to return.

Willie remained in Spain for eighteen months until the sulphur mine no longer contained sulphur. By then, Katharine's relationship with Mr Weguelin had run its course, and her life at Eltham had acquired the flow of a placid stream. She gave and was given dinners, made visits and was visited. Gerard, her eldest, attended a day-school at Blackheath; the two girls had a German governess. Willie's return was unsettling. Katharine walked into rooms she was accustomed to finding empty, and he was there, a new and unwanted ornament. He clashed with her life. She was no longer in love with him and she told him so. He rocked with mirth. She persisted, and at last he saw it was true: his Kate had ceased to adore her Boysie. He flung away from her; she pursued him; he would hear her out. She proposed an arrangement. She would pay him six hundred pounds a year to go and live in London, coming home at weekends for the sake of propriety. In addition, when Aunt Ben died, he would receive a cash settlement out of Katharine's inheritance. When she mentioned the sum of twenty thousand pounds the hurt quite evaporated from his face.

Willie liked London; it held pleasures that were not to be found at Eltham. And so for six days a week he became a bachelor and for one day a week a husband; it was, he felt, a desirable ratio. He continued to fail at one business and another, until the day came when, on learning that a general election had been called, he realised that his true vocation lay in politics. The revelation came to him on a weekday; nonetheless, he went directly to Eltham. How, he asked Katharine, could he have hoped to succeed in the marketplace when his real destiny lay elsewhere? Politics called for no business acumen, no abilities other than a superiority to the common herd. She was intrigued. For the first time, it came to her that she was ambitious. As a woman, she cast no shadow of her own; she walked in that of her husband; but as the wife of a member of Parliament, she would attain an importance. New doors would open. She gladly paid – or, rather, Aunt Ben paid – not only for his election expenses but for those of his sponsor and running mate, an elderly one-time soldier of fortune, duellist and philanderer who styled himself the O'Gorman Mahon. At election time the pair went to County Clare, where they drank poteen, made speeches at crossroads, sat with eyes smarting by the turf fires of a hundred cabins and – so he wrote to Katharine – joined in when the rabble sang 'A Nation Once Again'.

Now, in Thomas's Hotel, one of the two newly elected members for Clare was saying: 'Parnell? Personally, I can't abide the fellow. Too cold a fish for my liking.'

Katharine saw a flush rising in Justin McCarthy's face. Her eyes signalled a warning to Willie, who took no notice.

'And he thinks he's the Lord God Almighty. Tell you the truth, I'm delighted he didn't come. I wasn't exactly enchanted with the prospect of seeing the beggar drink my claret.'

Katharine said: 'Willie, your discretion is the envy of London.'

Willie smiled, sensing a compliment. 'Is it?'

She said: 'Mr McCarthy is one of Mr Parnell's admirers.'

McCarthy grinned. 'More than an admirer, ma'am. I'm his man . . . day and night, body and soul.'

Katharine was amused by his passion. 'Heavens!'

'Justin McCarthy, may God forgive you!' Mrs McCarthy's fan was now a humming bird. 'How free you are with your soul. Anyone,' she told the company, 'would think he owned it.'

McCarthy ignored his wife with the ease of long practice. He addressed Katharine.

'Dear lady, I am and forever will be the slave of any man who can work the miracle of making his fellow Irishmen pull together for more than five minutes on end.'

Katharine said: 'And how does he do that?'

'By letting them know, ma'am, that they are right to hate England.'

Small ripples of shock raced down the table. McCarthy seemed not to notice.

'Not only did he give their hatred an imprimatur, but he brought it into the enemy camp. Do you know, I'm inclined to believe that if any man can get Home Rule for us, Parnell can. Mind, he'd better make haste. Do you know their name for him? The Uncrowned King of Ireland. Now that's dangerous. Throughout history, the Irish never kissed a hand, but they ended up by biting it.'

Willie said: 'A charming people. Tell me, McCarthy –'

'Captain O'Shea, that's the second time you've so addressed me.' McCarthy was geniality itself. 'You seem to have picked up the curious English habit of forgetting to call people "Mr".'

Willie said: 'Have I? Perhaps that's because I regard myself as an Englishman.'

'Do you, now? What a pity you forgot to mention that to the electorate of County Clare! You might have increased your majority.' McCarthy gave Katharine his most seraphic smile. 'The sole is ambrosial, ma'am.'

'I was about to say, McCarthy . . . *Mr* McCarthy,' Willie said, his temper quite lost, 'that if you're such a devotee of *Mr* Parnell, you might persuade him to sit at my wife's table.'

'Persuade Mr Parnell?' McCarthy waved a hand at the contents of his dinner plate. 'Sir, that unfortunate fish could more easily jump into the Thames and swim home to Dover. And even if it were within my poor powers, I would not for the world deprive my hostess of the pleasure of achieving that miracle for herself.'

'How very disobliging,' Katharine favoured him with a pout wrapped in a smile.

'But forgive me,' McCarthy said. 'When and if the mountain does come to the most bewitching of Mahomets, I shall be infinitely disappointed if I am not invited to bear witness to your triumph.'

Katharine rose to the challenge. 'Mr McCarthy, before the month is out you shall have your invitation.'

'He ought,' Mrs McCarthy said, glaring at her husband, 'to wait till he is asked.'

'I'm so terribly ill-read,' Katharine said, 'but isn't there a proverb that says it is Mahomet who must go to the mountain?'

McCarthy sensed that there was sport afoot. 'You'd never beard the lion?'

'Tomorrow, I think.'

Willie said: 'Well, if the fellow does come, don't expect me to play the host.'

'Dear Willie, you know your word is law.' There was no mockery in her smile, but it was a close-run thing. 'I shall feed the lion on your behalf.'

She was aware that Justin McCarthy had begun quietly to choke. 'A bone, ma'am,' he gasped. 'A fishbone.'

In the darkness of the growler, Willie put a hand on his wife's thigh and squeezed gently. Anna sat opposite. It was Katharine's custom, whenever she came up to town for one of Willie's dinner parties, to spend the night at her sister's house in Buckingham Gate. Where Willie was concerned, *in vino veritas* did not exist; rather, he was one of those men of whom it might be said: *in vino amor*. Only Anna's presence saved Katharine from a frontal assault. There was a tremor in his voice as, already enjoying her in his mind, he said, quite by the bye: 'Kate, I forgot to ask. How is dear Aunt Ben?'

Katharine replied drily: 'Still eighty-seven, Willie. Going on for eighty-eight.'

She moved his hand from her lap to his. It returned. She snapped: 'Please! Do you take me for one of your drabs from the Lambeth Music Hall?'

'Kate!' He was shocked. 'Think of Anna.'

'Anna knows all about you, and your women. Now pay heed. You ask me to make much of Mr Parnell so that you – what is your phrase for it? – hang on to his coat-tails. Why? Why should I put myself out if you continue to speak ill of him?'

'He's so damned superior.'

Anna said: 'Willie, be a good boy. Listen to Katharine.'

10

'What kind of fool would he be,' Katharine said, 'to give preferment to a man who belittles him behind his back? I mean, I'm sure it was very clever of you to get into Westminster but how, if you blackguard your own leader, do you propose to stay there?'

Willie said, very grandly: 'I shall . . . prove myself.'

'That, Willie, is what I'm afraid of.'

The noise of the horse's hooves on the roadway changed to a scuffling. They were stopping outside Anna's house.

Katharine said: 'Yes or no? Am I or am I not to go on making a fool of myself for your sake? Well?'

He mumbled.

'Is that yes, Willie, or is it no?'

'Yes! Yes!'

He all but hurled the words at her. She said, 'Very well, then,' and made to follow Anna out of the growler. He caught at her cloak. 'Kate, let her go in. Come to Albert Mansions.'

'What an idea!'

'I say you will. Driver . . .'

'And I say I will not.' She jerked at her cloak, snapping it from his hand. 'Now that's my gallant captain. Come out on Sunday and take the children to Mass.'

'You are not a good wife,' Willie said sullenly.

'No, Willie, I'm sure I am not. But it's no matter, as long as the world and Aunt Ben think I am.'

Willie snarled at the driver to move on. As the growler reached the corner of Grosvenor Place, he put his head out of the window. He shouted back: 'You just swing his coat-tails where I can catch hold of them. You can leave the —'

A passing hansom drowned him out.

On the nights when Katharine stayed with Anna they shared a bed, as they had done when young. This evening, Anna had wined well. Listening to her snore, Katharine wondered if perhaps this was one of the reasons Lieutenant-Colonel Steele had left for India after only one week of marriage and was likely to remain there. She was methodical and, before sleep came, liked to go over her plans for the following day. She thought of Mr Parnell and what she knew of him. He was Irish, a landowner, a Protestant and a bachelor. Either he was averse to acting the gay Lothario or his followers were discreet.

At dinner, Justin McCarthy had told her: 'You see, ma'am, when Mr Parnell first came into the House the Irish members were the court jesters. The English have always sat back and let us play the dancing bears. They have a soft spot for us; to them we are characters. They call us Oirish and talk of Paddy's pig, and sure God help us, we're a race that likes to be liked. Only give us a good luncheon and we'll follow you to . . . well, let's say to dinner-time.

'Do you know the name Butt, ma'am – Isaac Butt? No? Ah well, so much for immortality! When the young Mr Parnell came stuttering and stammering his way into the House in '75, it was Butt the Irish answered to. A nice, fat, harmless old fellow who called everyone his dear boy and believed that the first duty of an Irish member was to drink port instead of porter. He welcomed the new member for Meath with open arms. Mr Parnell, so he said, would make a great addition to the party . . . good family, don't you know? Well, 'twas the rock he perished on. Inside of five years, poor old Butt was out and all but in his grave, and the upstart was in. Straight off, Parnell laid down the law: no more colloguing with the enemy. The good times were gone. Ah, ma'am, it was a great sinecure while it lasted.'

Katharine said: 'And now you say it is to be Home Rule?'

'Home Rule, land reform and the dear knows what else.' McCarthy sighed with mock martyrdom. 'It's a hard old station.'

Parnell, she thought, sounded uppish and arrogant. She routed him from her mind, but sleep would not come; she was in unaccountably low spirits. She felt an anger at herself that she should presume to be unhappy. She reminded herself that she had the affection of her children. She was free of worldly needs; her life at Eltham was untouched by care. On Aunt Ben's assurances, she had expectations. Willie's election to Parliament had been her triumph no less than his. There are women who like to inspire envy in others, and Katharine was of their number. She enjoyed going about as the wife of the handsome Captain O'Shea, M.P. – that her husband and she went about separately meant that she could enjoy the smooth without the rough. And if there were those foolish enough to believe that Willie's voice at Westminster – which, by the way, had not yet been heard – was no more than the echo of hers, she was not inclined to set them to rights.

She lay, rebuking herself for her melancholy. Then it came to her that she was thirty-five and had once been twenty, and that like all young girls, she had made promises to herself of a summertime ahead. At the rectory at Rivenhall Place, life had been a delicious preparation; the future, indistinct, had beckoned across the lawns. The love she bore her papa had filled her life to overflow, and yet she knew that it was but a prelude, that a vessel existed which could contain all she had to give. The promises had been answered with the years of Willie's careless affection and the intrigue with Weguelin. Better half a loaf, the saying went, than no bread; but it was the half-loaf in its meanness that betokened famine. She had not been ill-used; she had been hardly used.

She wept quietly, luxuriantly, pondering in a dry-eyed corner of her mind if it was not perhaps the evening's wine that wept. Beside her, Anna's snores had softened to a purr.

TWO

Timothy Michael Healy would one day have a mountain pass named after him; meanwhile, he stood clasping a dispatch case to his narrow chest and awaited his master.

He could have sat in relative comfort in the Commons library or amid the bustle of the great corridor which was the Members' communal office. Instead, he had stationed himself outside the entrance to the chamber, ensuring that his would be the first face the Chief would look upon when he emerged. He had been there since the debate began. He thought of the disciples dozing off in Gethsemane and of another Master saying: 'What, could ye not watch with me one hour?' He smiled at their want of substance. Tim Healy believed that devotion which was less than total was not devotion.

He was twenty-five, and his hair was close-cropped as if he were fearful of excess. He was temperate in all things except love and enmity. He was a Corkman, west and east; Bandon in West Cork had sired him, and the Christian Brothers in far-off Fermoy had taught him to abominate sins of the flesh. His eyes were a pale blue in which many had been judged and damned. For one so young, he had often found his faith in others to be misplaced, and, when disillusionment came, had cast them from him, recognising no court of appeal. He was foolish, he knew, to

trust in human nature when it was so unworthy of his faith and
yet he persevered. Now, in Parnell, he was vindicated; a leader
had arisen worthy of his passion. He had thrown up his trade of
journalism and become his idol's secretary, errand boy and bonds-
man. In Toronto, while accompanying the Chief on a fund-raising
tour for the Land League, it was he who had coined the title 'The
Uncrowned King of Ireland'. There were times when, he believed,
his Mr Parnell to be not quite sane, but it seemed somehow false
to his Irishness to rank madness as a sin.

Applause and a loud grumble of voices came from the chamber. Mr Gladstone had finished speaking. He would in a moment
appear; it was his custom, as Parnell had observed, always to set
sail on a high tide. A moment passed and he emerged: a lambent
flame ringed by moths, among them William Forster, the Irish
Secretary. Tim Healy's heart throbbed with loathing. The group,
murmuring, moved onwards. A voice pursued them.

'Mr Gladstone, might I have a word?'

To Healy's surprise, he saw that Parnell had come from the
chamber in unmistakable pursuit of the Prime Minister. Over
the past five years, the two had addressed each other on the
Commons floor and through the Speaker, but never, until now,
directly. Gladstone affected to be at a loss for words; it gave him
time to inspect his avowed enemy at close range for the first time.

He saw a bearded man of thirty-four, above six feet, with
dark hair becoming thin. He was gaunt, the eyes were sunken,
and the luminous pallor of the high forehead led Gladstone to
reflect without grief that here was one who would not make old
bones.

He said with antique courtesy: 'I think we have not met, sir.'

Parnell inclined his head in what masqueraded as a bow. 'I
am the member for Meath, sir. Or, if you prefer, for Cork – I
am doubly blest. You were good enough to read to the House just
now some inflammatory passages from a speech I made in Sligo.
Could I trouble you for a sight?'

It was many years since Gladstone had risen to impudence.

15

He did not do so now. In silence, he handed over to Parnell the papers he was carrying.

Parnell said: 'I am obliged. A portion of what I thought you said seemed unfamiliar. Of course it may have been the delivery. Now let me just see . . .'

He studied the papers unhurriedly while Gladstone and his entourage danced attendance. William Forster all but snarled. As Secretary for Ireland, he believed that the natural habitat for Parnell, architect of his troubles, was a prison cell. Once, as a fervent Quaker, he had in the House announced that the police would henceforth merely use buckshot against the Irish instead of bullets; and an Irish member at once called out 'Buckshot Forster!' It was a nickname that would stick to him for life, and, for the first and only time, he had seen his arch-tormentor laugh out loud. The wound, small as it was, had yet to heal.

Parnell, scanning the papers, asked without looking up: 'Have you been to Sligo, Prime Minister?'

Gladstone started at the pleasantry. Coming from such an unlikely quarter, it was as if he had been asked if he had of late enjoyed the favours of Mrs Gladstone. 'I have not, sir.'

Parnell said: 'The scenery is much admired. I recommend it.'

He swooped upon a passage. 'Ah, I have it.' He read for a moment, then said: 'As I thought, that passage is inaccurate. I never said it. Sir, I am obliged.'

He restored the papers to Mr Gladstone, again inclined his head in what would not become a bow, and set off briskly. Tim Healy, taken unawares and still hugging his dispatch case, was obliged to trot to catch up with him.

'Mr Parnell . . . excuse me, but, if you were —'

'Wait. We are within earshot.'

They rounded a corner, out of sight of Gladstone and his attendants. Parnell succeeded in not smiling.

'I think that was not badly done. Did you take note of my impudence, Healy?'

'In tackling the Old Man? 'Twas great.' Tim Healy spoke with the sing-song cadences of his native county, elongating the vowels so that 'great' was uttered as 'grey-et'.

'Healy, you miss the point. Any dolt could have waylaid him. Any clodhopper could have pointed out the inaccuracy. The impudence lay in not troubling to demand correction.'

'I see.' Plainly, Healy did not. 'Maybe a bit too subtle, sir.'

'Now you disappoint me, Healy. Too subtle for Gladstone? You have more to learn than I imagined.'

They made their way to the Members' Corridor. Unlike Gladstone and his ministers, Parnell did not merit a private room. His office was a table half-way along the cluttered hall; the archives and daily business of the Irish party reposed in Tim Healy's dispatch case. In the corridor, members' business was conducted in perfect bedlam. Visitors came and went, messages flew to and from the chamber; such was the uproar that conspiracies were hatched and schemes laid, not in whispers but shouts. Healy opened his case; it contained letters for signature, arrangements for the Land League meeting at Ennis in September, Irish newspapers, a list of the past month's evictions in the West, and accounts of the latest arrests and trials. Also from Ireland there came a daily homage of sprigs of shamrock. As instructed, Tim Healy had destroyed them on sight; his chief had a superstitious loathing of the colour green. The letters, written in Healy's copper-plate, were signed unread.

'This last one,' Healy said, 'acknowledges a donation of thirty dollars from the United States. The letter that came with it said "Five dollars for bread, twenty-five for lead." '

'The Americans have a passion for war and revolution,' Parnell said, 'especially in a country that is safely three thousand miles from theirs.'

Tim Healy giggled. 'That's good!'

He reached across for the signed letter and blotted it, his midriff all but nudging Parnell's forehead. The physical closeness to his idol gave him a frisson of pleasure; whereas to Parnell, looking up and seeing only waistcoat buttons, the world seemed to be full of Timothy Healy . For an instant he felt the unreasoning fury with

17

which is suffered the affections of a woman one does not love. The other at last moved away, and Parnell, his horizons restored, took a copy of *Freeman's Journal* from the dispatch case. While his amanuensis sat to one side and licked postage stamps, he flicked through the pages. He was expecting a visitor at noon.

At two minutes to the hour, a messenger escorted a tall, dark-bearded figure down the corridor.

'A Mr Davitt, sir.'

'Davitt, there you are.' Parnell waited until the messenger was gone. 'We could have met at my rooms in Keppel Street, but I thought Westminster might appeal to your sense of humour. You had no problems at the gate?'

'None, thanks to your *passe-partout*.' Davitt had been born in Mayo, but his accent was encrusted with the soot that darkened the moors above Haslingden where he had grown up. 'I told the chap at t'door I was on ticket-of-leave from Dartmoor.'

'And he thought you were joking?'

'Aye. He wants seeing to.'

'Have you met Timothy Healy?'

Healy sprang forward, his hand outstretched; then remembered what he had been told: that Davitt's right arm was missing. He reddened.

'I beg your pardon.'

Davitt said: 'Not at all. I'm used to being without it. It was mislaid in a mill in Baxenden when I was eleven.' He offered Healy his left hand.

Parnell waved him to a chair. 'Davitt, I have had a most entertaining morning. Mr Gladstone has been assuring the House that I am fomenting armed rebellion in Ireland.'

Davitt scowled. 'I wish to God it was true.'

'I know you do.'

Parnell said in mock appeal: 'Davitt, have pity. In Ireland, they complain that I am a pacifist; whereas in London, they swear that I am plotting murder and rapine. I seem to be having the worst of all possible worlds.'

'One of these days,' Davitt said, 'you'll fall off that bloody tightrope of yours.'

'Is that what you call it?'

'No, not a tightrope. You're like a man wi' two wives, praying they'll never meet.'

Tim Healy eyed the two, aware that a mutual respect did nothing to mitigate a mutual dislike. Parnell was an aristocrat; Davitt had been born as he would die, a peasant whose family had been evicted from their cabin near Lough Conn in the year of his birth. At twenty-four, he had been sentenced to fifteen years in prison for conspiring to smuggle guns to the Fenians. For seven years he had not been permitted a visitor; he had lived on decayed food, had broken animal bones in the Dartmoor charnel house, and, because of his disablement, had learned to pick oakum with his teeth.

Parnell was as aloof and ungiving of himself as Davitt was passionate. Parnell, since he had been sent down from Cambridge, had not since opened a book; Davitt, who had hardly seen the inside of a school-room, was well-read. Parnell had set his face against violence; Davitt would think victory incomplete if it were not achieved by force of arms.

They spoke of the meeting in Ennis. 'There will be eight priests on the platform,' Davitt said.

'Good God. It sounds as if we are becoming respectable.'

Davitt had no time for humour. 'At the meeting, you'll not deviate from your pledge?'

Without taking his eyes off him, Parnell said: 'Healy.'

The lid of the all-containing dispatch case flew open and Healy produced a sheet of paper. Parnell reached for it, but to the bemusement of both men Healy started to read, his Cork accent rising and dipping like a range of small hills.

'I, the undersigned, as President of the Land League, do solemnly agree: one, that I shall not discredit the ideal of independence to be won by physical force; two, that we shall demand no less than an Irish parliament with full power over national

19

interests; three, that the land question will be settled by tenant ownership; four, that —'

Davitt interrupted him. 'Look here, our agreement was verbal.'

Parnell said: 'Now it is written down. Healy, a pen.' He took the paper. 'By signing this, I give my word that I have promised no less.' He handed the pen and paper to Davitt. 'And by appending your name as witness you will be giving yours that I have promised no more.'

Davitt signed and, for the first time, grinned. 'You're a crafty bugger.'

He used his one hand to fold the paper. As he tucked it in his pocket, a messenger appeared at Healy's elbow, whispered and gave him a calling card.

Healy said: 'The devil she does! Well, now.' He turned to Parnell. 'It's Captain O'Shea's wife. She's in Palace Yard. Will you go to her?'

'Confound the woman. Does she never give up?' Parnell glanced at the card. ' "Will the Uncrowned King of Ireland deign to spare a —" Damn her impudence.'

Davitt asked: 'A lovelorn female?'

'Worse. A giver of dinners. Healy, go and tell her I am engaged.'

Healy said: 'She told the messenger that she will wait all day.'

'Am I to be spared nothing?' Parnell rose. 'Very well, if the lady invites brutality, then by heaven she shall have it. Davitt, forgive me. Stay, and we shall have lunch.'

He went off down the corridor. Healy's lip was trembling with a lover's indignation. ' 'Tisn't fair. People take advantage of him.'

Davitt said sourly: 'I can see that you're one of the idolaters.'

Healy said: 'If I have clothes on my back, 'twas the Chief who put them there. Whatever I am, he made me.'

'Did he, now?' Davitt said drily. 'Well, be merciful. Try not to punish him.'

His eyes were on the departing Parnell. He felt the old bitterness bite at his craw that he, who had set up the Land League, was not its president. His sense of what was fair reminded him that Parnell was a leader and he was not, and yet what rankled was that the Irish, consumed by self-hate or envy or whatever it was ailed them, would not accept one of their own. 'If a man is only as good as I am,' the reasoning went, 'then the back of my hand to him.' They wanted an autocrat who would despise and bully them, a cold fish who would move among them, untouching and untouched. An image crossed Davitt's mind; he had remembered the fable of the frogs who begged for a new king and were sent a stork, who devoured them.

Palace Yard was bright in the July sunshine. Katharine had thought to engage an open carriage, but Anna, who had opposed the expedition from its beginning, stood firm. Either they would go by hansom or her sister must find another chaperon. They were exposing themselves to the insults of a known boor, and the confines of an enclosed cab would help conceal any rebuff they might receive. 'This is not ladylike,' Anna said as they left the house at Buckingham Gate. She said it again, giving a disapproving glance at the red rose in Katharine's bodice as they drove under the trees of Birdcage Walk. As they waited outside the Houses of Parliament, she flinched at every carriage that passed. For a third time, she was about to remark upon the unlady-likeness of their adventure when Katharine said: 'I think the mountain approaches.'

It was common knowledge that the Irish leader was not robust, but Katharine was unprepared for his paleness. He came towards the hansom cab with long, quick strides. Here, she thought, is a man in a temper. In a moment, he was upon them.

'Mrs O'Shea?'

Replying, she marvelled that her voice could sound so calm. 'As you can see, Mr Parnell, a cat presumes to look at an uncrowned king.' As she gave him her hand through the open window, she felt rather than heard Anna give a tiny hiccup of terror. 'I think you do not know my sister. Mrs Steele.'

21

'An honour.' He was looking, not at Anna, but Katharine.

She launched her attack. 'Sir, you are unkind. You did not come to dinner last evening. Or to the three dinners before that. Am I to be told why?'

From his eyes, she knew that she was to be lied to. Probably it would be a well-turned lie, bright and handsome, but she would have the truth. She repeated: 'Am I, Mr Parnell?'

A minute had not passed and already their acquaintance had become too intimate for falsehood. He said: 'I did not come because I took my hostess to be the kind of woman she evidently is not.'

Without looking, Katharine knew that Anna's eyes were wide with shock. She said, enjoying herself: 'Honesty! What a bad beginning. And now that you are disabused, is your hostess perhaps the kind of woman who could induce you to grace her table?'

He thought for a moment. 'Tomorrow I go to Paris for my sister's wedding. Later on, I am to address a meeting at Ennis. That is in County Clare.'

Katharine said: 'So I have heard. My husband is the member for that county.'

'Is he?' There was bland insult in his voice, not directed at her but at Willie. 'It had slipped my mind.' Then: 'So shall we say between Paris and Ennis?'

'London, perhaps? How convenient.' It was a game now, and she was matching him. 'Do you like the theatre, Mr Parnell?'

'I detest it.'

She said: 'Good. I shall engage a box for after dinner. It will be your punishment.'

She extended her hand. He took it and bowed formally to Anna. 'Goodbye, Mrs Steele.'

As he turned away, Katharine gave a faint cry. He looked and saw that the rose had fallen from her bodice. For a moment he hesitated. 'Allow me.' He picked it up, raised it for a moment to his nose, then bore it away towards the Commons.

'Katharine!' Anna was shocked. 'You dropped that flower on purpose.'

'Nonsense.'

'Well, you flirted with him.'

'Nothing of the sort. I was the one who was flirted with. I simply retaliated.'

Furious, Anna told the cabman to drive on.

'Wait! Not yet!' Katharine watched until Parnell had disappeared indoors.

'Now drive.'

He came to dinner at Thomas's Hotel ten days later. Willie, who had vowed not to attend, grumbled that he might after all be persuaded to come. Katharine would not hear of it. 'How can I flirt and make great eyes at the dreadful man for your sake if you are looking on? What kind of fool would he take you for to permit it?' Willie laughed and agreed with her. 'Go it, Dick!' he said, using the nickname he had had for her in their courting days and which she loathed.

Again it was a party of eight, with Anna and the Justin McCarthys there to witness her triumph. Parnell paid lavish attentions to Anna throughout the meal, hardly glancing towards his hostess. Anna seemed to be quite won over, and McCarthy at one point looked wonderingly from the pair to Katharine. She smiled and said in a soft voice: 'Dinners have their separate courses, Mr McCarthy. So do evenings.'

She had engaged a box for afterwards at the Gaiety, where her favourite, Marion Hood, was playing. She sat with Parnell at the rear of the box out of sight of the audience. They spoke, his face made even paler than before by the light from the stage. She asked him why he had not married. He told her of a young lady in America several years before, whose father had forbidden her engagement to a young Irishman who lacked a title and was therefore only a gentleman by hearsay.

23

'I saw her again,' he said, 'on my fund-raising tour in March last. I escorted her to a ball.'

'Oh, yes?' Katharine realised to her annoyance that her voice had trembled. 'And of course you were now a famous man.'

'Yes, I daresay. As we were going up the stairs she pressed a paper into my hand. It contained a verse written, I believe, by a Mrs Browning. It is the only verse I ever put to memory.

> "Unless you can muse in a crowd all day
> On the absent face that fixed you,
> Unless you can dream that his faith is fast
> Through behoving and unbehoving,
> Unless you can die when the dream is past,
> Oh, never call it loving."'

'Well, of course,' Parnell said, 'I wasn't prepared to do all of that, so I went away and came home.'

Katharine endeavoured to keep her face straight. 'Quite right, too.' He nodded. 'I am told that my Miss Woods is now engaged to a prominent lawyer in Boston.'

Katharine started. '*What* did you say her name was? Did you call her Miss Woods?'

'Why? You cannot know her.'

Katharine said: 'Wood was my maiden name. Wood in the singular, that is.'

'Singular in more ways than one. Extraordinary.'

Katharine said 'Isn't it!' and began to laugh.

He said: 'You find it so amusing. May I know why?'

'No, it is too bad of me. I must not. And yet . . .'

Her laughter became quite helpless. Anna looked around, smiling, and put a finger to her lips. Parnell frowned, wondering if he was the butt of a joke.

He said peevishly: 'Whatever it is, it is quite over my head.'

Katharine touched a handkerchief to her eyes. 'It occurred to me . . . no, it is unforgivable. Mr Parnell, it occurred to me that you are not yet . . . out of the Woods.'

24

He stared at her, then gave a short explosive bark of a laugh that brought hisses from the neighbouring playgoers. On the stage, Marion Hood faltered in mid-sentence.

On the following Wednesday, Parnell looked up from his seat in the House and saw Katharine in the Ladies' Gallery. A few minutes later, he was at her side. She expected a greeting; instead he took her arm.

'Come away.'

'Where are we going?'

He hurried her down the stairs. 'I have no pressing business today, and clearly neither have you. We shall take a drive in the sunshine.'

Outside, he hailed a cab and they drove to Mortlake, where they walked in the meadows, found a bench to sit by the river's edge and watched the boats. Among the bright colours, Parnell, sombre in his parliamentary frock-coat, drew amused glances. Katharine spoke to him of Rivenhall where she grew up; in return, he talked of his estate in Avondale in County Wicklow. He had been thirteen when his father died. His mother was American and as a bride had brought to Ireland a dowry of fanatical hatred. A blind loathing of England had existed in her family since the War of Independence, and she tended it like a sacred flame. It was her life, her legacy to her children. It was venom in the bloodstream of Parnell's younger sisters, Fanny and Anna. Neither had married. No man, no footling sexuality, could match the ecstasy of their hatred for whatever was English. They offered up their separate virginities to the cause of enslaved Ireland. Their faces were gaunt, their eyes burned as if hungering for the pyre of martyrdom. They were high priestesses of the Land League, and, as if to add fuel to their fire, Fanny wrote impassioned patriotic verses.

'I think,' Parnell said, 'that my mother is perhaps not sane.'

Katharine looked at him in mild shock.

25

He smiled. 'In our family we have few bonds of sentiment. We are not close-knit.'

'They say that you too hate England.'

'They slander me. Hate England? Not at all. Only the English.'

She prayed that he would not be so coy as to say that there were certain exceptions. When her prayer was answered and he remained silent, she was both glad and annoyed. She punished him by bringing up the subject of Willie.

'About my husband . . .'

'Oh, yes?'

On the instant, she could have sworn that the sun had gone in.

'I would like you to do what you can for him.'

'Yes, I am sure you would.'

His eyes were suddenly cold. His displeasure frightened her. She affected the impatience of a nursemaid with a sullen child.

'Now for pity's sake, don't take offence and allow it to spoil our day. You know I must ask. It is my duty, so let us have it over and done with. My husband has many excellent qualities' – she wondered at how effortlessly she lied – 'but he is improvident. We exist by the goodness of an aunt of mine without whom we should starve. I want to see Willie live by his own efforts. Mr Parnell, if there is another election, is my husband likely to retain his seat?'

The answer came without hesitation. 'No.'

'You seem very certain.'

'I am.'

'May I ask why?'

Parnell's voice was contemptuous as he replied: 'Because he won it by fraud.'

'Mr Parnell!'

'Your husband put himself forward to his party and to the electorate as an Irish nationalist. He was and is nothing of the kind, and now he has been found out. The people will not have him a second time.'

'Then are you saying that there is no hope for him?'

He paused before replying. 'I will do what I can.'

On impulse she put a hand on his arm. He was not pleased that she took pleasure in her husband's well-being.

'I cannot help him, however, if he will not behave himself. In the House, he consorts with our enemies. He treats the other Irish members as if he were an English gentleman and they were rabblement.'

'Should I talk to him?'

'Certainly *I* do not intend to.'

She said, meaning it. 'I think he does not deserve your help.'

Parnell smiled and the day was saved. 'In that case I shall do my best.'

They drove back to London, but by the time they reached Cannon Street the train for Blackheath had gone. Parnell was pleased. 'It means I shall have another hour of your company.' He chose the sleekest horse in the cab rank.

When they reached the Wonersh Lodge, she begged leave not to invite him in. 'The house is unfit for visitors, and besides I must go at once to Aunt Ben.'

As he handed her down from the cab, he said jealously: 'What you perhaps mean is that your husband is at home.'

She looked puzzled for a moment. 'But of course you don't know . . . how could you? Willie and I live apart. He comes here only at weekends and by invitation.' She turned towards the house, then hesitated. 'When do you go to Ennis?'

He was still attempting to take in what she had told him. 'When do I . . . ?'

Katharine said: 'This is impudence, I know, in one who must as yet be less than a friend, but I think you are not well. You look most dreadfully pale. Please do not go to Ireland.'

'What? Not go home?'

'You do too much. You are stubborn and foolhardy.'

Parnell took her hand. 'You *are* my friend, and I thank you for your concern. Alas, the Irish think they can hold on to their land with pikes and buckshot. How are they to know they are fools if I am not there to tell them?'

She retrieved her hand. 'And I think that not only are you unwell; you are also conceited.'

He said: 'My American tour was more taxing than I had expected. The ill effects will pass. The conceit is, alas, incurable. Are you annoyed?'

'Yes.' Her lips twitched. She said, before the mask could slip: 'Goodbye, Mr Parnell.'

28

THREE

The autumnal gales had begun early. The mail-packet on which Parnell travelled from Holyhead bucked and yawed until in sight of Kingstown harbour. The same wind roared across the Earl of Erne's estate on the bleak Mayo uplands as a sergeant and six infantrymen escorted Cornelius Ring and his family to their new home. As a child, Ring had seen his parents and two sisters die of the famine in Black '47; now, in what were to be the last minutes of his life, he thought that his luck had changed.

The new home was a thatched cabin that until the previous week had been occupied by the Moone family. Michael Moone had made a mistake. He had worked his smallholding too diligently. When there was a good year and he prospered, the landlord's agent raised his rent. That was the way of things. When an early frost destroyed his crop and he fell upon evil days, the rent remained the same; that, too, was the way of things. The Moones were permitted three months of arrears; then, last week, they had been evicted. Already this year, more than seven thousand evictions had been carried out in Ireland. Michael Moone had no head for statistics; for the past week, his wife and the girls had bedded down on the mud floor of a neighbour's cottage; he and his son had slept in the byre.

Pushing a handcart on which his possessions were piled, and with room on it for twice as much, Cornelius Ring saw the cabin

29

come into view through the gaps in the whin. He nodded to his wife, Honor, indicating that they had come into their kingdom. There would be smoke from their chimney within the hour and tea in the cups. It was the custom on the occasion of an eviction to pull down the lintel after the departing tenants, making the dwelling uninhabitable. This time, knowing that the cottage would not stand empty for long, the bailiffs had merely boarded up the door and windows. Now, at a signal from the sergeant, two infantrymen went ahead at the double, heads bent against the gale, and ripped down the boards. The Rings, reaching the wooden front gate, waited.

'Sergeant.'

One of the soldiers made a signal. The sergeant looked and saw what he had expected: a crowd of perhaps a dozen men who had been watching them from the lee of a broken wall. They moved forward. Michael Moone was in front, not so much leading the men as being impelled by those behind. They were local smallholders, neighbours of the evicted family. They stopped, confronting the Rings across the threshold.

The two infantrymen had completed their task. The door hung open, waiting. The sergeant, ignoring the others, said formally to the new tenant: 'It's yours. Take possession.' As Cornelius Ring hesitated, the sergeant shoved him forward. 'Don't be afraid, man. Walk in.'

As Ring made to take a step forward, Michael Moone was all but flung into his path. 'Tell him, Mick,' a voice said. 'Tell the grabber.' Another man shouted at Ring: 'Go back to Leitrim, you whoor's melt.'

Moone's teeth were chattering as much from fear as from the wind that spat across Lough Mask, but he was a Mayoman and knew that he must at least put his anger on show for his neighbours to bear witness. 'No interloper,' he said, 'will set foot on my land.'

The sergeant, a Northerner by his accent, said: 'It's not your land, and it never was. You were put off it and these people are taking peaceable possession. Now stand back.'

Moone said, stammering: 'I say 'tis mine, and . . . and . . . and death to all grabbers.'

A voice from behind him said: 'True for you, Mick.'

The sergeant pointed at Cornelius Ring. 'This family is under the Queen's protection. I'm ordering the lot of you to disperse or be charged with riotous behaviour.' He turned on the new tenant. 'Man, you have a right to be here, and the law and your landlord say so. Do you mean to have us out here till winter comes?'

Ring looked at his wife. Her eyes went from his face to the waiting cottage. He took a step. Of a sudden, Michael Moone was shouting.

'Me and mine were put off that land for the want of a quarter's rent. I'll swing for any man that puts foot through my gate.'

The sergeant said: 'That will do us, that's a threat. Take him in charge.'

Afterwards, nobody could or would say if Michael Moone had brought the pistol with him for courage, or if one of his sympathisers had pressed it into his hand. He produced it from under his coat and levelled it, first at the sergeant, then at the two young soldiers who had come forward to seize him, and finally at Cornelius Ring. The muzzle shook.

It was starvation that had brought Ring from County Leitrim. He was not so different from Michael Moone; both had families; both, ill-used, were driven by desperation. He took a step forward, his hands extended, palms upwards in appeal.

He said: 'Decent man, y'are. Sure don't blame us. All we are is —'

Michael Moone shot him through the left eye.

For a moment, there was no sound but the whine of the wind. Then Honor Ring began to scream. The sergeant drew his own pistol and shot Michael Moone in the chest. He was thrown back against the wall, but remained upright. He began to hiccup blood.

The sergeant screamed at his men: 'What the hell are ye waiting for? Are ye bloody statues?'

31

He moved to one side, pointed at the wounded man and screamed 'Fire!' Five of the infantrymen let off a ragged volley at Moone, riddling him. The sixth aimed, hesitated and left it too late; he lowered his rifle and stood sheepishly. Two men lay dead. Nora Ring's keening had infected her children; they began to run about blindly. The sergeant looked at the bodies; there would be the devil to pay over this: outcries by day, acts of blackguardism by night, brimstone from the pulpits on Sundays.

As he turned, again to order the crowd to disperse, a heavy stone was thrown and caught him on the forehead. Another struck his chest. He staggered backwards through the gate. The men followed him, making ammunition of the unmortared wall. The sergeant raised an arm, too slow for the stone that shattered his face. If the Paddies would not have a care, he thought, they would kill him. Another stone put his eye out. He stumbled and fell. The men came and stood over him. In Mayo, stones are plentiful. The men pounded his head in, using both hands.

The five infantrymen who had been Moone's firing squad were young townies, half-trained and half-frozen. The sergeant's ill-judged order to fire had left them helpless; out-numbered, they made no attempt to reload their single-shot rifles. The soldier who had not fired was the first to walk away. The others followed. After a while, they began to run. Within minutes, they were scarlet flecks against the rain-logged bogland.

In Pall Mall, the Earl of Erne came out of his club, looked at the sullen sky, laughed and remarked to his companion that it was Irish weather.

The mail-packet docked late because of the storm. Parnell spent the night in Dublin and travelled to Ennis next day, by a mid-afternoon train. The Land League organisers had announced a Grand Torchlight Procession and had all but gored their President with an Irish bull by imploring that he would not bedim the lustre of the occasion by arriving during the hours of daylight. By the time he boarded the train in the company of Timothy Healy and one of his lieutenants, John Dillon, the Mayo killings had become the latest sensation. The Irish were martyrs and the Irish were murderers, and with scrupulous fairness demands for bloody vengeance went up, whichever side one took.

'I think,' Dillon said, addressing the air as they pulled out of Kingsbridge station, 'that any man who speaks of peace in Ennis this evening may save his breath to cool his porridge.'

Dillon, although the coolest of the Young Turks, was not so rash as to offer advice directly to his chief. Parnell did not reply; his thoughts were on a letter he had had that morning written:

> *My dear Mrs O'Shea,*
>
> *A line to say that after Ennis I go on to Avondale, Rathdrum, where I hope to hear from you.*
>
> *I may tell you in confidence that I don't feel quite so content at the prospect of a week's absence amongst the hills and valleys of Wicklow as I should have done some weeks since.*
>
> *The cause is mysterious, but perhaps you will help me to find it, or her, on my return.*
>
> *Yours always,*
>
> *Chas. S. Parnell*

At Ennis, the torches flickered in the rain, the crowds cheered and a fife-and-drum band played 'Let Erin Remember' and – in memory of the Manchester Martyrs – 'God Save Ireland'. Tim Healy held an umbrella over his chief's head as the procession moved off. Michael Davitt had materialised with a retinue of eight priests, as he had predicted, all of them suitably grim. His own face was, as usual, dour, but the eyes contained a glint of malicious delight. The Mayo killings had made his followers eager for blood. He would have his revolution yet.

As they marched, he said to Parnell: 'You'll want to watch out that you don't fall off that tightrope of yours. If I were you, I wouldn't misjudge the humour of this crowd.'

33

Parnell made no reply. He was trying to avoid contact with those along the route who attempted to shake his hand or – and at this his fastidious soul recoiled – were determined to kiss it.

A voice in the crowd shouted: 'The King! The King!'

'That revolting nickname,' Parnell said coldly, 'is your doing, Healy.'

The platform for the meeting had been erected in an open space on the edge of the town. The rain, which settled down to become a drizzle, had no effect on the size of the audience, many of whom had come north from Limerick and even south from Galway. Parnell suppressed a groan when he mounted the steps; he had resigned himself to the green leather benches of the House, but not to the Irish love of festooning public platforms with shamrocks and emerald drapes. To him, green was the colour of death.

The crowd patiently endured the preliminary speakers, none of whom made more than passing reference to the events in Mayo. Even Davitt, when it was his turn, held back. It was for Parnell, as dictator, to utter the awaited battle cry. If he summoned the crowd to arms, Davitt told himself, he was finished in Westminster; if he counselled restraint, he was finished in the Land League.

The rear of the platform was sheltered by an awning; when Parnell stepped forward bare-headed, Healy made to accompany him with the umbrella and was waved back for his trouble. Parnell faced his audience: he was erect, commanding: a demigod among earthlings. 'He *looks* like a leader,' Davitt growled to Dillon, 'and the bugger knows it.'

Parnell spoke for forty minutes by Tim Healy's watch. He was not a natural orator; those seated behind him on the platform saw that his right hand was clenched, the nails pressing into the palm. Towards the end, he spoke of next year's Land Bill and warned his listeners that its success depended on how they behaved during the winter. The crowd became restive; they sensed appeasement; he would counsel meekness and submission to the law.

He said: 'The measure of the Land Bill will be the measure of

34

your determination to keep a firm grip on your homesteads. More easily said than done! For what are we to do to a tenant who bids for a farm from which his neighbour has been evicted?'

For a moment, there was an amazed silence. They had wronged him; he had grasped the nettle.

A roar went up that shook Ennis. 'Kill him! Shoot him!'

Parnell started back in affected surprise. He put a hand elaborately to his ear and said: 'I beg your pardon. I think I heard someone say "Shoot him".'

A laugh went up. Bejasus, he only thought he heard it! That was a good one! Oh, leave it to the Chief!

Parnell looked down on the faces that in the light of the torches were a sea of glowing coals. 'No, I wish to point out to you a very much better way, a more Christian and a more charitable way, which will give the lost sinner an opportunity of repenting.' He took his time, knowing that the crowd was his.

'When a man takes a farm from which another has been evicted, you must shun him on the roadside when you meet him, you must shun him in the streets of the town, you must shun him at the shop counter, you must shun him in the fair and in the market-place —'

A voice parroted: 'Shun him!'

'. . . and even in the house of worship, by leaving him severely alone. You must show him your detestation of the crime he has committed, and you may depend upon it that there will be no man so full of avarice, so lost to shame, as to dare the public opinion of all right-thinking men and to transgress your unwritten code of laws. Such a man cannot survive; men such as you cannot but win.'

He went back to his seat, the applause welling up to follow him. As it spread and endured, Davitt found himself torn between admiration and anger. He could not make up his mind whether Parnell had given to the Irish a devastating weapon or a toy to play with. He was capable of either.

'Wasn't he great?' Tim Healy said.

'Aye,' Davitt replied. 'I'd applaud him if I had another hand.'

35

No man could have been in sunnier mood than Joseph Gillis Biggar, M.P., as he turned into Keppel Street. There was a bounce in his step that made his progress seem doubly incongruous in view of his height, or the want of it. There was in all no more than five feet of him, and he had just failed in an attempt to be a hunchback. Disraeli, on a first sighting of him in the House, had raised his eyeglass and asked: 'Do I espy a leprechaun?'

Joseph Biggar liked the ladies and, either in spite of or because of his appearance, they liked him back. One of the reasons for this morning's good humour was that he had just released from his bed a barmaid named Charlotte, who at three in the morning had begged him for mercy and, when it was offered, declined to accept. Among his mail, he had found a letter threatening an action for breach of promise action on behalf of an Irish lady living in Paris. Aside from reflecting that women were the devil for marrying, Biggar did not give the lady, or for that matter his children by various mothers, a further thought. There had been, for once, good news from Ireland.

A woman looked at him as he passed. He assumed that she was admiring the Wellington boots of which he was so proud that he kept his trousers cut short, the better to display them to the world. Or she perhaps recognised him as Joe Biggar, M.P., Belfastman, Presbyterian, demon lover, pork butcher and impassioned Parnellite and marvelled that so compact a frame could contain so many wonders.

The tidings had come from the estate of the Earl of Erne. It was there – fittingly at the scene of the Mayo killings – that Parnell's new stratagem had swiftly been put to the test. Because of a dispute over wages, no local man could be found to harvest the Erne crops, and so fifty Orangemen had been imported under the protection of two thousand troops. The harvesters and their bodyguard alike had all but starved. In the villages and on the roads, they might have been invisible and voiceless. No shopkeeper could be induced to serve them with food, and they lived off the crops they had come to save. In the end, the harvest was brought in, but the cost to the government was, so Parnell took pleasure in declaring, a shilling a turnip. Meanwhile, Lord Erne's servants and labourers had quit his service. Horses went unshod, cows unmilked, dinners uncooked. There was nothing for his lordship's land agent to do but leave Connaught or himself expire of hunger. Captain Charles Boycott had duly entrained for his native England.

And so Joseph Biggar all but skipped up the front steps of 16, Keppel Street, where Parnell lodged. He was not alone. A handsome woman was at the door awaiting admission. She seemed nervous, and Biggar came to the natural conclusion that he was the cause. He unbuttoned his coat so that she would have the benefit of his gleaming sealskin waistcoat. There were days on which he could not for the life of him explain how any woman in London could resist throwing herself at him.

A maidservant answered the door. Katharine asked if Mr Parnell was at home.

It was Biggar's chance. He leered up at her; women, he had discovered, enjoyed the novelty of being flirted with from beneath their eye level. 'If you'll allow me, madam. I myself am calling upon Mr Parnell. Joseph Biggar, at your service, ma'am.'

He took her arm and guided her upstairs to the first floor, where he knocked upon a door. John Dillon answered it. 'Joe! Come in, we're —' He broke off on seeing Katharine.

Grouped around the sitting-room table there were three men besides Parnell, who wore a dressing-gown and, beneath it, a collarless shirt. Katharine saw at once that he was unwell. He came towards her, hardly believing it was she. 'Mrs O'Shea!'

She had thought to find him alone. It had taken an effort of the will to come alone to his lodgings; even so, it was only now that she realised the impropriety of her visit.

She was flustered. 'I see I am intruding. Perhaps another time would be more —'

Parnell said: 'There is no intrusion, but I am less than presentable.' He moved to withdraw into the bedroom, lingering first to introduce his companions. 'May I present Mr Dillon, Mr O'Connor and Mr Healy? No doubt you are already acquainted with our Mr Biggar, who does not stand on ceremony.' He extended a hand towards Katharine. 'Mrs O'Shea.' He added: 'Mrs O'Shea's husband is . . . ah, our Captain O'Shea.'

John Dillon said: 'Oh?'

T.P. O'Connor said: 'Indeed?'

Timothy Healy said nothing, but regarded her with the eyes of an old Christian Brothers boy.

'Healy,' Parnell said, 'a chair for Mrs O'Shea.'

She said, faintly: 'No, I must not.'

Parnell was firm. 'You shall. I am delighted to see you. If you would permit me for just one moment . . .'

He stepped into the bedroom. Katharine sat. The constraint in the room was almost tangible.

'They told me,' Biggar said, addressing the four walls, 'that the Chief came back ailing from Ireland. Begod, they weren't drawing the longbow. I'd say that another clean shirt would do him.'

Katharine gave him so horrified a look that he changed the subject. 'Did yous hear the great news from Mayo?'

T.P. O'Connor said: 'Did we not!'

Dillon said: 'That's as stale as yesterday's bread. Look here, Joe. We were just now feasting our eyes on this.' He picked up a news-sheet from the table. 'A red-letter day for us. Number One. Volume One. Mrs O'Shea, ma'am, will you take a look?'

Katharine read aloud: '*United Ireland*. Is it a new newspaper?'

Dillon said: '*Our* newspaper, ma'am.'

Biggar said: 'Begod, lads, is thon printer's ink I smell off of it, or is it cordite?'

Healy said, and there was a catch in his throat: 'Now we have a voice.'

Dillon told her: 'The name says it all: what we want and what we mean to have.'

Katharine asked: 'Is Ireland not united, then?'

O'Connor laughed and affected a brogue. 'Lord save you, ma'am, to be sure 'tis, and forever 'twill be. From the dawn of time and down the ages, sure haven't the Irish always been firmly united in their disunity?'

The bedroom door had been left open, and now Parnell was in the room, pulling on a jacket, his face dark with sudden rage. He advanced on O'Connor.

O'Connor said: 'Sir, I was —'

When Parnell spoke, it was how Katharine had since childhood imagined that a snake would strike. He said: 'O'Connor, you will not within my hearing again cheapen what we hold most dear by making a vulgar joke of it. Do you understand?'

Dillon, intervening, said: 'With respect, sir, I think that what O'Connor meant was —'

Parnell snarled at him. 'I was not addressing you, Dillon.' He rounded again on O'Connor. 'Say what you have to say. Say it as truth or as your opinion or even as a damned lie, but not as a buffoon. While I am leader of the party its members will have self-respect. Do you mind me?'

O'Connor said 'Yes, sir' in a low voice. The tongue-lashing had been the more humiliating for the presence of a woman.

Katharine rose to her feet. 'Mr Parnell, I really think that I should leave.'

Her look spurned any attempt at protest. Parnell gave way and said that he would escort her to her carriage. When the leavetakings were done and the door had closed behind them, O'Connor collapsed into a chair. He looked at his hand and wondered when it would stop trembling.

Biggar said: 'Bejesus, T. P., I can't see your ear for the fleas in it.' He chuckled. 'I thought he'd be dug out o' you.'

Timothy Healy was all but weeping from anger. 'That woman,' he said, 'has the Chief persecuted. She thinks he will do favours

39

for her husband. She came to the Commons after him, and now she comes into his own home. She has no shame.'

He went to the front window and looked down mournfully at his afflicted chief assisting Mrs O'Shea into her carriage. Silently, he cursed Parnell's soft-heartedness. He did not actually give way to tears; had he done so, they would have dried instantly when he saw the carriage move off, not with one passenger, but two.

'The Strand,' Parnell said to the driver. He smiled at Katharine: 'I know where we may obtain coffee that is second to none. The place is quite respectable.'

'What of your friends?' she asked.

He corrected her. 'My subordinates. They have work to do.'

She said: 'Mr Parnell, I am not sure that I wish to take coffee with you. And I hope that what I have just seen and heard was the very worst of you.'

'Oh, no,' he said cheerfully. 'There are still depths to plumb. Chasms and abysses.'

She was silent for a time, then asked: 'Why did you abuse that poor young man?'

He said: 'Self-discipline is not one of the Irish characteristics. It requires to be instilled.'

'You instil it very well.'

'It is kind of you to say so.'

She thought bitterly that this was how he thanked her for inviting scandal for his sake. The brute seemed determined to make light of her vexation. She would not descend to his level.

She affected her most regal voice: 'By the bye, who was that repulsive little man?'

Parnell said: 'Who? Oh, if you mean Biggar, he is not at all repulsive, merely ugly. No man lives who is more staunch, and as a fighter he is the best in the world. He fears none.'

'Not even you?'

He did not reply. Instead, and as if divining her mood, he said: 'You have not told me why I have been so unexpectedly honoured.'

She said: 'I gave way to an impulse. It was foolishness.'

He looked at her keenly. 'Was it?'

'Let us wait until we have our coffee.'

When the carriage pulled up, she saw that they had arrived at the Savoy. 'Is this the place you described as "respectable"?'

Parnell said: 'It is only ten years old, but let us give it the benefit of the doubt.'

She doubled her resolve not to lose her temper. Parnell was rhapsodically greeted by the *maître d'hôtel*, who all but gavotted ahead of them to a table overlooking the Embankment. The coffee came.

'Last evening,' Katharine said, 'I entertained one of my husband's colleagues and yours to dinner. The O'Gorman Mahon. It is an Irish title, is it not?'

'Yes, which the rogue pilfered for himself. He has as little right to it as I do.'

Katharine said: 'I think he is not one of your admirers. He told us, and he smiled as he did so, that you had returned from Ireland in worse health than when you went there. He went so far as to say, even more gleefully, that you were unlikely to last out the present session.'

'Seeing that he himself is eighty,' Parnell said, 'I could return the compliment.'

She said: 'You look wretched. I think I agree with him.'

He said: 'I caught cold in Ennis. It was my own fault for striking bare-headed attitudes in the rain. At home in Avondale it turned to bronchitis, with a touch of rheumatism as a garnish.'

Katharine said: 'I came to Keppel Street because I wanted . . . I *want* you to come and stay at Eltham.'

41

In the act of adding milk to his coffee, he thought better of it. 'My dear lady . . . !'

'I know you neglect yourself. London isn't good for Irishmen; they die of it. My Irish cook, Ellen, and the parlourmaid, Mary . . . now *they* think that Mr Parnell is a god come down to earth, so at least you will have proper meals and be looked after. Dear heaven, look at the man!'

He appeared moved; at any rate, she noticed that he now took great pains in attending to his coffee. 'And for how long am I to be . . . what is the word for it . . . your patient?'

'Until you are well. A dead man could not be of much help to my husband.'

She saw the look come into his face that she had seen once before, by the river at Mortlake.

He said, offended: 'I see.'

She said: 'Is it the sight of the Thames that has that effect on you, or is it the mention of my husband?'

'You mean, that in return for your hospitality, I am to —'

'Oh, hush.' She glanced about her in case they were overheard. 'Mr Parnell, I am not clever or accomplished or a woman of the world. But I do know that if I were thought to invite you to my home for my own gain and my husband's, all society would applaud. They would smile and be wise and say: That is how affairs are managed. As my husband is so fond of saying, it is a market-place. Instead, let us suppose that you were to come to Eltham only as my friend, to be nursed back to health. Don't you realise that the impropriety of it would rock London?'

Parnell looked out at the river and smiled. He said: 'I may have to revise my opinion.'

'Of me?'

'I met you for the first time on the same day as I first met Mr Gladstone. I made the mistake then of thinking that my meeting with him was the more momentous.'

Her eyes were at once dismayed, and for a moment he saw the young girl she had once been. The woman she now was would not yield first place, even to Gladstone. She asked, almost tearfully: 'Did you really think that?'

He told her, and would have done so even if it were a lie: 'Not for an instant.'

She smiled, the victory hers. 'Then will you come to Eltham?'

'If it were only possible.' He shrugged helplessly. 'Perhaps when my affairs are less pressing . . .'

She said: 'Your affairs will always be pressing. You know where Wonersh Lodge is. I shall expect you at three o'clock.'

Her tone brooked no refusal; privately, she wondered if he would come. As if the matter were settled beyond debate, she looked about her at their surroundings. 'This is humiliating.'

'Being here with me?'

'No. I mean that I am an Englishwoman, and I have never been to the Savoy. You are Irish, and you walk in here as if it were your home. I feel quite dispossessed.'

43

FOUR

Ellen had ruinously over-cooked the luncheon sole. By two o'clock, she and Mary were useless; by three, they were panic-stricken; by four, they were wringing their hands in black despair. Katharine tended to the potted flowers she had arranged in one of the two sitting rooms in honour of her visitor. She resisted glancing at the time, but could not shut out the chiming of the quarter-hour from the grandfather clock in the hall. She felt a familiar fury, except that this time there was not an empty chair, but a room prepared, a fire blazing, a bed turned down. At going on for half-past four, she heard Mary scream from her outpost at the half-landing window; a moment later, from below stairs, Ellen answered in duet. Katharine untied her pinafore and went to receive her guest. How, she reflected, could he possibly not have come?

When Parnell had quite settled in, she took him for a walk in the grounds and pointed out her aunt's house, The Lodge, across the park.

'Perhaps you will meet her. I am sure that she is inspecting you at this moment.'

It was the moment of sunset; rooks in their hundreds wheeled over the autumn wood. Their cries echoed her own turbulence. She knew that he wanted her; she had known that from the moment of their meeting in the Palace Yard. It was why, when

44

she had deliberately let the rose fall from her bodice, he had in answer played the story-book lover and carried it away. To be sure, he wanted her; to be wanted, and by him, was glorious, but it was not enough. Mr Weguelin had wanted her, but in bed he had been less like a banker than a burglar who clumsily smashes down a door without thinking to discover that it is already open. In three months she would be thirty-five, and she wanted more than to be wanted. She was too old for an adventure, too proud now for an affair and its uses. She wanted what she had been denied: a life.

Playing the hostess, she told Parnell how Mr George Meredith came and read to Aunt Ben for three hundred pounds a year. He said: 'If he ever tires of his labours, pray let me know.'

'You are not wealthy, then?'

'My opponents say that I have a down on landlords because I am the least successful of the breed. And so I am. Instead of paying their rents my tenants make up sentimental songs – usually about me.'

'Was it they who called you the Uncrowned King?'

'No. For that I may thank Timothy Healy.'

'Was he the one who glared so hatefully at me in Keppel Street?'

'Did he?' Parnell did not seem surprised. 'Yes, he would. I deplore hero worship. Not from modesty – an odious virtue – but it's like a love affair: it always ends badly.'

She felt her breath catch; perhaps he was warning her. She said brightly: 'I disagree.'

'Do you mean about hero worship?'

She said: 'I mean, and you know I do, about love affairs. They end badly only if they are conducted badly.'

Although the sun had gone, she put a hand over her eyes as if to seek out a far-off object. She wondered if she had shocked him. He might even think her an immoral woman. From the house, a hand-bell rang. She was delivered.

She said, mocking him: 'Your American lady has made a cynic

45

of you. And that bell is to say that Willie has arrived from town. He has agreed to stay the night.'

'To stay the night?'

She exulted at the dismay in his voice. Or perhaps it was not on her account, but simply that he abhorred Willie's company. At the second possibility, she again felt an antipathy towards Parnell. This would not do; she was behaving like the wretched Alice in the song, who wept with delight when given a smile and trembled with fear at a frown.

She said: 'Of course. You know how tongues wag. And Aunt Ben would frown on any irregularity.'

He said: 'So you spare her feelings?'

'I must. It is she who pays the piper. Ah, here is Willie now.'

He looked and saw Captain O'Shea come around the corner of the house. Even at a range of fifty yards, his hand was extended in greeting.

Parnell said: 'How long does he think my arm is?'

Willie could not have been more affable. His home, he declared, was Parnell's. He was honoured. Long threatening, he said with a nudge to his guest's ribs, had come at last. It was time, he implied, that they pooled their superiority to the common herd.

Katharine had arranged for dinner to be served early. In spite of her attempts to keep the conversation untiring, Willie was determined to make a display of his political wares.

'What I suggest,' he said, 'is that I should be the one who takes the temperature of the water. You will have noticed that I choose to sit on the Government benches.'

'Indeed, everyone has noticed,' Parnell said.

The sarcasm might have been a cobweb in Willie's path. He soldiered on. 'Gladstone is too much the tin god to deal with the Irish Party directly. He will not condescend. So what you stand most in need of is a . . .'

'A go-between?'

'You have it. A man who is to be trusted. Discreet, reliable

46

and in the know. And,' Willie informed him impressively, 'that man is in this room.'

For a delirious moment, Katharine thought that Parnell would make a show of looking about him for a sight of Willie's discreet, reliable and knowledgable man; she even had a crazed vision of him glancing under the table. Instead, he appeared to be hanging raptly on Willie's every word. Even that, she thought, was too bad of him.

'Is he, now?' Parnell said, seemingly much affected.

'He is,' Willie confirmed. 'Look here, while we smoke our cigars —'

'There will be no cigars for either of you,' Katharine told him. 'Mr Parnell is here to rest. It is time he retired.'

Willie did not protest. 'Right, then. I'll just pop up and say good night to the children before I go.'

'Before you . . . ? Willie!'

'Shan't be a sec.' He went jauntily out.

She looked, disbelieving, at Parnell. 'No, now he goes too far. Excuse me.'

She waited, angry, in the dark of the stairhead while Willie bade the children an unlingering farewell. It was monstrous of him to return to London. She had no intention of becoming scandalously involved with Mr Parnell, but even if she were so lost to shame as to dream of tumbling into his bed, Willie had no business in making it easy for her. It was most discourteous, inconsiderate and unhusbandly.

'Willie, you cannot possibly go back to town. You gave me your word.'

He could not have been more rueful. 'I did, I did, and in good faith, my love, but dash it, some business has come up.'

'At this hour? With whom? One of your women?'

'Dick, for shame.'

'Don't call me that! Willie, for as long as Mr Parnell is here, so must you be. Or would you prefer a scandal?'

'My love, I trust you. Thingummy's wife, you know.'

47

'That is hardly the —'

'And as for Parnell,' he said, 'the poor fellow is as weak as a kitten. I'll warrant you'll get no trouble there.'

She said: 'Willie, that remark is worthy of you.'

A smile thanked her for the compliment. He preceded her downstairs at a happy trot. 'Well, I think you've done splendidly. But remember, now that we've hooked the fish, let's not lose him. Use the gaff.'

'The what?'

'Keep up the good work.'

She watched for a moment as he took his overcoat down from the hallstand and flicked a speck from his hat. She returned to the dining room, where Mary was clearing away, her eyes, twin birds' eyes, fixed on Parnell.

Katharine said: 'My husband finds that he has business in London.' She attempted a laugh. 'Mr Parnell, I do assure you that this is not a conspiracy.'

Parnell said courteously: 'I'm sure it is no such thing.' Then, as if in afterthought: 'A conspiracy to what possible end?'

There was no reply she could properly make. She longed to tell him that he was of no help whatsoever.

Drifting towards sleep, she imagined she heard the house sighing in the dark. In the daytime, there were noises: footsteps, the clatter of an iron lid on the downstairs range, the children shouting on the lawn, her own voice summoning Mary; in the evening, there was the purr of gas in the mantle, the drawing of curtains, the fall of a burning coal. The house hid behind these sounds and pretended it was not alive. At night, it tried to hold its breath and failed. It gave up its play-acting. She dozed further off. She was on the verge of a dark and vast and somehow familiar sea. She had taken ship upon it once before. At the water's edge, it came to her that she was again a maiden; her life, a voyage restored, was before her. She had been granted her wish.

The sound of coughing brought her fully awake. The walls at Wonersh Lodge were thick, the doors stout; small sounds were not heard. She got out of bed and put on her *peignoir*. Her fingers reassured her breasts. In the passage outside, the gaslight, turned low, was kept burning through the night. She saw that she had heard him because the door of his room had been set ajar. She moved silently and opened it more fully so that the light fell across his sleeping face. As she made to withdraw, his voice stopped her.

He said, speaking so quietly that she might not have been there: 'I have many fears, all of them absurd for a man of supposed intelligence. One of them is to sleep in a confined space. I must have an open door. And I abhor the number thirteen and to see three candles burning in a room. I fear the month of October because I have a presentiment that I shall die in it, and this year we are already in its fifth day. Most of all, I cannot abide the colour green. It surrounds me, in the House and on public platforms. Even at Avondale, when I look out of my window I see fields and, in summer, green woods as well.'

Katharine said, her voice gently mocking: 'Well then at night time you can see nothing, and so you have no reason not to sleep.'

He said: 'I was waiting for you to come in. I lied about being afraid of confined spaces. The open door was an invitation.'

'And the cough a summons? I am sure you are a very wicked man. The invitation is not accepted. Now go to sleep.'

'Stay with me.'

She said: 'You know that I cannot and I must not. Good night.'

Not leaving, she closed the door. She was aware that her decision was irrevocable and for always. She let her *peignoir* fall to the floor, then her nightdress. She moved to the bed and reached out for him. They became lovers.

At breakfast next morning, Mary served them and poured coffee. When she had gone, Katharine asked: 'Do you take sugar?'

49

'One.'

She said: 'Am I to remember that?'

'I should advise it. It would save years of my having to remind you.'

That pleased her. She was a tidy woman, who liked matters to be arranged, smoothed and laid away. She thought: good, then it is settled.

He said: 'Is O'Shea likely to come this evening?'

She marvelled at the amount of contempt he managed to put into the name. It was a pity that he should so dislike Willie, but if there was no help for it then she hoped, wanting the moon, that he would at least despise him out of jealousy.

Replying, she said, without stressing the ambiguity, that the Captain had affairs in London. She said: 'Last evening, he complimented me on getting you here.'

'Fool.'

'He said that we had hooked the fish, and I should' – she tried to recall Willie's exact phrase – 'use the gaff. If you please, what is a gaff?'

'It is an angler's pole for taking fish from the water, but in your husband's case it should be spelt with an "e" at the end, meaning a social blunder.'

She laughed, almost upsetting her coffee, then of a sudden felt ashamed. It was not for what she had done; rather, it was the shame of feeling no shame at all.

After the marriage, in reversal of the natural order, came the courtship: a ritual dance of small, careful steps, advances and retreats. She willingly laid her life before him; he, by nature, was more reticent. She pressed him for stories of his childhood. He told her of how, when he and his sister, Anna, played toy soldiers, they had laid their troops out in opposing ranks and fired upon the enemy with toy cannons. 'I invariably won,' he said.

Katharine said: 'I'm sure you did. Boys dote on wars and battles. They are much more at home with guns than girls are.'

He shook his head. 'Not I. I truly could not have hit the wall of this room. I won and Anna lost, because I nailed my tin soldiers to the floor.'

She said, fondly: 'What wickedness!'

He did not smile in answer. 'I hope not. I still do it whenever I can.'

He stayed for two weeks. In that time, their lives took on a pattern that alternated passion with tranquillity. Within days, they had acquired the easiness of a middle-class suburban couple; only the passion set them apart from the norm. Parnell's health improved. 'My recovery,' he told Katharine, 'must be laid firmly at the door of perfect rest, Ellen's cooking, Mary's devoted nursing, and I dare not suggest what else.' She blushed and told him he was dreadful. When, towards the end of his sojourn, he declared himself well enough to go to Westminster, returning to Wonersh Lodge in the evenings, she knew better than to protest. 'I must,' he said, 'nail Mr Gladstone's toy soldiers to the floor.'

The Irish Secretary had become peevish. In spite of the new fad for non-violence, there were still those in Ireland who preferred to settle their scores in the time-honoured way. Cattle were maimed and farm buildings set on fire, and now and then a new tenant was discovered dead and in undisputed occupancy of a ditch. Whenever an arrest was made, justice was swift and unvarying. The accused was brought before an Irish jury, tried with all the grim solemnity of the law, acquitted, and sent home.

'Buckshot' Forster vigorously condemned the lawlessness; but what really put him out of sorts was the success attending what had come to be known as the boycott. As an Englishman first and a Quaker hardly at all in such troubled times, the Secretary believed that it was the immemorial role of the Irish to murder the English and be hanged in return and at the exchange rate, if it could be managed, of five for one. Parnell, breaking with tradition, had cold-bloodedly incited the Irish to peace. Forster was shocked; it was not gentlemanly, and the success of such a strategy could not but give bad example for the future. Buckshot urged the Prime Minister to meet the outbreak of peaceful resistance with a Coercion Bill suspending habeas corpus and jailing members of the Land League without the tiresomeness of trial.

Gladstone thought it a capital idea. He prided himself, however, on being the kind of man who could not pick up a single stone without looking for two birds to bring down with it. A Coercion Bill, it occurred to him, would not only dispose of the more troublesome Parnellites; it would also in time rid him of William Forster.

An Irish Secretary might be likened to a pair of trousers that when new was a perfect fit, smart and faultlessly pressed. When it became frayed, as it always did, and the seat had begun to shine, then it was time to exchange it for another. Buckshot Forster, however, had attracted so much odium among the Irish that he was in tatters and had no seat to speak of. It was time, Gladstone thought, for him to go, and it was only fitting that his own bill should provide the means. Irony was the Prime Minister's long suit.

Parnell instructed Timothy Healy to convene a meeting for the following Monday. 'I want you to draft a motion. It is this: that all Home Rule members will henceforth sit in Opposition. Any dissenting member will be liable for expulsion.'

Healy began to write, the words hardly legible from excitement.

Parnell watched him, curious. 'You obey so blindly. Have you no questions?' Tim Healy mumbled. 'Speak up!'

Healy said: 'I wouldn't presume.'

What he meant was that he had no intention of going the way of others who, for their temerity, had incurred the slow, incredulous stare and the words, spat out with the deadliness of a striking snake: 'Are you asking me for an *explanation*?' A man in love, however, is of a mind to be tolerant of the world at large, and Parnell was in summer mood.

'Healy, if we sit as one party on the Opposition benches, then the passing of the Coercion Bill – and I believe that it will be passed – will seem to be an act of vindictiveness on the part of the government.'

Tim Healy, in his Bantry cradle, had gnawed on intrigue as his teething ring. 'A moral advantage. Yes!'

'There is a practical side to it. United, we shall one day hold a balance of power. Those who would form a government must pay our price, and need I say that that price will be a Home Rule bill?'

Timothy Healy's eyes were misting. The Chief was actually confiding in him, admitting him to the sanctum of his private self. Whatever about the paradise to come, earth had no more to give.

'If habeas corpus is suspended, we may be in for dark days. My purpose is to light a torch of hope. Healy, do you see this?' He extended his right hand, empty, the palm upwards. 'Therein resides a government for Ireland.'

Healy saw the reddish glint in the Chief's eyes as they burned into his. He all but swooned. He could not wait to put it in a letter to his brother Maurice.

On the Sunday morning, Parnell left Wonersh Lodge to return to Keppel Street. Swathed in greatcoat and comforter, he waited with Katharine in the front hall for Willie and the children to come home from Mass at Chislehurst.

'Willie, you are late. Our guest wishes to take his leave.'

Parnell said: 'To say "Thank you" at any rate. Captain O'Shea and I shall meet in the House tomorrow.'

Willie looked at him vaguely. 'Eh? Oh yes, this idea of yours that we should sit in Opposition. Yes, I'll be there.' He added, waggishly: 'I'm not saying how I shall vote, mind.'

Parnell said, coldly: 'Indeed? Then we must talk first.'

'Frankly,' Willie said, 'I'm a Government man. Always back the winner, that's what I say.'

'Is it?'

Willie's smile was threatening to become a grin. 'As for all this Home Rule hullabaloo, if you want my opinion —'

53

Looking at her lover, Katharine would not have taken him for the proponent of non-violence. She said: 'Willie, unless you have need of the carriage, our guest has a train to catch. I shall go with him to Blackheath.'

Parnell thanked Willie for his kindness. Willie laughed and said: 'Rot, old man. Send you a bill tomorrow.' When the carriage was out of sight, he closed the door and informed the hall mirror, speaking aloud: 'Thought we'd never see the back of him.'

On the station platform, Katharine said: 'Our first parting.'

Parnell said: 'Did you hear him? He is not saying how he will vote, mind!'

'Is it so important?'

'He is daring me to expel him from the party. Either it is the rankest stupidity or he wants to find out how far I may be pushed.' He took her hand. 'Well, this is the beginning of the price we pay.'

She looked nervously at the few other travellers. 'Then it is too high. We must stop now.'

'You know we cannot. I'll save his skin, and you and I will go on. We have chosen our road, or it has chosen us.'

At Monday's meeting, the motion was proposed, seconded and carried, with only Captain O'Shea dissenting to cries of 'Turncoat!' and (from Joseph Biggar) 'May you die roaring.' He strolled, whistling and unabashed, from the committee room. John Dillon, unable to contain himself, said: 'Well, that's the last of him.' Biggar said: 'And high bloody time.'

Parnell said: 'Let us not be too hasty.' The members looked at him, puzzled. 'I may have a use for the Honourable Member,' he told them, 'as a messenger boy.'

He smiled; they smiled in return. Some laughed. The notion of the exquisite Willie O'Shea running to and fro on errands appealed to them. It was sweet punishment, far better than expulsion. Only in Timothy Healy's literal mind did the thought alight that the motion had stipulated one thing and the Chief had done another.

Even Parnell was bemused at the ease with which he had pulled O'Shea's chestnuts from the fire. The wording had been all; if he had described him as a go-between instead of a messenger boy, the smiles would have been fewer and fainter. It was no matter; he had taken the hurdle with ease. It only momentarily occured to him to wonder if it was the first hurdle of others yet to come.

As soon as the meeting was over, he went to the Commons cloakroom and collected the portmanteau he had packed at Keppel Street that morning. He took a cab to Cannon Street and, from there and this time without O'Shea's knowledge, set out for Wonersh to continue his honeymoon.

FIVE

Timothy Healy had, to his great delight, been arrested, and, as if this were not joy enough, it happened in his native Bantry.

A local farmer, evicted with his family, had taken shelter under an upturned boat on the seashore. The man had died of exposure and, in a funeral oration, Healy had publicly denounced what he described as an act of legalised murder. He was at once seized by police officers who chanced to be in attendance – some said at Tim Healy's invitation – and put into handcuffs. His trial at the Cork Assizes was in the nature of a public testimonial. Once the formality of acquittal had been complied with, it took him no more than six weeks to be elected to Parliament as a member for Wexford.

A victory party was held in London upstairs from a public house. Tim Healy himself was a votary of the late Irish apostle of temperance, Father Theobald Mathew, but most of the others were journeying towards a long night and sore heads. Willie O'Shea alone was in bad humour. He had come only because he was damned if he would be excluded. With the pellucid vision of the morbidly drunk, he saw through them all; they were poor creatures, time-servers, upstarts, fleas on the lion's tail.

Thomas Sexton proposed that T.P. O'Connor oblige the company with a rendition of 'The Peeler and the Goat'. O'Connor said that Sexton, himself the son of a policeman, had the devil's own nerve. John Dillon called for a speech from the guest of honour. Timothy Healy accordingly stood and was told by Henry Harrison to sit down again. 'Not yet, Tim. Proper order. Save the speeches for the Chief.'

'Point taken,' Justin McCarthy said. 'Matter of protocol.'

McCarthy himself was now invited to contribute a few words. The novelist and doyen of the party declined with a show of modesty, but in the private awareness that his element was a sedate dinner party in Mayfair rather than what Joe Biggar termed 'a few wee jars and the singing of a couple of oul' come-all-ye's'.

A barmaid brought drinks from downstairs. When she had gone, Joseph Biggar invited the company's opinion as regards the ferocity of her good nature.

'Deuced bad form,' Willie said.

'What is?' Biggar wanted to know. 'Are you referring to me, sir?'

'Not you . . . *him.*' He waved a hand towards a place set at the head of the table. 'Why isn't he here? Is he trying to insult us? If you ask me, the fellow is riding for a fall.'

'Who is?' Harrison wanted to know. 'What is it he says?'

'He's a dull fellow,' John Dillon said. 'Ignore him.'

Willie drew himself up. 'Am I? Dull, am I? Well, I will not be rough-ridden . . .' He set about untangling his words. '. . . rodden . . . ridden . . . roughshod over.'

T.P. O'Connor said: 'O'Shea, will you kindly not be such a mouth.'

'He comes,' Willie said, 'when he has a mind to, he goes without a by-your-leave, and we are expected to dance attendance. Some of us . . .' He pulled out his watch. 'Some of us have appointments.'

Sexton winked at Biggar. 'With a lady, is it?'

Willie regarded him with half-cut dignity. 'And what if it is? The society of a true gentleman, Sexton, is always in demand.'

A group at the bottom end of the table had begun to sing 'The Bold Thady Quill'. Sexton gave Biggar another look that told him sport was afoot. To Willie he said: 'Oh, Captain, Captain, you're playing with fire. I have heard tell that . . .' He looked about him fearfully.

'That what?' Willie asked.

'Joe, should we tell him?'

Biggar felt the heel of Sexton's shoe gouge into his Wellingtons under the supper table. 'Aye, do . . . tell him. When all's said and done, isn't O'Shea one of us?'

Sexton spoke in a low voice and with great intensity. 'Captain, there is a shadow behind you that isn't yours. Don't you know that you're being followed?'

Willie began to turn pale. 'Eh?'

'Gawd's truth,' Biggar said, seizing on his cue. 'Och, but aren't wives fierce suspicious creatures all the same? Could you be up to them?'

'What? Look here,' Willie said, 'is this your idea of humour? Because if it is —'

Even in his agitation, he noticed that the room had fallen silent. All present were looking at a tall newcomer. He was dark, hollow-eyed and neither clean-shaven nor bearded; small clumps of dark hair were upon his face as if missed by a razor.

'I spy strangers!' a voice said and giggled.

Dillon moved towards the man. 'Your pardon, sir, but this function is private.'

Parnell snapped: 'Don't be a damned fool, Dillon.'

No one spoke as he made his way towards Tim Healy at the head of the table. Without his beard, he was almost unrecognisable. His face had the indecency of nakedness. He came face to face with T.P. O'Connor, whose mouth was open.

'Does something ail you, O'Connor?'

O'Connor started back as if touched by acid. 'No, sir.'

Parnell reached the new member, shook him by the hand and addressed the assembly. He had forfeited a secretary, he said, that the party might gain a fighter. In the days ahead, there would be need of such men as Timothy Healy. Willie O'Shea did not hear the speech, as brief as it was. He was out on the street, walking quickly and spinning around now and then to take unawares the person who was following him. In the November fog he saw no one, but he quite distinctly heard footsteps that stopped when he did.

Willie was nobody's fool; he did not need to think twice to fix upon the reason for his persecution. It was simple: the old woman at Eltham could not live much longer. Kate was her heir, and she wanted the money for herself. To this end, she would use his few moments of harmless diversion as cause for divorce. The thought of such stupendous greed took his breath away. Had it not been for his own good nature, he would have foreseen this long ago; after all, were he in Katharine's place, it was what he himself would have done.

In the 18th Hussars, Willie O'Shea had been known first and foremost as a man of action, and he did not hesitate now. He hailed a cab and told the driver to take him with all speed to Cannon Street Station. Let his shadow, he thought, follow him to Eltham.

It was late before Parnell could decently leave Tim Healy's celebrations. The guest of honour had become tearful to a degree that was unbecoming in a man who was not the worse for drink. 'I owe it all to the Chief,' he repeated as if it were an incantation. By the time Parnell broke away and arrived at Wonersh Lodge, it was past eleven. He had hardly reached the front door when it was flung open.

'Charles, Willie has been —' Katharine broke off and stared at him. 'My God, what has happened to you?'

He all but preened himself. 'It is my disguise. Do you like it, my darling? I am told that I am quite unlike myself.'

'A disguise? Is the world gone mad this evening? Come in.'

In the light of the hall, she thought his appearance even more grotesque. 'What in the world have you done to yourself?'

'I used my pocket scissors.'

She said: 'I have no doubt of it. Charles, I cannot bear to

see you in this condition. Go the bathroom. Shave. Then you shall hear my news.'

He looked, she thought, like a small boy who had offered his favourite aunt the gift of an earthworm, only to see it refused. When he came downstairs, he was clean-shaven and seemed absurdly young. His cheek was smooth against hers; it was as if she were embracing a stranger.

She said: 'Willie has been here. He came without warning. I kept listening for carriage wheels and thinking: what if you and he came face to face?'

He was unconcerned. 'It is the stuff of farce, I believe.'

'He was not sober. Worse, he was quite mad. He accused me of having him followed. He ranted. He said that I was bent on cheating him of Aunt Ben's fortune. When I denied it, he said he would retaliate. He would search the house and find evidence against *me*.' Her voice trembled. 'My darling, I think he has done so.'

Parnell seemed almost bored. 'Oh, yes?'

'Upstairs . . . he found your portmanteau and took it away with him. He said it was proof.'

'Did he, by Jove! What a scoundrel he is.' At last, she thought, she had won his attention. 'I say, does he keep clothes of his own here?'

'Well, yes, but . . .'

'That's all right, then. At least I shall not begin tomorrow without a change of linen.'

His calmness was maddening. She said: 'Charles, he has found us out.'

'Nonsense.' He pulled her to him. 'Now, as regards my beard, of which I was so proud, you see what sacrifices I make for you? Henceforward, we may go where we please, undetected. Now where shall it be? Eastbourne? Brighton?'

She broke away from him. 'Charles, it is useless.'

'Or further afield. Paris, perhaps?' He laughed, following her. 'My dearest, you make too much of it. Your husband was drunk . . . you have said so.'

60

'No, I mean there is worse, far worse.'

She kept him from her, her arms warding him off, the palms towards him. She could not bear to be held and then to feel his embrace die as she told him.

She said: 'If he does not know about us, he soon will. Do you know what I am saying?' Her eyes were of a sudden huge and filled with tears.

He said it for her, and the saying of it was an act of mercy: 'You are carrying a child.'

Henry Harrison said in warning: 'The O'Gorman Mahon, sir. Will you see him?'

'Briefly, yes.' Parnell watched the old man, straight as a lance, march towards him down the Members' Corridor. In a race that was now all but run he had been a despoiler of women, a friend of Talleyrand, a Chilean admiral, a colonel in Brazil and again under Louis Napoleon, and a lieutenant in the Tsar's bodyguard. He had fought for Uruguay, Austria and Turkey. Now, aged eighty, he could still lay claim to distinction. He was one of the two members of Parliament for County Clare, and he was Willie O'Shea's intimate friend.

He stood before Parnell's work table. 'My respects, sir. My business is —'

'. . . All the better, I am sure, for being done in comfort,' Parnell said. 'Will you not sit?'

It was not only a matter of courtesy. At six feet three inches, the O'Gorman Mahon had occasioned more than sixty years of craned necks.

'I thank you, I think not.'

Like Willie, the O'Gorman Mahon had been elected under the banner of the Irish party, but he regarded Parnell with deep suspicion. He believed any man to be effete who, aged thirty-four, had yet to fight a duel. He himself had in his time

61

issued twenty-two challenges, and now, although he seemed alas, doomed to die in his bed, he was requesting satisfaction on behalf of a comrade.

'Sir, Captain O'Shea asks if you will be kind enough to be at his disposal in Lille or any other town in the north of France which may suit your convenience.'

'In France, you say?'

'You are aware, sir, that under the laws of England affairs of honour cannot be settled as gentlemen would wish.'

'Affairs of honour?' Parnell affected to be momentarily at a loss, the enlightenment shone. 'Ah, you mean a duel? By all means. Done!'

'That is your reply? You accept?'

'Delighted. My new secretary will arrange the dates.' He turned to Henry Harrison, who, in attendance, had much the same look as a man freshly run over by a brewery dray. 'Choose a Saturday, will you, Harrison? Then I can enjoy the Sunday in Paris.'

He had thought to take Katharine to France; now it seemed as if his companion, however briefly, would be her husband. He turned back to the O'Gorman Mahon. 'As the one who is challenged, I believe the choice of weapons is mine. Pistols?'

Without waiting for an answer, he returned to his correspondence. The O'Gorman Mahon would have preferred an iciness of bowing and a hoar frost of 'sirs'. Reflecting that good manners had died with Isaac Butt, he was allowing Harrison to escort him to the entrance, when Parnell addressed him.

'One moment, sir. Since you appear to be a friend of Captain O'Shea's bosom, perhaps you would be kind enough to ask him what he has done with my luggage. I have searched half the cloakrooms in London, and not a trace of it.'

The O'Gorman Mahon bowed so stiffly that he all but snapped. As his beanpole frame receded down the corridor, Parnell made a mental note to warn Katharine not to unmask him to her husband as less than a dead shot.

He met her that afternoon in Cannon Street Hotel where

he had taken rooms. Over tea, he told her of the duel, and her response was, as he might have expected of her, unexpected.

'You fool. You cannot fight over me. My God, it is absurd. I am older than you are.'

Parnell, who could not see the relevance, contented himself with murmuring: 'Only by five months.'

She said, almost wailing: 'It is no matter. I am older, older! No, it is too bad of you.'

As they finished their tea and moved from the sitting room to the bedroom, he was at a loss, and remained so, as to whether his fault lay in accepting O'Shea's challenge or in being five months younger than she was.

Until the business with Willie was cleared up there was no question of Parnell accompanying her to Eltham. This evening, she refused even to let him wait with her on the station platform; instead, she dispatched him by cab to Keppel Street. When he was safely out of sight, she herself hailed a cab and went direct to Albert Mansions. She had, she decided, enough to contend with without the idiocy of duels. Willie, by chance, was at home; moreover, still worried that Katharine was having him watched, he was alone. Even with their relations strained, he was pleased to see her. It had been a shock when the O'Gorman Mahon reported to him that Parnell had accepted the challenge.

'Pistols,' he said to Katharine. 'Do you know that the fellow chose pistols?'

Parnell was not merely mad, she thought, but doubly mad.

It occurred to him to ask how she had known about the duel. 'From your friend Parnell, I daresay,' he said bitterly.

'I have not seen Mr Parnell,' she said, curling a lip that was swollen from Parnell's teeth. 'If you must know, your foolishness is the talk of London.'

He was aggrieved, a man tricked by underhandedness. 'I thought he would back down, damn him.' Contemplating his sudden and bloody end under French skies, he reached for the whisky decanter. 'But of course why should he? Living on that Wicklow estate of his, he's been used to handling guns since the year dot. Probably never misses. The more I think of it, the more I'm sure: the swine means to kill me.'

'Willie, have you forgotten? *You* challenged *him*.'

He scowled. 'Yes. Well. A chap has to think of his honour.'

'How does honour come into it? You told me to play up to him. You said to be agreeable.'

He blustered. 'Yes, I daresay, but hang it all, Kate, there are limits.'

For the moment, she forgot that Parnell and she were lovers. She went for Willie with the anger of the righteous. 'Are there indeed? Well, somehow, you forgot to tell me where the limits were. Will you never have sense? Don't you know that if you drag Parnell down, we go with him? Have you forgotten Aunt Ben? Do you want to see us disinherited because of a stupid scandal?'

He began to mumble. 'The man insults me. In my own home . . . in my own bedroom, I find his —'

She said: 'Yes! Because he comes for the quiet he cannot find in London. Because *you* told him our home was his. You were not there, you had business in town, remember? So I was the one who had to make it seem that he was welcome.'

Willie had been put to rout, the battle was over. All that now remained to him was to sue for peace.

'Well, if . . . if you were to say to me – honestly, mind! . . . I'll not have lies – that there was nothing improper between you and him . . .'

With a sigh: 'Yes, Willie, I say it to you honestly. Now, you goose, sit down, take pen and withdraw your silly challenge.'

He said, grumbling: 'Mind, he is not to stay at Eltham in my absence. Have I your promise?'

She spoke as if to a child. 'Yes, Willie, you have it.'

'Very well, then. But I am too easy-going, I know I am.'

She knew at that moment what she would do. She looked about her at his sitting room. There was no clutter, because Willie had few possessions; the furnishings were dull, the chair covers frayed, not because he was poor, but because a home meant nothing to him.

She said: 'On the contrary, Willie, I think you have behaved very well indeed . . . very sensibly. And I think you are deserving of a reward. Now, what shall it be?'

She looked at him provocatively. She gave him as wanton a smile as she could manage and slowly removed the long pin from her hat. Willie, unable to believe his good fortune, gulped down the remainder of his whisky.

It was still dark when she woke up. She slipped out of bed without waking him. In the sitting room, the letter withdrawing his challenge to the duel was on the table. She put it into her reticule just in case – although it was unlikely – Willie should think again. She went into the bathroom, washed and dressed. She stood, not moving, before the mirror. There was no sound except for the whisper of the gas in the mantle. She marvelled that her face was unchanged. It was the face of the previous day. It might even have been the face of last July when Parnell had been no more than an empty chair at Thomas's Hotel. There was no sign in it of wickedness. And yet she had sworn to what was never true, she had made promises she would never keep, and she had lied and been false as easily as if she had done so all her life. No hypocrite was ever so innocent and ill-used. She was a stranger to herself.

She caught the first train home to Eltham. Late in the afternoon, she returned to London and met Parnell at the hotel in Cannon Street. From his face, she knew that he had lived to see her. She owed him no less than to strike quickly and let the thing be done.

'I slept with Willie last night. Now he will think that your child is his.'

Later, they lay together, not making love. In the darkness she heard him weep.

It was cold in Dublin, even for February. Michael Davitt, coming out of the Land League office, could smell snow in the wind. He pulled up the collar of his greatcoat, and as he did so a man stepped into his path. Davitt could not only smell snow; he could smell policemen. Behind the man were two constables.

'You are Michael Davitt?'

'I am.'

The detective smiled. 'Grand. You're under arrest.'

'On what charge?'

'Charge?' The smile widened. 'Oh, the new Act won't bother its thatch about charges. Let me see now.' He made a show of consulting his warrant. 'Will this do? "Behaviour not in accordance with the conditions of leave for a convict." '

Davitt was incredulous. 'Are you mad?'

One of the constables came forward with manacles. 'Ah God,' the plain-clothes man said: 'Would ye slap handcuffs on a one-armed man?' He took Davitt by the arm. 'Come on with you. By tomorrow night we'll have you tucked up back home in Portland Gaol.'

To Timothy Healy, an emergency was food and drink. Although the Coercion Bill was not yet law, he saw Davitt's arrest as a straw in the wind. At a signal from him, the Land League funds were transferred out of harm's way to a bank in Paris. There, in the Hotel Brighton on the Rue du Rivoli, Healy, John Dillon, Joseph Biggar and two others of the executive met for a council of war with the Chief. They waited, and Parnell did not appear. Six days went by without sign of him. 'He's left us in the lurch,' Biggar said. 'Not he,' the faithful Healy replied. 'He's locked up in the Tower of London. Either there, or at the bottom of the Thames.'

Dillon said: 'I'm not saying a word against the man, but God almighty, he forbids us to act on our own initiative, and when we're most in need of him he goes to earth.'

Joe Biggar said: 'He's picked a right time. With Davitt arrested, it could be our turn next.'

James J. O'Kelly, who had run guns with Michael Davitt for the Fenians, had the idea of asking if letters addressed to Parnell had been delivered to the hotel; if so, perhaps they would yield a clue. Timothy Healy blushed and admitted that yes, there were letters, and they were in his keeping. A debate ensued as to whether in the circumstances they should be opened. One of them, that had arrived that morning, was in a woman's handwriting.

Biggar, who had spent the previous two nights renewing his promises to the Irish lady who was sueing him for breach of promise, said in mock horror: 'Och, the whoormaster!' Tim Healy rounded upon him. Dillon said: 'He's joking, Tim.'

The letter was produced and all but flung upon a table as if its touch would burn. They stood around and looked at it. All were agreed – Tim Healy reluctantly – that it should be opened. Each waited for another to make a move; no one did. 'We'll be here all flamin' night,' Biggar said.

The fourth member of the group was T.D. Sullivan, who had composed the words of 'God Save Ireland' in honour of the Manchester Martyrs. He said: 'It's a woman's writing sure enough.'

'Smell it,' Dillon said, 'for perfume.'

'I'll open it,' Tim Healy said suddenly. 'The Chief would want us to use our initiative.'

Biggar gave a crooked grin. Among others in the party, he knew Healy to be incapable of either holding his tongue or staying his hand. He deferred to Parnell; with others, if action must be taken, he would court ruin sooner than play the role of looker-on.

Dillon was suddenly cautious. 'There might not be an address in it.'

Healy said: 'And there might. If we don't find out what's become of him, let it not be for want of trying.'

He opened the envelope. As he read its contents, the others saw his face go pale. His hand shook. He was a man looking upon horrors.

Dillon said: 'Well?'

'Does it say where he is?' O'Kelly said.

Biggar, looking at Healy's face, said: 'Jesus, it can't be that bad.'

Healy giggled as if he were not quite sane. He looked at them wildly for a moment, then said: 'It's from Lizzie from Blankshire.'

'*Who?*'

Lizzie from Blankshire was an all-purpose, half-contemptuous nickname for the kind of barmaid or servant girl with whom a man far from home whiled away an hour and none the wiser.

'The Chief?' Dillon asked, incredulous. 'Carrying on with one of *them*? I don't believe it.'

The four men, including Biggar, were faintly embarrassed. Healy, still trembling, was putting the letter back in its envelope when there came a knock and the concierge appeared.

'*Pardon, messieurs. Monsieur Parnell est arrivé.*'

After almost a week, it seemed impossible that he had chosen that instant to appear. Dazed with relief, they were about to rush to greet him when Biggar nodded at the opened letter in Healy's hand. 'Sooner you than me, Timothy,' he said. At once, the four had second thoughts; hanging back, they allowed Healy to lead the way. He smiled at their cravenness and did so. He knocked at the door of Parnell's room; the familiar voice bade him enter.

Parnell, who was still in his travelling clothes, looked balefully at his visitor. 'What do you want?'

Timothy Healy said: 'We have been anxious about you. It has been six days.' He saw that Parnell's eyes were fixed on the letter he was still holding. He proffered it. 'This was our last hope. I took it upon myself to —'

Parnell snatched it from him, his face drained of blood. 'Get out of my sight.'

Healy stammered: 'Sir, it was with the best of all possible —'

'Do you hear what I say?'

For a moment, he thought that Parnell was about to strike him. He bowed, stepped to the far side of the door and turned. 'Sir, you must know that we were distracted with worry. We had no notion of where you were or —'

Parnell reached the door in three strides and slammed it in Tim Healy's face. Healy stood motionless for a time, his eyes only inches from the door, his slight frame rigid with shock and humiliation. He did not turn until the others, except for John Dillon, had gone.

Dillon took his arm. 'Tim, come on, we'll sit out of doors and drink coffee.' Healy shook his head. 'And I say you will. Damn it, aren't we in Paris?' He led Healy to a café in the Rue des Halles.

The trouble with Healy, Dillon thought, was that to him existence was either tragedy or triumph, famine or feast, and now as they waited for their coffee, he sat staring at his burnt-out life. 'Tim,' Dillon said, 'did you ever hear tell how a shilling piece changed the run of Irish history?'

Healy was in no humour for tales, but Dillon was hanged if he would allow the other's sulks to put a blight on the spring sunshine. There were attractive women all about them – French women at that – and, for all the pleasure the sight of them was affording Tim Healy, he might as well have been in Ballydehob. Dillon felt his own mood begin to darken, as if infected, and stubbornly he told of how, when Parnell was an undergraduate at Magdalene's College, Cambridge, he had one evening gone on a drinking spree.

'Well, by the time the champagne was all gone it was not far off midnight, and, while his companions went to look for transportation, the bold Charley decided to take his ease by lying in the gutter . . .'

'Gutter,' Healy said darkly. 'Oh aye, the gutter.'

'No, listen. While he was so reposing, along came a manure dealer and his servant, who, upon espying a fellow-human in distress, attempted to play the Samaritans. They raised the sleeping beauty to his feet, whereupon he proceeded to knock the pair of them off theirs. True. He flattened them.

'Next thing, a policeman is on the scene. Just strolling by, you understand. "What's going on here?" says he. Well, the Chief thinks to grease the constable's palm with a sovereign, but because of the darkness and the fact that he was peluthered, doesn't he give him a shilling by mistake. Well, the bobby didn't mind being bribed, but he was damned if he'd be insulted. Next thing, the young Charles Steward Parnell is up in court. He's expelled from Cambridge, and twelve years later the pair of us are not only members of Parliament but as good as on the run. Ah, the coffee . . . grand!'

Healy responded to the story with an indifferent shrug. To him, all that ever mattered was the here and now; the whys did not concern him. And yet, forty years in the future, when Parnell was dust in his grave and Timothy Healy was taking the inaugural oath as the first governor-general of the new Irish Free State, he would reflect that his life had assumed its course because of a letter opened a minute too soon and the slam of a hotel room door.

'Do you know,' John Dillon said, savouring his coffee, 'I thought he was going to murder you. Come on . . . between ourselves, what the devil was in that letter?'

'I told you,' Healy said. 'It was from one of his conquests. A girl in Holloway Prison who has had his bastard. She was looking for money.'

Dillon was incredulous. 'Do you mean she wrote to him in *Paris*?'

Healy was silent.

In the Hotel Brighton, Parnell at last forced himself to take the violated letter from its envelope. If Healy had read it, he reflected, he could not but have noticed that it was headed: Wonersh Lodge, Eltham.

My husband,
It is a short hour since you left my arms. For as long as you
are away from me, know that for good or ill I am your wife,
your lover and shall soon be the mother of your child. While you
are in France, write or wire me to say that you are well, and I
will try not to be unhappy until you are with me again ...

At the Café des Huguenots, Dillon was horrified to see that Tim Healy had begun to weep. 'Tim, for God's sake, what ails you?'

Hiccups shook Healy's body as he tried to speak. 'I . . . I know him now for what he is,' he said. 'He deceived me. I was a fool. The man is a fraud, a whited sepulchre.'

'Tim, go easy.'

'That's all right. I'll stick with him for the good of Ireland. As long as his path and Ireland's cause are the one, I'll not desert him.' With a knuckle he rubbed his eyes dry. His mouth was set and unforgiving. 'Bogus, that's what he is.'

He held the word as if it were a small animal he had trapped. 'Bogus.'

SIX

When they travelled together, he took childish pleasure in disguises and false names. His favourite name, because of the initials, was Clement S. Preston; he thought it ingenious. When, unaccompanied, Katharine took a room at Fox's Hotel off Piccadilly, she did so as Mrs Preston; the incognito, although unnecessary, made her feel that they were not apart.

He had given her two commissions. The first was to do with the sitting-room carpet at Eltham; he believed that the green threads in its pattern contained toxic matter that had given him a sore throat. She had cut out a piece of the carpet and brought it to an analyst; today, on calling for the findings, she was told with the most exquisite and insolent civility that no poisons had been discovered. Her second mission was more to her liking; it was to spy upon Gladstone and Buckshot Forster.

She stayed overnight at Fox's. Next day at two in the afternoon, a written message came to say that the Cabinet was meeting in secret council. It was unsigned, but the sender was a secretary employed by her uncle, Lord Hatherley, who had lately been Lord Chancellor – once, in a dark moment, Willie had been heard to enquire aggrievedly of his Maker as to how so well-connected a family could be so damnably hard up. She sent a telegram to Parnell in care of Morrison's Hotel in Dublin. The text was prearranged: RAIN ON

THE WIND. Not wishing to seem impersonal, she added of her own accord, YOURS VERY SINCERELY. When it had been dispatched, she returned to Fox's to await a second message from her agent.

At 10, Downing Street, 'Buckshot' was about to enjoy his proudest hour. With the new act and the suspension of habeas corpus, he had ordered the imprisonment of more than a thousand persons. There had been a set-back or two – in one incident, an old woman had been shot and a girl bayoneted – but Forster felt this to be a poor excuse for his new nickname, the 'English Robespierre'. There were times, he reflected, when the ingratitude of the Irish seemed boundless. He might have known despair had Mr Gladstone not cheered him onwards by paying tribute to his success at combining a 'cool head and warm heart'.

Early in the week at Wexford, Parnell had surprised even his enemies with an inflammatory speech. 'The Irishman,' he said, 'who thinks he can throw away his arms will find to his sorrow that he has placed himself in the power of the cruel and perfidious English enemy.' It was incitement.

'He is play-acting,' Gladstone said. 'I am inclined to think that his purpose is to test us.'

Forster said: 'Then, sir, let us be tested. Will you give the order for his arrest?'

'I? Never!' The Grand Old Man smiled upon him. 'My dear Forster, it is you who have sown the wind. The whirlwind is yours for the reaping.'

The benignity in his voice caused a warmth to spread within the English Robespierre. He and no one but he would be privileged to dispose of his arch-tormentor. He hardly dared ask for more, and yet he dared. 'Prime Minister, is it to be the one warrant . . . for Parnell alone?'

Gladstone made a cathedral of his fingers. 'Indeed, why should it be? No, I think that if the honourable members are in agreement we may as well rid ourselves of the limbs of the beast as well as the head.'

Forster's cup was overflowing. With the meeting's business

done, he sent a message to Superintendent Mallon of the Dublin police. It bore one word: *Proceed*. He himself would cross by mail-packet that night to sign the main warrant. Others could be prepared at leisure.

Within twenty minutes, Katharine had dispatched her second telegram to Morrison's Hotel. Like Forster's, it consisted of one word: in this case: *Deluge*. To add a salutation would this time, she thought, be excessive.

Before returning home, she visited her doctor, who assured her that her pregnancy was taking its natural course. At Wonersh Lodge, the chink of crystal against crystal told her not only that she had a visitor, but who it was.

'Willie! And upon another weekday! What is it? Have I been having you followed again? Or perhaps you are looking for Mr Parnell?'

'No, Kate, not any more. He has other lodgings from his day out.' Willie all but crowed; had it not been for the risk of spilling his whisky, he would surely have danced. 'Well, I said it would happen, and it did. He's got his come-uppance at last. Laid by the heels, by God.'

She knew what was coming and was prepared. 'Willie, must you swear? He? Who are you talking about?'

'Parnell. Joe Chamberlain told me there's a warrant out. He'll be arrested first thing tomorrow, thrown into Kilmainham Gaol and left to rot.'

His eyes were close upon her face, watching for a sign of shock or grief. Her voice betrayed nothing; she had done her weeping when she was writing the second telegram.

She said: 'Well, it is hardly a surprise. I did not think he could keep out of prison much longer, did you?'

He was disappointed. He had come from town, left the warmth and good fellowship of Chamberlain's club, expressly to bring her the news. He had at least expected dismay that the leader, the so-called Chief, had been brought low. She had begrudged him his moment of pleasure. Willie's was not the kind of brain that could accommodate two emotions at once. It only dimly occurred to him that Kate's unconcern was proof positive of her innocence. He would attend to that later; what filled his mind was that he had expected tears, caterwauling and wringing of hands, and the woman, born contrary, had let him down. He deserved better. In philosophical moments, it occurred to Willie that whenever life seemed about to yield up its perfections there was always a piece of cork in the wine glass, a fleck of mud on his shoe, or a handsomer woman at the next table. Perhaps, he thought, his standards were too high.

Katharine said: 'Willie, why did you think this news of such importance that you came from London to impart it?'

Aware that he could hardly admit to his eagerness to witness her distress, she was determined on a small revenge. He floundered.

'Ah.'

Pleasantly: 'Yes, Willie?'

'Fact is . . . the news was, ah, purely by the way. I thought I'd . . . um come and stay the night.' It was, he told himself, smart thinking. He could not deny himself a small out-of-the-woods smile.

She managed to look demure. 'Oh but, Willie, that would never do. Have you forgotten our arrangement?'

'Yes, but dash it all. I mean, that's gone by the board.'

'Has it?'

'Jove, yes. You can't have forgotten.' He gave her his masterful look. 'That evening a few weeks ago, when you came to Albert Mansions. And couldn't resist spending the night, what? I thought it rather like old times.'

'Oh, *that*?'

'So . . . ah, all wagers are off, eh, my dear?'

'How charmingly you put it.' She gave him her most compassionate look. 'But my poor Willie.'

'Eh?'

'How could you possibly have mistaken a treat for a pension?'

As he stomped off towards the railway station, nursing yet another hurt, she remembered that she had not yet told him she was pregnant. The urge to call him back was easily withstood. She decided to send him a note instead. The sight of William learning that he was to be again blessed with parenthood was a pleasure she could deny herself.

As he dressed, he asked if he might write a letter.

Superintendent Mallon could not have been more obliging. 'Most certainly. It won't take too long, will it, sir? I shouldn't like a crowd to gather and hinder us on our way.'

He wrote: *I have just been arrested by two fine looking detectives, and write these words to tell my wife that she must not fret over her husband . . .* In case the letter should go astray, he made no mention of her two telegrams, which had given him time to destroy or make safe his private papers. Instead of a police van, a cab was waiting outside Morrison's Hotel. On the way to Kilmainham, he espied a pillar-box, called upon the driver to stop, alighted, posted the letter and completed his journey.

Later, he wrote to tell her that he had been allocated two cells, one the size of his bedroom at Avondale. He had stayed in far worse railway hotels. For part of the day, on some days, there was sunlight. And he was not wanting for company; within the week, his lieutenants, John Dillon, Thomas Sexton and others, had joined him as prisoners.

'How goes the country?' Parnell asked of Dillon.

'Grief-stricken. There has been rioting.'

Parnell seemed not dismayed. 'It was inevitable. Captain Moonlight has taken my place.' He looked past Dillon as a uniformed convict entered his cell. 'Ah, Hurley.'

The convict, who had the red hair and pale eyes of Connaught, balanced a glass of aerated liquid on a makeshift tray that was the upturned lid of a biscuit tin.

'Hurley,' Parnell said, 'has been here these nine months. He seems to have appointed himself as my valet. Tell Mr Dillon what it was you did, Hurley.'

'If you plaise, yer honour, I pizoned a grabber's well.'

Parnell smiled, accepted the glass and sipped from it. To Dillon, he said: 'Soda water and lemon juice. Hurley declares that there is no mixture more refreshing.'

Dillon said sardonically: 'You seem not to go short of comforts.'

'Nor will you. The prison fare is as poisonous as the grabber's well, so our food is brought from the outside. My sister Anna has set up a welfare fund, and at the rate it grows it will soon feed every prisoner in Dublin. No, what you want to look out for here is the damp. I already have sciatica.'

They talked. Timothy Healy, on Parnell's instructions, had remained in England, where Coercion had no teeth. Joseph Biggar had fled to Paris and was diligently providing his lady friend, Fanny Hyland, with further grounds for breach of promise.

Weeks passed. Parnell reported to Katharine that for exercise he played handball, and he had at last taken up the reading of books. He received gifts from admirers. One of these was an eiderdown quilt; at the sight of its green satin covering, he was terrified and called for Hurley to come and take it away. His letters were lightsome; he made little of his confinement; his health was good; release could not be far off. He was playing a role; she was aware of it, and she read most attentively the words he had not written.

A fancy came to her and would not be put to rout. It clung to her mind as if with barbs that, as his love for her strengthened, his passion for Ireland had begun to ebb. It was as if she and his country drank from the same bowl, and there was perhaps not enough for two. He was still the Uncrowned King, the chief and prophet, but the letters whispered that now instead of creating history he was willing to be borne on its tide.

Her head swam. Perhaps she was misreading what was unsaid; perhaps, insatiable, she was deluding herself that she was first in his life, even above his countrymen. She wondered why a man who so despised the common herd could choose to be its leader. He had never spoken to her of that. In the matter of Ireland – that wretched country she had never seen and where she would never set foot – he had no confidants; he could speak to ten thousand at a time, but not to one.

'Let us,' Parnell said to Dillon in Kilmainham one day, 'inform the country that we still have a voice.'

He drafted a manifesto, to which Michael Davitt, in Portland Gaol, added his signature. It was published in *United Ireland* on behalf of the Land League, and it urged tenants to fight Coercion by non-payment of rent. To Parnell's surprise, it was an utter failure. The Irish clergy instructed their flock that the withholding of rent was as much a sin against nature as non-payment of parish dues. The sheep, ever obedient to their shepherds, rejected the manifesto. The clergy, Parnell noted, omitted to inform them that the murder of policemen, landlords and their fellow-countrymen might also be accounted a sin. 'It is just as well,' he remarked. 'In these hard times, the poor have so few diversions.'

Parnell was not accustomed to defeat, but at least in this instance there was more silver lining than cloud. His manifesto had wrecked the Land League. Not only was it now defunct, but the Government decided to suppress it, thereby shutting the stable door when the horse was dead. 'At least,' Parnell said, 'I am quit of Davitt and may climb down from my tight-rope.'

He had been four months in Kilmainham when the time came for Katharine's confinement. Willie kept a vigil in the sitting room, and the labour did not take much longer than a decanter of brandy. Towards midnight, he was summoned to her bedroom. Red with maudlin pleasure and Armagnac, he kissed her on the forehead, managing not to over-balance. He said, affectionately: 'Thank you, Dick!' As the doctor announced, 'Your daughter, sir,' the nurse put the infant in Willie's arms and as quickly retrieved it.

Next day, Katharine felt strong enough to entrust Mary with a letter for posting. It was addressed to 'Mr Carpenter' in care of Parnell's solicitor, who visited his client twice weekly.

For family reasons the child will be named Claude Sophie.
Willie comes to Eltham more frequently than I would allow.
He thinks that the birth will seal our reconciliation, whereas I
know it will only cement the cold hatred I feel towards him and
consummate the love I bear my child's father.

Within four weeks, she wrote to him saying that Claude Sophie
was failing and had not long to live.

On the heels of this came another letter by a more direct route. It
was from Willie O'Shea. He had formed, he said, a certain powerful
connexion through which the Irish leader might, if he so desired,
treat with the Prime Minister. He, Captain O'Shea, was prepared
to place himself at Parnell's disposal as an intermediary. He made
no mention of Katharine or the dying child.

Dillon read the letter. 'O'Shea's impudence beggars belief.'

'Not *my* belief,' Parnell said.

'This mysterious connexion of his. Do you believe that such
a person exists?'

Parnell said: 'You may bank on it. It is beyond doubt Joseph
Chamberlain. O'Shea has become his hanger-on.'

Dillon, unaware that his chief's intelligence network had its
headquarters in Eltham, was much impressed. 'Is he? Then I wish
them joy of each other. But what on earth has Joe Chamberlain to
do with us?'

Parnell said slowly: 'He is Buckshot Forster's sworn enemy.'

His face clouded; his thoughts had drifted away from Chamberlain and Willie O'Shea and were with Katharine and his
child. He only dimly noticed the presence of a newcomer in the
cell.

'Mr Parnell . . .'

He recovered himself and begged the governor to be seated.
'Sir, we are honoured.' He added, drily: 'You will overlook our
surroundings.'

It was his standard greeting. Usually it was as gravely received
as it was uttered; today, the governor was holding what Parnell

saw was a telegram. 'Mr Parnell, I regret that I am the bearer of unhappy news. A bereavement.'

He stared at the message without accepting it. The thought came that Claude Sophie was dead and that Katharine, demented by grief, had now telegraphed the news to him and the child's parentage to the world.

In the dim gaslight, he might have been a ghost. Katharine and Willie stared at him in amazement. She swayed upon her feet. Willie caught hold of her. He said: 'My wife is not well.'

Her eyes had not left Parnell's face. 'They have released you, then. I was . . . we had not heard.'

He told them: 'My sister's boy Henry has died of typhoid in Paris. I have been put on parole to attend the funeral.'

She said: 'I'm so sorry. You look unwell.'

'Nonsense, Kate. Where are your manners? The chap is as fit as a fiddle.' Willie bade his visitor welcome and, to prove that his simile was not a fluke, declared himself as pleased as Punch. He offered his guest a chair. Only when he had turned away to pour a whisky did Parnell and Katharine have an opportunity to exchange looks and each saw mirrored in the other the same unhappiness.

He wondered if the child was still living. He must tread carefully. In the circumstances, there was no reason why Willie should not have been here, but out of foolishness he had expected to find Katharine alone. Now he must make no mistakes. Willie placed a glass of whisky beside Parnell, then turned up the gas in the twin mantles over the fireplace. 'I take it you have come from Albert Mansions?'

Parnell looked at him blankly.

'And they told you I was here.' Willie gave him the smile of one who is magnanimous in victory. 'Yes, I thought that letter of mine would make you sit up and beg. You were anxious for a chinwag!'

'Naturally.' He caught Katharine's eye.

Willie all but gloated. 'I should say so. Well, now that you've tracked me down, you must stay the night. Eh, Kate?' His voice became confidential. 'Fact is, we have some melancholy news of our own.'

'I trust not.' Now he did not look at her.

'Did you know – well, of course you did not, how could you? – that my wife and I had been blessed with a little girl?'

Willie's face was for once open and empty of guile; it was almost good-natured. The lie was too great for utterance, even for a single word. Parnell shook his head.

'Alas, not long for this world.'

'Oh?'

'Poor little thing. At first she looked to be thriving. Then of a sudden she seemed to go from us. Kate sent for me because . . .' He sniffed and blinked back a tear. 'Sorry.'

She said: '. . . Because the doctor says that she will not live beyond tonight.' She said to Parnell, point-blank: 'Would you like to see her?'

Willie was shocked. 'Kate, no. Don't oblige him.'

He said: 'Yes. Yes, I would.'

As she and Parnell left the room, Willie had found a ray of light. He said: 'Luckily, I had her baptised a Catholic.'

On the stairs, she asked: 'When do you go to Paris?'

'Tomorrow. I must return to Dublin immediately after the funeral.'

There was a housemaid in the nursery attending the dying child. Parnell and Katharine looked into the cradle. She said to the maid: 'It is stifling in here. Will you fetch my eau-de-Cologne from the bathroom?'

When the girl had gone, she looked again at the child, so still as to seem already dead, and said softly to Parnell, 'Forgive me.' For reply, he touched her hand. Without warning, she flung her arms about his neck and thrust her body hard against his; her mouth was open on his own, working as if she would devour him. He felt his coat sleeve brush the cradle. When he became aroused, her nails gouged his neck. She whispered: 'Oh, we shall go to hell for this. We shall burn.'

After dinner, Katharine went upstairs to sit by Claude Sophie. At the dining table, Willie watched as Parnell wrote, struck out a word or a line and wrote again. When he had finished, Willie held his hand out for the paper.

'No. Hear me first.'

Parnell looked at the other's face and at the hand which did not retreat but was still outstretched, greedily like a beggar's on the street. He knew that O'Shea was not to be relied on. Whatever he was told to do, he would depart from it, perhaps from incompetence, assuredly to prove that he was no man's underling.

'What I have written may seem hard to grasp, so I want to tell you very simply what it amounts to.' Willie's face tightened; he was being taken for a fool. 'If the Government can devise a satisfactory way of dealing with arrears of rent, then I, as leader of the party, will denounce all outrages and resistance to law, including the boycott. Other matters may be adjusted; the arrears are our sticking point.'

Willie, man of destiny, all but swept the paper from Parnell's hand. 'I'll not give an inch. Joe Chamberlain will know he isn't dealing with a milksop.'

In his heart, Parnell all but groaned. He said: 'I have to be direct with you. If my conditions are departed from in the minutest, if you go an inch beyond my instructions, I shall disavow both the agreement and yourself.'

As he spoke, he knew that his breath might be better saved to cool his porridge. His threat was empty; whatever happened, for Katharine's sake, O'Shea's skin must somehow be saved.

Willie said: 'You can trust me. I'll have you out of Kilmainham in no time. By the time I've done —'

'You will do nothing! My release is secondary. Your only concern is to present that document to Chamberlain as it stands; you are not to cancel or enlarge upon one word of it.'

'Quite, quite, say no more. I'm not a greenhorn, you know.'

Willie thrust the paper into his inside pocket. It amused him that Ireland's leader should be such an old woman. Their business done, he hesitated, then spoke again. 'Ah . . . by the by, there is a personal matter.'

'Yes?'

'That . . . um, difference of opinion we had.'

Parnell's voice was cold. 'You held an opinion, did you?'

'I mean that . . . um, nonsense of me sending you a challenge. Didn't stop to think. I felt a complete ass.'

He hoped that Parnell would contradict him; instead, his guest regarded him as if it would be unmannerly to do so. Willie cleared his throat.

'So I hope it's all water under the . . .' Thirsting for a synonym for 'bridge' and unable to find it, he made what he intended to be an eloquent gesture of the hand. 'I mean, you've entrusted me with this matter, fate of nations and so forth, so as far as this house is concerned, from here on please feel free to —'

Shadows moved across the outer hall. Katharine, carrying a lamp, had come downstairs. When she was in the room, Willie stood up and said: 'It's over, then, is it?'

She said, to Parnell: 'Yes.'

Willie gave a fatalistic shrug. 'Sure it's the will of God.'

His accent had suddenly reverted to the purest Dublin. He attempted to smile bravely. The effort cost him his self-composure; he crumpled from within, his face screwed up like crushed paper. A great blubbering sob shook his body. He stood, alone and shuddering in an ague of grief. Katharine made no move towards him. Horrified, Parnell forced himself to touch Willie on the shoulder.

He said: 'I am extremely sorry.'

Willie clutched his wrist. Unable to speak, he jerked his head up and down in a grotesque, unending nod. Parnell, held fast, looked at Katharine.

William Henry O'Shea, statesman and architect of Ireland's destiny, had haggled, withheld, dangled, conceded, stood firm, cut the cards, dealt again and raised the stakes.

'What kind of man is your Captain O'Shea?' Gladstone asked of Joseph Chamberlain.

It was Buckshot Forster who, ignored by them both, now elbowed his way to the fore. He said: 'Clever enough, sir. No, not clever. Cunning, I should say. Vain. Untrustworthy.'

Gladstone granted him a glance: 'And what are his faults, pray?'

A dutiful laugh went around the cabinet table. Forster did not share it. Irish affairs were within his bailiwick, and 'Pushful' Joe was an interloper in his house. In keeping with his own best traditions, he attempted an eviction.

'With respect, sir, if we are to negotiate with Parnell or his followers, surely it becomes a matter for myself as Irish Secretary?'

Gladstone's eyes were hooded, as was his smile. 'Ordinarily, yes. Unhappily, Mr Forster, we have a conflict of interests, you and I.'

'Do we, sir? I was not aware of it.'

The old man regarded him mournfully: a father reproaching a wayward son. 'You, sir, put Mr Parnell into a Dublin prison and are determined to keep him there. Given that his imprisonment has led not to peace in Ireland but to virtual chaos, *my* present concern is to extricate him.'

Forster had the sensation of stepping out on to what a moment ago had been earth and was now boundless space. Falling, he felt the cold wind of outdoors and knew dimly that he, not Chamberlain, had been the one evicted. Gladstone's face, grave and noble, held in it no sigh of deceit. Like the fledgling chess player who has been outwitted by a master, Forster could discern checkmate a move ahead, but had not the least idea of how the old man had managed it. Worse, he had not even known there was a game in progress.

A week later, a late April sun shone upon Albert Mansions and Downing Street alike. Willie was usually liverish of a morning; today, and to the surprise of his friend, Mrs Jenny Armbruster, he was all but merry. Lying back on her pillow, she belched gently, put forefinger and thumb in a circle to her lips, little finger genteelly extended, and said: 'Pardon.' Willie did not hear; nightshirted, he was smiling at himself in the glass and passing a finger along the silkiness of his moustache. He had Chamberlain's word that today the Kilmainham Treaty would be ratified. He would be the talk of Westminster. The future was his; in time, he would oust Parnell as Parnell had ousted Isaac Butt. Kate would learn what a sterling man she had thrown aside; he could see her, perhaps on her knees, imploring him to return to her and the chicks.

'Willie, my gallant captain, I'm cold,' Mrs Armbruster said. 'Come back to bed.'

The wife of a naval officer, she was a theatre lover whom Willie had encountered on the promenade of the Alhambra Music Hall. Captain Webb, the Channel swimmer, had been the principal attraction, and afterwards Willie had taken Mrs Armbruster to his especial haunt, Evans's Late Joys in Covent Garden.

Willie, who had no place to go but the Commons, climbed back into bed. 'Do you know,' he said, 'that today, single-handedly, I shall have saved Ireland?'

'To hell with Ireland,' Mrs Armbruster said, hunting him through the bedclothes.

Willie laughed. 'That's what I always say.'

The hussar mounted his steed.

In Downing Street, too, there was happiness. Joseph Chamberlain was in festive mood, and Mr Gladstone was delighted to be indoors out of the sunshine, which, with the years, made him look increasingly like a ruined abbey. Forster alone was not happy as he faced the two in the otherwise deserted Cabinet room. All but naked to his enemies, he sought only to retain a poor tatter for his modesty.

'I take it, sir, that a condition of Parnell's release will be that he makes a public declaration of penitence?'

'Penitence?' Gladstone asked.

'For his crimes.'

Blandly: 'Were there any?'

This, then, was to be the measure of the betrayal. The smile on Chamberlain's face held undisguised mockery as Gladstone continued.

'My dear Forster, we would be poor men of business if we demanded that which we had no hope of receiving. If Mr Parnell were to wear sack-cloth at our insistence, his people would call it betrayal. It would be the end of him. And the end of him would be the end of peace in Ireland. No, I think we have done handsomely.' He turned away from Forster as a Caesar might turn from a suppliant. 'Well, Chamberlain, shall the man Davitt be released, too?'

Ignoring Forster, as Gladstone had done, Joseph Chamberlain spoke almost as to an intimate. 'I see no reason why not. With the Land League a spent force, Davitt has lost his sting. And Parnell will be glad to see the back of him. Let the fellow go.'

Gladstone, well pleased, rose to his feet, the meeting at an end.

'Prime Minister . . .' Forster's anger was hardly contained. He was aware that, as 'Buckshot' first and then 'Robespierre', he had been a well-hated Secretary. No one, however, had ever suggested that he was less than a slave to his office or that he wanted for courage – in his constant journeyings between Dublin and Westminster he had a hundred times risked assassination by the Fenians. He would not now be thrown aside.

He said: 'Sir, if Parnell is not obliged to render an apology before the House, it will be alleged that his imprisonment was an error, if not an outright miscarriage of justice.'

'It will be alleged?' The hooded eyes were wide with the innocence of age. 'Alleged by whom?'

'Prime Minister, the decision to commit him to prison was taken, you will remember, in a session of full Cabinet.'

Gladstone was never deadlier than at his most venerable. 'My dear Forster, my memory is nowadays a poor thing. I do seem to recall, however, that Mr Parnell was arrested on a warrant applied for by your good self as Irish Secretary.'

At once, the Prime Minister's words on that occasion came back to Forster: 'It is you who have sown the wind. The whirlwind is yours for the reaping.' If Forster was devastated at how he had been ushered into the trap, it was because he had the misfortune to be thrice honest: as a Quaker, as a Yorkshireman, and as the husband of a daughter of Dr Thomas Arnold of Rugby. It required no false dignity for him to reply: 'Sir, you shall have my resignation within the hour.'

Gladstone threw up his hands. 'Forster, surely not?'

'I regret that I have no choice.'

The old man, grave, afflicted, said: 'But you will reconsider?'

The commotion that attended Parnell's release caused Forster to reflect that yesterday's villain is today's hero; the world would otherwise expire of ennui. It might have cheered him to consider that time's revenges would ensure that the converse was also true, but for the moment and after nearly seven months in gaol, the liberated Parnell was as much a hero in England as at home. Timothy Healy was one of the group that journeyed to Holyhead to meet him and the other prisoners. He bowed to his chief, but did not offer to shake hands as he did with Dillon and William O'Brien. With what Healy regarded as intolerable arrogance, Parnell did not seem to notice the snub; he was more intent on sending a telegram before entraining for London. Watching him enter the stationmaster's office to write it, Healy thought: It is a message to *her*. By tomorrow evening, the rottenness will begin again. They have no shame.

William Forster's misfortunes were not yet at an end. He had chosen the afternoon of Parnell's return to the Commons to hold forth upon why he had felt compelled to resign as Irish Secretary.

'Poor Buckshot,' Parnell said. 'His timing could not have been worse.' Outside the chamber, he addressed Dillon. 'Will you and Healy go into the House first? I shall follow.'

Healy hissed at Dillon as they walked towards the Opposition benches: 'You see? He wants to make an entrance. Always the actor!'

In his speech to the House, Forster was unrepentant. He had properly ordered the arrest of Parnell and his followers for plotting to overthrow public order and render injury to the Queen's subjects. 'And now these criminals have been set free. Well, if England cannot govern the honourable member for Cork, then we may as well acknowledge that he is the greatest power in Ireland today.'

Forster's tone was bitter, but the appearance of Parnell at that moment gave his words the effect of an unqualified tribute. The Irish members cheered as their chief took his accustomed seat. He showed no emotion as the applause raged on, defying the cries for order. Instead, he let his eyes rest coldly upon the face of Buckshot Forster, who, a moment before, had unwittingly raised his deadliest enemy, the leader of a minor political faction, to a place in the pantheon.

As soon as the opportunity arose, Parnell spoke briefly, then left the chamber, again to applause. By six o'clock, he was at home in Eltham.

SEVEN

She wondered what the servants knew or suspected. They must at all costs not be scandalised. Mary and Ellen were devout Catholics; on Sundays, they accompanied Willie and the children to Mass at Chislehurst, and they were given an extra evening off each month to attend a mysterious ritual known as the First Friday. They each wore a gold locket containing a portrait of Parnell, and only at his command would they consent to keep them hidden under their clothing instead of in defiant view. In their eyes, Parnell could do no wrong; all the same, Katharine was determined that there would be no conflict of loyalties between God and god. She and Parnell must abide by rules. There would be no overt displays of affection. In the evenings, they would sit apart. At night, he would not come to her room until the servants, including the children's governess, were in bed. He protested only at her insistence that he return to his room before Ellen arose to rake out the kitchen range. 'Katey, she is two floors below us,' he pleaded. She remained adamant.

At breakfast, on his first morning after his return from Kilmainham, she asked: 'Do you go to town today?'

'I must.' As Party leader, he had been invited to take tea with the new Irish Secretary, Lord Frederick Cavendish. 'His most notable political coup so far has been to marry Gladstone's niece. Still, he can hardly be worse than poor old Buckshot.'

She asked him: 'Will you come this evening?'

He said: 'Forbid me.'

He met Lord Frederick Cavendish on the terrace at Westminster, as arranged. The new Secretary was by ten years Parnell's senior; his manner was easygoing and affable in contrast to his predecessor: a Yorkshire bull in an Irish china shop. This, Parnell thought, looking him over, is to be the new enemy.

'My congratulations,' Cavendish said, 'on your victorious return to the House. Your star seems to be at its zenith.'

'Not quite yet, I hope.'

Cavendish laughed. 'You alarm me. Still, I look forward to our dealings. Only be kind; tell me now what devilment you have in store for me.'

'None at all. At least not in Ireland. My devilment is wholly constitutional.'

Two days previously he had gone to Portland Prison to greet Michael Davitt on his release. On the train to London, he had made no secret of his pleasure at the demise of the Land League. 'With respect, Davitt, or perhaps with no respect, we've had enough of you and your religion of death, with the gallows as its high altar. We'll have Home Rule, and we'll have it my way.'

Davitt had looked at him in incredulity. He said: 'The blind, bloody arrogance. Old Gladstone will have you for his supper.'

Old Gladstone was now, in fact, two tables away, covertly watching over Parnell's meeting with Cavendish. Parnell said: 'The violence in Ireland is unorganised. It has no centre, and it will die out. As for my sister Anna, I have dealt with her.'

'Your sister?'

'She is the moving spirit behind the Ladies' Land League. A fearsome crew, not unlike the Furies of legend. She has been squandering party funds at an alarming rate, so I have ordered that the League be disbanded.'

'What does your sister say to that?'

Parnell was unemotional. 'She has sworn never to speak to me again in her lifetime.'

'Do you think she means it?'

'Of course. She is a Parnell.'

Gladstone excused himself to his companions and stopped by their table. He had four sons, but it was said that Lord Frederick Cavendish, although related only by marriage, was closer to him than any of them. At close range, Parnell saw that his affection went deep. The old man put a hand fondly on Cavendish's shoulder. He said, proudly: 'We expect great things.'

'So do we,' Parnell said.

The three men smiled. When Gladstone had moved on, Parnell asked: 'When do you go to Ireland?'

'This very evening.'

Early on the Sunday morning, Katharine accompanied Parnell to the station at Blackheath to await the mail-train to Cannon Street. Since Willie, after the exertions of Saturday night, would arrive for his weekly visit barely in time for eleven o'clock Mass, there was little danger that the two men would meet. Parnell went to the platform kiosk: 'I must see what the papers have to say about Davitt's release.'

Katharine said, gently mocking him: 'And, by the way, about your own triumphant return.'

He bought a *Sunday Observer*. As he walked back towards her, looking at the front page, she thought he was about to fall. He stood, his face draining of blood.

'Charley, what is it?'

'Cavendish is dead. They have done for him.'

'What?'

'In Dublin. And they have as surely done for us.'

At long last, Buckshot Forster's luck had been in. A group of assassins styling themselves the Invincibles had determined

91

to kill him as he left Ireland for the last time. To keep a dinner appointment before sailing, he had taken an early train to Kingstown, and so was saved, whereupon the gang looked about them for another victim. They were not proud; bilked of a florin, they were prepared to make do with eighteenpence in the person of Thomas Henry Burke, the Permanent Under-Secretary.

Leaving a function at Dublin Castle, Burke engaged a jaunting car to take him to the Vice-regal Lodge in the Phoenix Park. He had reached the Gough statue just beyond the park gates when he saw a familiar figure walking ahead of him. It was the new Irish Secretary, Lord Frederick Cavendish, who had arrived in Ireland that morning and was enjoying the balm of the Dublin evening. Burke climbed down from the car, paid his driver and accompanied Cavendish on his walk. They strolled arm in arm. There was a polo match in progress; there were ramblers and bicyclists. It was towards sunset; families were moving homeward.

The assassins were five in number. They walked past Burke and Cavendish, then one of them suddenly bent as if to tie a bootlace. His name, it was later discovered, was Joe Brady; he was a stonemason. 'Watch out, man,' Burke said, almost falling over him. Brady sprang up, wrapped an arm around his neck and stabbed him in the throat.

Cavendish cried out: 'What are you doing? Help . . . help, somebody!' He struck Brady on the head with his umbrella.

Brady said: 'Would you? Ah, you villain, you.' He stabbed Cavendish in the arm, then followed him into the roadway and drove the knife into his chest. Upon Brady's order, the youngest member of the gang cut the throats of both men. As the Invincibles fled, none of them was aware that they had killed not only their intended victim, but the new Irish Secretary and William Gladstone's surrogate son.

'Animals!' Parnell said, so loudly and with such despair that others on the station platform looked around.

'What does it mean?' Katharine asked. 'For you, that is?'

'Mean? Why, that once again we are villains before the world.

Who will trust us now? Who will say that we are fit to govern ourselves? Gladstone was ours . . . we had him. And now *this*.' He had taken hold of her hand, crushing it so that the rings bit into her fingers. 'I shall resign.'

'Nothing of the sort,' she told him. 'Here is your train. Go and see Davitt and as many of your people as you can find, only do it now. Resign, indeed! What do you take me for that I would call a coward my husband?'

Her manner was so fierce, her temper so real, that he was taken aback. He nodded, saying no more, and caught his train. In London, he called upon Willie O'Shea, who, having sped Mrs Armbruster homeward to Kensal Rise, was on the point of leaving for Eltham.

'O'Shea, I have a commission for you. It is urgent.'

Willie all but gaped at his visitor. Like a fiery wind, the vision swept through his mind of Parnell arriving a half hour earlier than he had done and meeting Mrs Armbruster on the stairs. He banished the horror from him and said: 'Today? It's Sunday. I am engaged to take the chicks to Mass.'

Parnell said: I want you to go and see the Prime Minister.'

When he had given O'Shea his instructions, he went to the Westminster Palace Hotel, where Davitt lodged. It was the agreed meeting place in the event of crisis, and Davitt, with Biggar, Dillon, Timothy Healy and others had forgathered in one of the private dining rooms. They were shocked to see that Parnell had been weeping. By way of greeting, all that Davitt could do was shake his head in bewilderment. To him, who could see little cause for outrage in the shooting of a bailiff from behind an Irish ditch, the killing of Cavendish and Burke was butchery, even if the end result was no different. It was worse than butchery, he had told the members, for there was no sense to it.

Timothy Healy said: 'The meeting thought that you would wish us to issue a statement. I have prepared a draft. Do you want to see it?'

Parnell said: 'No. Read it.'

93

Healy did so. The manifesto deplored the murders; it prayed that the perpetrators would be brought to justice; it emphasised that the assassins were the enemies of Home Rule. As he read, the others half-listened; their eyes were on Parnell. His loss of reserve frightened them, as children are unnerved at seeing tears in a parent's eyes. When Tim Healy had finished, he looked towards Parnell for approval.

'It will do. Who will make copies for the press?'

Henry Harrison said that he would see to it. Tim Healy handed the manifesto to him, shaking his head as if at a futility. Parnell asked: 'Something ails you, Healy?'

Healy said, bitterly: 'Yes, sir, and with respect, sir, fine words are what ails me. I wrote out that manifesto because the others here wanted it, but talk is cheap, no matter who does the talking. Even yourself. The way I see it, when they murdered Cavendish they put Irish freedom to sleep, too, maybe for a generation. I think all Irish members should resign.'

Cries of protest went up from the others. Tim Healy ignored them. Having had his say, he looked unflinchingly at Parnell; of the old idolatry, there was no sign. For the first time that day, Davitt smiled. He thought of an encounter going on for two years ago in the Members' Corridor, when Healy had said: 'Whatever I am, he made me,' meaning Parnell. Davitt had replied: 'Be merciful. Try not to punish him.' Now he thought: It's happened, then?

Parnell seemed not to notice Healy's insolence. He said: 'Let us hear another voice. Mr Biggar?'

Joseph Biggar said: 'My God, if you're inviting the rank and file to put an oar in, it must be the end of the world.'

'I'm not asking you for an oar, Mr Biggar, but for an opinion.'

'Then you can have it. I say that young Healy is wrong. I don't believe it'll take a generation; no, nor near it. But I say again, what if it does? Let us abide. Let us watch and wait.'

Thomas Sexton chimed in. 'Right, Joe! And what I say is —'

Parnell said, gently for him: 'Thank you, Sexton. I asked for one opinion, and it has been given.' He addressed the members at large. 'Not thirty minutes ago, I sent a message to the Prime Minister. I said that rather than endanger the policy we have embarked upon, I was prepared to resign my seat.'

There was a dismayed silence. After a moment, Dillon asked: 'And what answer did Gladstone give?'

'I am waiting for word,' Parnell added, offhandedly: 'My agent in this matter is Captain O'Shea.'

He affected not to hear Biggar muttering: 'Who, ye can be sure, will make a holy hames of it.' Parnell had beaten the party into shape upon an anvil of obedience. He commanded; they followed; he did not explain. Now he heard himself break his own commandment. 'As you are aware, alone among the Irish members, Captain O'Shea chooses to sit with the Government. On this tragic day, I have put his recalcitrance to good use. He will be the Irish presence that is least unwelcome to the Prime Minister.'

As the words turned to dust in his mouth and he felt rather than saw Timothy Healy's eyes upon him, he realised that explaining himself was the lesser sin; his words were hypocrisy.

They would wait, he said, for O'Shea's return from Downing Street. After a time, finding the room stifling, he went out and walked to the corner of Parliament Square. A man called down from the top deck of an omnibus: 'There's Parnell!' Further on, a woman shook her fist and shouted: 'Irish murderer.' Rounding the square, he saw Willie O'Shea hurrying towards the hotel.

'There you are,' Willie said. 'Good news. Gladstone says, no resignation. You're safe.'

Only O'Shea, Parnell thought, could put it so charmingly. The two men went to the room where the members were waiting. 'Captain O'Shea has brought me the Prime Minister's reply,' Parnell said. 'He —'

Willie not only committed the *lèse majesté* of interrupting, but all but elbowed his chief aside in his resolve that centre stage should be his alone. 'The P.M. has most graciously informed me that his duty does not permit him to entertain Mr Parnell's proposal. He is, however, deeply sensible of the honourable motives by which it

95

was prompted.' Like many a bad actor, Willie mistook incredulity for adulation. He beamed upon his astonished listeners.

Parnell said, softly: 'If I may serve as interpreter, it appears that Mr Gladstone has declined my offer.'

His gaze fell on Timothy Healy. 'And so in answer to the proposal that the members resign in the mass, that would leave me as the leader of a party of one. No, Healy, I think not.'

Willie cleared his throat. He stood fast; Henry Irving could more easily have been persuaded to forsake the stage of the Lyceum in mid-performance. 'Furthermore,' he announced, 'I have been to the police. All is arranged.'

Parnell's sense of danger warned him of a cliff edge. He seized O'Shea's arm. 'Come, we shall discuss this in private.'

Willie disengaged himself with a smile that told the world he was nobody's fool. He knew what Parnell was up to. The fellow was jealous. And, as usual, he wanted to come first, with the rest nowhere. It was time, Willie felt, for him to move over.

He shone his full light upon the members. 'I have applied for, and been granted, police protection for Mr Parnell and myself, both in London and at Eltham.'

Parnell stared at him in unbelief. 'You have done what?'

Willie said, with diffidence: 'I thought to include myself because, well, the world knows that it was I who engineered your release from Kilmainham. In the present climate, that will not be easily forgiven.' He noticed that Parnell seemed less than gratified. Jealousy again, he supposed.

Parnell said, glaring at him: 'Do you know what you have done? Do you?'

'I have ensured our safety,' Willie said, smiling at his unsmiling audience.

'Are you aware that, thanks to you, we are now tied in with the Dublin murders? And you have left me open to the inference that, since I feel myself in need of protection, there must exist on my part a consciousness of guilt.'

It was too deep for Willie. Plainly, since Parnell had failed to deprive him of his share of the limelight, he was now attempting to confuse him. He said: 'How d'you mean?'

'What is more, by inviting the police to act as our nurserymaids, you have given them their dearest wish: the opportunity to spy upon us in broad daylight.'

Willie might be too straightforward for his own good, but at least he knew an absurdity when he heard it. He smiled: 'Now, my dear sir, it is not a good day for us. You are out of temper, and you exaggerate.'

Parnell said: 'You damned fool.' He went from the room.

Willie saw the embarrassment on the faces of Dillon, Davitt and the others; only Biggar had the crassness to seem amused. Their concern touched him; in their rough way, they were worthy fellows. He said, lightly to put them at their ease: 'Well, that's the last time I'll do *him* a service.' No one spoke; he was doubly touched: they were taking it to heart.

He said: 'Do you know, I mean to demand an apology. Where d'you think he's gone?'

Timothy Healy said: 'You'll never guess.'

There was a half-sneer on his face. Willie thought Healy a queer fish; in a moment of insight, he marked him down as the kind who could not order a lamb chop without passing judgment on the waiter. As the meeting broke up, Joseph Biggar gave it as his opinion that on this dark day the only friend an Irishman had in London was a jug of ale. To no one's surprise, he added that, Sunday and all as it was, he knew of a place. Willie was not invited to join the party, and in any case would have refused. Public houses were for the lower orders.

Timothy Healy, at twenty-seven, had never been drunk before and would never be drunk again. On this Sunday afternoon, however, Father Mathew would have wept for him. Joseph Biggar had thrust a mug of ale into his hand and said: 'Here, young lad, take this because of the day that's in it.' The others, Dillon and

Sexton, looked on; their initial instinct had been to separate Healy from the ale, but the spectacle of a man taking his first drink is as fascinating as seeing an infant stand upright and embark upon its first tottering steps. Biggar was regretting that he had played the role of the tempter. Tim Healy was not a good drunk. There is the kind of toper for whom the world is bathed in sunshine and to whom plain fat women become slender creatures of desire. There are others who possess a quality that Timothy Healy shared with Willie O'Shea, whom he despised; they see human nature for the poor, sickly, self-deluding thing it is; if they are enjoined to silence, they stand in corners and smile knowingly. It had taken Timothy Healy only two pints to attain this state of all-knowingness, and, having been told repeatedly by the company to hold his tongue, he was sitting apart, his arms folded, looking at them through half-closed eyes.

They were in a public house named Sharkey's in Camden Town; although it was closed and empty, Biggar out of a passion for conspiracy had insisted that they sit in the snuggery. The conversation was Irish and therefore circular; which is to say that when a topic was talked to exhaustion it was laid to rest, to be revived when its turn came around once more. Biggar had returned to the subject of Willie O'Shea.

'If there's one kind of jackass that gets my dander up, it's the kind that thinks he's a bloody racehorse. God almighty in His wisdom, why does the Chief put up with him?'

'You don't know?' It was Timothy Healy again. His smile, intended to be inscrutable, succeeded only in being lopsided.

'Do *you*?' John Dillon asked.

Biggar said: 'Don't encourage him.'

Healy attempted to re-fold his arms and failed.

'Tim is silent,' Dillon said. 'It's John Barleycorn that speaks for him. Am I not right, Tim?'

Healy said: 'I'll tell you something for nothing, Dillon.'

Dillon winked at the company. 'This will be good. Fire away.'

As he spoke, Healy's face was suffused with contempt. 'The

Chief . . . there's an expression that the Chief . . . as *you* call him . . . an expression that Mr Parnell is very fond of. "I have a government for Ireland in the palm of my hand." And so he has. Fair dues to him, Ireland is in the palm of Parnell's hand. But God help him and God help us, because there exists another hand, and Parnell himself is in the palm of it.' Healy held out his own hand and closed it into a ball. 'The fine hand of Willie O'Shea.'

'Are you mad?'

'Tim, give over.'

Biggar said: 'Thon young fellow oughtn't to drink. Take it off him.'

Healy said: 'O'Shea sits with the Government. He votes with the Liberals and against us. Why does Mr Parnell not treat him like the . . . the pariah he is? Why does he employ him as his messenger boy and go-between . . . a blackguard I wouldn't trust to . . . to pour *that* from a barrel!' He brandished his ale mug, slopping the dregs.

Biggar said, as Sharkey the landlord looked in at them: 'Easy, easy, you'll have us thrun out.'

Tom Sexton said: 'But it's a question, Joe, it's a question.'

Dillon was fond of Healy; he admired the unashamedness of the kind of passion that might change sides but would never abate. He said: 'Tim, there was a time when you lived in the Chief's pocket. He was father and mother to you, patron saint and God almighty. What ever came between you and him? Did he fall out with you?'

Tim Healy said: 'I'll not have doors slammed in my face.'

'Is that all that ails you?' Dillon laughed. 'I was there, I saw it. Well, it takes little enough to turn you against a man.'

'That's a lie!' ('Jesus, keep it down,' Biggar said.) 'I've never turned against him.' He could hold the truth back no longer. 'He turned against me because I found him out.'

Dillon said, grinning: 'To be sure you did!'

'That letter I opened . . .'

'From what's-her-name? Tillie from Blankshire. The one in Holloway that had his bastard. You'll have one yourself some day.'

99

'He will,' Biggar said. 'Please God, he will so. Sure I have two of them myself.' His eyes became distant with affection. 'Grand wee things.'

Healy, no longer to be silenced, was on his feet, shouting at them. 'It was not from any girl in Holloway. I wish with all my heart it was, even if she was the lowest of the low. God, are the lot of ye blind? He is carrying on with a person who is – who must be – as evil a woman as ever lived. Do you need me to tell ye who she is? Go to Eltham and see for yourselves.'

It was done, it had been told; the burden was no longer his alone. They stared at each other, then at him, appalled, as Tim Healy, the lover betrayed, sat down, laid his head upon the ale-wet table and sobbed inconsolably.

When Willie O'Shea left the Westminster Palace Hotel, he walked for an hour, nursing his humiliation. P for Parnell, he thought, P for Pig. He made a litany of all that he had done for the ruffian and with little thanks; he recalled the delicacy of his dealings with Joe Chamberlain; how he had fetched and carried, and with nary a grumble; and of how he had told Parnell to look upon Wonersh Lodge as his home from home. Well, *that* at least was at an end; let him find another good-natured fool who would allow him to act the sponge. Willie would get his own back. Only days ago, Chamberlain had told him that after the next election, when he succeeded Gladstone as Prime Minister, he would be in need of an Irish Secretary. 'Do you mean . . . ?' Willie had said, hardly daring to hope. Chamberlain had tapped a forefinger against the side of his nose. 'Say no more. I do not forget the faithful few.' Well, when Willie O'Shea was Irish Secretary, he would make Parnell dance to his tune; by the time he was done with him, the ingrate would be pining for the departed days of Buckshot Forster. The thought put Willie in good humour; then he remembered today, the hour spent cooling his heels at Downing Street, and, at the end of it, to be humiliated in front of such ragtag and bobtail as young Healy and the whoremaster Biggar.

Moreover, it had cost him his Sunday at Eltham. He enjoyed not only seeing the chicks, but the luncheon that, in honour of his weekly visit, was more of a dinner. Now it was too late; on his way to Number 10, he had sent a telegram to Kate: CANNOT COME TODAY ON ACCOUNT EVENTS IN DUBLIN. MOST URGENT BUSINESS WITH PRIME MINISTER. LOVE. BOYSIE. He had enjoyed the look on the face of the post-office clerk as he read the message. Now he was at a loose end. He loathed spending Sunday in town. It was a gloomy day; all his haunts were closed, and his election to the brand-new National Liberal Club, for which Chamberlain had proposed him, still hung fire. As he climbed the stairs of Albert Mansions, he remembered that he had not eaten since his breakfast with Mrs Armbruster. Hunger made his hatred of Parnell a devouring furnace. He would never again address him or favour him with a look that was not the sum of his contempt and pity. In that resolve, he was unshakeable.

A telegram had come for him. COME TO DINNER. BRING MR PARNELL WITH YOU. DO NOT FAIL ME. KATE. Willie could not make out whether what he was not to fail in was arriving for dinner or bringing Parnell. He decided not to risk Kate's displeasure on either score. Inside of twenty minutes, he was at Keppel Street. He told the cab driver to wait. Parnell answered his knock and was amazed, not to see the face of Willie O'Shea, but that it was smiling.

'My dear fellow, come along. Kate says I'm to take you to dinner at Eltham, I shall brook no refusals.'

At Wonersh, as they gave their hats to Mary, Katharine came from the sitting room.

'Hello, Willie. Mr Parnell, what dreadful news from Ireland. And yet I must say how pleased I am that you are free from that terrible prison.'

She did it, Parnell thought, extremely well.

101

EIGHT

As he alighted from the carriage outside the Athenaeum, Gladstone noticed a young woman loitering by a doorway. One did not see many unfortunates in the heart of St James's; the Haymarket marked their western frontier, while, so he had heard, they promenaded the Strand in their hundreds. Evidently, this poor creature had been deluded into believing that the kind of personage who frequented Pall Mall would consort with women of the streets. The detectives who accompanied the Prime Minister watched as he engaged the drab in conversation. His tone was fatherly and concerned; he gave her a card bearing the address of the home he had founded for fallen women; he urged her to accept a sovereign – it was, although he was unaware of it, a shilling more than her asking price. His bearing told the woman that he was a person of importance; she had met his kind before; they derived excitement from venturing to the edge of the pit and peering within. When Gladstone had entered the Athenaeum, one of the detectives took the woman by the arm, told her, 'There's your road,' and thrust her in the direction of the Haymarket.

It suited Gladstone's sense of propriety to use his club for the kind of business that lay at the indistinct edge of what was parliamentary. He went to the smoking room, where his guest, Joseph Chamberlain, was waiting. When the pair had retired to a secluded corner, the Prime Minister took from his pocket a folded document.

'I shall not trespass on your time, my dear sir. Without doubt, you are anxious to return to your home and the bosom of your loved ones.'

Chamberlain blinked. Although he was as yet only in his late forties, he had been twice a widower. Even among Gladstone's intimates, it was a source of tireless surmise as to whether his lapses were due to old age or a propensity for malice.

'This is a report compiled by our agents on the activities of Mr Parnell and his followers. It tells us what we already know: that the Irish party had no hand, act or part in the Dublin murders. On the contrary, the crime has dashed their hopes for a Home Rule bill.' He passed the document to Chamberlain. 'Be good enough to turn to the last page.'

Chamberlain did so. He read. He said, 'My God,' and added, 'I beg your pardon, sir.'

Gladstone said: 'The report alleges that Captain O'Shea's wife is Mr Parnell's mistress.'

'Yes.' 'Pushful Joe' was seldom at a loss for words, but what he read beggared belief. It was a record of Parnell's nocturnal arrivals and morning leave-takings, the evening walks, the excursions to the country, the assumed names, the furtive embraces.

'You are on close terms with Captain O'Shea, are you not?'

'On amicable terms, yes.' Chamberlain stepped warily.

'Still, if what is written there is correct, you would have heard rumours?'

'I daresay.'

'And Captain O'Shea has never intimated to you . . .'

'Never.'

Gladstone smiled. It was as if a weight had been lifted from him. 'Then the report is a combination of evil gossip and incompetent surveillance. Good. I was sure of it.'

It seemed to Chamberlain that the old man had so far bounded to a conclusion as to put himself virtually out of earshot. Perhaps he was, after all, too unworldly to comprehend viciousness in others. An alternative was that he was on the verge of senility.

Gladstone took the younger man's arm as he walked him to the door. He asked: 'Is Mrs O'Shea a handsome woman?'

Chamberlain replied: 'I am told so. Men behave as if she is.'

'Ah, and that is what matters. Then I shall look forward to meeting her.' As the other glanced at him sharply, he said: 'I omitted to mention that she has written to me.'

'Mrs O'Shea has?'

'Did you know that her uncle is Lord Hatherley? She has the most impressive connexions. She writes to say that she is Mr Parnell's friend, and that he wishes her to act as his intermediary.'

Parnell's audacity, thought Chamberlain, was breathtaking.

'Naturally,' Gladstone continued, 'after the murders, any congress of a direct nature between him and myself is impossible. In the public eye, he is steeped to the lips in treason.'

He stopped and faced Chamberlain, his grip tightening upon his arm. 'And therein, my friend, lies the crux. Are we to believe that in the very crisis of his country's fortunes a leader would not only commit adultery with the wife of a parliamentary colleague, but go on to make use of her for political ends? No! I pray to God, sir, that we may never come to that.'

England itself was in his face, in the thrust of the jaw, the lofty brow, the steeliness of the eyes. Even Chamberlain, who had little use for sentiment, was touched to see that in a corrupt age the old values lived on. When Gladstone had taken leave of his guest, he returned to the fastnesses of the club and there meditated.

He wondered if Captain O'Shea was the kind of husband who would be likely to know if his wife were involved in a sexual intrigue. He had met the captain only once and briefly, on the day following the murder of Lord Frederick, when he had been all but overcome by grief. Nonetheless, the little he had seen told him that Willie O'Shea was both stupid enough not to know and cunning enough not to know.

104

In the beginning, she had wondered if so inwardly turbulent a creature as Parnell was containable by home and hearth. She discovered that his nature was as domestic as hers. For a time, he took up astronomy as a hobby, but the vastness of the universe tended to make Ireland seem small by comparison, and he regretfully decided that one of the two must go. Katharine had a new room built on to the rear of the lodge; it was both his study and the workroom where he assayed the pieces of quartz he had taken from the Avonmore river near his home in Wicklow. He told her that at Cambridge he had been fond of cricket, and so she employed workmen to convert a two-acre field and part of the garden into a pitch. A lily pond, she thought, was well lost for love. If he was away for a day, he sent two telegrams; if his absence was longer, there were letters as well. If the Commons sittings were late, she waited for him by pre-arrangement at one of the stations on the way to Blackheath. At Waterloo Junction, which stayed open all night because of the early-morning trains, she walked up and down, murmuring aloud: 'There is one great comfort, and it is that he always comes at last.'

She was half exhilarated, half fearful, when, in reply to the letter Parnell had dictated, Gladstone wrote inviting her to call upon him.

'What shall I say to him?'

'He will plague you with questions about me and the kind of person I am. He is one-third old man and two-thirds old woman. He adores gossip. And to be flirted with by beautiful women.'

It was night. They were in the sitting room, she on the sofa, he in an armchair, both waiting for Mary to go to bed.

She said: 'Then he will be disappointed.'

'Do you mean, you will not flirt?'

'I mean – and do not, if you please, contradict me – that I am not beautiful.' As he made to rise from his chair, she said: 'And you are on no account to sit next to me. Now be patient.'

She thought again of her meeting with Gladstone. 'I am terrified. And yet I must learn to concern myself with politics. It will prepare me for Ireland.'

He looked at her, amused. 'I had not heard of this. Are you going to Ireland, then?'

She resembled a child so filled with a secret that it would explode if it were not released. 'I have had a letter from Willie. He cannot come on Sunday —'

'But this is the best of news!'

'Hush . . . Because he is spending the weekend with Mr Chamberlain. You know that he and Willie are intimates?'

'I think you mean, as thick as thieves.'

'Well, Mr Chamberlain told Willie that as soon as he is Prime Minister —'

'The devil he says!'

'Charley, you interrupt so. He says that he will appoint him as Irish Secretary. Think of it, my darling; at last I shall see your beloved Avondale.'

In the half-light, he could not discern her face clearly. There was gladness in her voice. He wondered whether she was excited for herself or for O'Shea. The bitterness came to him that it was always so, that every moment of their contentment was clouded with the wraith of O'Shea and his ambitions.

His silence unnerved her. She said, hesitantly: 'I mean, to give Willie his due, he can be most statesmanlike when he sets his mind to it. We must grant him that when you were in prison, he was conscientious to a fault.'

For a time, Parnell said nothing. He had held from her the truth about Kilmainham: that O'Shea had botched his role as go-between. It might have been foreseen; the runner of errands had donned the cloak of envoy extraordinary. Without consulting his chief, he had made promises to Chamberlain in Parnell's name. Later, when these were repudiated, Willie was appalled; once again, his arch-enemy had done him down. Hand on heart, he assured Chamberlain that they had been duped by a liar and blackguard.

As a consequence, Parnell now found himself with two deadly enemies where there had been one.

Normally, he felt that there were worthier topics of conversation for him and Katharine than the exploits of Willie O'Shea. This time, there was a more compelling reason for silence: he lacked courage. He feared to see the face of a mother whose errant but still loved child had once again dashed her hopes. He could not bear it that she might retain an affection for O'Shea. If the chronically unfaithful are those who are most prone to jealousy; the converse is as true; Parnell, monogamous by nature, could not conceive how love, once given, could utterly die.

Katharine said: 'Charley, why don't you speak to me?'

The notion of O'Shea as Irish Secretary was one delusion which he could not allow her to nurture. He said, brutally: 'Joseph Chamberlain will never be Prime Minister. And your husband in ten lifetimes will never set foot inside Dublin Castle.'

'Charley!'

He pressed on, not sparing her. 'Chamberlain is a schemer who tells the fool what he most yearns to hear. Irish Secretary? After the election, your husband will not even have a seat in Westminster.'

She almost wailed. 'But he must.'

The despair in her voice enraged him. He said, intent that every bow should strike home: 'How? The Liberals won't adopt him . . . no one likes a renegade, not even the English. His own people – *my* people – won't have him at any price. He has betrayed them. He votes with the enemy. He's an outcast. Don't you understand what I'm saying? He is finished.'

She caught the cruelty in his voice. 'Why do you talk to me like this?' When he did not answer, she said: 'The Irish will accept him if you tell them to. Whatever you say, they will do. You know it.'

He looked at her with what was close to hatred. 'Are you telling me that for your sake I should force your scoundrel of a husband down the throats of honest men?'

She said, her voice small and wheedling: 'You make a small thing seem so terrible. Charley, you will do it?'

He arose and turned the gas up, not so that he could see her face, but so that she might see his. He asked: 'A small thing? Then why is it so important?'

'You cannot refuse me. Do it for us.'

He said, cynically: 'For us? Or for him?'

She would not meet his eye. 'So that he will leave us in peace.'

Now he had caught her out. '*Are* we not in peace? Where is the danger? Did you not say that we were safe from him as long as your aunt was alive? Did you not say that with her fingers on the purse-strings O'Shea was helpless?'

'And so he is.'

'Yet now you say that his silence must be paid for twice over. Why?'

She was in retreat. She said, sulkily: 'So that he . . . will be grateful.'

He blazed at her. 'Him? Willie O'Shea? Grateful to me? Grateful to anyone?' He seized her by the elbows, pulling her to her feet. 'What a liar you are. My God, you care for him.'

'No!'

'Then why?'

She wrenched herself free of him. Her arms went around her breasts as if to staunch a wound.

She said: 'Not because I care for him. I care for myself!' She walked away from him and turned to show a face that in their three years together he had not seen. 'You know what I am to you.' As he did not respond, she flung it at him: 'You *know*. And you know that what is between us must be hidden. Like any woman, I exist in my husband's shadow, and now you tell me that soon he will have no shadow to cast. I want a face that I may show to the world, even if that face is a false one. If he becomes a nobody, then, although estranged from him, so must I.'

He had mistaken her. This, at least, he could understand; they had in common what he had not suspected. He said: 'Ambition, by heaven!'

She no longer begged, but demanded, as her right. She said:

108

'If a part of me is to have a life in the open, it must be as more than the wife of a man who has neither position nor respect. If you want that for me, then you must help him.'

He saw her with a new clarity, as dispassionately as if she were a stranger; it might have been a trick of the light. Her face was dark, almost gypsyish, and within it a girl's face was lost; he noticed that her figure had become settled. He saw a woman being borne towards middle-age, determined to snatch what she could from life while there was still time. An instant later, as if he had blinked, the woman had become Katharine again.

He nodded slowly. He said: 'Help him? Rather ask how can I not help *you*?'

He would work the miracle. He would have O'Shea re-elected somehow, against his party members, even against O'Shea himself. She came over to him. He realised that she was aroused, perhaps by their quarrel, perhaps by the knowledge that he would do as she wanted. He looked towards the closed door.

He said: 'The girl . . . Mary.'

She laughed and put her face up to his. 'How nervous you are!'

Her visit to Downing Street was all that she could have hoped for. Gladstone arose from his desk, went quickly to an open door behind him and closed it. He greeted her and, instead of begging her to be seated, said: 'Would you mind walking up and down the room with me? I talk better so.'

She told him: 'Sir, I would be delighted to walk with you. But, Mr Gladstone, who or what is behind that door you closed with such haste?'

Her impertinence amused him; they would get along. He said: 'Only a secretary or so. Or, in these days of foolish panic, detectives.'

He offered her his arm. They walked to and fro. It was her zenith; at that delicious moment, she alone in the world could lay claim to the intimacy of the Prime Minister. He said: 'Tell me about your friend. You are in Mr Parnell's confidence?'

She said: 'I believe he thinks well of me.'

'Capital. Then you will help me to know him?'

She smiled. 'You ask for much!'

He was at his most benign. 'For the earth, dear lady. I see an Irishman who is as aloof from the Irish nature as I myself am. A man who in speech and temperament could pass for English and yet who professes to detest England. Come . . . indulge my taste for paradox!'

He had the most potent kind of charm: the gift of making others feel irresistible. There were further meetings; he introduced her to the Chief Whip, Lord Grosvenor. 'Dear lady, you quite overwhelmed him. Thanks to you, has he not adopted Captain O'Shea as the next Liberal candidate for Nottingham?'

She corrected him. 'For Liverpool, sir. The Exchange Division.'

'Is it so? Dear me, I had forgotten. The ravages of *anno Domini*.'

She knew him by now, and she was aware that there was no role he enjoyed playing better than the half-senile greybeard who dwelt as much in the next world as in this. If the truth were known, it was probably he who had signalled to Lord Grosvenor that Willie should be adopted for the safe seat in Liverpool. She felt a double satisfaction: her husband's future was assured, and it had been done without risk to Parnell.

Pleased with herself, she was almost glad to see Willie when he arrived for his Sunday visit. They kissed, not quite on the cheek, their lips making small noises against the air; it was a sight so diverting that Mary, who had opened the door to Willie, threw her apron up to her face and bolted below stairs.

They walked in the garden. It was early winter; leaves crackled beneath their feet. Willie told her that Lord Grosvenor, in selecting him for the Exchange Division, had shown more good sense than the Irish peasantry; he, at least, recognised a thoroughbred.

She said, as innocently as she could manage: 'Aren't there Irish voters in Liverpool, Willie?'

'A handful.' He dismissed them with a wave.

She made no mention of her part in his adoption as Liberal candidate. Had she done so, he would have smiled at her foolishness in expecting to be believed. To Willie, his qualities of leadership were so unmistakably of the front rank that an attempt to assist him in his ascent would be as redundant as offering wings to an eagle. He noticed that she did not congratulate him on his achievement; he knew that she had thought him a ne'er-do-well; it saddened him that now she lacked the grace to own herself in the wrong.

He asked with languid off-handedness: 'Has your friend been here this week?'

'My friend, Willie?'

'Not mine, surely.'

She was as casual as he. 'Oh, you mean Mr Parnell? Yes, last Wednesday he came to lunch.'

He said: 'I meant, in the evening. Because in a moment of weakness I —'

'Of which, Willie, you have so few.'

'. . . I told him he was always welcome.'

Katharine said with severity: 'Yes, you did, and it really was most impetuous of you. You have no regard whatever for my reputation. Fortunately, Mr Parnell has some sense of propriety.'

Willie was resolved that this time she should not get the better of him. He decided upon a direct approach. She might be evasive, but he knew that she would not stoop to an outright lie. He stopped in his walk, obliging her to do the same. 'Then he has not been here at night time?'

She replied unflinchingly. 'Most certainly not.'

'I take it that I have your word of honour?'

'You do. And you accept it?'

He said: 'Completely. And you accept that I accept it?'

She told him: 'Utterly.'

They looked into each other's face, and each saw the same expression of the profoundest sincerity.

They resumed their walk, rounding the rear of the lodge.

111

Aunt Ben's mansion came into view. Possibly, the old lady was at her window affectionately regarding Katharine – her 'swan' – and Willie, the tireless parliamentarian, whom affairs of state detained in London all week.

Willie, like a dog worrying a bone, had not relinquished the topic of Parnell. '. . . His tenants don't pay rent, because they know he doesn't dare evict them, so the Irish have passed the hat round.'

'The hat?'

'Every damned peasant and village idiot in the country. Instead of putting their money on the church collection plates, they've given it to Parnell.'

'Oh, yes?'

Katharine had already learned of the Parnell 'tribute' and from the person most directly involved. Near penury, he had first mortgaged Avondale for £12,000, then offered it for sale. What Willie said was true: the people had come to his rescue; responding to a newspaper appeal, they contributed £7000. 'And there,' Parnell had told her, 'it would have rested had not his Holiness, Leo XIII, condemned the tribute as unlawful. The Irish Catholic, my dear, is a contrary beast; use a stick on him and he moves backwards. Instead of paying the annual Peter's Pence to support the papacy, the entire nation withheld it and paid Parnell's Pounds instead. Next week, I go to Dublin to receive a cheque for £37,000.'

'And another three thousand is on its way from America,' Willie was saying. 'Into that humbug's pocket. It's true what they say: the devil's children have the devil's —'

He broke off. He had come into sight of his 'chicks', Gerard, Norah and Carmen, who were playing a ball game in what had been the meadow.

He said: 'Really, my dear, what are you thinking of? Allowing the children to play cricket on a Sunday. No, it is not proper. What will Aunt Ben think if she —' A look of stupefaction came over his face. 'Am I going mad?'

'I don't know, Willie. Are you?'

112

'Where is our lily pond? My God, that is a cricket pitch!'

'Yes, Willie. It has been there for some time now. You really are most unobservant.' She told him, pleasantly. 'Mr Parnell is devoted to cricket.'

His face had a pole-axed look. As he seemed not inclined to speak, she filled the silence. 'And since you invited him here, I thought that he might as well enjoy himself. In the daytime, of course.'

She called out to the children that their papa had come and that it was time to get ready for Mass. She made a note not to antagonise Willie today, but to be at her most charming. She would invite him to stay to dinner in honour of his adoption for the Liverpool Exchange Division. He might, she thought, even wish to spend the night. She was pregnant again.

For the first time in living memory, snow fell on Dublin in early December. It did not deter the crowds that turned out for the Lord Mayor's torchlight parade to Morrison's Hotel; rather, it gave the look of a stage setting to the city streets. It clung to the trees in St Stephen's Green, blanketed the grime on railings and sills, and spluttered on the gas lamps down Grafton Street. It muted the clatter of cart and carriage wheels on the new asphalt. The spinning flakes might have been confetti. The arrangements for the evening were that the mayor, in his ceremonial robes, would depart from Dawson Street to a skirl of pipes. Other carriages, containing members of the corporation and their wives, would follow the mayoral coach, the procession taking the longest feasible route so that two other bands – a fife and drum and a brass – might share in the occasion. On arriving at Morrison's, the Lord Mayor would greet Mr Parnell, deliver an address of appropriate weight, present him with the cheque and formerly invite him to a civic banquet in his honour.

A crowd had assembled outside Morrison's, their gaze upturned towards a first-floor window. As the curtains shivered and a face

113

looked out, a cheer began and torches were brandished. When it was seen that the face was clean-shaven and so was not Parnell's, the cheering died, the torches were lowered.

'Sexton, come away from the window.'

Parnell was in testy mood. Already, faint on the wind, he could hear the strains of

Down the glen came Sarsfield's men,
And they wore the jackets green.

Doubtlessly, he thought, it would be followed by 'Wrap the green flag round me, boys'. His fate was to be greenness without end. He made a sign to Henry Harrison, who poured a glass of claret. The others in the room were Davitt, Timothy Healy and John Dillon.

Parnell said aloud: 'Apparently I am to be spared nothing. I must jump through their hoops like a performing dog.'

'They mean to honour you,' Davitt said.

'They do no such thing. They give me my supper, and I must sing for it.'

It occurred to him that the others, Davitt most of all, thought him ungracious. They did not recognise the occasion for the abasement it was. All five of them were men of principle, but their pride was not as his. Davitt and Healy were peasants; strike at them and it was an affront to their race and ancestry. Dillon, Sexton and Harrison were town-bred and cerebral; with them, pride was a thing of the reason. Parnell was not merely an aristocrat, possessing the arrogance of his kind, but he himself knew it to be the conceit of Lucifer, who chose to fall sooner than serve. This evening, Lucifer was to be brought low. The people had saved Parnell and Avondale from ruin; their reward was to be his acknowledged benefactors, to see the godhead admit that for once he was the debtor.

Davitt was speaking. 'They pay tribute, and you honour them by accepting it. You really are their king, you know. Mind, for a monarch, you have an unusual distinction. They love you not

 114

for anything you've accomplished, but because you've made their enemies hate you.'

John Dillon, uneasy, went to the window and affected to peer out.

'Tell me,' Davitt went on, 'supposing you really were their king . . . crown, throne and the rest of it, what would be your first royal act?'

Parnell looked at him with an indifference which was more contempt than rancour. He said: 'I would at once put you back in prison.'

The music came nearer and a new outbreak of cheering told them that the Lord Mayor's party had arrived. Timothy Healy took note of the patrician distaste on Parnell's face as he started out of the room to face the ritual ahead. Healy shook his head in wonderment, that he could for years have mistaken vainglory for nobility.

There was some trouble in getting the banners through the front entrance of the hotel. Parnell waited, standing on the lowermost step of the staircase, his lieutenants and a dour-faced Davitt behind him. He had resigned himself to the colour of the banners; what caused him to recoil in revulsion was that the Lord Mayor was wearing not only his chain of office, but a wide sash of brightest emerald. The retinue squeezed into the foyer, the ladies blushing to see Parnell at close range. The brass band, just outside the door, caused the chandelier to play music of its own. A member of the mayoral party sent a message that the musicians should be quiet; meanwhile, Parnell and the Lord Mayor faced each other, the latter holding a cheque in one hand and several closely-written pages in the other. He was small and pink and wore mutton-chop whiskers that by the moment threatened to become wings and bear him off. When there was silence and the last onlooker had been wedged into the foyer, the Lord Mayor cleared his throat and addressed his prey, whose eyes were fixed, as if mesmerised, upon the green sash.

He began: 'Most gracious sir, how shall I call you as we mark this effulgent . . . nay, this golden page in our city's . . .

115

nay, in our nation's history? "Uncrowned King of Ireland"? Eh? "Blackbird of Sweet Avondale"? Or shall we say, he in whom all Erin's hopes —'

Parnell said: 'I believe you have a cheque for me?'

The Lord Mayor stared as if he had been addressed in an unknown tongue. An unnatural stillness fell upon the assembly. 'What? Ah. Yes.' He attempted to resume his speech. 'The one in whom all Erin's hopes repose. The —'

Parnell asked: 'Is it made payable to order and crossed?'

The Lord Mayor might as well have been asked a question concerning the moon and green cheese. He looked dazedly from his speech to the cheque and back again. He repeated: 'Payable to order and . . .'

'And crossed.' Parnell cocked his head, the better to see it. 'I perceive that it is. I am obliged to you.'

He took the cheque from the Lord Mayor, folded it in two, turned and went quickly back upstairs. For a moment, Dillon and the others, leaderless and taken unawares, stared haplessly at the crowd in the foyer, then followed Parnell as if fearful that they, the rearguard, might be set upon. The stunned dignatories parted their ranks as the Lord Mayor, twice as pink as when he came in, stomped back into the street. His reappearance was the signal for the crowd to launch into 'God Save Ireland'.

In the upstairs room and at a nod from Dillon, Harrison went to the window, pulled the curtains aside and thrust it open. The singing welled up.

Parnell, who was about to finish his wine, said, angrily: 'Harrison, what the devil do you think you're doing?'

Dillon told him: 'Mr Parnell, you must talk to them.'

'Must? "Must," did you say?'

It was the nearest that one of his followers had come to defying him. Dillon said, without flinching, 'Sir, you have no choice. They are our people. They have waited for you in the snow. They expect it.'

A long moment passed before Parnell, without giving a sign

of compliance, moved to the window. When he came into the crowd's view, the singing gained in volume and fervour.

> 'God save Ireland', say the heroes,
> 'God save Ireland', say we all.
> Whether on the scaffold high
> Or the battlefield we die,
> Sure what matter when for Erin dear we fall?

When it was over, they cheered him and cried 'God save the Chief' and 'Hail to the King'. In the room, Sexton said to Timothy Healy in an undertone: 'By all that's holy, a common workman would acknowledge the gift of a penknife more graciously.'

Parnell raised his hand for silence. When it came, and although the snow was becoming heavier, the men in the crowd removed their hats and caps. He spoke for twenty-two seconds by Timothy Healy's trusty watch. He said that he had not the power to express adequately his feelings with regard to the magnificence of the demonstration. He said that he preferred to leave to historians the description of the occasion, just as he proposed to leave to posterity whatever fruits the occasion should put forth. He bade his listeners good night.

When he moved in from the window, the crowd was still. They had come expecting a feast and he had thrown them a crust. Harrison was about to close the window when a solitary male voice was heard raised in song, a clear, tenor voice from the packed street. The song was the most popular of the ballads that had been composed in Parnell's honour, and from its title he had been visited with his second nickname, 'The Blackbird of Avondale'. It told of old Ireland's enchainments and of how a new hero, half-saint, half-giant, had arisen to deliver her from the oppressor. The words were banal, the rhymes uncertain, the emotion trite; and yet, the snow, the stillness, the hushed crowd and the play of light from the torches combined to move many of the listeners to tears. The evening had been given its epiphany. On the morrow, they would say: 'You should have been there.'

117

In the hotel room, listening, Timothy Healy wiped a sleeve across his eyes. As Parnell sat impassively, glass in hand, Davitt turned on him in anger. 'Damn it to hell, man, the song is about you. Have you no feelings?'

When Parnell replied, it was with the flat weariness of one who knew that he spoke not across a common ground of intellect, but to minds – even those of the townies, Dillon and Sexton – that were unreachable through the race memories that fattened on tyranny and believed that the sweetest embrace was the hangman's.

'It was feelings, Davitt . . . easy emotionalism and the singing of maudlin songs, that kept us in the gutter for seven hundred years. Ask me to shed tears, and you ask me to be no stronger than they are.'

He saw that Tim Healy's eyes were large and moist. He looked away quickly, but not before Healy had seen the faint, fleeting look of amusement. In the street, the song continued.

NINE

Months passed. In July, Katharine was delivered of an infant daughter whom she named Clare. In October, in Liverpool, a man emptied his pint pot of beer over Willie O'Shea.

Willie was at a loss to explain why. Amid the excitement of the general election, his own campaign speeches had gone well. He had sworn that Ireland possessed no better friend than Mr Gladstone and that a vote for the Liberals was a vote for Home Rule. Parnell sat behind him on the platform, demonstrating his support and coming forward to shake hands when Willie concluded his address with an impassioned cry of 'God save Ireland!'

Willie was not so foolish as to delude himself as to why the Irish community flocked to his meetings; sheep, he knew, often followed a dishonest shepherd. In the beginning of the campaign, Parnell had addressed the electors, assuring them that Captain O'Shea was manifestly their man. So tumultuous was his reception that Willie began to feel that he, the leading actor, was being outshone. He said as much. Parnell replied: 'Does it matter? Surely our sole purpose is to ensure that you are elected?' Willie was not mollified; he thought it demeaning that the loudest cheers should go to one who, on this occasion, was no more than his attendant. With a shrug, Parnell said that he would gladly remain silent. When he did so, Willie was no happier. Now the audiences were fretful;

119

they had come not merely to see the Irish leader, but to hear him. There were grumblings; a few voters had walked out when he was in mid-oration. He was a fair man; he admitted that it was at his insistence that Parnell had been silent, but he was nobody's fool; the silence was less eloquent than it might have been.

After the meetings, it was Parnell's practice to slip away quietly, leaving Willie to mix with his future constituents and be taken to supper or for refreshments. In a working men's club at Toxteth he made an impromptu speech, then sat privately and treated his hosts to a few insights concerning the seamier side of politics. The common voter, Willie knew, was an innocent; he could not suspect how even the most honourable of men must consort with strange bedfellows. He could not know of Parnell the ingrate, of the broken promises, of a deceived Willie O'Shea and Joseph Chamberlain. Willie spoke of how the Irish party was at the mercy of a scoundrel; he predicted that, once elected, he would turn the tables upon a rogue and a —

It was at this moment that the pint pot was emptied over Willie's head.

The assault could have been the work of a drunkard — this place was, after all, the haunt of working men; but Willie did not discount the possibility that his assailant had been a Conservative hireling. It troubled him that the incident might be the prelude to more grievous attacks. He wrote that night to Katharine:

I am worried, if not out of my wits, out of my hair. The little left came out this morning, and I am balder than a coot is. Such fun.

He went on to chastise her for not encouraging the children to write to their father: *No one cares a bit for me except my old mother.* While Katharine was reading this letter, a telegram arrived from Parnell. It was as cryptic as Willie's soul-barings had been piteous; it said: **SEND W. A TIP TO BE CIVIL.** It was all most puzzling.

Parnell waited in Liverpool until the day of the election. He stood with Willie outside the main polling station and shook hands with the voters as they streamed in. A high poll, he thought, was a sign of discontent; it could be a black day for Gladstone and the Liberals. Willie was fortunate that his was a safe seat.

Within the hour, Parnell was on a train for London. An autumn gale buffeted the window. He had a sense of well-being. He had played his part in buying Willie off and the price had not been unbearable: ten days in O'Shea's company, ten days out of Katharine's. O'Shea was greedy, but he could ask for no more than he now had, or rather for no more than he would receive when the returning officer declared him elected to the Exchange Division. The Irish cupboard was bare; if his stomach growled for more, let him go to his crony, 'Pushful Joe'. Parnell was rid of him.

The same gale was raging late the following night when Parnell, in Katharine's bed, was awakened by a knocking so violent that it threatened to out-rage the storm.

She whispered: 'There has been a result. He said he would telegraph from Liverpool.'

Parnell had lit the bedside candle. 'At this hour? And with such a pounding? I think not. Far more likely, the conquering hero comes himself.'

At once, there was panic in her voice. 'Willie? It can't be. Oh, say it is not.'

She got out of bed and was putting on her *peignoir* when a tapping came at the bedroom door. They heard Mary say: 'If you please, ma'am, 'tis the Captain. He's come home.'

Parnell said: 'Damn him.'

She motioned to him to be silent. 'Thank you, Mary. I'll come down.'

Instead of leaving, Mary opened the door by an inch so that she could whisper. Katharine had no fear that the girl would look into the room; like Ellen, the cook, she knew what she chose to know.

'If you please again, ma'am, and saying what 'tisn't my place to say, the master has a sup took.' The door closed.

121

Katharine said, blankly: 'A sup took?'

'It is the Irish,' Parnell said, 'for roaring drunk. The new member has been celebrating.'

Willie had yet to begin roaring, but he was unsteady on his feet. His mood was splenetic. The long train journey had given him time to brood, and thought was rarely good for him; Willie's mind was a phenomenon of nature, unimproved by additives. Without removing his greatcoat, he found the key for the tantalus, then discovered that it was unlocked. While he was looking at it accusingly, Katharine came into the room.

She said: 'Isn't this a trifle late, Willie, even for you? Was it such a victory?'

He said, thickly: 'Five and fifty votes.'

'As narrow as that? Well, never mind. To win is the main thing. Well done, Willie.'

His groan was the cry of a great animal brought down. 'I was *defeated*.'

She could not believe it. Nor, when he had been told, did Willie. He demanded and was granted a recount. He had looked on while it was done and, like a fool, had murmured aloud without meaning to: 'It is a safe seat.' One of the enumerators had giggled insolently. The result was unchanged; he had lost by a handful of votes.

'I am done for,' he told Katharine. 'What is to become of us now . . . of our chicks?'

She said: 'Willie, if you mean the children, say so.'

'And little Clare, still a babe in arms.'

Katharine had a mental image of little Clare's father, struggling into his clothes in the bedroom above. She felt a wave of anger against Willie; he had brought his ambitions to dust and her own along with them. She would give him cold comfort.

Willie groaned: 'It is ruin.'

She snapped at him. 'Yes, Willie, it is, and like a good many others in this election you are no longer a Member of Parliament. Now you – and I – must make the best of it.'

Willie smiled crookedly. 'I begin to see.'

'Do you? And what is it you see?'

He recalled that a dazzling thought had come to him on the train journey. It had either been in the nature of a revelation, searing in its totality, or it was a masterly stratagem against Parnell. He could not remember which; the whisky he had had at Cannon Street had burnt it from his mind.

She repeated: 'Willie, what is that you see?'

See? She was trying to sidetrack him. He said: 'I have been treated in blackguard fashion. If he had for a moment given thought to me instead of himself I would have carried the day.'

She said, her eyes sending darts of hatred: 'And who is "he", Willie? I suppose you mean Mr Parnell.'

'Yes, him! The imposter, the ingrate, the architect of my downfall. Deny it, dare to deny it!' He flung at her the ultimate, the irrefutable charge. 'Then why was I not elected?'

She said: 'Possibly, Willie, because the voters did not like you.'

He looked at her, a glass half-way to his lips. Obviously, she thought him drunker than he was. 'Don't be ridiculous.'

Parnell, his clothing in disarray, had come downstairs as far as the dark half-landing. He saw the light from the sitting room and heard voices, but was unable to catch the words. O'Shea was ranting. With a cold dismay, Parnell knew that he had lost the election, and safety was as far distant as ever. He moved down to the foot of the stairs. O'Shea was no more than ten feet away.

'Yes,' he was saying, 'trust you to take his part. The truth is that after all I have done for him he has failed me most shamefully. Well, he has mistaken his man. I am not one to lie in a ditch. I mean to hit back a stunner. All is ready. I have packed my shell with dynamite, and it will send a blackguard's reputation to smithereens.'

Katharine asked: 'What do you mean?' Parnell caught a note of fear in her voice.

Willie said: 'I mean that his ruination is in these hands.' There was the sound of a glass hitting the carpet. 'Damn. Sorry.'

She said: 'Leave it. I'll get a cloth from the kitchen. Now sit there and no more foolishness.'

She was startled to find Parnell so close at hand. She led him down the passageway to the head of the back stairs. He said: 'What has happened?'

'Hush. Nothing . . . he spilt his whisky.' She whispered: 'Did you hear? He lost at Liverpool. And now he's threatening . . . I don't know whom or what. You . . . us . . . he makes no sense.'

'I know. Look here, I must get away from here, back to London.'

She said: 'Are you insane? There's a storm out. It would be the end of you.' As he made to protest, she put her fingers to his lips. 'Wait. I must think.' She buttoned his waistcoat and tightened the knot of his necktie. She said: 'Listen to me.'

When she returned to the sitting room a few minutes later, Willie was asleep in an armchair. She dabbed with a wet cloth at the whisky stain on the carpet, then shook him awake. 'Willie. Willie, wake up. Didn't you hear the knocking?'

He grunted in protest. When he came to, he had no idea where he was. 'Eh? What? Hello? What's happening?'

'Really, can't you even be trusted to answer the door? Did you want poor Mary to be roused from her bed a second time?' She looked into his face. 'The *knocking*, Willie . . . are you quite deaf?'

He blinked and said stupidly: 'Knocking?'

As he came awake, he saw Parnell standing inside the door of the sitting room.

Katharine said: 'As soon as Mr Parnell heard the election result, he came to commiserate. And on such a dreadful night . . . Willie, is it not kind of him?'

Parnell came forward. Willie stood, swayed and extended his hand.

Of the three, in their separate rooms, Parnell and Katharine lay awake, thinking of each other and what lay ahead; Willie

124

slept the untroubled sleep of the drunk. Parnell awoke early, walked into the village and bought the papers. His party, the Irish Nationalists, had hoped to win sixty-five seats; instead, they seemed set to gain eighty-five out of a contested eighty-six. It was an undreamed-of victory. Now he who would rule England must first woo the Parnellites, and the price of Gladstone's survival would be a Home Rule bill. Parnell found an irony in the knowledge that while the election had delivered the next government into his hands, he was himself in the power of one who was no longer being even a member of the rank and file.

He wondered how much Willie knew, or if he might be likened to the child who brandishes a loaded pistol, believing it to be a toy. He had wholeheartedly accepted the new child, Clare, as his own; he would hardly have done so if the faintest possibility existed that her father was his sworn enemy. And O'Shea was ruled by his conceit; what others thought of him was what mattered most; not even for a score of Aunt Bens and a hundred seats in Parliament would he own himself a cuckold. And yet, if he did not suspect, his hatred was inexplicable.

When Parnell returned to Wonersh Lodge, he found his host in the garden surveying the storm damage. A sycamore had blown down. He hardly looked around as Parnell came over.

'I was fond of that tree. A damned shame. Well, at least now I have time on my hands. Henceforward, London has done with me, and I can be here all week.'

Parnell looked at him sharply. His face was empty of malice; he was looking mournfully at the fallen tree.

'Politically, Liverpool need not be the end of you.'

'No?' Willie's voice was bitter. 'I'm sure there are any number of seats going a-begging.'

Katharine appeared at the conservatory door and called to them. 'Ah,' Willie said, 'breakfast!'

At table, she asked how the election had gone. Willie seemed not at all interested; it was well, his demeanour suggested, for some. It took some minutes for the full import of the Irish triumph to sink

125

in; when it did, it occurred to him that if, as he firmly believed, Parnell was riding for a fall, the fall was taking its time to come. The scoundrel seemed glued to the saddle.

Parnell said, carefully: 'And we have a seat to spare. T.P. O'Connor has been elected from both Galway and the Scotland Division of Liverpool.'

He caught Katharine's eye. Willie, who was making heavy weather of his devilled kidneys, snorted in the manner of one who has been through the furnace. 'Liverpool!'

She asked: 'And what does that mean?'

Parnell said: 'O'Connor will find it more convenient to retain the Liverpool seat. That means a by-election in Galway.'

They both looked at Willie. Slowly, his jaws ceased to work. He blinked. He said: 'I say, look here. Why don't . . . why don't *I* run for Galway?'

The idea had taken root; Parnell watched as it grew.

'Yes,' Willie said. 'Good Lord, I'd be an odds-on favourite. The Irish voters think the world of me.'

'Do they? I had not heard.'

In his excitement, Willie missed the sarcasm. 'Mind, I should be sorry to have to rub shoulders with the rapscallions of the party.'

'Pray, don't be sorry.' Parnell now regarded him with open dislike. 'Your contempt for them is returned.'

He saw Katharine start and knew what, as always, was foremost in her mind. Willie must not be crossed; Willie must be kept sweet; Willie's feathers must not be ruffled. Parnell, however, was not in a giving mood.

He said: 'Look here, O'Shea, let us be outlandish. Let us suppose that the Galway seat was within your grasp. Would you agree to take the pledge?'

'The pledge?' Willie grinned fatuously. 'Give up drink, you mean?'

Parnell ignored the attempt at humour. 'I am speaking of the mandatory pledge that you will sit, act and vote with the Irish Parliamentary party.'

126

'Oh, *that* pledge.' Willie's tone was still jovial. 'Do you mean, sit with your lot? And vote with them? No fear. Joe Chamberlain would never speak to me again.'

'Willie!' Katharine stared at him in unbelief.

Parnell said: 'You would refuse to take the pledge?'

'Absolutely. I mean, damn it, a fellow has his principles.'

'*Principles!*' Parnell, now on his feet, almost spat the word at Willie, who sat, serene. 'Captain O'Shea, at personal cost – I do not know what cost, as yet – I am prepared to offer you the last chance you will ever have of regaining your seat at Westminster. The pledge is obligatory. I cannot work miracles. Refuse to take it, and my people will reject you out of hand.'

Willie was imperturbable. 'I don't really believe that, do you? No, sorry. Can't be done.' He snapped his fingers at Mary, who was in attendance. 'Noonan . . . more coffee.'

Parnell said: 'I think, Mrs O'Shea, that I must return to London.'

As he carried his bag downstairs, he heard Katharine's voice. She was storming at her husband. He entered the dining room in time to hear O'Shea tell her: 'After the services I've done the fellow, he owes it to me. Besides, he as good as lost me the seat in Liverpool . . . I'm entitled to redeem my honour.' When he saw that he had been overheard, he affected to look out of the window.

Parnell took his leave, saying that he would walk to Blackheath station. Katharine offered to drive him in the dog-cart; he saw the hurt in her face when he declined. His anger needed time to cool, and it would not happen if she spoke to him of O'Shea. She would tell him, he knew, that if only Willie were elected for Galway, all danger would be past. It was a myth, and, if he said so, she would in one breath weep that she should so selfishly ask this thing of him and in the next plead that it must be done.

He was a realist; he knew that arguments, refusals, bargains and strategies were a waste of time; at the end of the road the Galway seat must go to O'Shea and none other. It was impossible, and it was inevitable. For her sake, Parnell would force him down

127

the throats of the voters and the party members alike. If need be, the dictator would play the despot.

The roadway was so littered with twigs and branches blown down by the storm that he was obliged to pick his way through the debris. He half-regretted not having allowed her to drive him to the station. This evening, he would return to Wonersh Lodge and tell her that Willie was to be the new candidate for Galway. He would not say that for the first time in his political life he proposed to betray his party and use power for dishonourable ends. There were reasons for this. One was that the telling would smack of the emotionalism he detested. Another was that Katharine might weep and declare that the blame was hers. A third was that she might humour him in the way that women did and privately find amusement that in a world so ungiving he could find time for scruples.

A shout from the driver of an overtaking vehicle caused him to leap to the side of the road. He felt rainwater seep into his shoes. He cursed the driver; his doctor in Dublin had warned him of rheumatic fever and said that at all costs he must keep his extremities dry. He cursed the driver twice over when he saw that he was Willie.

'Hello. Glad I caught up with you. Thought we might go up to town together. Climb in.'

Of course, Katharine had sent him to make amends. On the station platform, Willie said: 'Look here, about this proposal of yours that I stand for Galway . . .' Parnell stared at him; the man's effrontery was sublime. 'I do flatter myself that I get on with the people of the west. The scum in Liverpool are renegade Irish. With that crowd, I hadn't a chance.'

There were people about. A devil entered Parnell's brain; with gleeful malice, he replied to O'Shea, using his orator's voice; and each word was enunciated clearly and from the diaphragm. 'The reason the scum in Liverpool turned against you, O'Shea, was that you continually spoke ill to them of me.'

His voice rang down the platform. People stared. Willie's face began to redden. 'I say, let's have a care. We're in a public —'

Parnell raised his voice. 'Insult yourself, if you will, with a denial; kindly do not insult me. While I was working to secure your election, you were proclaiming me a villain the length and breadth of Liverpool. Did you think I was not aware of it? If so, you take me for a fool. Play that double game with the Galway voters, and you will receive a dusty answer, do you understand me?'

From the first days of steam, the English railway traveller, when aware of raised voices, had so perfected an innate talent for looking the other way that it had come close to being an art form. Here, however, the passengers had been taken unawares. There was no ignoring the spectacle of one gentleman, who was unmistakably the man Parnell, delivering so fearful a wigging to another. They could as soon have ignored it if Mr Gladstone had appeared to deliver a comic song.

Willie, mortified, said: 'For God's sake, man.'

'Captain O'Shea, I said that slander will cost you the Galway seat as well, and I asked if you understood me. I await an answer.'

It was too much. Willie's nerve broke; he walked very quickly away from his tormentor to the far end of the platform. Later in the day, he would write to Katharine to say that Parnell was quite mad. Meanwhile, travellers grinned at him openly. Left alone, it was Parnell's turn to flush with embarrassment, but a beleaguered man was entitled to a small revenge.

The knocking was loud and imperative. Joseph Biggar said to the woman in bed with him: 'Jesus, you aren't married, are you?'

T.P. O'Connor's voice said: 'Joe, are you in there? I've got Tim Healy with me.'

Biggar said: 'Away to hell wi' youse. I'm smothering with a cold.'

'Joe, it's life or death. There's news. Bad news.'

'Och, holy shite.' A public man, Biggar thought, could no longer lay claim to a private life. He whispered to the woman: 'Flossie, my love —'

'Molly.'

'Molly, my sweetness, my life, would you ever like a decent girl go and stand behind yon screen while I transact a wee bit of business. And not a sound out of you.' Aloud, he said: 'Gimme a minute, lads.'

With a flicker of lust, he watched her naked rear end as she disappeared behind the tall screen which served to hide from sight the performance of private rituals. The bed was covered with an immense bearskin which he wrapped about him as he went to admit his callers. It dragged behind him like a grotesque bridal train.

It was true that he had a cold; his eyes were streaming. He said: 'Make it quick, lads. I'm not long for this world.'

Timothy Healy said: 'Right, then. Here it is, plump and plain. Mr Parnell is running O'Shea for T.P.'s Galway seat.'

Biggar was stunned. 'Ye liar, ye.'

O'Connor said: 'It's God's truth. I saw the Chief an hour ago. I told him I had my own candidate for the seat. I might as well have been talking to that wall.'

'Christ almighty. Wait . . . you mean O'Shea has agreed to take the pledge?'

Tim Healy pitied his credulity. 'Not he! Isn't it exquisite? The bold Captain Willie is to be on this evening's Irish Mail. By midday tomorrow, he'll be in Galway.'

'Then we'll go, too!' Biggar almost let go of the bearskin in his excitement. 'We'll oppose him, we'll fight, we'll take it to the people. Tim . . . decent man, hand me me trousers.' The true implications of the news were beginning to sink in. He said: 'Is Parnell lost to all decency? He's sold himself, and us along with him, and for an English whoor.'

At that moment, Timothy Healy, who had been rummaging in a pile of clothing, discovered that he was holding Biggar's trousers in one hand and a woman's stays in the other.

Biggar, Healy and O'Connor were on the mail train to Holyhead. They caught sight of Willie O'Shea leaving the mailboat at Kingstown and again as he waited for the Galway train at Westland Row. Either he failed to notice them or affected not to. At the station newsstand, O'Connor bought that morning's *Freeman's Journal*. It carried the news that Parnell had formally endorsed O'Shea.

'He didn't waste much time,' Biggar said.

They walked down the granite steps to the street. At the corner of Merrion Square, O'Connor stopped. He said, miserably: 'Joe . . . Tim . . . I'm no longer with you. I hoped we might turn the Chief in midstream. It wasn't to be. It's a disgrace and an outrage, but if he has come out publicly for O'Shea, I can't oppose him. I'm sorry, Joe.'

Biggar nodded. He admired integrity, and he understood the Irish temper. He said: 'There was never one of us yet who knew what side he was on. Good luck, T. P.'

O'Connor shook hands with Biggar and Timothy Healy.

Watching him go, Biggar said: 'Come on, young lad. I'll treat you to rashers and eggs and tea you could walk on. Then we'll follow Captain Willie to Galway. And first thing we do when we get there will be to send Mr Parnell one o' them billay-doos.'

By five that afternoon, they were in a public room of the Railway Hotel in Eyre Square, where Biggar drafted his message. Like its author, it was short and blunt. It said: MRS O'SHEA WILL BE YOUR RUIN.

Tim Healy turned pale. 'Jesus, we can't send that.'

'Why the hell can't we? You're a fine one to say "can't". Who was it told all of Sharkey's snuggery he was carrying on with her?'

'I'll not put my name to it.'

Biggar grumbled, but in the end agreed to modify the wording to THE O'SHEAS WILL BE YOUR RUIN.

As a city, Galway ranked sixth in Ireland, but if it had come

131

first it would have still been too small for secrets; before a day had passed, the telegram, even in its amended form, was food for scandal. It was part of Willie's election strategy to walk about the city bidding the top of the morning or a kindly good afternoon to the natives. He smiled a great deal, but it took him a day or two to realise that the smiles he received in return were either far cooler than his own or disquietingly broad. He could not shake off the impression that a tide was running against him. The two rebels were fomenting mutiny, each in his own style. Biggar forthrightly declared Willie to be a Whig, an opportunist and a Government toady; Tim Healy, on the other hand, went about his work with careful smiles, half-sentences and the wry, time-honoured disclaimer of, 'Mind you, I've said nothing.'

This time around, Willie had taken care not to speak ill of Parnell; it was torture, but he had been discretion itself. In spite of it, the smiles became no warmer. There was, he thought, no pleasing people. From his window in the Railway Hotel, he saw Biggar and Healy address an open-air meeting in the square. The jackanapes Healy had the audacity to point up at him and shout: 'If we have to raise other issues in this election, we shall not fail to do so before we allow the honour of Galway to be besmirched.' The crowd had followed the aimed muzzle of his finger, seen Willie before he could back out of sight, and sent up a coarse jeer. He at once went downstairs and sent a wire to Parnell: ALL HOPE GONE UNLESS YOU CAN COME AT ONCE. The message, like Biggar's before it, went in two directions: to London and, less officially, around Galway and half-way into Connemara, and within hou.*s the local bookmakers had lengthened the odds against Willie. As if to prove that his misfortunes had not yet had their second wind, he that day received an invitation to call to a local address. The writer declared himself to be Willie's, in Christ, Thomas Carr, Bishop of Galway.

Next morning, Willie sat, facing a life-sized statue of his Redeemer and in an aura of beeswax that made his eyes smart. Even Parnell's answering telegram – WILL ARRIVE TUESDAY. BE-

LIEVE CAN OVERCOME DIFFICULTY – gave him little joy. Footsteps echoed on the tiled floor, and he saw that he was to face not one prelate, but two. Dr Carr advanced with hand extended, episcopal ring jutting. Willie genuflected and kissed the ring. He had regained his feet when the bishop said: 'Have you met the Archbishop of Tuam?' To Willie, again going down on one knee, it was as if, summonsed for recklessly riding a bicycle, he had found himself arraigned before the Lord Chief Justice.

It was February, but the day was mild, and Dr Carr suggested a stroll in the garden. Willie wondered if it was significant that there was no offer of hospitality. Flanked by the churchmen and strolling along the gravel path, he spoke to them of his children and how, overcoming the impediment of a mixed marriage, he took them to Sunday Mass in rain or shine.

Dr Carr owned himself delighted. The Archbishop spoke not at all, but inhaled the salt breeze from the Atlantic. Willie made a mental note to go to confession when he returned to London.

'The reason,' Dr Carr said, 'that we intrude on your most valuable time has to do with a certain pernicious rumour.'

Willie, who was by now almost the only person in Galway who had not heard it, said: 'To do with me?'

The bishop looked at the archbishop, who had plucked a sprig of mint and was rubbing it between his palms. 'This is most distressing. You will understand that since such rumour has come to our ears, we are in conscience bound to lay it to rest.' The archbishop cupped his hands, raised them to his nose and sniffed the fragrance. 'The person who has been making this allegation is a colleague of yours, a Mr Biggar.'

'Him?' Willie was genuinely outraged. 'With respect, your Grace, not only is that man a Presbyterian, but a tradesman, a known blackguard and a person of low morals. He is no colleague of mine and, I assure you, never will be.'

As if Willie had not spoken, Dr Carr continued on the same even note. 'Mr Biggar claims that there exists an improper . . . I should say a scandalous relationship between your wife and Mr Parnell.'

133

Willie felt perspiration start out on his forehead and at once turn chill. In his days with the 18th Hussars, when his horse, Early Bird, had tripped and thrown him, he had lain in the barracks with broken ribs and concussion. He had seen a tall woman with holes for eyes and a wound for a mouth walking between the cots. He knew that she was not real, for no one else looked in her direction, and, as his injuries healed, he saw her no longer. With Kate and Parnell, he had taken the same comfort. An inner voice told him they were lovers, but no fingers pointed, no eyes looked; it was as much of an illusion, his reason told him, as the woman with no eyes. Now, someone besides himself had seen the phantom, and it was a phantom no longer.

His voice, he thought, feigned disbelief quite convincingly. 'Biggar says what?'

'Unfortunately, the more vile such rumours are, the harder they die. We are informed that this allegation is already the occasion of ribald gossip about the city.'

'Well, I'll sue him,' Willie said, disposing of the matter. 'I'll bring an action.' He looked at the Archbishop of Tuam, seeking and not finding a nod of approval.

'That,' Dr Carr told him, 'is a matter for your good self. However, if there were only an iota of truth in the charge, then the hierarchy would be compelled to direct their flock not to accept you as a candidate for Galway. To do otherwise would be a grave sin and an offence to God. His Lordship and I are of a mind that you should be given the opportunity to deny the allegation. Or, unhappily, to confirm it.'

Willie said: 'I see.'

The prelates had paused in their stroll. He realised that they were waiting.

He said: 'Do you mean now?' He adopted a declarative voice. 'Your Lordships, on bended knee, I swear —' He broke off, realising that he was not kneeling and that in his present company a figure of speech would not suffice. He flopped down on both knees on the grass verge.

'On my knees, I swear to you that there is nothing between my wife and Mr Parnell.'

For the first time, the archbishop spoke. 'You foolish man.'

Fear took Willie by the heart. He squinted up at the figure, dark against the winter sun.

Archbishop McEvilly said: 'You're kneeling on wet grass.'

For luncheon, Willie could manage no more than a dozen of the local oysters. In the afternoon, he walked out of the city to Salthill and on by the sea road to the thatched cottages of Barna, where, across the half-doors, there were smiles that were neither too cold nor too knowing. The tide was out. He had bought a blackthorn walking stick to give himself the air of being Irish, and he sat poking its ferrule at a crab in a rock pool. He thought of Parnell and Kate. He wondered if he could possibly have sworn the truth without meaning to, if the rumours had indeed been fabricated by Biggar and Healy. If so, if they were false, why was he constantly devoured by hatred for Parnell? He thought of Kate's protestations of innocence. Faithful or false, truth or lies: the opposites spun in his head, one putting horns upon the other. He started the walk back to the city. Yes, well, he would play the game out. Parnell owed him the seat; it was neither favour not debt; he, Willie had earned it. He would bide his time; Aunt Ben would soon make up her mind to die, and then he would know what to do.

He was cheered up and himself again when he returned to the Railway Hotel. He bathed, put a dab of pomade on his hair and combed it carefully to disguise the thinning. The long walk had given him an appetite, and as he passed the entrance to the hotel bar on his way to the dining room, there was an explosion of raucous laughter. A group of men were exchanging stories. Willie heard one of them speak a name he had not heard before. Although the woman mentioned was a namesake of his, he was seated at his table before he connected her with himself. He would hear the name many times again, always spoken by an Irishman and with a snigger or a guffaw. Kitty O'Shea.

135

Parnell came ready to do battle. Fifty of those loyal to him had already signed an appeal to the Galway electors, urging them to stand by their chief. As his train entered the dim cavern of Galway station, he saw that the platform was thronged. There were shouts of 'To hell with O'Shea.' What he had not expected was that others would cry: 'To hell with Parnell and Whiggery.' He was glad; their mood tested him. He stood at the open carriage door and stared the crowd down until the booings died away. He waited, like an actor holding a silence, then stepped down and made his way, unhindered, to the private stairs leading up to the hotel. He had instructed Thomas Sexton and William O'Brien, among those who had travelled with him, to prevent Willie O'Shea from publicly shaking his hand. Out of the corner of his eye, he caught sight of them holding a protesting O'Shea back on the pretext of being delighted to see him.

A public meeting was to be held in the Young Ireland Hall, but first, among the piled-up tables and chairs of the hotel dining-room, he confronted Biggar and Healy. The pair entered to find him already seated in the middle of the room, attended by Sexton, O'Brien and T.P. O'Connor. Biggar had shaken O'Connor's hand when they parted in Dublin; now, seeing him in Galway among Parnell's stalwarts, he started and muttered to himself: 'Et tu, bloody Brutus, begod.' Chairs had not been set for Biggar and Healy; they were obliged either to find their own or remain standing like suppliants. Biggar, his face thunderous, wrenched a chair from a pile and planked it down facing Parnell. When he sat, his feet hardly touched the floor. Timothy Healy was nervous; fumbling, he got one chair entangled in another and brought them both.

Parnell waited until the small farce of the chairs was done. He knew that Joe Biggar was not to be brow-beaten. The other Irish members were hot-blooded; Biggar alone would destroy an enemy pitilessly and yet without a trace of malice. In the early days, he had been Parnell's mentor and accomplice. He had shown him how to waste the Government's time with speeches as interminable as they were pointless – it was a lesson put to good use, particularly when matched with Parnell's flair for never wasting his own time. For all his lusts, Biggar, the retired pork butcher, was not a man of sentiment; he could admire a fine animal and yet unhesitatingly see it put down if it went to the bad. He would do no less with Parnell.

Timothy Healy was chalk to Biggar's cheese. His forebears were god-fearing in the sense that they worshipped a God of vengeance rather than of love. Healy might in grief and disillusionment turn from Parnell; actually to pull him down was to incur hellfire. Facing him, he began to tremble.

In Parnell's mind, the fate of Willie O'Shea had assumed a minor importance. What mattered more was that Biggar and Healy had opposed his will and must be brought to heel. He had shaped the party; it was his element, and within its greater purpose there were strengths to be tested. The Fianna, the warriors of the golden age, interspersed their wars with contests of fitness; it was such a game that Parnell now played. He knew that of his opponents, Healy was doubly the weaker; his enmity had its roots in the emotions, and he was afraid.

Biggar made no show of courtesy; he might have been a bailiff assailing a cottage door. 'The reason me and young Healy are opposing Captain O'Shea —'

'*I* summoned *you* here, Biggar. *You* did not summon *me*.' Parnell's voice was at its most glacial. He feigned to address both men, while favouring the one who would break. 'A rumour has spread that if Captain O'Shea is not returned, I shall resign from the party. I have no intention of resigning. I would not resign if the people of Galway were to kick me through its streets.'

He made the familiar gesture of extending his left hand, palm facing upwards. He said: 'I have a parliament for Ireland within the hollow of my hand.' He slammed his right fist into the palm. 'Destroy me, and you destroy that parliament.'

'We've heard that song before, sir,' Biggar said.

'You will hear it again at this evening's meeting. And you

will hear me say that if the people reject Captain O'Shea, if they set their faces against me, then the word will go out through the universe that a disaster has overwhelmed Ireland. There will arise a shout from our country's enemies: "Parnell is beaten. Ireland no longer has a leader." '

His eyes rested upon the younger of the two men. 'Timothy Healy, is that to be the sum of your achievement? The destruction of Home Rule?'

'Blackmail, begod,' Biggar muttered. Without heeding him, Healy shook his head dumbly.

Parnell was relentless. 'Answer me!'

Healy whispered: 'I will fight you another day.'

It was as much courage as he dared muster. He stood, avoiding Biggar's eyes and went from the room.

The public meeting was turbulent. It should also have been brief, but nobody in the history of such occasions had ever gone home at nine o'clock, and so the speeches expanded to fill the time available. Biggar spoke forcibly. If there were those who willed him to hint at Parnell's reasons for championing Willie O'Shea, they received no joy; hinting was not part of Biggar's stock in trade. Loud groans came when Tim Healy withdrew his resistance. God would bear witness, he exclaimed, his voice breaking, that it was a bitter cup for him to drink, but it was a cup he would drain for the sake of the party he loved.

Only Joe Biggar stood his ground. One of the many folderols he despised was graciousness in defeat. He told Parnell: 'Mr Chairman, you have carried the day, but I'll say this to you. You've drawn on the reserves of the party's loyalty and affection. If you attempt to draw on those funds again, you'll find the account empty.'

He stomped, applauded, from the hall. Parnell, paying his departure no more outward sign than the passing of a cloud, declared the meeting closed. The crowd departed, grumbling, home or to the public houses. They had hoped for revolution, bloody for preference, and instead had been given Willie O'Shea.

 138

Tim Healy fled from Galway by the last train for Limerick; on the morrow he would visit his brother Maurice in Cork. He had been put to shame: a defeated intriguer. The winning cards had been in his hand, and he had not dared to play them. He had held back from speaking the words that would topple the idol. Parnell was committing fornication, the most loathsome sin of all, with O'Shea's wife. No matter; he could wait; he had the patience of his race. One day, when the 'king' was no longer also a god, he would speak the words aloud.

Parnell sent a message in a pre-arranged code to Katharine at the Piccadilly hotel she used to keep vigil. In the morning, she would return, content, to Eltham to await him. Meanwhile, he knew that Biggar had spoken the truth; his credit had been drawn to its limit. At least, the danger was past; there was only one Willie O'Shea in the world and his price had been paid. There could be no more demands, or at least none that he could be asked to meet, and Katey would again be the wife of a personage.

Two evenings later, he arrived at Blackheath station. Again by arrangement, she was there to meet him. For once, she did not care that the place was public; she held and kissed him.

She said: 'My darling, you did it. He won. Thank you.'

He took her arm and they walked towards the waiting dog-cart. He said: 'Yes, he won. Nobody else did.'

TEN

It was an important morning in the life of Joe Brady.

Four years had passed since he and his friends had killed Lord Frederick Cavendish and Thomas Henry Burke in the Phoenix Park. Usually, he began his work as a stonemason at eight o'clock, and so today it was no hardship for him to be awakened at seven. He was dressed and ready when the time came to keep his appointment. He had not far to go, no more than a few paces along a corridor and up a flight of stairs.

His arms were already trussed. With demonic speed, the hangman bound his legs with a strap, put a white cloth hood over his head and pulled the noose tight about his neck. Brady hardly had time to say 'Poor Ireland . . . poor old Ireland' before the trap door opened under his feet.

Among the crowd waiting outside Mountjoy Prison was a young man named Edward Caulfield Houston. He took note of the names on the notice of execution: Joe Brady, Daniel Curley, Michael Fagan, Thomas Caffrey and the twenty-one-year-old Timothy Kelly, who had cut their victims' throats. A sixth name was missing, Houston thought. He caught a train to Kingstown and walked along the path of the sea wall to Sandycove Avenue. He knocked at a door which wanted for a coat of paint. He heard the caterwauling of children. A slavey told him that the 'Major' was at

140

the Forty Foot, a men's bathing place a hundred yards away.

Houston had been told that the self-styled major was short, balding, pot-bellied and spade-bearded. The description was accurate. Also, he wore an eyeglass and, at the moment, nothing else. He was strolling about near the diving place. The swimmers at the Forty Foot had not adopted the new custom of wearing bathing drawers; their nakedness had become a matter of principle; it proclaimed that the place was out of bounds to the lesser sex. The thought occurred to Houston that his man, when fully dressed, would cut less than an impressive figure; without clothes, he was a sight upon which the eye was not tempted to linger.

Houston introduced himself. 'Have I the honour of addressing Mr Richard Pigott?'

Mr Pigott was charmed to meet him. With his bare stomach nudging Houston's privates, he declared himself to be at his visitor's disposal. Houston, retreating, said that their business could wait until he no longer had his new acquaintance at a disadvantage. Pigott was about to reply that he felt perfectly at ease, but the other had already vanished around the Martello tower that overlooked the bathing place. When Pigott, clothed, came in pursuit, the shabbiness of his clothes told of hard times. The two men strolled and talked. Edward Houston had a commission for Pigott. It was to find evidence unmasking Parnell as the ringleader of the Phoenix Park murderers.

Pigott seemed to him to qualify for the task. He was hard up and unable to feed the young and hungry family on which he doted; he was a spendthrift; he had a nose for smelling out secrets; as a journalist, he danced to the sweetest fiddler, using pseudonyms to eulogise Parnell one week and 'expose' him the next. And he had pursued a brief but lucrative trade as a blackmailer. Now, looking across Scotsman's Bay to the spires of Kingstown, he shook his head and said that no one seriously believed Parnell to have had hand, act or part in the Park murders. Houston replied that he proposed to pay him a guinea a day and full travelling expenses. Pigott was silent for a time after this. On the other hand, he said, there was no smoke without fire and still waters ran deep.

They were sitting on an outcrop of granite overlooking the little beach from which Sandycove derived its name. Houston took a small bag from his pocket and set it to rest on the stone surface. The contents clinked.

He said: 'The patience of the people I represent is infinite. But bear in mind that we can find out mere rumours for ourselves. We require evidence . . . letters, documents, whatever will put Parnell at the end of a rope.'

Richard Pigott touched the bag with his fingertip. Within, a coin slid and made a noise. He said: 'Trust me. I'll give you proof.'

Within the hour, Houston was at work in his office in Molesworth Street. The brass doorplate identified the house as the headquarters of the Irish Loyal and Patriotic Union, of which he was the newly engaged secretary. It was an organisation devoted to the overthrow of Irish nationalism in general and Parnell in particular; its watchword, Houston liked to say in irreverent moments, was 'Ireland for the English'. Both its pedigree and funding were British and impeccable. Houston wrote to his superiors of the meeting with Richard Pigott. Pigott, he told them, would draw his guinea a day and expenses and give next to nothing in return. From a rogue, one could expect roguery. After some months, Houston would threaten to cut off the golden flow; it was then that Pigott, who had become used to easy living, would go to work in earnest.

At that moment, the 'Major', as he liked to be called, was packing a bag. He would visit Lausanne first. It was years since he had been to Switzerland, and it was as likely a place as any in which to find a Fenian conspiracy. He decided that he would stop in Paris on the way. Among his hobbies was the study and appreciation of pornography, and his collection had of late begun to pall.

    142

A famous composer, Willie thought, should at least look the part, and Johannes Brahms, wearing baggy trousers and a plaid shawl fastened with a safety pin, was a distinct disappointment. Nonetheless, Brahms he undoubtedly was. Willie, who was watching him from behind the previous Saturday's *Times*, did not much care for music without tunes, but to share a roof with persons of importance, even if they resembled pastry cooks on holiday, helped to restore the sense of one's own eminence.

Willie's customary good opinion of himself had been taking a buffeting. He had come to Carlsbad, not only for the sake of his liver, but to escape an uncordial Westminster. On his return to the Commons after the Galway by-election, there had been the feeling of revisiting a scene of past happiness only to find that the wind was chill and the landscape bleak. The fact was that his fellow members were snubbing him, and he had no idea why. He did not, of course, count the Irish, who could not abide being the natural inferiors of any man, but even Liberals had begun to remember pressing business when he came up. Invitations had become fewer; his mantelshelf looked positively naked. Willie was a natural mimic, and his imitation of Joseph Biggar – 'Misther Spayker . . . Misther Spayker, sorr!' – was especially acclaimed. Last week, it had not brought a titter. Even Joe Chamberlain was deucedly cool these days. And so Willie had taken his liver to Carlsbad for the waters and a fortnight of congenial society. There were many English guests at the hydro; one of them, a Mrs Pell, came into the sunlight and joined Willie in his contemplation of Johannes Brahms. When the composer began in his turn to contemplate Willie and Mrs Pell, she opened her newspaper.

After some moments, she said: 'Captain O'Shea, how famous you are. Your name is here in the *Pall Mall Gazette*.'

Willie smiled and reached out his hand for the paper. Mrs Pell read on. Her expression changed to dismay; she began to blush. She said: 'Oh, no. I'm so sorry. It's a mistake.'

Willie took the paper from her. The item was headed: MR PARNELL'S SUBURBAN RETREAT. It told of how, while the Irish

143

leader was driving a brougham from Blackheath to Eltham after midnight, he collided with a cart belonging to a market gardener. Mr Parnell was described as being the guest of Captain and Mrs O'Shea of Wonersh Lodge.

Mrs Pell was distressed. There seemed to be nowhere to look except either at Willie or Johannes Brahms. Willie smiled in the manner of one who accepted that to be famous was to be regularly traduced. 'It is a pity,' he said, 'that these newspaper johnnies tell only half the truth. They might have mentioned that in my absence my wife's sister stays at Eltham as chaperon.' He rose and said: 'Will you excuse me?' He went indoors to the concierge and sent off a telegram demanding to know what Parnell was doing at Eltham after midnight.

A reply came next day: DEAR BOYSIE, MR PARNELL INFORMS ME NEWSPAPER REPORT WAS FABRICATED BY TIMOTHY HEALY IN REVENGE FOR HIS DEFEAT AT GALWAY. YOUR ACCUSATIONS ARE MOST UNGENTLEMANLY. KATE.

Her brazenness was breathtaking. Willie had been the butt of the Galway gossip-mongers; now it seemed that his good name was to be dragged in the London mud as well. He re-read the telegram. He could understand equivocation from a faithless wife, but so unblushing a denial was disquieting. He wondered if, after all, he had wronged her. He walked under the plane trees of Carlsbad and considered the case for the defence. First, she was his own Kate – Dick, as, in spite of her protests, he knew she liked to be called. She was his wife and the mother of his children. That counted for much. Secondly, he was, after all, Captain Willie O'Shea. Putting conceit to one side, he asked himself if any woman, never mind Kate, could spurn him for a sickly wretch who was neither in his right mind nor, by the look of him, long for this world. He found it unlikely, and yet he could not reach a verdict. Uncertainty of any kind was upsetting to Willie, and the more he thought of Kate and the bounder, Parnell, the more it undid the benefits of his cure.

Within days, he received two letters. One was from Kate in

144

which she said that Parnell had put his two horses out to grass on Bexley Heath, and that this was why he may have been in the neighbourhood at midnight. The business of working out why anyone would go looking for his horses on heathland in the pitch dark gave Willie the beginnings of a head pain. He read on. She said again that Timothy Healy had given a garbled story to the *Pall Mall Gazette*. She wrote: *In a letter, Charles tells me that he has called Healy a chimney-sweep to his face*. The name 'Charles', so effortlessly set down, sent his bile leaping into Willie's throat; his headache no longer threatened, but raged.

In his reply, Willie adopted an Olympian attitude. He neither swallowed her explanation nor choked on it; whichever he did, the future might prove him wrong. Silence, he thought unhappily, would sweep the ground from under her. Besides, her Aunt Ben, at ninety-two, seemed determined never to die. *Aunt is well*, Kate had written in a postscript, as if to indicate to Willie the buttered side of his bread. His tone, when he wrote, was perfectly cool and amiable, but he deliberately signed himself 'W.H. O'Shea' rather than 'Boysie'.

His second letter of the day had been written by Henry Harrison over the signature 'Chas. S. Parnell'. It reminded the member for Galway that the vote on the second reading of Gladstone's Home Rule bill was to be taken on the 7th June and that he was expected to do his duty. Crumpling the letter, Willie thought he knew where his duty lay. Unswervingly, and with all the force at his command, he would abstain.

Home Rule was to be the gateway to full independence for Ireland. Gladstone, as the Lord God Jehovah, had beckoned, and Parnell, the new Moses, would lead his followers to the Promised Land. The path lay clear and golden in the sun. When the division bell rang, Willie took his seat in the Visitors' Gallery where he could be unostentatiously neutral. He sighed at the futility of it all. Gladstone had been hoodwinked by Parnell, and Home Rule would be entrusted to a race of peasants: uncouth, mutinous and feckless. There was little point in a man cutting short his well-deserved holiday; it made a mockery of abstention.

Willie had deliberately missed most of the preliminary debate; long speeches bored him. It took him a little while, therefore, to realise that there was mischief afoot. His crony, Joseph Chamberlain, had turned against Gladstone and mustered his own faction of radicals to oppose the bill. When it came to the vote, Home Rule was declared lost by thirty votes. It was Pushful Joe's revenge on Parnell.

Parnell sat as if carved in stone. Some of the Irish members bellowed in anger; others wept openly. Willie wept, too, but for the joy that exploded within him. At last, his enemy had come to grief. When he saw Chamberlain assemble his papers and prepare to leave the chamber, he hurried down from the gallery to congratulate him. On arriving at the lobby, he was taken aback to see that although the time was going on for two in the morning, most of the Irish members still lingered, speaking in quiet voices like mourners at a wake. Joseph Chamberlain appeared and walked through the lobby.

Willie heard Parnell say loudly: 'Mark him! There goes the man who murdered Home Rule.'

Chamberlain smiled faintly to himself as if the slur were a compliment. He did not falter in his walk. Willie found himself obliged either to run the gauntlet of the Irish members or lose him. As he started forward, he heard Tim Healy say: 'And there, sir, goes the man who poisoned the murderer's mind against you. The wastrel you forced down the party's throat.'

Willie stopped in his tracks. Turning, he saw Parnell stride away. He heard Thomas Sexton say: 'Healy, you have the devil's own luck. After tonight, you're lucky he didn't kill you.'

Healy made no answer; he was regarding Willie with a look of intense hatred. Of a sudden, Willie remembered Kate's letter and the insult Parnell had supposedly delivered to Healy's face.

He took a step forward. 'Chimney-sweep!'

As Willie walked away, all but snorting with self-approval, Healy had not the faintest idea of what he meant.

'I suspect, Mr Stewart, that you are suffering from nephritis
. . . it goes by the more common name of Bright's disease. I
shall require to examine you again in a week from now.'

Sir Henry Thompson was at a loss to understand his patient's
passion for secrecy, especially since his likeness was to be found in
every newspaper in London. In the actual flesh – what there was
of it – he had a more cadaverous look, and the eye sockets were
caverns, but there was no mistaking him. Evidently, he enjoyed
the playing of games.

'Also, I find that your reserves of strength are used up to
a degree that, quite frankly, gives grounds for alarm. Complete
rest is essential, and I would recommend sea air.'

For the first time, the woman spoke. 'Mr Stewart has taken
lodgings at Eastbourne.'

Sir Henry wondered if she, too, was using an assumed name.
He said: 'No better place. Do you happen to have children, Mrs
O'Shea?'

'My youngest is two.'

'Then you will be the perfect nurse for a grown man.' Sir
Henry bathed her in the lambent smile which, although he was
unaware of it, had put his name among the Birthday Honours.
He again addressed his patient: 'Sir, your doctor in Dublin . . .'

'Dr Kenny.'

'Did he prescribe a regimen?'

'He said that at all costs my extremities were to be kept dry.'

'Your Dr Kenny is to be cherished, sir. You must on no
account catch cold. I suggest that you carry a change of socks
with you always.' Sir Henry's smile, which had not quite guttered
out, glowed back to amber life. 'And let the spare socks always be
of a different colour to those you are wearing.'

Parnell was at once on his guard. The fates were forever
conspiring against him; only the previous week he had been
sitting on a sofa for all of ten minutes before it occurred to
him to lift its loose cover and look beneath. His sixth sense had
not deceived him: it had originally been upholstered in the colour
that spelt his ruin.

He gave Sir Henry a knowing look. He said: 'I suppose you are going to suggest that I wear green socks?'

The physician was taken aback. 'Not at all. A difference in colour is important so that this lady, this ministering angel of yours, will know at a glance if you have changed them in accordance with my instructions.'

Parnell was not merely relieved; he smiled. Sir Henry had the kind of Jesuitical mind he admired. Forgetting himself, he said: 'You, sir, should be in Westminster.'

Sir Henry said: 'I could say that of you, too, sir.'

Katharine was asked if she would wait in the outside room while the doctor had a parting word with his patient. When the two men were alone, Sir Henry said: 'You must take better care of your health, Mr Stewart. We live in stirring times. It would be a pity not to see them through.'

Parnell said: 'You think there is that possibility?'

If patients could play games, so could their physicians. 'Let us say,' Sir Henry said, 'that I wish you occupied Mr Parnell's shoes at this moment.'

Parnell smiled again. He was in even better company than he had supposed. 'And if I *were* in his shoes, would I be in better health?'

'Perhaps not. But what a delightful prospect lies before him. With the Liberals defeated and out of power, he is in the wilderness. In his place, only think, sir, of what a peaceful convalescence you might have.'

'Somehow,' his patient said, 'I do not believe that peacefulness is what Mr Parnell prizes most.'

Katharine wished to visit her own doctor while she was in town and so proposed to stay overnight with her sister, joining Parnell on the morrow in Eastbourne. He had asked if she was ill; she laughed and made mention of 'women's matters'. As they drove to Anna's house at Buckingham Gate, he attempted to keep his tone casual. 'While you are in town, will you visit O'Shea?'

She avoided a direct answer. 'These days Willie and I are barely on speaking terms. I doubt if he would make me welcome.'

His eyes were so dark with pain that she knew he suspected the truth. She squeezed his arm fiercely and said: 'My heart's darling, there is nothing that touches us. Always remember that you and I are outside the world.'

She had tea with Anna and afterwards called upon her doctor, who confirmed what she already suspected. She took a cab to Albert Mansions. On finding that Willie was not at home, she left her card with the message that she would return later in the evening. It would be the third deception of its kind, always supposing that Willie's lusts were a match for his sense of grievance. The physical part of it was not repellent to her; it was no more than a thing between bodies. Men were romantics; they thought of women as sacred vessels; they could not understand that the mind was the seat of the affections, that caring and being cared for was what mattered.

The phrase 'hardened sinner' came into her mind. It was said that when a sin was repeated the soul grew calloused and insensitive. It was untrue; the evil, repeated, was a wound reopened. To justify what she had twice done and was prepared to do again, she arraigned Willie in her thoughts. His hatred for Parnell was blind and out of all proportion to the wrong done to him – a small wrong, if truth be told, for nothing had been taken that he had not long since thrown away. He had had his women. His men friends knew, even as Katharine welcomed them to Willie's dinners in Thomas's Hotel. They regarded a wife as of no account, whereas a man was a complex being: a good fellow in town and a good man in the country. It was modern times; the world had shrunk, and its adventures with it; a woman's thighs were the Tahiti of the age. And, as a father, Willie could hardly be more remiss. Like his Mass-going, his affections were on the surface. He played so small a part in the shaping of the children's lives that it seemed hardly to matter whether their paternity was his or another's. The thought had hardly formed than she knew it to be a lie. Only the thin paper wall of self-delusion kept Willie's destruction at bay; if it ruptured, he would be revealed to the world as a fool and a dupe who did not even know his own children, and the blame would be hers.

As she returned to Anna's house to wait for evening, she put from her mind all thoughts of right and wrong. Necessity was stronger than either, and the child she would bear must be her husband's, or she and Charles were lost. When Anna was inquisitive about the day's comings and goings, Katharine said that she was on family business. When, a minute later, she laughed aloud, she did not explain why.

Willie, on arriving home at Albert Mansions, tore up Katharine's visiting card. He had been at her beck and call for too long. If she did not need his presence in her life, he would answer in kind. Besides, he had a more pleasurable evening in mind than putting up with her evasions and, for all he knew, out-and-out lies. He shaved, washed, applied cologne water, changed into evening dress and took a cab to Mudie's Banqueting Rooms in South Street. Earlier, in the New Liberal Club, he had looked in vain for Joseph Chamberlain.

'Not here,' Willie was told. 'No doubt you'll see him later at his party at Mudie's.' Then, a smile. 'I say, aren't you going?'

Unhesitatingly, Willie had replied that of course he was going, try and keep him away, perish all thought to the contrary. It took him a little while to realise that what Chamberlain was celebrating was the victory over Home Rule, and that he, Willie, the very power behind the throne, had not been invited. He ordered a brandy and soda, and brooded. It was he, after all, who had exposed Parnell to Joe Chamberlain in his true lights. If Chamberlain was the powder keg, Willie had been at the very least the fuse. He ordered another brandy and soda and a third, and, for once, drink had a mellowing effect upon him. He looked for extenuation, an oversight. He recalled that he had mentioned to Chamberlain that he proposed to move to a new flat in Charles II Street, off the Haymarket. Almost certainly the invitation had been sent there. He was sure of it. After the fifth brandy and soda, he went home and dressed for the occasion.

At Mudie's, a damned flunkey looked at the guest list and told him that he was not on it. Willie declared himself to be Captain William O'Shea, M.P., and an intimate of Mr Chamberlain. He attempted to brush past; his way was politely barred. A kind of senior flunkey appeared; there were words, heated on Willie's part. Finally, Chamberlain was sent for. Meanwhile, guests arrived and were admitted. Willie was mortified to recognise them from the House. One of them nodded to him.

Joe Chamberlain, dressed up to the nines, came quickly downstairs, bidding his guests welcome as they passed. 'Hello, O'Shea, you here? What can I do for you?'

It was not the greeting of a host to a guest, but Willie had decided upon the card he would play and saw it spinning to the table. 'Thank heaven, now all will be set to rights. Through some oversight, I did not receive my invitation, and these people of yours have been damned officious.'

Chamberlain seemed genuinely baffled. 'Forgive me. D'you say, your invitation.'

'To our victory celebrations.'

His bewilderment deepened. 'Victory? O'Shea, I am at a loss. What victory have you in mind?'

Willie began to be annoyed. 'My dear sir . . . no games, I beg of you. I mean the defeat of Parnell and the end of Home Rule. We routed him. We —'

Joe Chamberlain was actually laughing. It was a silent, careful laugh, as befitted him. He took a step away from Willie, shaking his head.

Willie, now angry, said: 'It amuses you, does it? Well, see here. If I, who have played a vital role in the overthrow of a consummate blackguard, am now to be denied a glass of wine —'

151

Chamberlain's laughter was put to rout. He looked about him. 'O'Shea, we are in a public place . . . have the goodness to lower your voice.' He sighed at the need to explain. 'Victory celebration! If I smiled, it is because I have brought down my own party and put myself out of office. In my constituency, I have been hanged in effigy on the town hall steps, and yet you believe there is a cause for jollification.'

Through the mist of Willie's five brandies-and-sodas came the realisation that he had made a mistake. And yet, even as he stared haplessly at Chamberlain, three other guests came in in their evening clothes. He stammered: 'But there is a celebration.'

Chamberlain said: 'Indeed there is. You seem not to know that tomorrow Miss Mary Endicott and I are to be married. This evening's occasion is my bachelor dinner . . .'

'Oh, my God.'

'. . . although I confess that the name "bachelor" sits uneasily on one who has been twice a widower.'

Willie was put to rout. He began to yammer. He told Chamberlain that he was lost for words, then babbled a hundred of them – regrets, felicitations, his best respects. When he was done, he went, almost blindly, towards the entrance.

Chamberlain spoke his name. Willie stopped. He was being recalled. He would not, he thought, steeling himself, be invited to attend the party out of the other's pity – at any rate, not for more than a brandy or two, from graciousness.

'Come with me.'

Chamberlain did not lead him upstairs to his celebrations; instead, he steered him to a public room at the rear of Mudie's. It was discreet, softly lit; the velvet drapes and upholstery were of a deep, sullen red. It was a place where a gentleman who had dined well and did not wish his evening to end might find the means to prolong it. At this early hour, the room was empty except for two women drinking wine. Their dresses of fine silk suggested that they were ladies of quality; their feather boas and a suspicion of rouge

152

said that they were not. One of them glanced up as Chamberlain and Willie came in. As Chamberlain ordered brandies, Willie's eyes met the woman's. He liked to look at handsome women. He liked even more to be looked at in return. The woman was not above five and thirty, the best age. Her throat was enclosed by pale lace fastened with a cameo brooch. She had long black hair, worn in a chignon. He wondered how it would look spread out upon the white of a pillow.

Willie was paying only half-attention when Chamberlain spoke. 'I must return to my guests, so I'll be brief. You have been of service to me, so the least I can do is repay you with good advice.' He paused for a moment before saying: 'Resign your seat. Don't delay. Do it now.'

The words did not at once penetrate; then Willie's head came around slowly. His eyes took a moment to focus. He said, dully: 'Pardon me?'

Chamberlain said: 'Save whatever honour you can. Get out.'

Willie said: 'I think you mean to insult me.'

'Don't be a fool.' Chamberlain's voice was impatient. He was a businessman who had amassed a fortune partly by looking reality in the face. 'Politically, you are done for. You have allowed your hatred of Parnell to poison your mind and your life.'

'He is vile. You yourself despise him.'

'I can't stand the fellow, but I am hardly in your position.'

Willie looked at him sharply. He had been deemed not good enough to attend the blow-out upstairs; well, he was hanged if, in addition, he was going to be the butt of scurrilous rumours, even from Joe Chamberlain. With the Bishop of Galway, he had had to bow the knee and kiss the whip; here, it was different.

He said, with cold dignity: 'My position? What position is that?'

Chamberlain's voice was no less cold. 'I do not owe my seat in Westminster to the man I detest. I tell you, O'Shea, there is not a member on either side of the House but believes that that seat was too dearly bought.'

Willie reddened. 'Damned hypocrites. Call themselves gentlemen!'

Chamberlain said: 'They do not call *you* one.'

The brandies arrived. Chamberlain paid for them and counted his change. Willie smarted as from a slap, but contained himself, waiting to see how close to the wind the other would sail. Chamberlain pushed his drink away from him as if in sudden distaste.

'They say that you take from Parnell with one hand and stab him in the back with the other. Is that what is called an Irish bull? Well, if so, it fits you as equally as it fits him. Your fellow members will have none of you.'

'Then,' Willie said, 'to the devil with them.'

'Listen to me. One day, I shall be in power again. That old hypocrite is well nicknamed the G.O.M. – God's Only Mistake – and if he decides not to live forever, I may even be Prime Minister. I could use your services.'

A flame of hope flickered in Willie's heart.

'But before I could do so, you would require to be re-elected. And that, Captain O'Shea, will never happen. You have had my advice, and now good evening to you.'

He arose and was gone. Willie sat alone, emptied his glass and wondered if Chamberlain was perhaps drunk or even slightly mad. The Galway seat had been hard won in the face of envy, calumny and the scurrility of the mob; only a fool or a coward would surrender it and provide his enemies with comfort. Parnell, most of all, would be in a very transport of delight. Willie sent the idea packing. He noticed, now that he was on his own, that the woman was looking at him with naked invitation. He felt his loins stir.

He summoned a waiter. 'My best respects to the lady and ask her if she could care to join me in refreshments.'

Without ceasing to hold her with his eyes, he drew Joe Chamberlain's untouched brandy towards him.

Katharine returned to Albert Mansions towards eleven in the hope that Willie had come home. She knocked at the door of his flat; there was no reply. She said: 'Willie, are you there? Answer.' She felt the beginnings of panic; if she did not see him this evening, there might not be another day. At this hour, there was no respectable place where she could go to wait for an hour and call again. She resigned herself to returning to her sister's house for the night. More from pique than to any purpose, she turned the doorknob and was surprised to see the door swing open.

The sitting room was lighted. A dark-haired woman was facing her. She was dressed for the street. One hand held her hat in place; the other was holding a hatpin. She had been frozen in that attitude, not answering the knocking. Now she looked at Katharine. She thought: If this is his wife, she seems remarkably unperturbed.

Katharine had never knowingly seen one of Willie's creatures at close quarters. She now made use of her opportunity, examining the woman in as much detail as the moment afforded. Willie's tastes, she thought with some satisfaction, tended towards the common. The dark-haired woman, who was not accustomed to being looked at as an object, stabbed home the hatpin.

Katharine said: 'Good evening. Is Captain O'Shea in?'

The woman replied: 'Out, some would say.'

She snatched up her reticule; the door slammed behind her. Katharine went into the other room. Willie was lying on his back on the bed, wearing only his socks and his dress shirt. It was hiked up about his midriff. His member, pink and flaccid, was a slow-worm on his thigh. His mouth sagged open. He made a continuous rasping noise. She called his name several times and shook him. He snorted and flung up an arm, almost striking her. He was unwakeable. She tugged the bedclothes free from under his dead weight and covered him.

She drew up a chair and sat for a time, almost like a mother watching over an ailing child. A thought came to her and grew, and she wondered if she dared. She knew that if she tried and

155

failed, there would be no second chance. And yet, if she left now and went to Anna's for the night, she might be throwing away her only hope. She arose, bent over and caught him by the shoulders. 'Willie, wake up!' Again, there was a martyred groan. It decided her. She took off her street clothes and shoes, then her bodice, skirt, outer petticoat and corset. She let down her hair, turned the gaslight lamp off and slid into bed beside her husband. She lay, without touching him, on her back. It occurred to her with wry amusement that she was trembling like a bride.

She awoke at dawn, starting up guiltily. At her side, Willie was still sleeping, but quietly now. She was vexed with herself that she had not stayed awake; sleep, it seemed to her, had been a kind of self-indulgence. She arose quietly, found a dressing gown of Willie's and put it over her shoulders against the cold. She stood by the window and looked out at the London morning: crooked chimneys, a wreath of smoke, the rattling of carts. She felt, rather than heard, the sound of Willie awaking. She knew that he was staring at her; his look was fingers laid against her skin. She whirled around and smiled at him brightly.

'Good morning, Willie!'

'Kate . . .'

She said: 'Well, awake at last. Willie, you drink far, far too much.'

Sleep made blind windows of his eyes. He said: 'When did you get here?'

It was now that play-acting was called for. She summoned up the beginnings of outrage. 'I can only think I have misheard. Would you repeat that?'

Willie's face had the blankness of panic; he was in a room of many doors, each one locked. Did he, she wondered, remember taking the black-haired woman to his bed? He began to bluster. 'Eh? No, what I mean is —'

Katharine drove harder, allowing him no escape. 'When did I get here? Willie, if that is intended as humour, I find it in extremely poor taste.'

156

She hardly believed that she could be so righteous. His eyes still had a blank look, not now from sleep but confusion. He was in utter disarray.

She went from vexation to distress. 'Oh, but no, I cannot believe it. Surely you'll not tell me that you don't remember?'

She wondered if she was overplaying her part, but Willie's face was a perfect mask of dismay. 'I . . . ah, I'm not quite awake yet. Just trying to get my wits about me.' He looked about the room as if in search of a third person. 'Did I . . . uh, happen to be alone when you arrived?'

Katharine gave him the look of a woman much wronged. There was the faintest catch in her voice. 'It is true, then . . . you have no recollection. I knew I should have gone home. Why did I not insist?'

She gave a shiver of revulsion and reached for her outer garments where she had placed them. The dressing-gown fell from her shoulders. As she bent to retrieve it, she was aware that Willie, as he was intended to do, was staring at her unconfined breasts.

As she straightened up, his eyes came, too late, to her face. He began to improvise, the while trying to work out in his mind how the woman of last night could have been metamorphosed into his wife. 'Kate, you are perfectly right to take me to task. I over-indulged myself. I admit it. Fact is, I was with Joe Chamberlain, and the fellow upset me.'

She said: 'Willie, you might at least have the civility to get up and see me to a cab.'

'What? Yes, I beg your pardon.'

He got out of bed. Katharine gave a small maidenly gasp and looked away. Willie, finding himself wearing only shirt and socks, snatched up his under-drawers and put them on; flustered, he hopped about on one foot. He said, grunting: 'In my place, any chap would have drunk too much. Do you know, he told me I should resign?'

Katharine said indifferently: 'Resign from what? Who told you?'

157

'Joe Chamberlain. According to him, I'm finished in politics.'

She turned to face him, abandoning the pretence of offended modesty. There was alarm on her face. 'Do you mean, resign your seat? You cannot.'

Willie had begun to struggle into his trousers. 'Chamberlain says that a gentleman would not stay.'

She said: 'Resign now, four months after the election? Willie, for heaven's sake! Mr Parnell all but lost his leadership because of you, and now you talk of resigning. How can you? He would be a laughing st —'.

She broke off, too late. She had betrayed herself. A slow dawning came upon Willie's face. He had been wrong. He had thought that to resign would be to do what Parnell most desired. The opposite was true; how could he not have seen it? If he were now to abandon his seat, the Galway uproar, the loss of face, the breach with Biggar and Healy – all would have been for nothing. In the world's eyes, Parnell would seem a fool. And Willie would be a man of principle, resigning his seat because its price was too high for a gentleman to pay.

He smiled at Katharine. 'Your friend would be a laughing stock? Would he, indeed?'

She said, knowing that it was futile: 'Willie, at least think of the children. With their father in Parliament, they have a standing in the eyes of others. At school, they are looked up to. And what of me? Am I not to be thought of?'

Willie's tartan dressing-gown hung open on her shoulders; its male roughness made her skin seem all the more delicate. He seized her by the arms. His voice was hoarse. 'Damn it, Kate, you're still a handsome woman.'

Even as she deceived him, she had felt a kind of pity. Now, knowing that he would resign his seat to spite Charles, she allowed her hatred of him to bloom again, more luxuriant than ever.

As he mumbled her name and pulled her to him, she said, her

voice flat and remote: 'Twice in a night? Willie . . . you greedy pig.'

He made no attempt to resist when she pulled her arms free and began to dress.

As stipulated, Edward Caulfield Houston and Dr J.F. Maguire of Trinity College travelled to Paris and took rooms at the Hotel des Deux-Mondes in the Rue de Clichy. There, in Houston's room at midnight, Richard Pigott came to them. He produced a folder and from it took a sheaf of letters.

'Gentlemen, there are two men waiting for me downstairs. They must not be named and they must not be seen. If you wish to buy these letters, the price is five hundred pounds. You have a quarter of an hour to decide, otherwise the men will reclaim them and be off.'

Houston and Dr Maguire took the letters into the other bedroom. It was the full fifteen minutes before they returned. Houston said: 'There is a letter here that shows Parnell to be in sympathy with the Park murderers. It does not prove his complicity.'

Pigott smiled. 'The men downstairs say there is a letter that does. They mean to strike another bargain.'

Houston said: 'For thrice the money, I daresay.'

He looked at Dr Maguire, who nodded. As Houston counted out five hundred pounds in bank notes, the doctor made a contribution of his own. 'And we of the Irish Loyal and Patriotic Union are pleased to pay you an additional hundred guineas, both as a reward and an incentive.'

Pigott bowed his head and said: 'My four little boys will pray for you.'

Houston noticed that Pigott made no attempt to keep the moneys separate, but put them into the one inside pocket. When he had gone, Dr Maguire examined the letter in which he was most interested, holding it up to the gaslight. Houston went to

159

the bedroom window, which fronted on to the Rue de Clichy. He saw Pigott emerge into the street below and go quickly down the Rue d'Amsterdam towards the Gare St Lazare. Of the two men, there was no sign. A notion had half-formed in his mind when Dr Maguire, almost purring as he examined the letter, said: 'This is excellent.'

Houston nodded and continued to look out of the window. Still, the two men did not appear.

ELEVEN

'They seem to think they are invisible,' Parnell said one day.

His presence at Wonersh Lodge attracted sightseers. They stood, a row of human headstones, confronting him over the low wall that separated the front garden from the road. They were patient and steadfast; when rain thinned their numbers, they came out again with the sun. When Katharine, vexed beyond endurance, rushed from the house and shouted: 'Be off with you! Leave us alone!' they stared back at her, expressionless. Their stillness was unnerving. Eventually, she had a seven-foot paling erected and planted a rose hedge. It discouraged onlookers, but, as if to show that some at least were not deceived, the anonymous practice began of pasting newspaper cuttings to the bolted carriage gates in the early morning.

Before breakfast on the 18th April, Katharine came from the house to tear down the latest clippings. She thought with longing of the cottage they had lately found on the cliffs near Beachy Head. As soon as it was ready for occupation, it was to be their refuge. Today, as usual, excerpts from *The Times* fluttered against the gates. She saw the headline PARNELLISM AND CRIME. Further down the page, a letter was reproduced in facsimile. It was dated nine days after the Phoenix Park murders and bore the signature 'Chas. S. Parnell'. She read it, at first uncomprehending, then again in horror. She tore the cutting across and flung it from her. When she returned indoors, Parnell was already at breakfast and spreading marmalade on his toast. The morning paper was in front of him, propped up against the coffee pot.

He said, still reading: 'I think I shall have to cancel *The Times*. It is becoming far too sensational.'

The letter said:

Dear Sir,

I am not surprised at your friend's anger, but he and you should know that to denounce the murders was the only course open to us. To do that promptly was plainly our best policy.

But you can tell him and all the others concerned that, though I regret the accident of Lord F. Cavendish's death, I cannot refuse to admit that Burke got no more than his deserts.

She said: 'Charley, it is villainous.'

He nodded. 'Indeed it is. Look at my signature . . . I haven't made an "S" like that since 1878.' He sipped from his cup. 'Ellen surpasses herself. This coffee is excellent.'

'Is that all you have to say?'

He gave her a smile of connubial affection.

She stormed at him: 'Really, sometimes you are as stupid as Willie.'

He said mildly: 'Now you go too far.'

She thought him the very picture of domesticity. The newspapers portrayed him as one whose demeanour was so glacial that Irish members dared not address him unbidden. There were times when, for amusement, she imagined two Parnells: the one who was her true husband, a creature of habit, devoted to the small pleasures of the home; the other, the cold, unyielding autocrat and master of his party. She could scarcely envisage the two within the same one skin. By right, they should be separate beings, like his two horses, the one named President and the other, appropriately, Dictator.

She said: 'Charley, you must take action.'

He looked infuriatingly wise. 'And, by so doing, give credence to a clumsy lie?'

She almost shouted at him: 'It is in *The Times*.'

He said: 'Which you, my love, in common with others of your benighted race, confuse with the Book of Common Prayer.'

She resorted to martyrdom. 'Then you won't defend yourself? You break my heart.'

At once, the impossible man was tenderness itself. He sighed: 'And so saying, you break mine. Very well, I shall finish my coffee, smoke a cigar, spend another hour at my assaying —'

'Oh, the devil take you and it!'

'. . . and then go to Westminster, where I shall inform the House that the letter is an audacious and unblushing forgery, and that *The Times* has allowed itself to be hoodwinked, hoaxed and bamboozled.'

At this, she came around the table and threw her arms about him. He held his buttered toast out to one side as she kissed him.

He managed to say: 'And, with the possible exception of members of my own party — I say the *possible* exception — not one person in the House will believe a word I say.'

She said: 'Dearest, don't wait. Do it now.'

With affected sternness, he pointed to her side of the table. She pouted, planted a defiant kiss on his forehead and returned to her chair. Her letters had, as usual, been placed beside her plate. She read them while Parnell skimmed through the allegations that his party were the instigators of crime in Ireland. The exposé, he thought, had the substance of cottonwool in a chemist's bottle. He turned the page. Now *this* was of interest: another gold field had been discovered in the Transvaal. It was a pity that one such could not be found in County Wicklow. He would be fortunate if, by the time Kate was free of O'Shea, the quartz stones from the Avonmore yielded sufficient gold to line the inside of her wedding ring.

She said: 'Willie is coming tomorrow.'

'Oh?'

163

'He sounds fearfully cross. Did I mention that he has taken to signing himself "Very truly yours, W.H. O'Shea"?'

At least, Parnell thought, however O'Shea styled himself he could no longer put M.P. after his name. It was the way of a bad tooth to rage for a time and hurt most of all at the moment of its departure; but then there descended a quiet so exquisite as to be audible. So it had been with Willie's resignation. He had gone without ripple or trace.

A disagreeable thought occurred. Parnell looked at Katharine in the manner of a host who has been too often imposed on. 'The fellow isn't staying the night, is he?'

To call oneself an English gentleman, which Willie did at every opportunity, entailed the fulfilment of various moral obligations so that the breed might endure. One of these was, at least once in one's lifetime, to write a letter to *The Times*. For Willie, the moment could not be any longer deferred. He had opened the morning paper and read the text of what Parnell had told the House late on the previous evening.

He had said: 'The letter is a villainous and bare-faced forgery. The signature in question is written by a ready penman who has evidently covered as many leagues of letter paper in his life as I have yards.'

Willie's intended visit to Kate could bide its time while he laboured with pen and ink. The villain, Parnell, must not wriggle out of another trap. He had denied authorship of the letter; Willie had no evidence that would say otherwise, and yet now surely was the time to strike. A display of enmity would be self-defeating; with Willie's known dislike of Parnell, it would be seen as a familiar venting of spleen. Ideally, he thought, what he should strive for was a note of artlessness. In Spain during his army days, he had seen a trooper get into difficulties while swimming. A comrade had gone to his aid, only to succeed, through an excess of zealousness, in drowning his friend. Willie wondered if there were some way in

164

which he could, with similar results, swim to Parnell's rescue.

Journeying from North to South by way of West was not in Willie's nature, but after several drafts and a grievously chewed penholder, his letter was finished. He had been, he wrote, in Mr Parnell's company on the day following the Park murders; indeed, at his request he had called upon Mr Gladstone and conveyed to him the Irish leader's willingness to resign. He had been a witness to Mr Parnell's deep and unfeigned distress at the murders. Then, poisoning the cup, Willie wrote: *He was filled with horror that day, not only that two lives had been sacrificed, but that a third was in danger.*

It was deuced neat. The third life, it would be inferred, was Parnell's. He would seem to be a coward, frightened for his own safety. And Willie had not lied; with hindsight, he knew that Parnell *had* been mortally afraid.

He closed and addressed the envelope. As he got ready to go to Eltham, he found that what he had written nagged at his mind. It seemed as if his own words were speaking to him. He opened the envelope, re-read his letter, was bemused and sealed it again. He had posted it and was on his way by hansom to Cannon Street Station when, like a sunburst, it came upon him. He had, unknowingly, hit upon the truth. There had been no forgery. After the Park murders, Parnell had, out of terror, written the disputed letter to appease the Invincibles.

What Willie had done was not, as he had thought, merely neat, but masterly. He had, by apparent accident, drowned the swimmer. All of England, reading his letter when it appeared in *The Times*, would be quick to see that he had solved the mystery. The Parnell letter was not sedition; it was a contemptible expedience. Willie all but danced for glee on the station platform. He had put the last nail in his enemy's coffin.

He walked from Blackheath to Wonersh Lodge, swinging the ebony cane he used when in town. He was in holiday mood. He would not, he decided, mention his letter to Kate; she was no longer to be trusted. Outside the lodge, he saw three street

165

urchins attempting to look through the paling and the rose hedge beyond. He brandished his cane.

'What do you want here? What's your business? No answer? Then be off with you.'

One of the urchins said: 'Please, sir, we've come to see 'im.'

Him? Again, Willie tasted the familiar bile. He ran at them lashing out with his stick and they scampered off, happy to have found a new playmate.

Kate looked well; she was blooming, he thought. He refused his customary whisky and Seltzer; it seemed more formal to accept in its stead a glass of sherry. As she brought it, he looked around the room for a sign of Parnell's tenancy. There was none. It proved nothing; he should, he thought, have arrived without warning. When they were seated opposite each other, he began.

'Madam . . .'

She laughed. 'Oh, Boysie.'

He was unbending. He told her that he had come to a decision. Now that he had retired from working himself to death on behalf of peasants, he saw no reason why they – Katharine, the chicks and he – should continue to live in or near London. Devon or Cornwall would be equally salubrious, or it might be beneficial to be close to his mining interests in Spain. What mattered was that the children be removed from unwholesome surroundings.

'Do you mean this house?' she asked. 'Or this street? Or London?'

'I say nothing,' Willie said with aloof dignity.

'On the contrary.' She felt her temper beginning to rise. 'What you are saying, and very distinctly, is that you and I are once more to live together.'

'As your husband, I have the right to require that.'

She said: 'Yes, I suppose you do.'

He was suddenly on firm ground. 'Then you agree?'

'Most certainly!' She rejoiced to notice that he had so easily become sure of himself and of her. She said: 'Yes, Willie. By all means bear us off to Spain or remote Torquay. I hope I know my duty as a wife: "Whither thou goest, I will go, and where thou lodgest I will lodge." ' As Willie blinked, she smiled and explained: 'That is in the Bible, you know.'

It had been easier than he had expected. Lost for words, he said: 'Yes. Well, then.'

'Mind,' she went on, 'if a husband has rights, so do his wife and his chicks.' She flung his pet name for them at him like a stone. 'They have the right to be provided for. Do you agree?'

In his face, a small light went out.

'How do you intend to provide for us, Willie? Out of what you are pleased to call your mining interests? I thought the sulphur had quite run out. Or do you expect Aunt Ben to help you? She won't, you know, not on this side of the grave. Not a penny piece . . . I'll see to it. So how do you propose that we shall live?'

He did not reply, but looked at her with gathering hatred. Willie was so accustomed to having money at all times within his reach that he had forgotten from whose bounty it came.

She said: 'Another glass of sherry before you leave, dear? We see so little of you these days.'

It seemed that luncheon was to be denied him. She took his glass and brought it to the decanter. He felt swelling within him the rage of impotence. He could no longer hold his tongue; all roads led to the root of his madness. 'Kate, you have no shame. You seem not to care that you have become the object of common gossip.'

She said, unconcerned: 'I am well aware of it. Common gossip by common people.'

She gave him the recharged glass. Her calmness scourged him. He said: 'That man has been here against my express wishes.'

'You invited him.'

'The invitation was withdrawn.'

Her look of surprise was brazenly insincere. '*Was* it? I didn't know.'

He said: 'This house has become his club . . . his hotel.'

She was anxious above all else to be fair. 'Yes, his club, perhaps, dear . . . but not residential. Charles has been very ill.'

167

'Charles!' He thought he would choke on the word.

'He comes here to be undisturbed. Because you so foolishly threw your seat away, was I to close the door in his face? He rests and he pursues his hobby.'

She led Willie to the room she had added on at the rear of the house. In a corner was Parnell's assaying equipment and his specimens of ore.

She said: 'This balance is the latest thing. It can accurately weigh the most unbelievably minute particles of ore. Don't you find that fascinating?'

Willie wondered if her reason had quite gone.

'You see,' she explained, 'his hotel in town refused to allow him to work there with a torch, so I thought to put this room at his disposal. Now and then, he allows me to help him. I keep his blow-pipe at work while he attends to the crucibles.'

For a surreal moment, Willie, who was used to the salacities of the musical halls and Evans's Late Joys, wondered if she was uttering a kind of outlandish *double entendre*, but her face was innocent of all impropriety. Nowadays, it was easy for him to forget that Kate's father, as a young clergyman, had administerd the last rites to Queen Caroline, consort of George IV.

She said that she would walk part of the way with him to Blackheath. The leafy roadway had not long ago been a country lane; now, houses along the way interrupted the expanses of parkland on all sides except the west, where the yellow-brown halter of London's grime tethered the city to the sky. When they were quite on their own, with no one in sight, she turned on him with a suddenness that in itself was as startling as its ferocity.

'I did not want the servants to hear what I have to say. Your jealousy of Charles has made you so blind to all reason that you run to believe whatever most vilifies me and degrades you. Your name has become a byword for hatred. You feed on it; your letters become more insolent by the week, and I will endure no more. Now I'll speak plainly. If you want to share in Aunt Ben's fortune, you will not come to Wonersh again, weekdays or Sundays, without my

168

consent. And if you cannot be civil when you put pen to paper, then you will address me through a solicitor. Do you understand?'

He was so taken aback by her outburst, that he could summon no more wit than to say: 'I see.'

'I want to return to the house now. I asked if you had understood.'

He said: 'Yes, I do see. I am to leave a clear field for *him*, is that it?'

Her indignation and loathing of him were such that a lie was not a mask but an honest face. 'How dare you? Have I not given you repeated tokens of my affection, however ill you have deserved them? Well, you shall have a final proof. Six weeks ago, I called upon you at Albert Mansions.'

'I remember.' He was afraid of her. 'What of it?'

'You remember! How very kind of you. On the morning after, you seemed to remember so little else.' She said with a bitterness as deep as if it were unfeigned. 'No, I was at fault. I could have gone; I chose not to, and by staying I was as much to blame as you were.'

A moment before, she had been speaking of tokens of affection; now, somehow, there was talk of blame. He was attempting to find the bridge that led from one to the other when she walked away from him, back towards Wonersh. She had gone a few steps when she turned.

'Goodbye, Willie. This time I shall not ask you to share the responsibility. I prefer to be quit of you.'

He watched her small figure go out of sight with the turn of the road. Once again, he thought of his awakening in Albert Mansions to find her standing, half-clothed, by the window. In a small, rueful corner of his mind, he reflected that a pleasure unremembered was a pleasure wasted.

Two days later, his letter appeared in *The Times*, but the correspondence on the subject was so vast that his own voice went unheard. And yet, in one particular, he was rewarded; the editor,

169

George Buckle, invited him to dine at the Reform Club. At their meeting, he spoke of the possibility of Parnell sueing the paper for libel. He asked if Willie would in that event testify for the defence. Willie at once saw himself in the witness box, reducing the case for the plaintiff to chaff in the wind. He declared himself to be Mr Buckle's servant.

To his disappointment, the authorship of the Parnell letter fell into the limbo of yesterday's news. There was no action for libel. As for Katharine, the next time Willie spoke to her was in church at the christening of the new-born Frances, who, like Clare before her and the lamented Sophie Claude prior to that, was a seven-months baby. To mark the occasion, Willie was invited to come to lunch. He declined stiffly, shook hands with the priest, bowed to the godparents and stalked off. She wrote that evening, upbraiding him for his want of manners. He replied, taking a leaf from her book, and invited her to consult a solicitor. *I shrink*, he wrote, *from the possible eventualities of discussion with you, especially before our daughters.*

As for Parnell, the most significant event of that month was that Richard Pigott, out of funds, was dunned for payment of school fees.

The new letter was as terse as its predecessor. It was dated six years previously.

> *Dear E.,*
> *What are these fellows waiting for? This inaction is inexcuseable. Our best men are in prison and nothing is being done. Let there be an end to this hesitency. Prompt action is called for. You volunteered to make it hot for old Forster and Co. Let us have some evidence of your power to do so. My health is good, thanks. Yours very truly,*
> *   Chas. S. Parnell.*

'Christ,' Joseph Biggar said.

'Whoever the author is,' Parnell said, 'spelling is not his strong suit.'

'Yes,' Timothy Healy said, jabbing a forefinger at the facsimile, 'the mistake is glaring.'

Parnell looked at him coldly. 'Is it, indeed? If you will take the trouble to read the letter again, you will see that there are *two* misspellings.'

'*Are* there?' Biggar said. He re-read the letter. 'You're right. "Inexcusable" and "hesitancy". Like I observed a few seconds ago . . . Christ.'

Parnell's inner circle had come together in a private room in the St Pancras Hotel. The earlier letter had accused Parnell of being in sympathy with the Park murderers; this second showed him inciting them to the crime. It had been read out in open court by the Attorney-General, who, in a private capacity, was defending a libel action against *The Times*. As a result, it was today blazoned in the public prints.

Entering the hotel, Biggar had all but collided with a tall, scarecrowish figure attired in a tweed jacket over a scarlet knitted waistcoat. He carried a small black leather bag – an anarchist's bag out of a penny dreadful. His hair had not been cut in months. His eyes were hollow and large; the skin was waxen. Biggar stepped back to avoid contact. A familiar voice asked: 'Are we enemies, then, Biggar?'

The Belfastman was shocked. With a Home Rule bill in abeyance, Parnell had become lax about attending the House. Gossip flew; illness had made him apathetic. With his passion for secrecy, he was rumoured to move from one sanctuary to another. It was said that he had rooms in Regent's Park; there was talk of a hideaway cottage on the cliffs near Eastbourne. And of course, he stayed with *her* at Eltham. The newest letter had brought him out of seclusion. In the hotel room, they stared at him as they would at the walking dead.

As usual, Biggar was the only one who dared not to be diplomatic. 'It's time, sir, to pay the piper. With the last letter, you

171

were too lofty, too grand to take action. "Never apologise," says you, "never explain." Well, this time you'll have to act. Aye, and quick about it.'

Parnell said: 'What are my choices?'

'None!' Dillon had not meant to raise his voice. More quietly, but still with passion, he said: 'With respect, what I mean is that you must issue a writ. What else is there?'

Parnell said: 'I don't know.'

Biggar sat sideways on his chair in disgust, his arms folded. 'Ach, for God's sake!'

Parnell said: 'Very well, I sue for libel. But where? In an Irish court? In Dublin, I could throw an infant from Carlisle Bridge into the Liffey at midday, and a jury would not only acquit me, but award damages for my embarrassment. It would be a mockery, and seen as such.'

Biggar whirled around to face him. 'Then take your fight to the enemy, sir. Do it here.'

'Have sense, Biggar. They would rake up every outrage that has happened in Ireland in the last ten years. With perjured evidence and an astute counsel for the defence, what I now stand accused of would seem a venial sin.'

Timothy Healy said: 'Mr Parnell, as Dillon says, what else is there?'

Parnell remained vile in his eyes, the immoralist who had dragged the party through the mud of the streets as the price of his depravity. He had no claim on the goodwill of any man. And yet Tim Healy was incensed by the forgeries. The letters had brought alive in him a hatred of England so abstract that it was almost a thing of purity. It had festered in him in the womb; it had been taught to him at school and thundered at him from the pulpit; it was in every room of the Healys' granite house in Bantry, among the cornerboys of the town and in the office, painted in workhouse green, where his father had been a Poor Law Union clerk. With Parnell's encouragement, Timothy Healy had studied law and was now an advocate of the front rank. His intelligence, it was agreed, had no equal among the Parnellites, and yet his detestation of all that was English had no basis in reason; it might have been a bit of madness brought about by poteen or a full moon. Tim Healy was not unique; at home in Ireland, he might be counted by the million. The letters were simply another example of the treachery and double-dealing of perfidious Albion. If Parnell was to be brought down, his own people would do it by entitlement and without the underhandedness of England.

Joe Biggar crunched *The Times* in his fists. 'Sir, this is more than a lie, it's a monstrosity. If it was a living thing, it would be a snake. You must cut the head off it, or you're done for. Aye, even you.'

There was a sardonic amusement in Parnell's face. 'Where were you last night, Biggar?'

'Me?'

'It's a plain question. Where were you . . . say, at midnight?'

Biggar thought it none of his damned business, but assumed that the question had a purpose. 'I was on my own.'

Tom Sexton grinned and muttered to Dillon: 'That makes a change.'

Parnell said: 'You were on your own. Very well, prove it.'

'How?'

'Provide a witness who saw you.'

Biggar all but spluttered at the affront to reason. 'No one saw me. If I'd a had a flamin' witness, I wouldn't have been on my own, would I?'

Parnell said: 'Exactly. So who is there to say they saw me *not* write this letter?'

No one replied. He arose, thanked the members for their attendance and went out. After a moment, Biggar said: 'He's forgotten his bloody bag. John . . . decent mon, go after him.'

As he handed the black bag to Dillon, an impulse caused him to open it, look quickly inside and slam it shut again. When Dillon had gone in pursuit of Parnell, Biggar said, softly: 'And Christ, for a third time.'

173

Sexton said: 'What was in the bag?'

'Socks,' Biggar said. 'Yella woollen socks.'

When Dillon restored the black bag to its owner outside the hotel, Parnell detained him for a moment. 'Do you know, Dillon, with all my heart, I hope not only that the forger is brought to book, but that he is unmasked as none other than —' He broke off.

'Than whom? Dillon asked.

Parnell, who had almost committed the unthinkable folly of imparting a confidence, said: 'It is no matter.'

He nodded to Dillon and strode across the street towards Bloomsbury. That evening after dinner, he and Katharine sat at either side of the sitting-room fire. She was sewing.

He said: 'My dearest, I have an idea in my head, and, try as I may, I cannot be rid of it.'

She looked at him, waiting.

'Do you think your husband could be the forger?'

She said: *Willie?* and laughed so loudly that Mary, who was clearing away next door, looked in, smiling, to share in the merriment.

Timothy Healy was in love again. It was short-lived, but ennobling while it lasted.

It had begun in the House when Parnell spoke of the letter linking him with the Park murders. 'I never wrote it, I never signed it, I never directed it to be written, I never authorised it to be written, and I never saw it.'

He had asked that a select committee of the House be set up to investigate the forgeries. What he had been offered instead was a judicial commission. He said: 'It is not to be an inquiry into the vilification of one man. It is to be a trial, not merely of myself, but of the Irish people.'

Joseph Chamberlain arose, fixing his eyeglass into place. (A Cyclops, by God! Tim Healy thought.) The honourable member, he said languidly, did not welcome the setting up of a commission. It was understandable. No one in his senses would wish to be proved an assassin.

Biggar, seated behind Parnell, jumped to his feet. He was hardly visible as he shook his fist and shouted, 'Ye, blackguard, you.'

Parnell was not a natural orator. He disdained tricks, and he was incapable of passion. Now, he spoke, in a calm measured voice that was the more deadly for its want of emphasis. He accused Chamberlain of having in the past used cat's-paws to perform his acts of roguery, and of betraying Cabinet secrets. ('Judas!' shouted Tim Healy, and the cry was taken up by the Parnellites.)

'This is not the first time,' Parnell said, 'that you have poisoned the bowl and used the dagger against your political opponents when you could not overcome them in fair fight. To your cowardice and treachery, you add hypocrisy. You spike our guns, then sneer that we have not the courage to man them. I say to you, let us have your commission, then, and the sooner the better. We welcome it. We shall be a match for it.'

Under his breath as he sat, he said: 'And I wish to God I knew how.' The Irish members cheered; Parnell was himself again. Hands reached out to touch his arm and pat him on the back. He made no sign; it was enough that he resisted an urge to wince.

At that moment, Tim Healy's manhood was tested. He forgave his enemy, not out of Christian duty, but because he wanted with all his heart to do so; and, in making mortal clay of Parnell, he himself became more than mortal. It was, after all, to be expected that in a man who was great the flaws must perforce be great as well. Parnell would never again be a god come to earth – that golden age was beyond recall – but only one born to lead could so magnificently have thrown down the gauntlet to the antichrist Chamberlain. Not a god, then, but a prophet.

As Parnell left the Commons, Tim Healy caught up with

175

him in Palace Yard. 'Sir, that was very fine. May I say that I was moved. It gave heart to us all.'

'You were heartened?' Parnell said. 'Good.'

He made to move on, but Healy was before him. 'Sir, as an advocate of, I think, some experience, I intend to represent myself before the Commission.'

'Indeed? Then you will have the rare comfort of knowing that your client is innocent.'

Tim Healy said: 'I would be most willing to appear as counsel on your behalf as well.'

'Would you, now?' Parnell's voice had become flat.

In his eagerness, the younger man did not take warning. 'In a junior capacity, I need hardly say. If your solicitor will be good enough to offer me a brief —'

'Healy . . .' Parnell paused, as if unwilling to inflict hurt. 'With all due respects, I think you should act as counsel only for yourself.'

'It is not in the least an imposition. I would be more than willing.'

'Thank you, no.'

His voice was flat, the tone final. Tim Healy was stunned. 'Mr Parnell, do you mean to insult me? Are you saying that you reject my offer?'

'I . . . decline it.'

One word was no better than the other. Healy had humbled himself; he had gone against his own nature; he had forgiven. Parnell could not but see that his manner was conciliatory, that he was almost the worshipful Tim Healy of old. He had offered to take up the lance on behalf of his Chief. He had been spurned.

He said, bitterly: 'I see. Michael Davitt told me that you would neither forgive nor forget that I opposed you in Galway over Captain O'Shea. Is that it? Is this my punishment?'

Parnell said: 'I do not wish you to be my counsel. The reasons are my own.'

Members passing through Palace Yard looked curiously at the two men; the taller waiting for the other to clear his path; the younger man's body taut with anger.

Healy, almost in tears at the injustice that had been done to him, said: 'My God, I have put up with much. Sir, five years ago, at a time of crisis and when you were not to be found, I opened a letter addressed to you. As my punishment, I was —'

At the mention of the letter, Parnell forced his way past Healy, almost throwing him off balance. Healy, not to be robbed of his say, attempted to keep up.

'. . . I was expelled thereafter from your good regard. And yet not for a moment did I waver in my loyalty.' As Parnell's pace quickened, Healy stopped, no longer demeaning himself, and called after him. 'You are a law unto yourself. You treat not only me, but all of us, like —'

He gave up. He stood, forlorn in his misery as Parnell walked towards the cab rank. His anger would return later and this time for always. He had been a fool; it was his reward for sentiment. He had been right those years ago in Paris. The man was not only an immoralist; he was a play-actor, a humbug. Tim Healy would come to be glad that today had happened; it renewed and breathed new life into his enmity.

At Wonersh that evening, Parnell told Katharine of the incident. 'Young Healy's a good man, none better, but in my own case he either adores or hates, and there's nothing in between. If it comes to a choice, I prefer his hatred.'

'Surely not!'

'When Healy is my enemy I at least know where I stand. Hatred can hardly change for the worse.'

The Special Commission began its work in September. Its briefing was vast: no less than to investigate all the allegations made by *The Times* in its series, 'Parnellism and Crime'. There

177

were to be more than four hundred and fifty witnesses, one of whom, to his own joy, was to be Captain W. H. O'Shea.

After the first day's hearing, Parnell asked his senior counsel, Sir Charles Russell: 'When do we get to the forgeries?'

'In a few months. February, perhaps.'

He had thought, a few weeks at the very most. '*How* long?'

'I believe,' Russell said, 'in keeping the good wine until the feast's end.'

'But February . . .'

'Come, sir, what kind of play is it that unmasks its villain in the first act?'

Russell was arrogant and a show-off. To him, a client was a barely necessary evil, an irritant that constantly came between him and his sport. In spite of his seigneurial flair for putting litigants in their place, he suspected that Parnell, given a chance, would oust him from centre-stage.

As they left the Royal Courts of Justice and crossed the Strand, Parnell said: 'A villain, you say? Is there one?'

Russell steered a course towards the Middle Temple. He walked with the lofty mien of one who had his sights on a destiny denied to lesser men. Parnell disliked affectation; it required time that might be employed more gainfully.

'Do you know a Richard Pigott?' Russell asked.

'I know *of* such a person. He lives by his wits. In Dublin, he is a person more despised than most.'

'Indeed?'

'Given the Dublin character, that is no mean achievement.'

'Well, sir, Mr Pigott is our man.'

'*Pigott?*'

'You really should attend more to gossip, Mr Parnell. It's an open secret that our fox is endeavouring to go to ground even before the hounds are on his scent. Let us hope he does not succeed. You find it amusing?'

Parnell was laughing softly to himself. He said: 'Forgive me. I had quite set my heart on the forger being someone else.'

As they parted, he asked: 'Why on earth did Pigott do such a stupid thing?'

'For his children,' Russell said.

A week or so later, when Parnell alighted from the train at Blackheath, Katharine was not waiting for him with the dog-cart, as usual. Instead, Mary was at the station entrance, a dark shawl held tight across her throat.

'Begging your pardon, sir, 'tis the old lady.'

'Mrs Woods?'

'She's dying, God help her. The mistress said I was to give you this. Good night, sir.'

She gave him a small cardboard box, then was gone into the darkness of the road to Wonersh. He knew what the box contained. Each morning, Katharine gave him a white rose to wear before the Special Commission. He went back into the station, crossed by the iron footbridge and waited for the up train.

The funeral had brought out the best in Willie; one would think there had never been a discordant word between Katharine and himself. When she wept as Aunt Ben's coffin was lowered into the ground, his manly arm was about her shoulders. When rain fell softly, he all but snatched an umbrella from one of the undertaker's men and held it tenderly over her head. He agreed with one of the lesser mourners that the old lady's ninety-seven was a tremendous age, without giving the least indication that he privately thought it a most inconsiderate age.

After the interment, the funeral party returned to the departed's home, The Lodge, for refreshments and the necessary legalities. One of Aunt Ben's rules had been that her rare visitors should not walk upon her polished floors, but should use the Turkish rugs instead, as if they were islands; today, her two Georgian halls, the one opening upon the next, echoed to the sound of feet hurrying towards the library for the reading of the will. As

179

the mourners were seated, they exchanged smiles. For the fourth time that morning, Anna came and kissed Katharine. Willie's sister, Mary, had journeyed from Paris. There were cousins, near and distant on both sides, the Woods and the O'Sheas.

The terms of the will were so brief as hardly to justify the occupation of the library. Aunt Ben's estate amounted to £145,000 in Consols and land in Gloucestershire. The Woods ceased to smile when the estate went in its entirety to Katharine; the O'Sheas followed their example when it was disclosed that the legacy had been left to her outside the provisions of her marriage settlement. Willie seemed perfectly content; either he did not grasp or would not believe that he would have no claim on her inheritance.

Katharine asked Anna if she would stay to lunch.

'I think not. I really haven't the inclination. Goodbye, Kate . . . Willie.'

There was no parting kiss. The other mourners left in a spectrum of coolness, all save Willie's sister, who said that she would come to lunch once she had sent a telegram to her mother at their home in the Avenue de Wagram. The rain had stopped, but the parkland surrounding The Lodge was a quagmire, and Katharine and Willie went the short distance to Wonersh by carriage. As they drove, Willie gave it as his opinion that the other mourners had shown poor sportsmanship. Certainly, he would have expected better of Anna.

'Would you, Willie?'

'There is no excuse for bad manners.'

The springs of the carriage creaked and rain from the sodden trees drummed upon the roof. Again, it occurred to her that his flair for never seeing from any point of view but his own verged upon genius.

She said: 'Willie, supposing that it was Anna who had been left a fortune, and if you and I had ended up with not a penny . . . would *you* have been sportsmanlike?'

He said, unhesitatingly and with utter sincerity: 'I think I can fairly say that I have always taken life's reverses as they came.'

Candour compelled him to add: 'Mind, I don't deny that to be a man of means at long last is not unpleasant.' His happiness was almost infectious.

She said: 'And *are* you a man of means, Willie?'

The day was overcast, but his face had the sun in it. 'Well, as good as. You know.'

'I am glad you think so.'

'My dear Kate, a wife's property —'

She said: 'Yes, dear, I know. It is no property at all; it belongs to her husband. Unless, of course, as in this case, it has been bequeathed to her outside of her marriage settlement.'

Willie's happiness ebbed. Surely, he thought, she could not mean to spoil his day. 'Now, Kate, look here —'

She patted his hand. 'Dearest Willie, I shall be generosity itself. As long as you are an agreeable and well-behaved Boysie, you shall have no cause for reproach.'

Really, the woman was extraordinary. 'And when have I not behaved agreeably?'

'Quite right,' she said. 'What can I be thinking of?'

At Wonersh, he helped himself to a glass of whisky to overcome the rigours of the funeral. When Katharine heard a bell jangling below stairs, she knew that his sister Mary had returned from the telegraph office. There was a matter that must be settled while she and Willie were still alone.

She asked: 'Willie, when shall you be testifying before the Commission?'

'Eh? Oh, next week sometime.'

'And on behalf of *The Times*?'

'Naturally. Why do you ask?'

She gave him her most disarming smile. 'Why? I thought that I might like to come along and see my Boysie in the witness box and hear what he has to say. How exciting it will be.'

There was in her smile a quality that put him not at ease. He did not care for the way she had said 'and hear what he has to say'. He looked down at the carpet as if it were quicksands. It

181

began to occur to him that he was no longer his own master.

When Mary came in and saw Willie's face she thought that, good-natured fellow that he was, he had taken Aunt Ben's death to heart.

'Call Captain William O'Shea!'

He had not expected that in the witness box he would be no more than six feet away from Parnell. He had never, he thought, seen such a look of hatred upon a human countenance. Parnell's eyes were fixed on him without blinking; they seemed to contain flecks of red. Willie flinched and shifted his gaze to a point above Parnell's head. He saw a familiar face. Katharine was sitting at the front of the public gallery. She smiled at him. It was a blank slate of a smile into which a beholder would write his own meaning. He searched it for a hint of warning. He looked back at Parnell, who was now savouring the fragrance of a white rose he wore in his buttonhole. As the Attorney-General came forward to ask his questions, Willie produced his gold eye-glasses. He had of late become short-sighted, but he flourished them with the air of a Regency dandy wielding a quizzing-glass. The years had not been kind to Willie; middle age sits naturally on some, but he seemed to be imprisoned in a corroded youth. Watching him as he lolled against the edge of the witness box, the correspondent of the *Dublin Daily Express* wrote that his 'well-oiled poll shone beautifully in the electric light'.

In reply to Sir Richard Webster, Willie spoke of the Park murders and their aftermath. He was asked about the signatures on *The Times* letters.

'I know nothing about signatures,' Willie said.

Webster said: 'I know that you are not an expert. But as far as you can say, in whose handwriting do you believe the two signatures to be?'

'My opinion is that they were signed by Mr Parnell.'

From Parnell, he heard an intake of breath that was a hiss. The

Attorney-General withdrew, and Sir Charles Russell took his place. Willie looked up at Katharine. She was no longer smiling. Her face told him that he had a choice; he could do his part in exposing Parnell before the world, thereby incurring the punishment it was in her power to inflict; or he could hold his tongue, embrace the kind of easeful life that had long been his due, and return to fight another day. He realised that Sir Charles had asked a question.

'I beg your pardon?'

Russell said: 'I asked you, Captain O'Shea, if, during your membership of the House of Commons, you were on friendly terms with Mr Parnell?'

Willie said: 'I was for a time. Then I changed my opinion of him.'

Russell looked at Parnell, who made a slight motion with his forefinger. It was a signal that the question was to be pressed. Willie was not to be allowed to make a flanking attack and then withdraw; he would either charge the guns or leave the field.

'At the suggestion of my client,' Russell said, 'I wish to know what it was that altered your good opinion.'

Timothy Healy, who was in court representing his own interests, received a violent dig in the ribs from Joseph Biggar. Willie looked from Russell to Katharine, whose face was darkening with anger. He needed only to say that Parnell and she were lover and mistress; then it would be over.

He said: 'Certain things came to my knowledge which absolutely destroyed the good opinion I had hitherto held of Mr Parnell.' He was on the edge of the precipice; it was as if the court held its breath. Parnell himself was daring him to speak.

He heard himself say: 'I wish to add that I believed Mr Parnell to be absolutely free from any connivance with outrage. I still did not think him implicated after I had changed my opinion of him.'

There was a sigh of almost palpable disappointment. Willie had sheered away from the edge.

Russell said: 'And yet you have said to the Attorney-General that you believed Mr Parnell's signature on *The Times* letter to be genuine. Do you stand by that answer?'

183

For Willie, the comedy was over; now he was intent only on making his exit. He replied, almost carelessly: 'When I first saw the letter in *The Times*, I did not think it genuine.'

It was one of Sir Charles Russell's principles never to be amazed; he nonetheless much enjoyed seeming so. 'Well, now!'

Willie endeavoured to be of assistance. 'Not that I thought that the handwriting was not genuine, which I did, but I did not think the letter was genuine.' As the advocate all but reeled, he added: 'I trust I make myself clear.'

Russell said: 'As crystal, sir.'

There was laughter in the courtroom. Willie's face reddened. As he made to step down, a new voice was heard. It spoke in a Cork accent.

Timothy Healy, upon his feet, said: 'Before the witness is dispensed with, I have a question, and it is of a personal nature.'

'Healy!' Parnell had spoken involuntarily and in alarm. Willie O'Shea could be made to bend under pressure; Healy was of tempered metal.

Healy gave no sign that he had heard his name uttered. He asked his question: 'Captain O'Shea, when you were parliamentary candidate for Galway, did not Mr Joseph Biggar and I oppose you most vigorously?'

Willie looked at him with disdain. 'The word I would prefer to use is "viciously".'

Healy said: 'Thank you, that is all.'

Willie hurried from the box, not noticing that Parnell's glare of hatred had been transferred from him to Tim Healy. Joseph Biggar again nudged the younger man. This time, he asked: 'Healy, what the hell was that about?'

The other did not reply, but smiled, cat-like, to himself. The question to O'Shea had itself been unimportant. Tim Healy had wished to show the adulterer that he possessed the power to unmask him whenever he chose. If he had spared him, it was not a matter of whim; Parnell and Home Rule were of one flesh; until they became separate, to destroy the one was to tear down the other.

184

As for Willie, he was on the evening boat-train for Dover. He had more than earned his share in the estate of the late Aunt Ben, but probate would take its snail-like course, and meanwhile he was short of funds. Through his mining contacts, he had obtained a commission to act as agent for a Madrid banking house. He was not averse to work in moderation and welcomed the prospect of a winter of Spanish sun.

It became his custom, while in Madrid, to walk from his lodgings to the Plaza Mayor and there enjoy a *cafe solo* and *tapas* while reading the three-day-old London papers. The Special Commission continued to sit, and Willie looked forward to learning more of *The Times* letters, forged or not. As the weather became colder, he moved from an outdoor table to the warm interior of the *bodega* in the basement of Butin on the Calle de Cuchilleros. It was there, as he opened his paper, that he saw at another table a man who trembled when he, in turn, looked up and saw Willie.

The man was in his middle fifties, stout, bald, round-shouldered and bearded. He affected an eyeglass. He was reading *The Times* and drinking beer. Willie knew him, either by sight or from his likeness, but the name eluded him. That the man recognised Willie was certain. He gulped down the remainder of his beer and called for the reckoning. Before the mystery could go unsolved for ever, Willie got to his feet.

'My dear sir, will you forgive the intrusion? Captain William O'Shea, at your service. Fact is, I believe we have met. Can it be so?'

The man's trembling became more violent. 'No, I think not. Excuse me.'

He flung coins on the table and went out. The devil take him, Willie thought as he went back to his seat and his own copy of *The Times*. The man's likeness was staring out at him. In the drawing, he was standing in what seemed to be a witness box and holding a piece of paper on which was written the single word 'hesitency'. His name was Richard Pigott.

TWELVE

The encounter, Pigott told himself, had been the wildest coincidence; no one could have known that he was in Spain. He had put up the previous evening at the Hotel Embajadores, calling himself Roland Ponsonby. He thought the name had a certain resonance; certainly, it was to be preferred to the porcine 'Pigott'. On arrival, he had telegraphed for money to his solicitor, whose name was Shannon. He trusted Mr Shannon; one Irishman would surely not inform upon another. As for so unexpectedly meeting the famous Captain O'Shea, it signified nothing. The money would arrive in the afternoon; meanwhile, he went to the Prado, visiting a church or two on the way back. He lit candles for his parents and the wife who had died, leaving his four sons motherless. He knelt, but the prayers would not come; his thoughts kept returning to the courtroom.

As he walked towards the witness box, he had heard Parnell say: 'The rat, caught in the trap at last.' It was really most unkind and unfair. Life was hard and a man had his way to make in the world. What mattered was that no one could point him out as a bad father.

Young Edward Houston of the Irish Loyal and Patriot Union had been of little help. When asked by Sir Charles Russell how he could have been sure that *The Times* letters were genuine, he had answered: 'Because of their intrinsic probability.' There had been sniggers at that. It was not a good start.

He, Pigott himself, had been too eager at the beginning. He had told the court, straight off, that he had not forged the letters. He was taken aback when the Attorney-General asked: 'Has anyone accused you of forging them?' Before he could answer properly, Sir Richard Webster had resumed his seat and in his place there was the overbearing and affected Sir Charles Russell.

First, this Russell had commanded Pigott to sit at a table, take a sheet of paper and write down a number of words. Long words, regular jaw-breakers. He had done as he was bid and wrote 'likelihood', 'inexcusable' and 'livelihood'. As he was returning to the witness box, he was recalled and asked to write another word, 'hesitency'. 'With a small "h", if you please,' Sir Charles had said.

Then, with the paper put to one side, Pigott was shown a letter he had written to Archbishop Walsh of Dublin warning him that there was a plot afoot to destroy Parnell. 'Why did you write to his Grace?' Sir Charles asked. 'Had you qualms of conscience because you knew that *The Times* letters would wreak such mischief?'

'I did not forge the letters,' Pigott had said.

He was muddled as to what had come next. There had been so many questions. Seated in the gloom of the cathedral of San Isidro, he opened his newspaper and held it close to the glow of the candles he had lit. He read the transcript:

> Q. If you did not forge the letters and in fact did not know of the letters, what was your purpose in writing to Archbishop Walsh?
> A. I cannot tell you at all.
> Q. Try.
> A. I cannot.
> Q. Try.
> A. I really cannot.
> Q. Try.
> A. It is no use.
> Q. But when you wrote the letter, you had locked up in your bosom a plan to foil the designs against Mr Parnell?

187

A. Had I?

Q. So you told the Archbishop. I have here your written word.

A. In that case, yes, I suppose I must have done.

Q. And could it not still be hermetically sealed within your bosom?

A. Oh, no, because it has gone away out of my bosom.

Pigott, who prided himself that he could take a joke as well as the next man, could not see why the court had rocked with laughter at this. Even Parnell had smiled, but of course, being a Protestant, he had not a drop of Irish blood in him, any more than the rest of them. They were laughing at his native simplicity and lack of guile. That was the measure of the Old Enemy; in an English court no Irishman had ever stood a chance.

There were more questions, a whole day of them, coming at him like midges; then Sir Charles Russell returned to the words that Pigott had written at his request. It seemed that he had made the same mistakes as were in the letters allegedly written by Parnell. 'Excusable' and 'hesitancy' had both been misspelled. Could Mr Pigott account for that?

'Yes,' he said calmly, 'as a matter of fact I can. Ever since the letters appeared, those misspellings have become famous. The world knew of them. In fact, I thought so much about it that the rightful spellings went clear out of my head, and the wrong spellings went into it.'

'And that is your explanation?' Sir Charles had asked.

'It may perhaps seem unlikely,' Pigott told him, 'but it is the gospel truth.'

'I could almost believe it,' Sir Charles said.

Pigott said: 'Sir, you may believe it.'

Without taking his eyes off his man, Sir Charles had stretched out a hand. Another lawyer – a Herbert Asquith, who was not a Sir but a plain Mister – gave him a sheaf of papers.

'These,' Sir Charles said, 'are letters written by you to sundry persons eight and more years ago. Mark the dates. Some of them

188

beg, on various pretexts, for money. Others my Lords may construe to be attempts at blackmail. In each one of them, either the word "hesitancy" or the word "inexcusable" has been misspelled. How do you account for that?'

There had been silence in the courtroom for a time, then Pigott said: 'My children will starve because of this.' Still, no one spoke. It seemed to him that the mood was accusatory. He had wanted only fairness. He said: 'I have never pretended to be very virtuous.'

No one had hindered him when he left the court. That evening, he went to the Alhambra Music Hall to see Dan Leno. When his name was called in court for the following day's sitting, he was on the Channel steamer bound for Calais and the journey south.

Now he left the Catedral de San Isidro and emerged, blinking, into the Calle de la Colegiata. By now, his money should have arrived. He walked back to the Hotel Embajadores and asked at the desk if there was a message for him. There was not, but two Spanish policemen were waiting. They had received a telegram from London authorising his arrest on a charge of perjury. His Irish solicitor, Mr Shannon, had not, after all, served him faithfully.

Pigott asked if he might be allowed to pack his bags. The policemen consented and followed him upstairs to his room. He went to a small handbag and took from it a pistol. Before he could be prevented, he put the muzzle in his mouth and blew the top of his head off. At the morgue, they discovered that he was wearing scapulars on which there was a cross and the intertwined letters *I.H.S.*

As Parnell and John Dillon arrived by hansom cab at Palace Yard, a great crowd surged to the railings. They cheered and waved their handkerchiefs and scarfs. They shouted 'Bravo' and 'Long live Parnell'. Some implored him only to touch their hands.

Dillon said: 'You have become the most popular man in all England.'

189

Parnell said: 'Yes, isn't it wonderful? And, if they could do so, they would be at my throat inside a week.'

'But aren't you moved? Not even in the slightest?'

'Why should I be? It isn't I they are cheering, but the vindication of British justice in acquitting me.'

In the chamber an hour later, he rose to contribute to a debate. As he did so, Gladstone also was on his feet. It was the signal for both government and opposition to follow suit. Their homage was thunderous. Gladstone bowed to him. 'Give us another election,' his look said, 'and your day will be at hand.' Their new idol stood, seemingly indifferent to the applause. 'He has no heart,' Timothy Healy said.

Parnell heard him. Without looking around, he said: 'Healy, I did not ask them to rise. Come to that, I did not ask *you* to rise.'

As the cheering persisted, it occurred to him that whereas the Irish were ruled by their religion, the English bowed down and worshipped the law as if it were a god, and when one law became obsolete they made another and knelt before it with the same idolatry. There were times when he derided the Irish peasants as rabble, and yet in the middle of a crowd in a country town he felt a warmth that was absent at this moment, as if Katey were smiling at him across a street a moment before they met. The English had thought he had written the letters; now they were applauding him because he had not done so. They might as well have shouted themselves hoarse that Gladstone had not beaten his wife or broken into a pawnbroker's.

The applause subsided. Parnell spoke briefly, as he had intended, making not the smallest reference to the ovation. Later, he caught a train to Brighton where Katharine and he had taken a house. Wonersh Lodge had been her home; Number 10, Walsingham Terrace, she said, would be theirs. On the journey down, he thought again of the House rising and of its cheers. Beneath his disdain, he detected what for him was an unaccustomed emotion. It was fear. Adoration alarmed him. It could change only for the worst. Cheering, he thought, was not dissimilar to the baying of hounds.

Katharine was waiting on the platform at Brighton, discernible amid a confusion of scaffoldings and builders' rubble. The station was being rebuilt and expanded. It was Parnell's latest passion to make detailed plans of the new structure, including the width and depth of its roof span, from observation and his own measurements. He saw nothing incongruous in his intention to build a scaled-down replica in Avondale to serve as a cattle shed.

A porter offered to find them a carriage. 'Hansom or brougham, sir?'

He blew his whistle twice. One blast for a hansom, two blasts for a brougham. On the way home, she asked about his return to the Commons. 'Was there a great commotion?'

'There was a kind of fuss.' She made a face; she was hungry for details. Instead, he said: 'What of the house? Are you settling in? Is it too much for you?'

She told him that the children had spent the day by the sea. To the west of the new house, cornfields stretched all the way to Shoreham harbour; from a back window the little church at Aldrington was visible against the Downs. It was a perfect location for children or a convalescent in need of sea air.

She said: 'I have had a letter from Willie.'

'Impertinent?'

'Not in the least. Since Aunt died, I am back in his good books. He signs himself "Boysie" again.'

Parnell made a small, contemptuous noise. Against all reason, his jealousy of Willie still lurked.

She said: 'He is coming home from Spain.'

He sighed. 'Damn the fellow. Shall we never be rid of him?'

'Sooner than you perhaps think.' She had the satisfied smile of a woman who has solved a particularly irksome household problem. 'I intend to make Willie a gift. I thought of twenty-five thousand pounds.'

'So much? You mean, then, to buy him body and soul?'

191

She said: 'Willie never had a soul that I noticed, except perhaps on Sundays. But the money may help to rid me of his body. All he has to do is allow me to go into court and name one of the women in his life. Heaven knows there have been so many of them.'

He shook his head. 'He'll never let you go. He hates me too much.'

She smiled knowingly. 'Not as much as he loves money. I know him . . . he'll agree.'

Katharine's letter telling Willie of the move to Brighton passed him in mid-France. From Paris, he sent a telegram saying that he would call upon her and the 'chicks' on the morrow at Wonersh Lodge. He was profoundly shocked on going to Eltham to find the house locked and the windows shuttered. A few relic-hunters roamed through the garden, scavenging. Willie's ears burned on hearing one of them say: 'The great Mr Parnell didn't leave much, did he?' They were people of the lower orders. When one of them looked at him, curious to see a person of quality in the garden, Willie said carelessly, without knowing why: 'There may be cricket stumps at the back of the house.'

As he walked to the station, his mind was prey to an absurd fancy. He had been cheated of his due; Kate had taken the old woman's money and gone abroad. He would never see her again, any more than he would set foot in Eltham. He turned as he walked, conscious that he was looking back at Wonersh for the last time. Perhaps, money or no money, she was with *him*. Willie had read of Parnell's vindication and accounted himself fortunate to be out of the country, away from the madness. He had written to Joseph Chamberlain: *I begin to despair. Will he never get his deserts?* In reply, Chamberlain, back from his extended American honeymoon, had invited Willie to come to dinner.

Perhaps Kate had overcome the coolness with her sister and was staying at Buckingham Gate. He went direct to Anna Steele's house. She was not at home. A servant told him that Mrs O'Shea

192

had not been a visitor these many weeks. He left a note, conscious of the indignity of confessing that he had no notion of his wife's whereabouts. That evening, to his surprise, Anna came to his rooms.

'My dear Anna, what a pleasure. Do take a pew. A glass of sherry?'

She nodded. Willie was a creature of habit, and, as anxious as he was to know about Katharine, he treated his sister-in-law, as he did all handsome women, to a swift appraisal. She was older than Kate and taller, with the same gypsyish looks. She had kept her figure, perhaps because she had not been troubled with children. Her face had a fine tightness over the cheekbones. Her lower lip was full and protruded slightly. Biteable, Willie thought. Her husband, Lieutenant-Colonel Charles Steele of the 17th Lancers, had died five years previously in India, not much to her grief. They had parted after only a week of marriage, and she was nowadays escorted to dinner parties and occasions by this gentleman and that. Her name had not been touched by rumour, and Kate believed her to be disinclined towards adventure. Willie disagreed; he divided good-looking women into two kinds: those who admitted that they enjoyed men, and those who denied it and were liars.

When he had completed his assay of Anna, he raised his glass to her. 'I'm delighted to see you. I was under the impression that we were no longer on the best of terms.'

She said: 'Did that surprise you? Aunt Ben was my aunt as well as Kate's.'

He gave her his best smile. 'My dear girl, I'm wholly on your side . . . couldn't sympathise more.'

Oddly, she seemed relieved rather than merely glad. 'I'm glad to hear that, Willie. And I know that you will bear no malice.'

'Malice? Why should I?'

She put her glass to one side. 'Willie, I know I do my reputation no good by coming here, but your note was urgent. Besides, I thought that you and I should talk. I wanted to —'

193

He asked: 'Do you know where Kate is?'

She went on as if he had not spoken. 'I wanted to make it quite clear that in our contesting the will there will be absolutely no enmity towards you.'

Dismay laid a familiar hand on him. 'Contesting the will?'

'The family and I are bringing suit.'

He might have been an animal she had struck. She glared at him; she would not be in the wrong.

She said: 'Well, what would you expect? It was monstrous that Aunt Ben should have left all she possessed to Kate and not a farthing to us. Our solicitor says that we have an excellent case, even if it takes years.'

'Years?'

Deep in his gut he had known. He had played the game of pretence, but his wiser self was not deceived. Always, the prize had been there, barely out of reach, and at the end as unattainable as ever. A man's luck did not change.

Anna said: 'We shall claim that there has been – what is the word for it? – undue influence.' She again became defensive. 'You may blame Kate, not me or the others. She cheated you as well as me. We don't want all of the money, we never did . . . only our fair share. Now she has every penny, or thinks she has. To share with him.'

He had been half-listening, staring into a future that was no better than the past. Now his head came around.

She said: 'To share with Parnell.'

He would not have it. 'No.'

'Willie, you know it is so. She is his mistress, and she deceived me as well as you. She swore to me that it was no more than friendship, that she was making use of him so that your star might rise. She betrayed us both.'

He would not listen. He would oblige her to leave.

Now she was standing over him, the words coming in a torrent. 'Are you insane? All London knows it . . . the *world* knows it. At this moment, she is with him in a house in Brighton. And she

194

bought you, bought you with promises. All these years, you were cajoled with talk of Aunt Ben's inheritance, of how if you and she were to be rich there must be no impropriety, no scandal. I heard her, I was there. Well, now she will never be rich . . . no, nor you. Greed has undone her. She betrayed us both, and she will pay.'

Of a sudden, her hatred was a match for his. With a great joy, he realised that he was no longer alone. He could say what he wished, knowing that her hunger was equal to it and more.

He said, eagerly: 'Yes. Yes, she swore to me . . .'

'Falsely. Of course she did!'

'. . . that she was innocent, and I was the blackest scoundrel to doubt her word. I believed her. No . . . no, I knew, I always knew, and yet I denied it for her sake and the children's, even when she and that devil were plotting against me. It was not enough for him to take my wife and make her his harlot . . . he must drag my life in the dirt as well. God, what I could have amounted to!'

She brushed past his self-pity. 'So what would you have me do? Look on while our family's money goes to her and him and their children? We lead good lives and go poor, while they can —'

Now he was angry and a little afraid. 'Children? Children? What do you mean?'

There was contempt for him on her face. She said, brutally: 'I am telling you what you know and pretend not to. That Clare and the baby Frances and the little one who died . . . all three are his.'

Anna knew that she had gone too far. His face became contorted with rage. 'No. No, I'll not have that. The children are mine.'

'Willie, they are not. The —'

'Liar, liar, I say they are!'

He grasped her by the shoulders, his thumbs pressing into her flesh. He shook her so that her sudden gasp became a hiccup. His face, one she had never seen, glared into hers. There was spittle on his lips. Of the blustering Willie O'Shea, whom Kate knew as Boysie and whom they had both once looked upon with fond disparagement, there was no sign.

195

She said, in terror: 'Willie, do you mean to kill me? What are you doing? Please, I beg, don't hurt me.'

His grip eased and his face became his own again. He said, more calmly: 'Why would I hurt you? She is the one I will hurt.'

When he made to remove his hands from her shoulders, she took him by the arms so that they were holding each other. She thought that for an instant she had come close to death. It had aroused her. It was more than the danger; it was the room, their safety, his roughness, their enemy in common.

She looked up into his face. 'Willie, shall I help you? Would you like me to? Very well, then. Let us hurt her.'

Her mouth was open. Willie remembered his inventory of ten minutes before. His eyes were upon the lower lip that he had thought to be biteable.

At that moment in the house in Brighton, Parnell and his harlot were spending a quiet evening. He had mentioned that he was descended from the English poet, Thomas Parnell, who had died in 1718. 'And so I, too, am a poet.'

Katharine said: 'I do not think that quite follows, dear.'

He took pen and paper and began to write. When he had finished, he said: 'I composed this while digging in the garden today, and I think it as good as any of Tom Parnell's stuff.'

She doubted that in his life he had ever read a line of poetry, including his ancestor's. She took the paper from him and read:

> The grass shall cease to grow,
> The river's stream to run,
> The stars shall ponder in their course,
> No more shall shine the sun;
> The moon shall never wane or grow,
> The tide shall cease to ebb and flow,
> Ere I shall cease to love you.
>
> Chas. Parnell.

Meanwhile, in the bedroom of Willie's new flat off the Haymarket, Anna was vigorously deploying her best resources, the admired

196

nether lip included, to embolden the battle-weary Hussar for a second mounted attack.

'There is no great trick in having twenty people to dinner,' Joseph Chamberlain told his bride. 'To entertain only one guest is the rarest of accomplishments.'

At twenty-four, Mary Chamberlain, née Endicott, was less than twice her husband's age. She had so adored her father, who was the American Secretary of War, that she could not see a man of her own age without wanting to box his ears. Joseph Chamberlain had European manners – his monocle had been the talk of Washington, D.C. – and, like her father, he was a self-made man. To her delight, he did not out of false modesty conceal from her that he was quite unscrupulous. He was not used to American artlessness, and she startled him by accepting his proposal at the first time of asking. She had had misgivings that he might not prove as passionate a lover as she would have liked and was more than prepared to make allowances, but on their honeymoon she discovered what a more worldly upbringing might have led her to suspect: that middle-aged men were more persevering. He adored her; she responded, especially when he made her his fellow conspirator. She combined an all-consuming curiosity with tirelessness and her native belief that the Methodist deity had created days of thirty hours each.

Chamberlain told her that Willie O'Shea was both indiscreet and dangerous, but that he and the Captain were bound together by a shared passion: the destruction of Parnell. Thus warned, she was at her most vivacious when Willie came to dinner.

Anna's revelations of the previous evening had put him out of sorts. His appetite was poor; he stared at his place and would not have spoken except that Mary Chamberlain plied him with charm and questions in equal measure. When dessert was over, he said: 'I must apologise. I fear I have been a poor guest.'

As far as natural resilience was concerned, Mary Chamberlain could have been the model for Jo March in the late Mrs Alcott's chronicles. She smiled and said: 'Not at all, Captain. Your silence has been positively poetic.'

Chamberlain's eyes flickered towards the door in a signal that she should withdraw.

She said: 'I think I shall leave you gentlemen to your port and cigars. When I see you again, Captain O'Shea, I know you will be cheered up past recognition. It is a gift my Joe has.' As a manservant held the door open for her, she said: 'You may serve your master.'

When host and guest were quite alone, Chamberlain went through the ritual of lighting a cigar. 'Well, my friend, whatever it is, it seems to weigh heavily. Is it to be shared?'

Miserably, Willie said: 'She has betrayed me.'

'She? Do you mean your wife?'

'You have heard, I suppose.'

Chamberlain was not so reckless as to betray information that Willie might not possess. 'More. Say more.'

Willie said: 'She is Parnell's mistress.'

'Oh, that.' Chamberlain was airiness itself. 'I believe I heard something of the sort, but I never pay heed to scandal if it affects my friends. It is true, then? When did you find out?'

'I don't know.'

Chamberlain, reaching for the decanter, stared at him in bemusement.

Willie stammered: 'I mean that I suspected . . . then I was given assurances . . . then I suspected again. I have been treated most shamefully.'

'I see. You knew and yet you did not know. How vexatious for you.'

Vexatious, Willie thought, was hardly the word for it. He said: 'I have even been told that my two youngest children and the babe who died were not mine at all, but his.'

'My dear fellow!'

'That, at least,' Willie said, 'is the vilest of lies. I do not believe

198

it and never shall. I impressed as much on my informant..'

Chamberlain sat with an arm flung carelessly over the back of his chair. He saw no need to speak. Willie, unaided, was moving towards the destination which his host had not dared to name.

'I am a simple man. I cannot comprehend baseness in others. When at last I could no longer avoid the truth, I stayed my hand. There was the expectation of a legacy, money that would at last have enabled me to provide for my poor chicks. After all, what kind of father would I be to endanger their prospects with a scandal? So I held my tongue, and in the end it was all for nothing. The lawyers have it.'

'The money?'

'It is in dispute.'

'Oh, my poor fellow.' Joe Chamberlain could not have been more solicitous. 'At least now, if it is any poor consolation, your tongue no longer requires to be held.'

'Pardon me?'

'Or so you seem to be saying.'

'Ah.'

Willie's eyes glazed over. In the Hussars, his skill at taking a double fence had been the envy of his fellows. As if not wishing to seem over-lavish with her bounty, nature had withheld from him the agility to clear two mental jumps at once.

Chamberlain, seeing Willie cantering in his wake, performed a turn-about. He said: 'No, I must have a care. Let me not invite the fate of one so imprudent as to step between husband and wife. Instead I shall think out loud, and my thought is that the boldest course is sometimes the wisest.'

Willie had no wish to seem obtuse, but he wished the fellow would say whatever it was he was driving at. Meanwhile, he endeavoured to look profound and replied: 'You would say so?'

Chamberlain did not look at Willie, but held his glass up to the candlelight. A spot of red swam on his cheek. 'In the case of the man Parnell, he may be triumphant now, but he will one day press the wrong adversary too hard. And then, my friend, what a

199

fall there will be. There is a saying, is there not? "He who smashes Parnell smashes Parnellism." Now there indeed would be boldness!'

A shiver went through Willie. Out of nowhere, it had come to him what he must do. His shackles had at last been cast aside, leaving him free to bring down Parnell and be revenged on both of them. He looked at Joe Chamberlain who was regarding him through a coil of cigar smoke. The cure-all for his ills was as clear as the crystal glass in his own hand, and yet it had not dawned on Joe Chamberlain, who was supposed to be a kind of genius. Not for the first time, it occurred to Willie that it had been the world's loss when he resigned his seat.

Chamberlain saw a smile start upon his guest's face. His task done, he said: 'I say, my dear fellow, might I change the subject and be so inhospitable as to plead that I am as yet an affectionate bridegroom?'

Willie thought: Now what the deuce is he trying to say?

His host came to the point. 'Might we, do you think, join Mrs Chamberlain in the drawing room?'

Why had he not said so in the first place? 'By all means,' Willie said. 'A pleasure.'

He was on his feet, anxious to establish himself in his hostess's eyes as a paragon among guests and the life of every table. He had entered the Chamberlains' house as the most miserable of mortals; now, and thanks entirely to his own resourcefulness, he would leave it as the happiest.

Because it was Christmas Eve, the process-server was particularly anxious to have his work done and get home to his family. On calling at the house on Walsingham Terrace, he told Mary that he had a paper requiring the urgent attention of her mistress. Mary directed him to the road that led to Mile Oak, and there, a half mile or so along, he came upon a woman sitting in a trap and wrapped up against the cold. She was watching a bearded man spurring his horse to a gallop over a rise of the Downs.

'I beg your pardon, madam. Would you be Mrs O'Shea, by any chance? Mrs Katharine O'Shea?'

'I am.'

'Glad to have found you, ma'am. One of your servants said you might be hereabouts. I have this to serve upon you.'

Katharine looked at the paper. 'To serve, you say? What is it?'

'Copy of a petition for divorce, ma'am. O'Shea versus O'Shea.'

She took the paper and sat, too stunned to speak. The rider came up, reining in his horse. With a gladdening of the heart, the process-server recognised him; he was as good as home for Christmas.

The man said: 'What is it, Kate? Who is this person?'

The process-server asked: 'Mr Parnell, sir?'

'My name is Stewart.'

'Yes, sir, I have that name down as well.' He had produced a second paper and gave it to Parnell. 'Served upon you, sir, as co-respondent.' He raised his hat. 'My best respects, sir . . . ma'am.'

He turned and went back the way he had come, towards the sea. He was bow-legged. Parnell looked at the petition, then at Katharine.

'Oh, Charley.'

At least, Parnell thought, the process-server had been merciful. He had desisted from extending to them the compliments of the season.

THIRTEEN

It seemed absurd in a man so tiny in stature, but Joseph Biggar was shrinking.

So Michael Davitt thought when he met him in the company of Healy, Dillon and others in Sharkey's snuggery. Not only was Biggar becoming smaller, but he had a hacking cough and there was a look on his face that Davitt thought familiar. He had seen it on other faces in the past, but had always chosen to forget what it portended. Now he remembered and knew that Joe Biggar would die soon.

Davitt was a teetotaller, but he felt protected, when in London, to be in an Irish public house. The city at large was the camp of the enemy; while in it, he half-expected to be taken as a spy. That morning, he had kept an appointment with Parnell on the terrace at Westminster, and he was no less uneasy than he had been almost ten years ago when, as a ticket-of-leave man, he had met Parnell in the Members' Corridor. Today, the river shone; across it the Lambeth slums, dark against the sun, were kept at bridges' length. Women of fashion took tea on the terrace. All about, there were men who had never known hunger. It was true what Dickens had written: the Commons was the best club in London; certainly, it was the most privileged. As Parnell had come towards him, Davitt had seen a man who was more in his natural element here than in Ireland.

'He granted you an audience?' Healy said with a twist to his mouth. 'Well, weren't you the honoured one!'

Dillon said: 'I'd say it's the first time he's been at Westminster in a month. He no longer runs the party; *we* do. He hasn't made a speech in Ireland in four years. If the sky fell, we wouldn't know where to find him.'

Sexton said in a voice that was a nudge: 'And if we did know, we daren't let on.'

Biggar said: 'We're in the . . . the . . . ' He tried to draw breath and had a choking fit. He gasped: '. . . in the hands of a madman.'

In Ireland, the news of the imminent divorce case had come like a summer storm: at first, a far-off rim of darkness, then a great looming of clouds, one tumbling upon the other until the sun was gone and the sky could hold no more. As always and as in all things, the Irish were divided. There were those who held that wherever there was smoke there must be fire; the majority, however, looked back to the fiasco of the Pigott forgeries and believed that here was yet another English plan to dishonour their Chief and bring him down. If the Saxon tyrant could not do it one way, he would find another. As the months passed and the case impended, Davitt's people – the countryfolk, the tenant farmers, the old Land Leaguers – looked to him for reassurance. Like him, they were of peasant stock; generations of priests had dinned it into them, perhaps because they themselves were celibate, that unchastity was the vilest sin of all and adultery its most loathsome manifestation. It was, after all, only human to deny to others what was forbidden to oneself.

Davitt's countrymen might have tolerated a furtive lust, spoken of only out of the sides of mouths. They would not, however, accept a leader who, whether from brazenness or stupidity, had committed the sin of being found out. Davitt himself, as incorruptible as Robespierre, would not ask them to condone by silence. He had come to London expressly to see Parnell and demand that he declare himself. As they sat on the terrace and tea was ordered, Davitt realised that several of the women guest were staring at Parnell with a naked and unflinching sexuality. The most abandoned creature in Mayo, he thought, would show more seemliness.

Parnell, he saw at once, was as arrogant as ever.

Davitt had, straight away, come down to business. 'In bringing suit for divorce, Captain O'Shea has named you. My people want to know what's going on and where it's leading.'

Parnell affected to be amused. 'Your . . . people? Are you saying that my private life is their concern?'

'Your leadership is.'

'Is it?' The voice was flat and barren of interest. 'My leadership will not be touched upon. Tell your . . . your people that they may sleep easy.'

The contempt in his voice was undisguised. Davitt kept his temper. He had had to scrape together the expenses of his journey to London, and he had not come so far to be treated as if he were a tradesman brandishing a bill.

He said: 'I see. And with that there's an end to it? The book is closed?'

Parnell caught the eye of one of the women who were staring at him. He looked at her coldly, until, with a small, shrill laugh, she found the Thames to be of more interest. To Davitt, he said: 'If O'Shea's case comes into a court of law – and I take leave to doubt that it ever will – you may rest assured that it will be shown that the dishonour and discredit are not on my side.'

'I have your word for that?'

Parnell raised an eyebrow. 'Naturally. Since I have said it, it is my word.'

Davitt, smarting from the patronage, thought that the audience was at an end. To his surprise, Parnell had not finished. His voice was suddenly angry.

'They could not destroy me with public scandal, so now they attack my private self by tarnishing a woman's good name.' He had spoken loudly; at a neighbouring table, heads turned.

204

'If they only knew what a broken-kneed horse they are riding.'

Davitt asked: 'Do you mean Willie O'Shea?'

'A spavined beast that will never see the starting point. I have his measure.'

He uttered a small, sardonic laugh, as if rebuking himself for wasting speech upon Willie O'Shea. Tea was brought. They talked about Irish matters, then Parnell had walked with his guest to the omnibus stop at the corner of Broad Sanctuary.

As they waited, Davitt asked: 'If O'Shea persists in his suit, what of your comrades? Will they stand firm?'

Parnell had looked at him as if his hearing was at fault. 'My what, did you call them?'

'Your stalwarts, then. Dillon, Sexton, Healy and the rest of them . . . no fear of them breaking ranks?'

Parnell saw a bus approaching. He replied quickly. 'Davitt, if I suffered your catechising, it was because there are those to whom you must answer. The people you have named are answerable to *me*. Healy? Healy, did you say? I would as soon solicit the opinion of a sewer-rat.'

Davitt smiled for the first time. 'I'll tell him you said so.'

Now, in Sharkey's snuggery, he kept his word. As he repeated the sneer, Tim Healy flushed angrily. Davitt took note that none of the others smiled in the Irish manner. All was not well, he thought, if they had lost their taste for malice.

Davitt told Healy: 'I don't say it to carry tales. The man despises you, and I'm asking why.'

Healy's voice was tight with pride. 'Because I know him for what he is.' He had come to thrive upon Parnell's contempt.

'Ach, for Christ's sake,' Biggar said, trying to catch his breath. 'It's in the bloody opera you ought to be, young Healy. You've become a right whooring prima donna.'

He started to cough. In spite of all, he was Parnell's friend. If he opposed him, he would do so now as in the past: broadside on, his guns spitting fire. In his life, he had not held a grievance;

his quarrels were as quickly over with as fiercely fought, and he had come to be out of patience with Tim Healy's bravely-borne anguish.

'And yet,' Davitt said, ignoring Biggar's outburst, 'for all your poor opinion of him, you're still his creature.'

'Yes.' Healy's reply was instant.

'Why? What's the magic?'

'The magic,' Healy said, 'is that what we want for Ireland has become flesh of his flesh. As long as it remains so, then yes, I am what you are pleased to call his creature.' He looked at the others in the snuggery. 'I am *one* of his creatures. God in heaven, why else do you think we allowed him to force Willie O'Shea upon us in Galway? He made us eat the dirt of the road, and for what? He thought it was the price of O'Shea's wife.'

'True, Tim,' Sexton said. 'It's true for you.'

Davitt looked at them in dismay.

'And all for what?' Healy went on. 'Now the man he's put horns on has spiked his guns.'

Davitt said: 'Less than an hour ago, I had Parnell's word for it that as far as Mrs O'Shea is concerned he's guiltless.'

'You what?' Joseph Biggar could not believe that Parnell would stoop to an outright lie, except as he himself would and frequently had done, for the worthy purpose of deceiving a husband. He made to say more, but in his indignation he had drawn too deep a breath; his lungs rasped and tore.

Healy said, mockingly: 'He denied it? To be sure he would!'

'He assured me,' Davitt told them, 'that the dishonour and discredit would not be on his side.'

'Ah, that's different,' Dillon said.

'How is it?' Healy's manner was belligerent. He would not let Parnell be shown as less than a brazen liar. 'How is it different?'

'Adultery is a fact,' Dillon said. 'Honour is a matter of opinion.'

Davitt would have no truck with niceties. Whether because of a plain lie or an artful evasion, he had come within an aim's ace of returning to Mayo to swear on his honour that Parnell was innocent.

He said, angrily: 'To hell with whatever it is. If I've been made a fool of . . .'

Biggar stood, holding the table for support. His already hunched back was further bent as a coughing fit racked his frame. He swayed, and the table rocked. He said of it: 'The leg's bockety.'

John Dillon put an arm around his shoulders. 'Joe, you're sick.'

'Jesus, don't I know it? Give me a wee minute; then I'll go to my bed.'

'Right, Joe. Take your time. I'll see you safe home.'

Biggar said: 'Go 'long with you . . . I mean my bed in Belfast.' The spasm was easing; he was beginning to recover his breath. He gave them a crooked grin. 'Do you know, the cold fish he is, I'll lay odds on that he won't even come to my funeral.'

It was extraordinary, she thought, that Willie could have been so reckless.

She watched Frank Lockwood for the aeon he took to read the enquiry agent's report. He had a mannerism that threatened to drive her to distraction: while reading, he repeatedly drew a forefinger very slowly down one cheek from eye socket to jawbone as if tracing a chalk line.

As the finger began its tenth journey, she said, abruptly: 'When I engaged the agent, I thought it was time and money wasted. I —'

He said: 'Presently.'

She waited. When he had finished reading, he laid the report face down on his desk, stood, walked to the window and looked out. There was a growler waiting at the kerb below. He saw a man's lower arm resting on its sill and wondered if his client had been so imprudent as to come for her appointment in the company of the co-respondent. It would not surprise him. Her husband, almost on the eve of his action for divorce, had provided the defence with prima facie evidence of his own adultery. Frank Lockwood was inured to human foolishness; it had, after all, brought him

207

to the brink of a knighthood. The unwisdom of Captain O'Shea, however, was on a scale not far short of the monumental.

Lockwood, who had a fondness for understatement, turned to Katharine, gave her the quick smile of a friend, and said: 'The Captain has been indiscreet.'

She said: 'As I say, I thought that to employ an enquiry agent so late in the day was to take a chance in a million.'

But you were cleverly advised, Lockwood thought. He picked up the report and said aloud: 'This Mrs Anna Steele who was seen to visit your husband on four nocturnal occasions . . . she is not known to you?'

Katharine said: 'Oh, yes. She is my sister.'

Lockwood stared at her.

She had been shocked and hurt by the discovery that Anna was the latest of Willie's women. There was, admittedly, bad blood over Aunt Ben's will, but Anna had often and tediously declared that, when it came to gratification of the senses, men were no better than beasts of the field. It had to be a measure of her ill-will towards Katharine that she had submitted, not once, but on four known occasions, to the ordeal of bed with Willie. Katharine had wept that her sister could have been so vengeful, but Charley had dried her tears and pointed to the silver lining. As far as the divorce was concerned, he said, her husband had cooked his own goose, and to a turn.

Lockwood was taken aback by her apparent calmness. She seemed to be unaware that if her own sister was involved, then the proceedings threatened to become as lubricious as the case, four years earlier, of Sir Charles Dilke, M.P., who had taken his present and past mistresses to bed simultaneously, the better to indulge in sexual practices of a cross-Channel nature.

His client had the demeanour of a schoolgirl in a classroom as she asked, apropos of the enquiry agent's report: 'Is that what you would call evidence?'

He inclined his head. In twenty-three years of marriage, Willie had spent less than four hundred nights under his connubial roof.

In law, that alone was hardly a presumption of adultery, nor was there corroboration for Katharine's claim that over the years she had known of seventeen specific instances of infidelity on his part. 'But if this report is attested to,' Lockwood said, 'his Lordship could do no other than deny the petition.'

Still the schoolgirl, she all but clapped her hands. 'Thank heaven. I shall be set free.'

'Free? My dear lady . . .'

'At last I shall be quit of him.'

He said, as gently as he could manage: 'I am afraid that is not possible.'

Her delight was not quite dispelled. She knew that Frank Lockwood liked to put his clients at ease with a witticism or a piece of wordplay; mischief was part of his stock in trade. She clutched at the possibility that he was joking now.

There was no smile to answer hers. He said, still softly: 'Mrs O'Shea, on this new evidence, you can block your husband's petition. But it will be stalemate. In the eyes of the court, you are both guilty, and so an action brought by either side could not possibly succeed.'

It had been her one sustaining hope, and now it was crushed. She said, almost with a moan: 'Are you saying that I am to remain tied to him? Then may my death be not long.'

He said: 'The alternative, I am afraid, would be unacceptable.'

'I have a choice, then?'

'You can let the case go undefended.'

She almost laughed. 'And be beaten? By him? And see Mr Parnell ruined? Never.'

She stood to leave. Lockwood rose, too, and picked up from his desk the agent's report. He did not proffer it, but it was hers to take.

He said: 'Well, then?'

She hesitated only for a moment. 'Use it. Defend me. Protect him.'

When she joined Parnell in the brougham, she took his hand

and said, with a false lightness: 'Yes, my love, it is as we thought. Willie has been very foolish indeed, and now he must pay for it. He is not, after all, going to be rid of me!'

He looked at her sharply. They were passing the site of an extension of the new electric tube railway, and the odours of tar and oil gave her an excuse to put a handkerchief to her face. 'What an uproar,' she said. Then she cried openly. It was not simply that she would be tied to Willie until one of them died; now she and Charley could never be married. Their existence would be even more stealthy than before, for the divorce hearing would focus every eye upon them. They would be social outcasts and yet still be ruled by society's laws.

He made her go over what Lockwood had said. She told a tale poorly, and it took him a while to piece it together. When he had assured Michael Davitt that honour would be on his side, it had not been a bluff. When he had met Katey, he was a bachelor. At Cambridge, there had been an affair with a girl named Daisy, the daughter of a fruit farmer. She was sixteen, and for a time kisses sufficed; then he begged her for more. He, too, was young. He told her that if she loved him she would yield; when she did so, he said that if she had been the chaste person he took her for, she would have refused. His passion chilled; with the terrible morality of youth, he thrust her from him. It was the oldest story in creation, but it had a sequel. By coincidence he was strolling upon a bank of the Cam at the moment when her body was taken from the water. She had done it, he knew, because of him. His remorse made him a prey to nightmares; when he was at home in Avondale, the dead girl came to him from across the sea; his cries awoke the house. The years dulled the edges of his conscience, but as far as women were concerned he was circumspect. In America, when Miss Woods refused him, he was almost relieved. There was no other woman until the day, ten years ago, when he and Katey had first met in Palace Yard. Her marriage was over in all but name, and neither she nor Parnell was held back by moral ties. O'Shea, on the other hand, was a philanderer, a walking phallus; and yet it was he, the

210

hypocrite, who now played the part of the betrayed spouse. The court and – more importantly, Ireland – must be told where the true dishonour lay. He knew beyond doubt that the adoring Irish would never desert him, but they deserved to know that their adoration had not been misplaced.

The brougham brought them to Thomas's Hotel, where she would stay until the case was over. Parnell, who had declined to instruct counsel on his own behalf, went to his old rooms in Keppel Street. There was mail for him, including a package heavy for its size; it was from his brother John and contained a specimen of quartz from the Avonbeg River near its confluence with the Avonmore, the scene of Thomas Moore's *The Meeting of the Waters*. He put it in the black bag that always accompanied him; on his return to Brighton, he would make an assay. He thought of the ring that over the years he had lined with Wicklow gold; it was to have been Katherine's wedding band. Now, still married to O'Shea, she would have no use for it.

At that moment, he made his mind up. He thought of his followers: the party members and the Irish people at large. They would, as ever, stand by him. He bathed, dressed for the evening, hailed a cab and went to Thomas's Hotel. When she came down-stairs, he called for another cab.

'Charley, where are we going?'

'Where else, but to dinner?'

To her dismay, they alighted at Claridge's. In the sitting room, a string quintet was playing. Conversations broke off as he and Katey were shown to a table that was out of the way.

He said to the head waiter: 'No, that won't do at all. Why not that one?'

The man bowed and led them to a table in the middle of the room. Katherine heard a woman say: 'Well, really.'

She knew that she was blushing. She whispered: 'Charley, this is too bad of you.' When they were seated, she said: 'We make ourselves public. We shall give scandal.'

He was unconcerned. He said, calling her by the pet name he

211

had given her: 'My dearest Queenie, already we are an appetiser for the world's table. Tomorrow, the main course will be served, and the day after, the dessert. Think what a banquet they will make of us.'

It was cruel of him, she thought, to taunt her with what she most dreaded. She said: 'Don't.'

He said: 'Do you fear it so much?'

'Charley, I'm not inhuman. Of course I do. The courtroom, the questions, the faces. What they may say of us. And yet I think I could bear it ten times over if it were not that at the end of it all I shall still be his.' She caught sight of his face and thought she saw pity. She wanted to touch his hand, but knew that their every action was under scrutiny. She said: 'Forgive me. I am selfish; I put myself first. I have nothing to lose, while you have your entire life at stake and perhaps a country as well.'

She fumbled for a handkerchief. It was time, he thought, to make her free. He signalled to a waiter. 'Give me the bill of fare.'

Katharine said: 'I cannot take food. I marvel that you can.'

When the menu card was brought, he took a pencil from his pocket and told the waiter to summon the hotel porter. He tore the card in two and began to write on the reverse of one of the pieces.

She asked: 'Charley, what are you doing?'

He smiled, still writing: 'I am committing yet another crime. This time, forgery?'

She smiled. 'Really? And in whose name?'

'Yours.'

She became alarmed. 'What are you writing? Charley, I must know.'

He said: 'I am burning a boat or two. Look here, tomorrow, if it is fine, what do you say to a day on the Downs? Ellen shall provide us with a picnic.'

'Tomorrow? You know we cannot. We must —' She broke off. Now, with certainty, she knew what he had written in

212

her name. 'No, you mustn't. I forbid it. Whatever else, not that.'

She reached for the card. He held it from her. He said: 'The first day I met you in Palace Yard, I made up my mind that you would be my wife. I don't know why I even wavered. You will forgive me, I hope?'

The head porter came up. Parnell gave him the card. 'Will you have this telegraphed at once at the express rate?'

'We have forms for telegrams, sir.'

'Excellent. Then copy this on to one I trust that you can read my hand?'

She attempted to speak. He motioned her to silence, his eyes on the porter. The message was addressed to Frank Lockwood. It read: THIS INSTRUCTS YOU TO WITHDRAW MY DEFENCE AGAINST CAPTAIN O'SHEA'S PETITION. MY DECISION IRREVOCABLE. KINDEST REGARDS.

Parnell asked: 'Any difficulties?'

'No, sir. Thank you, sir.'

Parnell tipped him. When the porter was gone, he took hold of Katharine's wrist. 'Now listen to me, Queenie. Frank Lockwood will quite properly send to know if that message is genuine. You will not countermand it.'

It was not a question. She was to abide, he was telling her, by his decision. No longer concerned that they were in a public place, she covered his hand with her own. She said: 'You fool. You really are the most foolish man.'

He retrieved his hand, sat up straight in his chair and looked pleased with himself. 'I think I'm rather a clever one. And, now that the die is cast, a confoundedly hungry one.' He looked blankly at the table. 'Except that I seem to have torn up the damned bill of fare.'

Willie could hardly believe his good fortune. Frank Lockwood had stood up and informed Judge Butt that Kate had withdrawn her defence. He, Lockwood, would hold only a watching brief on

213

her behalf. It had been a close-run thing; with the evidence they had found of his skirmishes with that damned sexual madwoman, Kate's sister, he might have found the going not to his liking. Now, he was safe. And the day was to yield even more exquisite rewards. He heard his own counsel, Sir Edward Clarke, address the judge.

'Your Lordship, although Mrs O'Shea has at this late, this very late juncture seen fit to withdraw her defence, the charges made by her against my client remain on record. I ask that Captain O'Shea be permitted to give evidence to refute allegations which, we maintain, are as base as they are baseless.'

What sounded like a purr went through the public gallery. They were not, after all, to be cheated of their sport. Willie felt his eyes mist. The golden apple had at last fallen into his lap, and now, with Sir Edward's help, he would crush from it every last drop of juice. Judge Butt acceded to counsel's request, and Willie was bidden to enter the witness box.

It was the happiest hour of his life. In reply to questions, he told of his early suspicions of Parnell and how he had challenged him to a duel.

'Did Mr Parnell accept your challenge?'

Willie said: 'He did not, sir. He showed the white feather.' His staunchness of tone suggested that Parnell was wise in his cowardice.

'Did he offer guarantees as to his future good behaviour?'

'He did. I demanded and received an undertaking that he would not again visit my home except by daylight and at my express invitation.'

'He gave this undertaking in person?'

'No, sir.' Willie's lip all but curled. 'Rather than meet me like a man, he hid behind a woman's skirts. The assurances were conveyed to me by my wife.'

'And you believed at the time that they were honourable?'

'God help me, I did.' Willie's face shone upon Judge Butt. It was a good face; there was trust in it and the untarnished simple faith of a child. 'I am a simple man. To me, a word given is a word kept. I am foolish, I know.'

He heard a woman in the public gallery whisper 'Poor soul.' Nobody laughed. Sir Edward moved on to Parnell's sponsorship of Willie during the Galway by-election.

'I had been of much service to him in the past,' Willie said. 'He professed to be grateful. He said that I might be of service yet again.'

'Do you now believe that to be true?'

'I do not.' Willie's voice was bitter. 'I know now that he wanted to have me at a disadvantage. He thought that he had bought me, that I would look the other way while . . . while he and my wife were . . .'

The words would not come. Most of those in the public gallery wished fervently that they would.

Sir Edward was so moved that he pinched the loose skin between his eyes. 'Quite so. And when you discovered this, what did you do?'

Willie said, stiffly: 'I did what any man of honour would do. I resigned my seat.'

A solitary handclap from the gallery was silenced by the Clerk of the Court.

'And yet,' Sir Edward said, 'you did not at once file for divorce.' Willie, mute, shook his head. 'Will you tell his Lordship why?'

The truth, held back for so long, poured forth in gouts of grief. 'Because beyond all reason I hoped that my wife might turn from the folly of her ways. I thought . . . I *prayed* that she would find him out for the devil he was. I pleaded with her, on my knees I begged her, if not for my sake, then for our little ones. It was hopeless. His evil was in her blood.'

He fell silent, a man whose task was done, whose race was run. There was a stillness in the courtroom. Sir Edward let it ripen for some moments, then said, his voice soft: 'One last question, Captain O'Shea, and your ordeal will be at an end.'

215

Already? Willie thought, with a twinge of disappointment.

'You are aware, are you not, that your wife alleges instances of misconduct on your own part?'

Willie felt his heart leap. The question was perilously close to home. He stared at Sir Edward, wondering if he was, after all, a kind of fool. If Willie were to say, as he must, that he had never been unfaithful to Kate, half the women in London would know him for a liar and the other half would take him for a fool. Then Judge Butt said, as Sir Edward had known he would: 'I think that question need not be put. The witness may step down.'

Willie mouthed an elaborately unspoken 'Thank you' to the judge and left the box, resisting the temptation to limp.

There was one other witness, by name Caroline Pethers. She was stout, red-faced and of near middle age. She had worked as cook at 8, Medina Terrace, Hove, eight years before, when it had been rented by Mrs O'Shea for a summer holiday. She came, as she said, 'with the house'. Shown a photograph of the co-respondent, Parnell, she identified him as a Mr Charles Stewart, who was an overnight visitor whenever Captain O'Shea was absent.

Judge Butt interrupted: 'He called himself Stewart?'

Sir Edward said: 'It was a frequent pseudonym, my lord. He used other false names, including Clement S. Preston – your Lordship will take note of the initials – and Mr Fox.'

'Fox.' Mr Justice Butt had never been one to resist an opportunity to display his mastery of repartee, and he did not resist this one. 'That at least was well chosen.'

There was laughter in the courtroom.

'Tell me, Pethers,' Sir Edward said, 'during the times when this Mr Stewart was in residence, did Captain O'Shea happen to call?'

Caroline Pethers liked to be the centre of attention. In her life, she had never been at the centre of anything, except perhaps a kitchen. She was determined now to make the most of it.

'Didn't 'e just!' she said, vivaciously. 'That was something!'

 216

'Was it, so?' Sir Edward said, with great complicity, all but winking at her.

'Not 'alf. The Captain 'ud come to the front door, and the Irish girl, Mary, 'oo's the parlourmaid, she'd look out and say, "Oh, Mum, the master 'as come!" And straight off, Mr Stewart 'ud go tearing upstairs and out by the . . . by the wotsit, the fire-escape, same as if Old Nick wus after 'im.'

'He went out by the *what*?' Sir Edward asked, cupping his hand histrionically to his ear.

'Well, 'e must 'ave, mustn't 'e?' She grinned at the courtroom, enjoying herself hugely. 'Not unless 'e flew.'

The court shook with laughter. The reporters scribbled. Judge Butt gave her the cold look of a comedian who had unexpectedly come upon another comedian.

Almost alone in the body of the court, Frank Lockwood did not laugh. Two years previously, he had heard Parnell addressing the Eighty Club, and knew he was not one to go scrambling down a rope ladder in flight from a duped husband. A man, Lockwood held, could not overstep the bounds of his own nature, and fire-escapes and the remote, unemotional Parnell existed in worlds apart. As for the witness, Caroline Pethers, she was another Vesta Tilley, and her public were clamouring for more.

She waited until the laughter ebbed, then obliged. 'And then, not ten minutes later, before the Captain 'ad 'ardly got 'is 'at and coat off, Mr Stewart 'ud come ringing at the door to say as 'ow 'e just 'appened to be in Brighton and thought 'e'd drop in.'

Again, the courtroom convulsed. It was not, as in the Dilke case, three in a bed, but it would do. Lockwood, who had no voice in the proceedings, reflected that he would have let a term's retainers go hang in return for a ten-minute cross-examination of Caroline Pethers.

By the time Judge Butt had granted the decree nisi, Parnell, Katharine and the two youngest children, the others being at

217

school, were having their picnic on the Downs. Parnell himself, as usual and to Ellen's affected outrage, had made the salad. They brought chicken, a game pie and another of veal and ham. There was ginger beer in stone jars. They sat in the lee of a rise, with the sea, an arctic blue, in the distance. Parnell rode his hunter, President, first with Clare on the pommel, then Frances. At about the time they were clearing the picnic things for the journey home, Mr Justice Butt was nearing the climax of his philippic.

'Mr Parnell,' he said, and each word was a plum, ripe for the picking, 'is no mortal man, as others are. He is a Member of Parliament; he is the leader of his party and of his people; he is a being so exalted, so godlike, that his countrymen have bestowed upon him their title of uncrowned king.

'Today, we have been shown not a god, but a cold-blooded voluptuary who could and did accept the hospitality of a husband, the better to debauch the wife. No lie was too base, no deception too shameful for this man and the woman whose accomplice he was in the fouling of the marriage bed. All right-thinking men can do no other than express their disgust and revulsion.

'I grant a decree nisi and rule that the plaintiff shall have custody of all his and the defendant's children below the age of sixteen.'

He quitted the courtroom as if fleeing an unholy place.

At dinnertime, Katharine received the expected telegram from Frank Lockwood. In the few moments before tears came, she passed it to Parnell. He read it and got up from the table. He said: 'I have that piece of quartz to assay.'

At the door, he turned and said: 'I had not thought that we would lose the children.'

Willie's mantelpiece was itself again.

Invitations jostled for space. He was a public benefactor; he had shown up the blackguard Parnell, whose worst crime in the eyes of the English was not Irish brigandry or even adultery, but having become their hero. They had wronged him and in consequence were in his debt. He had drawn from them their adulation; they had cheered and feted him; the Prime Minister had bowed to him. It was too bad of him.

One of Willie's invitations was to accompany Mr Herbert Tree's party to the St James Theatre. The Irish playwright, Dion Bouciault, had died in September, and his play *The Shaughraun* had been revived as a tribute. Willie sat with the party in the stage box and, at the intervals, noticed that women in the stalls looked up at him admiringly. He was fifty, and a malicious journalist had described him as 'shabby genteel'. Willie thought that he had a look that the French called *distingué*; moreover, the éclat of the divorce case had renewed him. He felt aggrieved that until the decree became absolute he must avoid indiscretions. He hoped that his new fame would last until then.

During the last act of *The Shaughraun*, there was a thrilling and yet highly comical scene in which the hero, Con, was trapped by two ruffians in an Irish cabin. They came at him, brandishing daggers. He ran this way and that and at last seemed to be trapped. It was the scene Willie was waiting for. He had heard that a new line had been interpolated by the actor, and he leaned forward to hear it.

The cornered 'Con' said in an aside: 'Oh, Hivven help me, I'm moidhered and deshtroyed entoirely. What am I to do at all, at all? Is there no door or winda I can go through?'

He came downstage and said, confidingly, to the audience: ' "I haven't even got a fire-eshcape!" '

There was a roar of laughter that welled into applause. Willie's companions joined in and clapped him on the back. Instead of abating, the hilarity continued in great waves so that the actor could not continue with the scene, but simply stood and grinned. Willie, red with pleasure, turned to Herbert Tree.

He said: 'Do you know, the real fun of it is that there *was* no fire-escape.'

The smile went from Tree's face. Willie did not notice and in any case was amused enough for both of them.

FOURTEEN

Joe Biggar had not, after all, been well enough to make the journey home to Belfast. He remained in his lodgings in London and died there, although not before converting to Catholicism, to annoy, so he said, the Presbyterians. His friends buried him in Belfast, huddling against the sleet that spat down from Cave Hill.

Timothy Healy gave the oration. He said that Joseph Biggar was crooked of body, and there it ended, for no man ever lived who was truer of heart or as straight in the ways of truth. Nor was there one who flinched less from the saying of what he knew must be said.

'We have need of him today,' Tim Healy said. 'There are powers in England who demand that we should abandon our leader because of a momentary outcry that will be forgotten tomorrow. I know what answer our departed friend would make to these people. He would say, as I do in this place, that Mr Parnell is less a man than an ideal. Since Joe Biggar has gone from us, let me be his voice. I tell our enemies, as he would: let the wolves among you howl for our leader's downfall. He is not your leader, but ours, and we shall never forsake him.'

As they walked away down the long avenue of stone angels bowed under the weeping sky, Tim Healy said to John Dillon,

'Joe said the blackguard wouldn't come, and he was right.'

His graveside oratory was much admired; even Joe Biggar would have thought it not bad. All agreed that Healy had given England a good piece of his mind, and his championing of Parnell had won him many a firm handshake. He was, it was agreed, not the worst of them. Pint mugs were raised to the memory of the deceased, and, as the day wore on, feelings became heated at the impudence of the Saxon crew in daring to suggest that the Irish people should forsake their Chief. It occurred to few that Healy's speech had been nothing but rhetoric; the truth was that since the divorce not a single English voice had been raised against Parnell's leadership. Tim Healy, who had expected a gale of fury was puzzled by the dead calm. John Dillon, too, wondered why Liberals and Tories alike had so charitably stayed their hands, but he made no comment. None of the mourners would dishonour Joe Biggar's funeral by speaking well of the English.

The cold north-westerly rain that fell on Belfast had become a morose drizzle by the time it crossed the Irish Sea to Hawarden, the family home of William Ewart Gladstone. The old man waited for his servants to assemble for evening prayers, and he, too, was perplexed. Parnell, he told himself, could not survive. It was a belief that had nothing to do with divine retribution; he had long ago learned that the wages of sin was not death but, frequently, a seat on the Government front bench. Parnell would fall because the divorce case had put his fate beyond his own control. Gladstone did not know from which quarter the storm would come, or when, but he sensed its approach. As always, he trusted to his instincts. It was partly because of them that he had thrice been Her Majesty's first minister and would as such serve her again.

In the library at Hawarden, the family and servants knelt in prayer. Gladstone intoned a passage from Ephesians: 'For we wrestle not against flesh and blood, but against principalities, against powers, against the rulers of the darkness of this world, against spiritual wickedness in high places.'

His thoughts remained earthbound. They concerned a proposed

221

wedding. At the next election, the Irish party would take him and his party in marriage. Their espousal would secure a Liberal victory, and in return he would bring to the union the dowry of a new Home Rule bill. The alliance was agreeable to Gladstone, but Parnell would prove a domineering bridegroom: demanding and impatient, even brutal.

Life without Parnell would be Utopian, but Gladstone was too old for daydreams. As the saying went, if 'ifs' and 'ans' were pots and pans, there would be no trade for tinkers. No, he told himself again, the man could not survive; yet on Tuesday next in Westminster, the Irish party would meet and re-elect him as their leader. And so Gladstone shared Timothy Healy's puzzlement.

When he had disposed of Ephesians 6: 12–24, he implored the Almighty to give ear to His servants' prayers, provided that they were uttered in a spirit of submission to the divine will. He said 'Amen', his own servants dispersed, and the family said their good nights. He slept for six hours as he had always done, and rose to a clear sky and the news that his own prayers had been answered.

'Whatever happens,' John Dillon said outside the Athenaeum, 'don't let the old man detain you. If we're late for the meeting, the Chief will skin us alive.'

Justin McCarthy nodded. He had no idea why Gladstone should ask to see him, a stranger, only an hour prior to the meeting to elect – or, more accurately – to re-elect their leader. He left Dillon to wait in the hansom and entered the club.

Fifteen minutes later, he returned. As the cab drove off, Dillon saw that McCarthy's face was ashen. When addressed by name, he emitted a low groan. Dillon wondered if he had been taken ill.

'Justin, for God's sake, what is it? Are you sick? What did the Old Man want with you?' To his horror, he saw that McCarthy had begun to cry. 'Jesus, man, what ails you?'

222

McCarthy said with a sob of despair: 'We're finished. The old devil has done for us.'

He had found Gladstone waiting for him, attended by his staunchest supporter, John Morley, M.P., who had at one time been Irish Secretary and regarded his loss of that office as an insignificant hiatus.

Morley rose. 'McCarthy, there you are.' He smiled, as if he had just produced the Irishman from a silk hat. 'Sir, I do not believe you have met Mr Justin McCarthy.'

'Alas, no.' Gladstone was at his most venerable; ivy entwined his words. 'I have read Mr McCarthy's novels, and I have heard him speak. He is one of Mr Parnell's most able lieutenants.'

McCarthy had expected to be put at his ease; instead, he was conscious of a foreboding. As it darkened by the moment, he looked at the noble forehead, the resolute brow, the awesome jut of nose and chin. It was as if an intending statesman had been invited to sculpt the likeness he would choose for himself, but had gone too far. The side of McCarthy that was a novelist looked forward to witnessing a performance; the side that was a Parnellite was mortally afraid. He was reminded of one of Gladstone's nicknames: the Grand Old Spider. He declined an offer of refreshments. 'Thank you, I am on my way to a meeting.'

Morley smiled. 'Indeed, yes; a meeting at which Mr Parnell will be returned as your party leader.'

'Unanimously,' McCarthy said.

'And no doubt,' Morley said, 'he will, as is his custom, appear out of thin air ten minutes beforehand, like a pantomime demon. Since the divorce case, he has quite gone to earth.'

McCarthy said: 'I think in his place I would do the same.'

Morley made no reply. He seemed faintly startled that any man would wish to imagine himself in Parnell's place.

McCarthy said: 'Mr Gladstone, you must know that I am not charged to speak for Mr Parnell. As to why I have been brought here, I am at a loss.'

It was Morley who replied. 'Mr McCarthy, you are here because in a sea of passions you are a moderate. Mr Parnell is nowhere to be found. We have looked for him. And we have waited. We have prayed that he would come to us.'

Gladstone sighed and shook his head. 'Too proud.'

McCarthy wished that he himself had not come. There was some double-dealing afoot, and he was to be caught in the middle.

It was as if Gladstone had read his thoughts. He said, almost pityingly: 'I am an old man, Mr McCarthy, too old for the setting of traps. Sir, indulge me . . . how goes it in Ireland? The people there, the clergy . . . after what has occurred, where are their loyalties?'

McCarthy said: 'They are for the Chief . . . for Mr Parnell.'

'Their lordships, too? The hierarchy?'

Since the divorce, there had been hardly a flutter from the sacred dovecotes of Armagh and Maynooth. Silence, McCarthy thought, could be fairly interpreted either way. He said: 'Sir, they are for him with all their hearts.'

The old man smiled wistfully. 'How good that is to hear. What constancy in a changing world. And what a noble race yours is. Would, sir, that the Nonconformists of my own party were as rich in forgiveness.' The great head came up; the hooded eyes now fixed themselves upon McCarthy's face. 'There has been a meeting of the National Liberal Federation, and do you know, they say that Mr Parnell must resign.'

His meaning was too vast for Justin McCarthy to take in at once. He stared at the mask of Gladstone's face and thought he saw beneath it a kind of exultation.

Gladstone went on. 'Heartless, is it not? I have implored. I have appealed to their better selves. All to no avail. They, unlike your fine Irish clerics, cling to morality. They are resolute.'

Morley said: 'You can see that Mr Gladstone is devastated. The Nonconformists threaten to desert him.'

Gladstone made a gesture of frail helplessness. 'And so they will do if Parnell stays. In that event, the Liberal party will forfeit

224

the next general election. And the Irish party will as surely forfeit Home Rule.'

McCarthy got unsteadily to his feet. He said, hoarsely: 'I think I should not hear this.'

He was not to escape. Morley rose also: he held an envelope.

He said: 'Mr Gladstone has written a letter It is not addressed to Mr Parnell – that would seem to be a provocation – but to myself as Shadow Secretary. Not to detain you from your meeting, its burden is —'

'They have defeated me!' Gladstone groaned.

'. . . that if Mr Parnell remains as leader of his party, Mr Gladstone must resign as leader of his.'

'My heart breaks,' Gladstone all but wailed. 'It is the end of me.'

The letter was put into McCarthy's unresisting hand.

In the hansom ten minutes later, he wiped his eyes and said to Dillon: 'My God, I've lived for sixty years and haven't wept in thirty of them.' He buried his face in his hands. 'What is to become of us?' As the Houses of Parliament came in sight, Dillon suppressed an urge to leap from the cab and run back the way they had come.

The meeting had been called for a quarter to one. McCarthy waited outside the door of Committee Room 15 as the Irish members arrived. His eyes were red, and a few looked at him with curiosity. Against reason, he prayed that Parnell would stay away and allow the members to re-elect him *in absentia*. His heart sank when, with a few minutes to go, he saw two figures approach; one was unmistakably that of Parnell; the other, short and stocky, assumed the likeness of John Redmond. On the day after the divorce hearing, Redmond had convened a meeting in Dublin to pledge support for Parnell; for his steadfastness he had at once been raised to the thinning ranks of the élite.

'Mr Parnell . . .' McCarthy stepped into their path, the letter in his hand. 'I have just come from Mr Gladstone.'

'*You* have?' Parnell seemed faintly amused.

McCarthy felt himself redden. 'He sent for me. It could have

225

been anyone. I mean, I am inclined to think it was a random choice.'

'This is a sudden modesty, McCarthy.'

'I was given this.'

Parnell's eyes fell upon the envelope. He took it and looked at the writing.

'Addressed to the Shadow Secretary.'

'Mr Morley was also present. In fact, I received it from his hands, to do with as I pleased.'

'And so you are showing it to me?'

Parnell tapped a fingernail against the envelope. A game had begun, and it would not go forward unless he read the letter. He yielded – Gladstone's games were usually worth the playing. He opened the envelope and read quickly through its contents. Merely to know the substance of what was written had brought McCarthy to tears; now, watching Parnell, he thought that he would have shown more emotion in perusing a tailor's bill.

Parnell put single page back in its envelope. 'Clever. Yes, they play the game well, those two.'

He returned it to McCarthy, who asked: 'What am I to do with it?'

'My dear McCarthy, how should I know? It is not my letter. Why do you show me other people's correspondence?'

As he and Redmond were about to enter the committee room, McCarthy said, weakly: 'Mr Parnell, I think they may publish it.'

Parnell said at the door: 'They will, if they have any sense. There was little point in writing it otherwise.'

He was gone. McCarthy heard a loud cheer go up from the members. He wondered whether it was he or Parnell who had gone mad. He went into the room, and Sexton made space for him at the large horseshoe-shaped table.

He said: 'God, but you missed it. He just now walked in for all the world as if *we* had been committing adultery with *his* wife.'

Parnell was surrounded by a group of members, all attempting

   226

to shake his hand. Across the table, Dillon was employing elaborate dumb show to ask McCarthy about the letter. Had he shown it to Parnell? Were the contents to be placed before the meeting? In whose possession was it? McCarthy was in no humour for pantomime. He felt his heart pounding. Instead of a letter, there might have been an anarchist's bombshell in his inside pocket, ready to explode.

Maurice Healy had come from Bantry to visit his famous brother and was to look for him on the Members' Terrace after the meeting. Given that Parnell conducted party business at a breakneck pace, they appointed for four o'clock, in time for tea. Maurice had set out early – he had no intention of getting lost and seeming like a country mouse – and was seated at a table by the balustrade when his elder brother appeared. Timothy Healy saw him at once. As he started joyfully across the terrace, the figure of the Shadow Irish Secretary rose into his way.

Morley indicated a chair. 'Mr Healy, I am delighted to see you. Will you grant me the pleasure of your company?'

Full marks, Healy thought, for brazen impudence. Aloud, he said: 'Now there's an honour. Thank you, but perhaps another day. I have an appointment.'

As he attempted to go by, Morley all but danced in his path. 'Pray, let it be soon. For now, however, will you at least slake the fires of my curiosity? May a waiting world know who your new leader is?'

Healy looked at him with amusement. 'Your fires are easily slaked, sir. Our new leader is our old one.'

The smile died upon Morley's face. 'Do you mean Mr Parnell?'

'Did you expect another?'

The Shadow Secretary passed a hand over his forehead. 'Are you all quite mad? You re-elected him?' As Tim Healy stiffened in anger, he said: 'Sir, forgive me, but how is it possible? After Mr Gladstone's letter, how could you do it?'

227

'Letter? What letter?'

'Surely Mr Parnell was given a sight of it?'

From the table along the terrace, Maurice Healy saw his brother staring at the other man, who spoke at length. There was incredulity at first, then anger; Maurice thought he had never seen Tim in such a wax. Then an extraordinary thing happened. Without as much as another glance towards his visitor from home, Timothy Healy turned and went indoors. Minutes passed. Maurice sat, not knowing what to do. He realised that his was the only tweed suit on the terrace.

A waiter came over: 'Will you have tea, sir?'

Maurice did not like to put the man to trouble. He said: 'Ah sure, no. No, I won't. I will not. Thanks all the same.'

The waiter bowed and went away. Maurice thought that the man had been wanting in manners not to insist, not to say, 'Ah, you will,' and oblige him to have a cup, like at home. He wished that Tim would come back. He thought that London was vastly overrated.

It took Timothy Healy ten minutes to find Justin McCarthy, and as many seconds to ask a question and be answered. He went directly to the Members' Corridor, and strode up to where Parnell was conferring with Henry Harrison and John Redmond.

Without salutation, Healy said: 'I want to talk to you.'

Redmond and Harrison looked at him, open-mouthed. Parnell glanced at Healy, then affected to interest himself in the progress of a messenger along the corridor. He said in a detached voice: 'I am afflicted with several ailments, Healy, but until now I was not aware that stone deafness was one of them. Or could it be that you have forgotten to beg the pardon of those you intrude upon?'

This time, Healy would not be cowed or ignored. He thrust the letter at him, his voice shaking. 'Is it true? Did Justin McCarthy show this to you before the meeting?'

Parnell hardly looked at it. 'He did.'

'Why, then, was it not shown to the members?'

'It was not addressed to the members. Or, for that matter, to me.'

228

Healy's face was burning with rage. 'So you kept quiet. You knew what was in it, but you sang dumb and let yourself be re-elected.'

Parnell said coldly: 'I paid the members the compliment of assuming that they would not yield to blackmail.'

'Blackmail be damned.' Healy all but pushed the crunched-up letter into Parnell's face. 'Do you know what this says? It is to be either Gladstone or you, and if it is you who stays, then Home Rule is gone. Do you think we're going to throw it away for your sake?'

Parnell's voice dropped to a hiss. 'How dare you speak to me in that manner? Get out of my sight.'

Henry Harrison was aware that the long corridor, which was the communal working place of members and their secretaries and drudges, had begun to fall silent. He said: 'Now, Tim, that'll do. Don't let old Ireland down.'

Tim Healy was past caring; the spellbinder of the law courts had become a shouting youth. 'No, you haven't changed, and damn you, you never will. You'll be answerable to no one, isn't that it? Well, by Christ, you'll answer for this, and to all of us. You're finished, do you hear me? You're over and done with!'

The onlookers might have been graven images. They hardly attended to Healy's words; their eyes were upon Parnell. When he spoke, his voice had murder in it. 'Get out!'

Outside of a private room, no one until now had ever seen him abandon his composure. His gauntness made him seem wolflike; his eyes, flecked with red, were on Healy's throat.

Before Healy could launch into another tirade, John Redmond seized his arm and marched him quickly down the corridor, holding him not roughly, but with the easy firmness of a barman removing a valued customer. He said: 'Sorry, Tim, sorry.'

Timothy Healy did not struggle. When Redmond released him, he made his way out of the building. He thought his head would burst. He went into Parliament Square and sat on a bench. By degrees, he began to be conscious of the breeze from the river, the traffic and the sky; he heard carriage wheels and the commotion of horses. He wanted his anger to become a furnace that would consume even himself if need be, and yet he became aware that a new and disturbing emotion was elbowing it aside. He resisted, denying it admittance, and so for a time did not recognise what had come to him. It was happiness.

On the eve of the divorce, he had told Michael Davitt that for as long as Parnell and Home Rule were of one flesh, he, Tim Healy, would be Parnell's creature. Ireland above all else, he had said. Now the two were separate, and he was free. Old Gladstone had delivered him, and he was no longer bound to the adulterer and hypocrite. For Ireland's sake, he had been faithful; now, for Ireland's sake, he would be his enemy. He thought of the humiliations he had endured, of the opened letter, of Galway, of the day he had offered to be Parnell's counsel and it had been flung back in his face. He had seen his country's name dragged through the mire of the divorce courts. Now it was his turn, and he would drive Parnell either into the asylum or the grave.

He rose from the bench, his mood lightsome. He had walked half-way up Whitehall before he remembered that his brother Maurice was still on the terrace.

While Mary fetched a kettle of hot water from below stairs, Katharine removed his socks. 'Walking abroad in this weather . . . you will catch your death.'

He said: 'Not in November, Queenie. Remember it is October that is my unlucky month, and once it is past I am safe for the year ahead.'

Mary poured the hot water for his footbath. Katharine watched her so zealously that the maid exclaimed: 'Lord, madam, do you think I'd scald the poor man?'

Parnell said: 'My dear, you stand rebuked. If Mary is not to be trusted, who is? Mary, you may pour away.'

Katharine was not amused. In spite of her watchfulness, he

 230

had taken a wetting from the sea spray during the south-westerly gales. Years previously, he had abandoned his hobby of astronomy because the vastness of the heavens made Ireland seem by comparison almost non-existent. He discovered that coastal storms had a more salutary effect: they reduced Westminster to a comprehensible size. High seas fascinated him, and today he had walked a mile beyond Shoreham before realising that he was almost soaked through. As he turned for home, a passing carter agreed to take him to Walsingham Terrace. He sat, shivering, on the creaking seat. He attempted to forget his discomfort by preparing in his mind for next Monday's meeting. In Committee Room 15, where they had elected him as their leader, the Irish would attempt to undo their handiwork.

He believed that the key to the future was, as always, an understanding of the past. He had no trouble whatever in coming to terms with Gladstone's villainy; from a tactical viewpoint, he even admired the art with which the old man had concealed his malignity under a veneer of regret. It was not he, but the Irish, who were to Parnell objects of bafflement. At times, he wondered if the labyrinth that passed for the brain of an Irishman was evidence for the existence of God, on the grounds that only a divine hand could have fashioned such a wonder, or whether the opposite was the case and the Irish mind was simply one more token of a chaotic universe.

Gladstone's letter had been published in the *Pall Mall Gazette*. As its author had intended, it created a sensation. The English press declared that Parnell, the messiah of Home Rule, was now its Lucifer. One newspaper added that a man who could defile a marriage bed would as readily put horns on his own countrymen. Those who expected Parnell to play the sacrificial lamb were disappointed; instead, he issued a manifesto addressed to the people of Ireland. In it, he disputed the right of the Liberals to veto the Irish party's choice of leader. He asked if he was to be thrown to the 'English wolves' who were howling for his destruction. To his bemusement, the manifesto

231

caused more outrage within his own party than had Gladstone's letter.

The language, it was generally agreed, was intemperate. Now, Thomas Sexton protested, was not the time to go giving offence to the English people.

Parnell asked, coldly: 'Then when *is* the time?'

Sexton, who thought the question unfair, came back with an aggrieved 'Ah, but still.'

Dillon said, reasonably: 'Mr Parnell, surely at this critical moment the last thing we would wish to do is make an enemy of Mr Gladstone?'

Parnell had stared at him, reminding himself that this was the member of his inner circle who, more than any other and now that Biggar was gone, held compromise in contempt.

He said: 'Am I hearing aright? Dillon, from the beginning of time, Gladstone has been our enemy. Have you not grasped that? Have I not told all of you often enough? He has plotted against us, weaving his webs. He knows that for as long as I am leader, there will exist a party that will fight him and give no quarter. He knows, too, that without me, that party will disappear. Instead, there will be factions and cliques. He will roll over you like a juggernaut, so that if Home Rule ever comes it will not be on your terms, but on his. Cannot you see that he has been against us from the beginning? Now that he has come into the open, do you imagine that he cares two farthings whether this manifesto is published or not?'

He had hammered the words at them, and when he was done they looked at him sullenly. Justin McCarthy said: 'Mr Parnell, I did wrong to show Mr Gladstone's letter to you alone. I should have disclosed it to the members. Well, I'll not do wrong a second time. This manifesto of yours . . . it is too violent. It will give offence. That reference to English wolves!'

Parnell said: 'I trust, McCarthy, that I am not being thrown to the *Irish* wolves?'

At that, they had taken offence. They were fiercely protective of their own honour, yet could with equanimity accept Gladstone's insult to their leader. At the nub of it was their fatal Irishness; they craved to be liked, even by their enemies. All were educated men; John Dillon had studied medicine; McCarthy was a popular novelist and historian; and yet the centuries of servility had left their mark. They could not raise a clenched fist in defiance of tyranny without the forefinger going instinctively to the forelock. They kissed the rod even as they strove to break it.

It was Thomas Sexton, red-cheeked and consumptive, who made the first move toward open mutiny. He said, direct to Parnell: 'Rather than go down alone, you mean to drag the party after you for company. I give warning that if this manifesto is sent to the press, we are done with you.'

'*We*, Sexton?'

'All of us.'

No voice was raised in contradiction. Parnell looked at the set faces before him. He said: 'What I have written will stand.'

John Dillon said, his face pale: 'In that case, we shall meet on Monday. Then there will be an end to it.' He walked from the room, followed by Sexton, and McCarthy.

Now, seated before the fire at Brighton, Parnell looked down upon Katharine's head as she dried his feet. A scene from the New Testament came into his mind. He thought: if Timothy Healy were a fly on the wall, what a blasphemous parallel he would draw. He laughed to himself; the small muscular spasm caused her to look up.

'What is it?'

'Nothing.'

'Are you in pain?'

He told her no, although rheumatism made his right arm feel as if it were a lead weight. He put a hand beneath her chin and said: 'Queenie, we shall have to make a fight of it. Can you bear it? I'm afraid it's going to be tough work.'

She said, as lightly as she could: 'You speak as if it were I who was going to the wars.'

233

She took his change of socks from where they were warming before the fire. He knew what she longed to say and yet would not. She craved for him to break the spell that bound him to her rival, to a country that was a keening woman who knew only songs of death. It would take so very little for them both to be on their way to the vague place she often spoke of as 'a sunnier land'. Since he could deny her nothing, he would grant her this, too. There was only one more hurdle, one more ditch to be cleared. At Monday's meeting, if he could induce the members to make a stand against Gladstone's dictatorship, then he would know that he had created a party strong enough to fight alone. When the time came, he could take his leave with honour.

Thinking of the Old Spider, he said: 'My darling, do you know what is the most exquisite pleasure in life? That old humbug, Gladstone . . . *he* knows. It is to display one's morality as if it were a show horse, and yet make the poor brute perform the most degrading of tasks. To rid themselves of me, they must pretend that a man's private life is not his own.'

Katharine said: '*Pretend*, did you say?'

'What else?'

She wondered that he could so delude himself: 'My darling, you are a public man. Your life is not your own and never can be.'

Parnell put his arms around her. 'True, it is not mine; it is yours. But it is no one else's. Queenie, do you know where Healy is at this moment? I have had a telegram. He is in Dublin, trying to turn the people and the priests against me.'

He laughed. 'The fool might as well be trying to uproot Gibraltar.'

Since his arrival in Ireland, Timothy Healy had been a positive whirlwind. That morning, he had called upon Dr William J. Walsh, Archbishop of Dublin. He informed his Lordship that at Monday's meeting the Irish Nationalist party would overwhelmingly depose Parnell as its leader.

'Do you tell me?' Dr Walsh said. 'Poor fellow.'

Tim Healy did not wish to offend the Most Reverend ear with explicit references to adultery, cuckoldry and such. He said: 'We . . . ah, the members, that is, will no longer be led by such a man.'

'I am sure,' the Archbishop said serenely, 'that that is for the members to decide.'

He sat, his eyes as blue as a summer sky, quietly waiting for his visitor to come to the point. The pulpits of the land had been silent on the subject of the divorce case. It was hierarchical policy to issue directives to the laity only when there was a better than even-money chance that the laity would obey them. In the case of Parnell, the odds were long. He excited blind loyalty to a degree that quite pre-empted Mother Church's natural claim to that commodity.

Tim Healy said: 'I don't wish to presume.'

The Archbishop made a small gesture inviting him to do so.

'The people will turn against Parnell.'

Again, Dr Walsh said: 'Do you tell me?'

'I am certain of it. Once he has been overthrown, they will have no use for him. He will be as a leper of old. I thought that your Grace should be aware of this, seeing as —' He broke off. It required tactful phrasing, lest the lamb seem to be reminding the shepherd of his duty. He made a fresh start.

'With respect, your Grace, I thought it only good and proper that if the Irish people are to . . . ah, go down a certain road, they should, as always, be guided by their pastors rather than by . . . ah, by their politicians.'

Dr Walsh looked at him for a moment before enlightenment came. 'Ah, I begin to see. You mean that the Church is to be given the opportunity to cast the first stone.'

Timothy Healy felt a pink warmth begin to seep upward from his neck. 'Your reverence . . . I mean, your Lordship . . . please —'

'No, no.' The Archbishop waved his embarrassment to one side. He rose from his chair, went to the window and looked

235

across the lawns towards the small defile that marked the course
of the River Tolka. He sighed and said:

> 'And common is the commonplace,
> And vacant chaff well meant for grain.'

Tim Healy said: 'Excuse me?'

The Archbishop turned with a smile that, on the contrary,
begged his visitor's pardon. 'The Poet Laureate. Alfred Lord
Tennyson, Mr Healy. In other words, what is opinion and what
is fact? How truly do you judge the mood of the people?'

Tim Healy said: 'I know them. They will say that he has
betrayed them for a . . .' It took him an effort to speak the
word. '. . . for a woman.'

Dr Walsh noted the hesitation. Once again, he marvelled at the
squeamishness of the laity. 'The meeting is to be on Monday, you
say?'

'In Westminster, yes.'

The Archbishop paced the room, silent in his brocaded slip-
pers, his hands clasped behind his back. Tim Healy found himself
wondering why it was that episcopal hands were always so pinkly
immaculate, as if their anointing had an outward sign. The pacing
ceased; the most charming of smiles returned.

'In that case, Mr Healy, would it not be wise for you to
proceed there with all haste?'

Tim Healy returned to London, but by a circuitous route. He
caught a train for Thurles, in County Tipperary, where he had
appointed to call upon the Most Reverend Thomas Croke, Archbishop of Cashel and Emly. He flinched on entering the hall of
the palace and seeing there a marble bust of Parnell. He need
not have worried; his Grace was even more receptive to his news
than Archbishop Walsh had been and, unlike his colleague, did
not count self-restraint as a blessing. 'Tell me, then, of Parnell,'
he said, and, as Tim Healy embarked upon his litany, Dr Croke

provided the responses: 'Oh, a blackguard,' 'To be sure, a whited sepulchre,' and 'A mongrel, sure what else?'

Tim Healy declined Dr Croke's invitation to stay the night, pleading that he must travel on to Cork to catch the mail-boat to Fishguard. The Archbishop thought for a moment, winked, and tugged at a velvet bell rope. Almost at once, one of his housekeepers – a Sister of Charity – appeared. He addressed her as Sister Agnes, drew her aside and spoke to her in whispers. Her mouth opened; it seemed to Healy that she was scandalised. As she made to back away, Dr Croke said: 'No, come here to me.' He spoke again, his voice low, as before. Now, her shock ebbing away, she emitted what was almost a laugh and went from the room.

'Will you follow me?' the Archbishop asked.

He led Tim Healy through the French windows into the garden. It was mid-afternoon; the shadows were lengthening. Healy said: 'Your Grace, I really must be —' Dr Croke put a finger to his lips.

After a minute or so, Sister Agnes reappeared. She was carrying the bust of Parnell. She was followed by another, younger, nun, who was carrying a coal hammer. At a signal from Archbishop Croke, Sister Agnes knelt and set the bust before her upon the crazy paving of the path. She took the coal hammer from the other nun and looked up at the Archbishop. He nodded.

A smile came upon her face and widened into a grin. She giggled, daringly in the presence of Archbishop Croke. An irrational fear took hold of Timothy Healy as he saw a hatred that eclipsed his own. She raised the hammer high above her head with both hands and brought it own with force upon the marble bust. She struck repeatedly and demonically, her breast heaving, until at last the features of the image had been pulverized into granules of white.

Long before then, the smiling Archbishop said: 'Good girl, good girl, grand, that'll do you.'

237

FIFTEEN

The hatred on Parnell's face gladdened him.

The days were past when Tim Healy was a creature to be ignored or, at best, fobbed off with the short commons of contempt. Now, from three paces away, his eyes met Parnell's; he saw the enmity, and his heart leapt. He had at last attained his desire: to be detested as an equal.

The meeting had no sooner begun than a member named William Abraham rose, addressed the chair and proposed a motion. It was that Mr Parnell be deposed as president of the Irish Nationalist party. There were cheers and groans, but in his eagerness to get a foot inside the door of history, Mr Abraham failed to take note that the chairman and Mr Parnell were one and the same person. Both summarily ruled his motion out of order.

The members had come to attend a trial at which, it transpired, the accused was also the judge. It had the elements of an impasse. A member named McDonald, who was blind, was heard to mutter that they would be there all day. They were, and, with adjournments, for the next week.

There were seventy-three members in attendance. They read out messages for and against Parnell. They made speeches. They quarrelled. English members, passing the door of Committee Room 15, heard the uproar, the execrations and the oaths, and told each

238

other that the honourable members from the Emerald Isle seemed to be engaged in an exchange of views. They came and stood outside the door of Number 15 like children on excursions to the seaside.

During a particularly loud exchange, the Irish Shadow Secretary and a colleague chanced to be passing on their way from the library. They stood for a moment and listened.

As they resumed their progress, the member asked Morley: 'My dear fellow, own up. When old Gladstone thew that bomb into the Irish camp, did he know it would do so much mischief?'

Morley smiled. 'How could he? Who could guess that when it burst they would pick up the pieces and cut each other's throats with them?'

He stopped and looked back towards the shouting. 'Extraordinary, is it not? No one but Parnell can unify the Irish, he can even preside over their mass suicide.

Within the committee room, Parnell sat, refusing to yield. Years ago, when he had first entered Parliament, he had been schooled by Joseph Biggar in the art of obstructing his enemy, and what he learned then served him now. He parried every blow with the powers of the chair, and the longer the debate threatened to last, the more it pleased Tim Healy. He did not want to see his enemy dispatched at a single stroke; he preferred to witness a slower death, from bleeding.

Swords were crossed within the first hour. Healy reminded the members that if Parnell remained, Gladstone would go. 'If that happens,' he said, 'then what we have worked for – a government by, from and within Ireland – will be forever lost.'

There were cries of 'Rubbish!' and 'Not at all!'

Parnell said: 'Gladstone is and has always been our enemy.'

Healy had drawn him; it was more easily done than he had imagined. 'Is he now?' he said, almost languidly. 'Is that a fact? You did not tell us so in the past. Were you lying to us then, or are you lying now?'

Parnell, on his feet, said: 'I will not stand for an accusation

239

of falsehood from Timothy Healy. I call upon him to withdraw.'

As from a cloud of rooks wheeling at sunset, came the cries: 'Withdraw! Withdraw!'

Healy was unruffled. 'Most certainly. Out of respect for the chair I will happily withdraw. Mr Parnell is not a liar. But neither is he the leader of this party. What we are witnessing today are the last twitchings of a beast that is already dead.'

At this, there was a great clamour against Healy. The cry of 'Renegade' was taken up and bayed. One voice, above the rest, said: 'Crucify him!' The sentiment was loudly cheered.

Thomas Sexton said: 'Mr Chairman, I protest. Blasphemy has been uttered. I appeal to you to exert your authority.'

Tim Healy mocked: 'Authority? He has none.'

The jeering had begun to ebb like the trough of a wave. Now it welled up again, and Parnell was on his feet. With his hands he tamped down the noise.

He told them: 'No, you do Healy an injustice. Listen to me.' They did so, wondering what wrong could ever be done to Healy in Parnell's eyes. He said: 'For once, this person is in the right. I know that for him I have no authority. There speaks a man whose genius I was the first to see. A man I raised from the gutter. A man I educated. A man to whom I gave a seat in this parliament. A man in whose hand I put the knife with which he now attempts to destroy me. Tim Healy speaks true . . . I have no authority. I deserve none.'

He sat. The silence did not break. A faint smile clung to Healy's lips as his supporters and enemies alike looked at him. He had not flinched. Parnell's thrust had not as much as pierced his skin; a corpse could not inflict wounds.

The nearest the debate came to reasoned discourse was on the third day, and again the ending was a bedlam of oaths. And this time there was an end to friendships, not for life, but generations – the Irish had never mastered the English political art of impersonal hatred.

John Redmond spoke. 'In ten years, Mr Parnell has turned a rabblement into a nation.'

Cries of 'Shame!' deplored the insult, and a member from Carlow was heard to tell his neighbours that if the Irish had ever been rabble, it was of a vastly superior kind.

'Yet now,' Redmond said, 'we are to be rid of him. Very well, let him be gone. But when we sell out our own leader, should we not at least enquire what we are getting for the price we pay?'

Parnell put in: 'Don't sell me for nothing. If you get my value, then change me now.'

'Who is the man,' Redmond continued, 'to take his place? I tell you there is none.'

Tim Healy was lolling back in his chair, his jacket unfastened, his thumbs hooked in the pockets of his waistcoat. He drawled: 'What if Mr Parnell should die?'

Parnell said: 'I don't intend to die.'

'The look of you says different.' The Corkman's native inflections had not diminished with the years; he all but sang the words. There was a storm of booing. To Tim Healy, it was spring rain; he seemed to blossom. 'Whether you go under or not, you are only one man. Men far greater than you have been brought low before now.'

Henry Harrison said: 'Not by their own friends. Not by their comrades.'

Healy ignored him. 'They have gone, and the Irish cause remains. You declare that the country is for you. Then go to it. Obtain your mandate.'

Parnell said: 'So I shall.'

'And you will perish.'

The taunt in Healy's voice impelled John Dillon to rise in an attempt to lend the debate a measure of dignity. He addressed Parnell.

'Mr Chairman, you engineered – and more credit to you – an alliance between this party and the Liberals. You said, and I have it here' – he consulted a notebook – 'an alliance which I venture to believe will last.' Now this alliance is no more. It is sundered. Why? I ask you to tell the members, what broke it off?'

241

Parnell looked at the solemnity of Dillon's face and thought him a melancholy humbug. Aloud, he said: 'Come, you know the answer to that as well as I do. It was Gladstone's letter.'

At this, Tim Healy was on his feet again. He leant across the table and screamed at Parnell: 'Never! No letter was needed. Home Rule perished in the stench of the divorce court!'

There was a gasp of shock that was expelled as a moan of grief and in turn became a howling. It disturbed English members in the library fifty yards away. It was a peculiarly Irish sound; it came when a man had been called out of his name, when what had been spoken of in whispers was at last uttered aloud, and behind the grief there was a lurking glee. As the shouts of protest raged on, Parnell's awareness was not of Healy and his malice; the face of Willie O'Shea came into his mind. It was impossible, he thought, an affront to nature, that a fool could wreak such havoc. To his amazement, Tim Healy saw Parnell shake his head and smile to himself as at a private joke.

The deadlock was unbroken when the meeting adjourned on the Friday. There was a feeling that the sport had become stale and that Saturday would see the last of it. It was of secondary importance that at the week's end the sergeant-at-arms would demand that the building be cleared for the Christmas recess. The struggle would end for the best of reasons – that it could endure no longer.

On the final morning, Tim Healy was standing outside the committee room talking with a group of his supporters when Parnell appeared, flanked by John Redmond and Henry Harrison. To avoid a confrontation, Healy turned to enter the room.

'Healy, a word, if you please.'

He was taken aback. Parnell stood a short distance away, giving him no choice but to leave his comrades. Healy was of slight build; as Parnell loomed over him he saw, too close for his liking, the now almost skeletal face and the translucent skin. Only the eyes were as of old, and today he discerned no scorn in them. They were the eyes that ten years before had held him in a lover's thrall.

'Healy,' Parnell said, 'I am told you believed yesterday that I had a gun in my pocket and was about to use it.'

Healy said: 'I had heard so. 'Twas pure nonsense. I gave it no credence.'

'I am glad to hear it.' Parnell extended his hand. 'Healy, let us shake hands now, for it will be the last time.'

It was a public gesture. Healy, taken by surprise, had no choice but to accept. As he touched the proffered hand with his own, he said: 'Most willingly. Thank you, Parnell.'

Parnell gave him a smile that absolved as it rebuked. He said: ' From your lips, Healy, it is *Mr* Parnell.'

He entered the committee room. As he did so, one of the group of loiterers, a member named John Barry, cried out to Healy: 'Tim, wash your hands after him. And don't believe a word he tells you.' He hissed into Parnell's face. 'Trickster, that's all you are. Dirty trickster.'

Parnell did not look at him or reply. As he passed the man, he suppressed a shiver. He had remembered Barry's hand clapping him repeatedly on the shoulder on the day of his return to the House after the Pigott affair. He took his seat. Healy, following him, wondered what motive lay behind the handshake. Had Parnell been showing off, letting the lower orders see how a gentleman fought his wars? Or perhaps he was hoping to buy himself an easy passage on this last day? Tim Healy could think of no other reason.

There was a feeling of end-of-term. The members were tired of wrangling, and a consensus of opinion held that the worst – or best – part of the week had come and gone with Healy's 'stench of the divorce court'. Now, as the winter day closed in, the thoughts of many were of the Holyhead train, the mail-boat and home. The Houses of Parliament were being wired for electricity, and so paraffin lamps were brought in. As Parnell stood to address the meeting, his shadow stretched immensely to the ceiling. He spoke of Gladstone's refusal to discuss his proposals for Home Rule.

'He will say nothing until I am gone and you are in his power.

What will he do for you then? Nothing. There is not a single one of them who can be trusted. The Irish must trust themselves.'

Sexton said, with a hint of weariness in his voice: 'Can we trust *you*?'

Parnell replied: 'I think I have that right, and it is not an unfair thing to ask that I should come within sight of the Promised Land.'

There was applause from a minority. He sat, put on his glasses, took up a copy of the *Freeman's Journal* and affected to read it by the lamplight. It was a deliberate gesture of contempt for the proceedings; it said that he would thus wait out the remaining hour until five o'clock. Others spoke. Then Parnell became aware that William Abraham was on his feet again and to the same purpose as on the first day. 'Mr Chairman, let the talking be done with. I move that the chair be vacated.'

Parnell looked at him over his glasses. Abraham was balding and ferret-like, and he had a ferret's tenacity. His family name was the cross he bore; on meeting strangers, it was his custom to inform them, apropos of nothing whatever, that he was not in the least Jewish but Protestant.

Parnell said, with the sigh of one much put upon: 'I rule the member out of order. The motion before the party is that the Chairman reconsider his position.'

As he returned to his newspaper, Abraham began to rant. 'Then, sir, reconsider it, and be off with you. I have here a telegram —'

Parnell said: 'The member will —'

'. . . a telegram from the Archbishop of Dublin.' He brandished it and began to read: '"CATHOLIC IRELAND WILL NOT ACCEPT AS ITS LEADER A MAN DISHONOURED AND —"'

Parnell threw his newspaper aside. 'The member does not have the floor.'

Timothy Healy's heart was pounding; his visit to Ireland had borne glorious fruit. The members were galvanised; the clergy had shown their hand. At once, it was not Parnell's shadow that loomed largest in the room, but a mitred bishop's. Around the table,

244

through opposing camps, went the common thought: Christ, now we're in for it!

Abraham did not defer to the chair; he would finish reading, or die. He said, almost panting in his excitement: ' "... A MAN DISHONOURED AND WHOLLY UNWORTHY OF CHRISTIAN CONFIDENCE." '

Parnell was shouting now. 'The member is out of order.'

'I will not be silenced.' Abraham, having thrown his bombshell, was determined to make the most of it. He sent the telegram spinning across the table. 'McCarthy, here . . . you read it. See what it says.'

Justin McCarthy had no choice but to pick up the message. He had hardly done so when Parnell, his face rigid with fury, was out of his chair and behind him. He snatched the telegram from his hand and tore it to shreds. A cry of protest went up. Unheeding, he turned on Abraham.

'How dare you, sir? How dare you attempt to usurp me in the chair? Until the party deposes me, I am the chairman.'

Sexton said: 'Then depose him. Away with him.'

Dillon shouted: 'Resign!'

The cry was taken up by forty voices. Parnell, giving no sign that he heard, went back to his chair and took up his newspaper. Redmond attempted to make himself heard above the shouting. 'For God's sake, let us have sanity. Are we savages?'

Harrison shouted at them. 'Do you know what you are asking for? Do you? If he is deposed, Gladstone will be the party's new leader.'

Dillon said: 'Rubbish. He is not a member of the party.'

Redmond retorted: 'Are you mad? By our very presence here, we do his bidding. He is already master of the party.'

Timothy Healy had been biding his time, and now he saw his chance to strike a death-blow. He leaped to his feet. 'Is he? Is he, indeed?' He said, almost fondling the words that down the years he would repeat to the applause of a thousand dinner tables: 'Who, then, is to be mistress of the party?'

245

A bellow of 'Shame!' went up. There were shouts, one drowning out the next.

Parnell attempted to rise from his chair, only to fall back, the power gone from his limbs. Then, as if employing all his strength, he sprang at Healy, but the moment of delay had given time for others to step into his way. Hands pulled, restraining him, as he struck out.

One of Healy's defenders, Arthur O'Connor, stammered: 'This is not seemly. I appeal to the chair.'

The banality of the words dissolved the madness. Parnell saw the room again, the faces made yellow by the lamplight. He said: 'No, not to me. Better appeal to your friend there. Better appeal to that cowardly little scoundrel who dares in an assembly of Irishmen to insult a woman.'

Tim Healy remained sitting, as if in a void. A small, distant smile masked his exultation. Parnell resumed his chair. He thought of his Queenie and told himself that, at whatever cost, he must not weep.

William Abraham was one of those mortals to whom cataclysms in the lives of others were but interruptions to his own train of thought. As soon as he could again be heard, he said: 'I will rephrase my original motion to the chair . . .'

Parnell's voice was dead as he told Abraham yet again: 'The member is ruled out of order.'

For Justin McCarthy, the comedy had gone on for long enough. Facing Parnell, he said: 'Through the chair . . . I see no further use in continuing a discussion which must be barren of all save reproach, ill-temper, controversy and indignity. I suggest that those who are of my opinion should withdraw with me from this room.'

The twist of his mouth was an appeal for understanding. Parnell had once described him to Katharine as a nice old gentleman for a tea party. There was truth in it. McCarthy was soft; he was not a turncoat, but he bent to the prevailing winds. He led an easy life; he was no longer young, and Parnell's unyielding ways asked too much of him.

As the members followed McCarthy from the room, Parnell again picked up his newspaper, this time to shut out the sight of the Irish party taking its own life. He heard the scraping of chairs, the snufflings and murmurs and clearing of throats, the footsteps going past. The tongues of light dipped and cowered in the draught from the outside corridor. Finally, there was the soft closing of the door, and the flames rose straight and clear again.

He put down the paper and said, as if remembering a detail of not much importance: 'Count the members, would you, Harrison?'

At this sixth and final meeting, there had been an attendance of seventy-one. Now, two chairs out of every three were empty.

Harrison completed his count. He said, mournfully: 'Twenty-six.'

Parnell clapped his hands. 'Capital!' He chuckled, as if at the boundlessness of human folly. 'The idiots could have deposed me by signing a declaration. Now it is they who have gone, and we remain. Gentlemen, I believe that we have won the day!' He folded his newspaper, stood and picked up his black bag. 'The meeting is closed.'

Harrison knew that John Redmond was looking at him. He avoided his eyes.

Meanwhile, as Timothy Healy came out into New Palace Yard, he found himself in near darkness. Because of Westminster's conversion to electricity, storm lanterns had been fixed to the outer railings. There was hardly sufficient light to pick one's way towards the gas lamps of Parliament Square. Stepping into a pool of blackness and certain that he was unseen, Tim Healy did what, for him, was unthinkable and executed a small, brief, careful dance of happiness.

The house had been alive with noises since dawn, and at five o'clock he tapped at her door. 'Mrs O'Shea, will you get up, if you please? It is time to become Mrs Parnell.'

Katharine had already been up for an hour, and her personal

247

maid, Phyllis, was helping her to dress. Six months previously, the devoted Mary had received word that a match had been made for her at home in Leitrim with a farmer whose drudge of a wife had died, leaving him in need of an unpaid servant who would rear his brood, cook the meals, scrub the floors, feed the hens, milk the cows and help with the harvest. Devoted as she was to Katharine and Parnell, Mary could not resist such a golden opportunity. With much lamentation, she had returned to Ireland to achieve her apotheosis to wifehood, and, to take her place, Katharine had discovered Phyllis Bryson, whose own intended would, she declared, wait.

Yesterday, Parnell had driven to the registrar's office at Steyning to make final arrangements for the wedding. When he returned, he told her: 'The registrar, one Mr Cripps, informs me that the newspaper people have already been asking their questions.'

She almost wept. 'Then they'll be there tomorrow, waiting. Charley, they'll spoil it for us.'

'Not at all. Cripps is an admirable fellow, a very sphinx. He told them nothing. And I have instructed my own man to have Dictator harnessed in the phaeton for eleven o'clock, sharp. Under pain of death, he is not to breathe a word to a living soul.'

'Can we trust him?'

He smiled at her, incredulous that she should need to ask. 'Queenie, you disappoint me. Trust him? Not while there's a guinea loose in a journalist's pocket.'

'But then —'

'I myself will bring the phaeton around at seven in the morning. We'll be man and wife while the pack of them are still in bed.'

'Charley!' She pretended to be shocked. 'What a schemer you are.'

He shrugged. 'I am a politician.'

Her wedding dress was of dark blue silk, with leg of mutton sleeves, its line unbroken by flounces. There was Alençon lace at the throat and wrists. She wore a wide-brimmed picture hat, trimmed with roses. The servants were to travel to Steyning by train, and, as Parnell was hustling them out, Phyllis attempted to fasten a posy at Katharine's breast.

He said: 'No, Phyllis. Today, she must wear my white roses, but she shall carry yours.'

As Katharine waited, alone in the house, he went to rouse the groom, who, having made an evening of it with his windfall from the journalists, had slept not only in his livery but, apparently, in the stables. He was unshaven; there was straw in his hair. He made to excuse himself. 'I begin to suspect,' Parnell told him, 'that you are of Irish blood.'

It is said that a man in love rarely notices the clothes his mistress wears; her person eclipses all else. Parnell settled Katharine into the carriage and quite took her breath away by saying: 'My darling, you look lovely in that . . . ah, lace stuff and the . . . ah . . .' At which, his descriptive powers having run their course, he caused his forefinger to describe a number of vague circles.

She said, gravely: 'Thank you, Charley.'

'Not at all.' He seemed, she thought, rather pleased with his eloquence.

Katharine took the reins. Parnell, although an excellent horseman, was a poor driver, letting the reins lie so slackly along the horse's back that in a crisis the animal followed its own counsel. It was, he told her to her disbelief, how jarveys drove in Ireland. As the bedraggled groom climbed up behind the hood, sporting an immense buttonhole in honour of the occasion, Parnell said: 'Now, my dearest, let Dictator go with all his might.'

Their way took them between hedgerows of wild roses and traveller's joy. At Lancing they followed the bend of the Adur, then were through Bramber at a fast clip and into Steyning. The registrar's wife had decorated the parlour with flowers, and, while they were waiting for the servants to arrive, Parnell caught sight of his face, the eyes and cheeks sunken, in a mirror.

'It isn't every woman who makes so good a match as you are making, Queenie.' He patted the white rose in his lapel. 'And to such a handsome fellow.'

249

With a great commotion, Phyllis and the other servants appeared. Mr Cripps arranged all in their places. Words were spoken; the couple were joined. Afterwards, as they drove off for home, Katharine said: 'It was over so quickly. How long did it take, Charley? How long for us to be married? Ten minutes?'

He said: 'I make it eleven years.'

On the way, they passed two hansoms packed with reporters. As the drivers reined in and attempted to turn their horses, Katharine smiled to herself, snapped the reins and gave Dictator his head. The hunter stepped out, seemingly tireless. Parnell pushed back the hood of the phaeton so that the June sunlight was full on their faces. The breeze doubled back the wide brim of Katharine's hat. There had never been such a wedding.

Other pressmen were waiting at Walsingham Terrace. Parnell said: 'They have their work to do. Once we have had our breakfast, I'll speak to them.'

As they alighted from the phaeton, he took great pleasure in saying loudly: 'Stand back, there. Let Mrs Parnell pass.'

Later, when the reporters had gone, he put on an old coat, sat in his accustomed chair and looked at her so steadily that she became uncomfortable. 'Charles, you are not polite. I don't stare at you until you are shy.'

He was unrepentant. 'A cat may look at a king, and surely a man may look at his wife?'

She got to her feet. 'I am not going to stay indoors talking nonsense on such a lovely day. Short as our honeymoon is to be, let us make the most of it. Charley . . . come, walk with me.'

They strolled on the foreshore at Aldrington, taking with them their two dogs: Grouse, an Irish setter, and Pincher, a mongrel terrier that Parnell had found roaming the streets of Killaloe.

He said, basking as he walked: 'This weather is far too good for England. Avondale's the place for it.' 'D'you know, now that you and I have become' – he made a banquet of the word – 'respectable, perhaps I shall take you there before the leaves turn.'

She looked to see if he was in earnest. She said: 'Where,

did you say? To Avondale? Charley, I'm sure I have already been burned in effigy in Ireland. Would you see me set fire to in the flesh as well?'

He laughed at what he took for banter. Today she had not wanted to be reminded of Ireland or the Irish. With a flash of bad temper, the true-blue Englishwoman in her thought: What is more, he begrudges us even our weather!

They had walked for another while when she said, suddenly: 'For how much longer?'

Misunderstanding her in this, too, he said: 'I thought we might stroll as far as Shoreham. Is it too far? Are you tired?'

She said: 'I mean, how much longer will it be before you kill yourself? Seeing as I am now your wife in name, I thought you might be so kind as to enlighten me.'

He stared at her in part-amusement, part-shock. 'Queenie!'

They had never quarrelled. She could not believe she had spoken with such bitterness on this of all days. She heard herself go on to say: 'How many more hurdles, as you are pleased to call them? How many more ditches to clear?'

'Shall we sit?'

They walked to a groyne that jutted out from the sea wall and rested for a time without speaking. She was angry. This day should have been a new beginning; instead, by its transience, it mocked them. The very fall of the sun from its zenith was a reminder that today would end and, with it, the illusion of peace. Tomorrow, he would return to Ireland. The old adventurer, the O'Gorman Mahon, had at last died, aged eighty-nine, and there was to be a by-election. It would be the third in Ireland this year. Twice already, the seceders had proposed their own candidate in opposition to Parnell's, and twice they had won. Now, wearily, he must fight again.

Six months ago in Committee Room 15, he had blundered. It was not to be admitted to any man, still less even to Katharine, for whom he could do no wrong. To his private self, the knowledge came by stealth at moments when he was at the edge of sleep,

251

and, even as he chased the intruder from him, he knew that the Gladstone manifesto had been an act of folly. Joseph Biggar, M.P., had he lived, would have told him so. The misshapen, uncouth, fearless pork butcher of West Belfast would have read it through, torn it across and told Parnell: 'Resign, sir. Don't delay. Go this instant!'

Above all men, he would have heeded Joe Biggar. He could have resigned and played the martyr; instead, he had chosen the role of the deposed tyrant. He had taken hold of the tiger's tail and now could not let go. And that itself was a lie. There had been opportunities for him to step down with honour, and he had refused. Whether it was out of principle or from the pride of Lucifer, he could not go. Uncrowned or not, a king did not abdicate.

She waited for him to reply to her question. When he remained silent, she asked again. 'Charley, I would like an answer. You know that you are very ill. When you are absent from me, you do not spare yourself. So for how long am I to be a wife, and how soon a widow?'

He said: 'Once Home Rule is achieved —'

'Oh, my God.'

The rainbow's end, Utopia, the New Jerusalem, Avalon, the Promised Land: his eyes saw nothing else. It was hopeless; she would never have him to herself.

He knew what she was thinking. He said: 'My belief is that Ireland will have self-government within two years. Four or five at the utmost.' When she would not take heart, he said: 'My darling Queenie, you behave as if I were as ancient a monument as Gladstone. Have you forgotten? . . . the day after tomorrow, I shall be an old dodderer of forty-five. We have time . . . oceans of it.'

As they walked home, the dogs played the game of dawdling and catching up. He shooed the terrier from their path. Now that the bitterness had spent itself, she was remorseful.

She said: 'Have I spoiled our day? If so, I didn't mean to. It is only that I want us to have other days.'

They had come within sight of Walsingham Terrace. There were two figures on the front steps: journalists, craving to be told the secret of marital bliss. Parnell stopped so suddenly that she thought the terrier had tripped him. 'Darling, what is it?'

He took her arm and turned her so that she faced him. He said: 'My candidate in Carlow is an old Land Leaguer named Andrew Kettle.'

'What of it? Charley, those two men are watching us.'

'If Kettle is defeated, I'll resign as leader.'

'You'll . . . ?' She held her breath.

Her face was so childlike that his heart was touched. 'If that is what you most want, then let it be a wedding gift. Yes, young Redmond's a likely fellow. He has been a good deputy. Now let's see how he leads troops into battle.'

'Charley, do you mean it?'

'Mind, Redmond will never be royalty, as I am. A life baron at best, I should say.'

She stamped her feet. 'I forbid you to make jokes.'

He said: 'At any rate, don't let me catch you praying for poor Andy Kettle's defeat. I intend that he shall win.' He looked at her, now serious. 'Well, are you pleased?'

'Pleased?' She knew how much the decision had cost him. This day had been so happy, and now it was doubly so. She said, anxiously, still hardly believing: 'Darling, I do have your word? You'll not go back on it? I mean, if this man Kettle should lose, you will on your honour —'

'Well, not immediately.'

She felt the joy begin to ebb inside her. Now, the reporters had left the front steps and were coming towards them.

Parnell said: 'No, that would make it look as if I, too, had been defeated. Better that I should stay on for a time for appearances' sake and then hand over the traces.'

His words were too off-hand. She said: 'When? But when?'

He said, still vaguely: 'Oh, in a month or so. After October.'

SIXTEEN

He was about to leave for the railway station when the afternoon post arrived. Katharine looked at the envelopes, tied into bundles. 'Goodness, the entire world seems to have written to us!'

She took a telegram from a smaller pile. 'Charley, look here, I am addressed as Mrs Parnell for the first time ever.' She opened the envelope, saying as she did so: 'I shall keep the rest for your return.'

Parnell watched uneasily as she read the message. She laughed. 'It is signed "Six Irish Girls". It calls down upon our heads more blessings than heaven could ever afford. How kind they are.'

She saw the relief on his face. She said lightly, as if he were journeying no further than Westminster: 'Well now, I think it is time you were off.'

The maid picked up his suitcase and with it the small black bag. 'No, Phyllis, not that one.' Katharine took it from her. 'This bag and Mr Parnell are never to be parted.' She gave it to him and said with mock severity: 'Do you mind what I say?'

He said meekly, playing his role: 'Yes, Queenie.'

'Be sure, now.'

Her mood was too bright; it was not the kind of leave-taking he was used to. Then, when he made to embrace her, she moved back. She said: 'No, my darling, I'll not say goodbye to you. If

254

you want to kiss me, then come back to me. You may do so then.'
As he looked at her, puzzled, she told him: 'I want there to be all
the reasons in the world for you to live. Even one as small as this.
Do you understand me?'

He laughed silently. 'Small, you say!'

As the hansom drove away, he looked up and saw her at
the drawing-room window. Neither of them waved.

That evening, when the crying was done and she knew that
he was on the Irish mail, she looked at the piles of letters. She
would hold to her decision not to open them, but a package excited
her curiosity. She weakened and unwrapped it. To her surprise, it
contained what seemed to be a child's toy, a hinged ladder down
which a small wooden figure tumbled. It was some moments before
she realised that it was meant to be a fire-escape.

On coming ashore at Kingstown, Parnell was handed her telegram
greeting him on his birthday; at midnight, he had turned forty-five.
He bought the Irish papers, wondering in an idle way if the news
of the marriage had appeased the clergy. To his bemusement, it
seemed to have maddened them. It appeared that by cloaking their
sin in a pretence of decency, Katharine and he had befouled the
sacrament of matrimony. During the Kilkenny by-election of five
months before, Timothy Healy had publicly referred to Katey as
a 'convicted British prostitute'. Yesterday, the Bishop of Raphoe
had from his pulpit vied with Healy in gallantry – although, lest he
offend his congregation, he employed the less graphic term 'woman
of the streets' – and went on to describe the union as the 'climax of
brazoned horrors'.

Neither Healy nor Parnell had emerged from that Kilkenny
campaign unscathed. On a visit to Cork, the former had been
set upon by a gang of youths; blows to the face had cost Tim
Healy several teeth and a week in hospital. He had written home:
Apparently, we have the voters, whereas Parnell has their sons.

'At least that will curb his tongue,' Parnell said.

'Do you think so?' John Redmond asked sceptically.

255

'Oh yes, it is bound to,' Parnell told him. 'It is not easy to say "prostitute" with four teeth missing.'

His own arrival in Dublin had augured well. It was as if the olden days had come again. Torches blazed and a band played 'God Save Ireland' as the horses were unyoked from his carriage and he was drawn through the streets to the Rotunda. His every mention of Tim Healy was received with groans. When he said 'I don't pretend to be immaculate', the crowd shouted him down, refusing to let him continue in such a vein. When he said 'I believe you will stand by me to the end', the building shook as they roared back at him 'We will!' Dublin was with him still, and what Dublin said today Ireland would say on the morrow. All was well.

Kilkenny was not Dublin. There, Parnell was greeted with a woman's torn undergarment hoisted on a pole. A woman's shift, the cry went out, had become the flag of Ireland. Timothy Healy had already addressed a meeting in the city, and the crowds had taken up his rallying cry of 'Three cheers for Kitty O'Shea.' There were ribald jokes. In the streets, the vendors of ballads hawked come-all-ye's that had the name 'Kitty' in every verse. Parnell wrote to Katharine: *There is no such woman, and never was. It would really have hurt if those devils had got hold of your actual names, Katey or Queenie, or even the ridiculous 'Dick' that O'Shea called you.*

Wherever Parnell spoke, the tireless Healy had already been at work, backed by a phalanx of priests whose eyes raked the crowd as if for signs of allegiance to the man whom Healy called a putrifying political corpse.

'Mr Parnell,' Tim Healy told his audience, 'has made a new law, and it is this. While you have his name upon his lips, there is one name that you must not mention at all. It is the name of a precious personage who is more dear to Mr Parnell than Ireland itself, and that name is . . .'

He had only to wait a moment before the crowd, in perfect unison, chorused: 'Kitty!' They applauded, and Tim Healy smiled broadly, forgetting for a moment the loss of his front teeth. The priests, not wishing to be a party to sexual innuendo, inspected their feet. One of them said, mildly: 'Oh, terrible, terrible.'

At Castlecomer, twelve miles from Kilkenny, Parnell made derisive mention of Michael Davitt, who had come out on the side of the seceders. 'He calls me false to friends and false to Ireland. These are fine words from a chattering jackdaw.'

At this, there were miaowing noises from the crowd and cries of 'Here, Kitty'. After the meeting, as he was being driven away in a brake, someone in the darkness called out 'Whoormaster'. Another voice shouted: 'God damn your black soul to hell.' Stones were thrown, then a paper bag burst against Parnell's right eye. He felt his skin burn and was later told that the bag had contained slaked lime. He covered the inflamed eye with a bandage, but made light of the injury in a telegram to Katharine. The message was intercepted and shown to Tim Healy. 'You see?' he told the pressmen. 'A liar and a fraud, even in this. What a splendid comedian he is!'

On election day, there were priests outside the polling stations, waiting to engage their parishioners in discourse. Some of the younger clerics walked up and down with placards that said: VOTE FOR GOD AND IRELAND. Others had volunteered to give of their time as personation agents, assisting those voters who were illiterate.

Parnell's candidate was defeated by a two-to-one majority. In London, the Grand Old Man professed himself delighted. The next by-election, in North Sligo, had gone the same way. Now, facing John Redmond and Henry Harrison across a train compartment, he thought of his promise to Katharine. He imagined their consternation were he to tell them that the Carlow election, if lost, would be his last. He looked out of the train window; the Curragh was past, and now through the rain he saw the broken round tower of Kildare town. Of whatever tender promises were made on a wedding day, only one, he told himself, should be binding.

John Redmond looked up from his newspaper. 'Archbishop Croke has found another stick to beat us with.'

257

'Indeed? Another crozier, I think you mean.'

Redmond said: 'To beat *you* with, rather. He asks where you have obtained the funds to travel the length and breadth of Ireland. He says that you have ignored his request for an audit of the party accounts.'

'And so I have. Let him stick to spiritual book-keeping.'

'He goes so far as to suggest dishonesty.'

When Parnell did not reply, Henry Harrison said, nervously: 'I wonder what Tim Healy will make of that.'

Parnell was wondering, too. Dillon, Davitt, Sexton and the rest of them – the courtly Justin McCarthy excepted – were now his implacable enemies, but they had endistanced themselves from the demonic Healy. He, with the clergy for his hounds, was not content with the defeat of Parnell; instead, the pack was set on hunting him to the death. It was inevitable that Tim Healy, accompanied by an acrid whiff of hellfire, would appear in Carlow, seemingly on a dozen platforms at once, hands clutching his lapels or one hand held limp within the other.

Parnell had actually begun to dream of him. Dreams, he had thought, were for lovesick girls; now, in sleep, he walked into a room and saw the domed forehead, the pale eyes and the glint of the eyeglasses on their black ribbon. In one dream, Healy had even risen to utter Parnell's own words, spoken in Cork six years before: 'No man has the right to fix the boundary to the onward march of a nation.' He had said it in a toneless Cork drawl, directing the words at Parnell himself before passing from the room. In another dream, Parnell was, ludicrously, at the music hall. He looked up and saw Katharine and Healy in a box together, seemingly the best of friends. It made no sense. Last night, he had not slept on the mail-boat because of the pain in his arm; now he resisted the urge to doze lest his enemy came to him while he slept. Healy was no longer simply a man; he was the vengeful underside of the Ireland that Parnell had begun to fear; he would meet all men face to face as his equal, not by raising himself, but by dragging them down.

On the Sunday in Carlow town, a Father O'Connor informed his congregation that there were Parnellites among them. He said: 'You will know what to do with them when you get outside and are no longer on consecrated ground.'

On the Monday, an article headed 'Stop Thief!' appeared in the *National Press*. It was inspired by Archbishop Croke's allusion to party funds and signed 'Timothy M. Healy'. The final paragraph read:

> If Mr Parnell debauched Mrs O'Shea, one of the commandments delivered to us by Moses called this 'adultery'. If he appropriated the moneys left in trust with him – and we are prepared to prove that he did – the same old-fashioned law-giver called that 'theft'.

In Bagenalstown on polling day, a youth shouted 'Up Parnell!' and was beaten unconscious by a curate's blackthorn. When one of the onlookers protested, the priest threatened to turn him into a goat.

Katharine met him at Brighton station. He said, with a lightness that she had not expected: 'Not such a good showing, Queenie.'

Her small, shame-faced smile did not meet his look. When his telegram had come with the news that Carlow was lost, she had willed herself to be dismayed for his sake; instead, a small, traitorous joy told her that perhaps now he would be spared to her. In the cab on the way home, he squeezed her hand and said: 'Well, we must determine to do better next time.' Her heart seemed to falter. She could not find the courage to ask if he had forgotten his promise.

That evening, he slept on a sofa by the fire. She looked at his face and was shocked that she could see the skull beneath. At dinner, he had eaten poorly, but his humour was almost jaunty. He spoke of Carlow as of a minor setback. The cities – Dublin and Cork – were as steadfast as ever, he said; the true battleground was the smaller towns and villages, where the laity fought the priests' wars.

She thought, but did not say: All this, because of me.

'The country people were ours once,' he told her. 'They'll be ours again.'

His optimism confused her. In his absence, Justin McCarthy, an old acquaintance, had called upon Katharine. He paid his respects, extended his good wishes and stayed to lunch. As he was leaving, he suddenly looked as if he would weep.

'Why does he drive himself? To what avail? The people have turned against him. His followers desert him by the day. Will he not see that he is alone?'

As she offered him her hand, she said: 'Excuse me, Mr McCarthy, but are you not one of those who, you say, deserted him?'

He said: 'Yes, so I am. Except that in my case it was not out of badness.'

Now Parnell stirred in his sleep and the rug that covered him slid away. As she moved to replace it, he opened his eyes. 'Queenie, what were you doing in a box with —'

She said: 'A box? What are you talking about?'

He came fully awake, blinking. 'Nothing whatever. Arrant nonsense. Now I have had a splendid rest, so why do we not open our correspondence?'

In his absence, so many more letters had come that by the time they were half-way through the pile he was tired again and made a pretence of boredom. To her agreeable surprise, less than half of the letters were scurrilous.

He rose early next day and installed himself on the glass-enclosed terrace that faced the sea. Katharine found him transcribing notes into his diary.

'Darling, don't you ever rest?'

'If I lose track of these engagements, there'll be the devil to pay.'

'May I see?'

To her dismay, she saw that his diary was filled for ten weeks ahead with dates and the names of Irish towns that were as far apart as Listowel was from Belfast and Westport from Drogheda.

She flipped the pages so that they made small angry sounds, then passed the diary back to him. Her voice trembled. 'What about your promise to me?'

He said, mildly: 'My dear, if we were moving out of this house of ours, would we not leave all in order for the next tenant?'

During the weeks that followed, he addressed meetings in Ireland, returning to Brighton at the weekends. He said, only partly in jest, that the remotest bogland in Mayo was preferable to Westminster. Maurice Healy was now an M.P., and there had been a day when Parnell found himself wedged between him and his brother on the Irish benches, being talked across as if he were not there, and yet himself affecting that neither of the Healys existed in this world or another. As before, Katharine refused to take leave of him; the kisses and endearments were saved for his homecomings.

August passed. On September 20th, he spoke at Cabinteely outside Dublin, standing bareheaded in the rain that strode across the summits of Kippure and the Two-Rock. Later, he met his older sister Emily and her daughter Delia for dinner at the Royal Marine Hotel in Kingstown.

'Charley, your clothes are wet. You're soaked to the skin.'

He held up the small black bag. 'I'm well used to it. The extremities are what matter. As long as the feet are dry, all else is unimportant.'

She looked steadily at him for a moment, then gave her attention to the bill of fare. 'I have suspected as much for years, Charley, and now I know it. You're mad.'

A week later, he spoke at Creggs, six miles from Roscommon town. He spoke so slowly that the reporters took his words down in longhand. The pain in his left arm had drained him of strength. It rained again, more heavily than it had done at Cabinteely, and on the train for Dublin he realised that he had left behind him his black bag with the change of socks. He thought of Katey and how she would fuss and perhaps scold. He longed to be home and have the world put back to rights.

261

At Kingstown, a horror of solitude overcame him. He stood on the mail-boat deck, content to be jostled by the other passengers until the whistle blew and the gangways were dragged ashore. Sailors saluted and addressed him by name, and the yellow clock face of the town hall clock was a receding moon as the S.S. *Leinster* moved towards the harbour mouth. He went to his berth in the forward part of the ship. He lay down, feeling the racing pulse of the engines, and knew from the yawing when they were clear of Dublin Bay. First, the Bailey light was passed to larboard; then, after the Kish lightship, they were in the open sea. He thought of Ireland, astern in the dark and already half-asleep. At midnight, when the Welsh coast was still twenty miles distant, September ended and the month became October.

By the time he reached Brighton, he had forgotten the loss of the black bag, and his first words to Katharine were: 'You may keep me for a bit now.' He had delayed for an hour in London to take a Turkish bath in the hope that it would ease the pain in his arm; instead, it had drained him of strength. After dinner, he threw a cigar into the fire, half-smoked, and she heard him say: 'Queenie, I can't stand up. My legs won't support me.'

With her help and by leaning on his stick, he managed to climb the stairs. As they made their way, a step at a time, she said: 'What a foolish promise that was, Charley, to give up the leadership, and how foolish I was to let you make it. No, let us decide to go on as before; then you won't become ill trying to fit too much into too little time. What do you think?'

He had not heard. He was watching the Irish setter, who was trying to take the walking stick between his teeth. 'Grouse thinks all this is for his special benefit.'

When he was undressed and in bed, she rubbed his shoulders in firwood oil and wrapped his arm in layers of wool. Next morning, he was better, eating, and working on a speech for the following

Saturday in Macroom, thirty or so miles from Tim Healy's native Bantry.

He said: 'I'll beard that mangy lion in his den.'

She smiled, remembering how, eleven years before, she herself had vowed to beard another lion in *his* den. The lion had been Parnell, and the den had been New Palace Yard on a July morning. In its turn, a more recent memory stirred. Perhaps three years ago, she had emptied the pockets of Parnell's suit to have it cleaned, and an object had fallen from his pocket book. She wondered if he still carried it.

His improvement was short-lived. On the third day, he was in pain and feverish. She sent at once for a local physician, Dr Jowers. He stayed an hour with Parnell, then sat with Katharine on the terrace. Phyllis brought them tea.

He said: 'I have given Mr Parnell a draught to ease the pain.'

'And he will get better?'

Jowers seemed to choose his words too carefully. 'There may be a rheumatism of the heart. Or possibly the merest lumbar pneumonia. A man in good health would shake off either in a trice. What is disquieting is that Mr Parnell has no strength left.'

'I see.' When he gave no sign of continuing, she spoke for him. 'Then he will require complete rest, and that is what I assure you he will have. Doctor, should we go abroad, do you think?'

Jowers said: 'Mrs Parnell, you seem not to grasp what I say. I am a person of literal speech.'

A wave of faintness came upon her and swept past like a shadow. 'Well then, what is it you say?'

'There is nothing left. Mr Parnell is quite used up.' He said again, anxious that she should not cling to hope where there was none. 'There is nothing left.'

'Thank you.' She inclined her head as if to a shopkeeper bowing her out. She said, her voice almost bright: 'Then his murderers have done their work well.'

Late that night, Parnell told her that a malign invisible power was holding him down. He struggled; there was horror on his face.

263

He implored her help. She held him until he was calm. He seemed to doze; then she heard him say, murmuring: 'The Conservative Party.'

She said: 'Sleep, darling. Sleep and be well.'

His eyes were open and upon her face. He whispered: 'Kiss me, and I will try.'

She lay by his side and kissed him on the lips. His face was burning. Within moments, he was asleep. He dreamt again for a time, and then the dreaming stopped.

Next morning, she went to where his jacket hung and took out his pocket book. She opened it and searched; it was still there: a pressed red rose, long faded. She remembered the flower that she had coquettishly dropped from her bodice on the day of their first meeting. She knew that it was the same rose. Even if it were not, she was determined that it should be. It would go with him to Ireland when they took him from her.

As a woman, her life was over; she had died with him. As the girl who one summer's day had married Willie and given romance up for dead, she could not, without ingratitude, have asked for more.

Willie O'Shea, alighting from a hansom, could not believe the words he saw on a newsvendor's placard. He bought a paper and read. It was true, and there was a tribute from Gladstone. Next week in Dublin, Parnell would be given the greatest funeral since that of Daniel O'Connell – it was his reward for having had the good breeding to die. A broad smile came upon Willie's face. He went directly to his club and drank several brandies. Then, to his utter surprise, he began to cry. It was embarrassing; he went quickly downstairs to the washroom. He immersed his face in cold water, but the weeping would not stop. The attendant looked at him with curiosity.

Willie dried his face with a hand-towel. Straightening up, he caught sight of himself in the mirror, the eyes red-rimmed and still filled with tears. He was weeping, not for Parnell, but for himself, a man alone and wretched, who no longer had an enemy in the world.